Merry Christmas, everyone!

It's my 27th novel (yikes!), and it sees a welcome return of the lovely Chocolate Lovers' Club ladies.

My two previous novels featuring these girls are *The Chocolate Lovers' Club* and *The Chocolate Lovers' Diet* and they've proved to be my most popular books with readers at home and around the world. It seems we women share a love of chocolate! And romantic stories, of course.

As a writer there are some characters that never leave you. Each time I finish a chocolate lovers' book, I think it's the last, but those ladies keep telling me that they have more to say. Their friendship endures, even off the page. That's why it was so lovely for me to be able to write this book and delve into their world again.

If you haven't read the other books, I hope you enjoy meeting these ladies. To those who have read and loved them, then I hope you'll enjoy catching up with old friends.

Just make sure that you're stocked up with chocolate goodies when you read them and, at Christmas, you have a particularly good choice!

Wishing you a Christmas filled with love, happiness and a great big selection box.

Carole ☺ xx

The Chocolate Lovers' Christmas

Carole Matthews

sphere

SPHERE

First published in Great Britain in 2015 by Sphere
This paperback edition published in 2015 by Sphere

A CIP catalogue record for this book
is available from the British Library.

ISBN 978-0-7515-5213-3

Typeset in Sabon LT Std by Palimpsest Book Production Limited,
Falkirk, Stirlingshire
Printed and bound in Great Britain by Clays Ltd, St Ives plc

Papers used by Sphere are natural, renewable and recyclable
products sourced from well-managed forests and certified
in accordance with the rules of the Forest Stewardship Council.

MIX
Paper from
responsible sources
FSC
www.fsc.org   FSC® C104740

An imprint of
Little, Brown Book Group
Carmelite House
50 Victoria Embankment
London EC4Y 0DZ

An Hachette UK Company
www.hachette.co.uk

www.littlebrown.co.uk

To Karen Phillips – my lovely friend and honorary
Entertainments Executive. You are funny, feisty, caring
and kind beyond measure. I love my outings with you
even when they involve near-death experiences.
What's the worst that could happen?

Chapter One

It's a well-known fact that if you break chocolate outwards, all the calories fall out. Fabulous. I put this theory to the test and snap a piece off a chunky bar of 70 per cent Madagascar chocolate to set myself up for the day. Hmm. Certainly looks lower in calories to me already. Popping it into my mouth I enjoy the intense, dark sensation of paradise on my tongue. I, Lucy Lombard, manager of Chocolate Heaven and self-confessed chocolate addict, sigh happily into the ether.

It's coming up to Christmas and, due to an unfeasibly early morning start on my part, Chocolate Heaven is now decorated in its finest festive garb. Designed by me and sourced entirely from the bargain basement of eBay, I've tried to aim for tasteful instead of Santa's grotto. I think I may have nailed it. Now the busy café and emporium of all things chocolatey is dressed in a most restrained theme of silver, white, chocolate brown and Dairy Milk purple. Perfect.

Groups of baubles in co-ordinating colours dangle attractively from the wall lights and there are pretty, blinking fairy lights across the wall behind the counter. I've changed the usual brown velvet cushions on our leather sofas for white felt ones adorned with a sprinkling of glittery, sequined snowflakes. Classy. Flanking the front door there are two beautiful, tall Christmas trees, also dressed in what I'm calling my 'signature' festive theme. There's a wreath on the door made of baubles too – bought rather than fashioned by my own fair hand. It's possibly more restrained in colour palette than in sheer volume of decorations which, I think, is straying towards the outer reaches of excessive.

It's nearly opening time now and so I stop fiddling with the decorations and take my station. Checking the counter in front of me, I make minor adjustments to the trays of hand-baked brownies, chunky chocolate-chip cookies, and rows of colourful melt-in-the-mouth macaroons sandwiched together with a rich chocolate ganache. I'm proud to say that I've introduced several new ranges since I took over – more cake-based than the straightforward chocolate selection that the owners, Clive and Tristan, favoured – and they're all flying out of the door. Cake is the new sex, isn't it? And chocolate cake is, of course, the best of all. I don't think it's bragging to say that the dark chocolate and pistachio rocky road has already become a legend throughout the land. Well, north London. I fuss with my devil's food cake, turning it so that it's showing its best side to the world. With a last proprietorial glance at my goodies, I go to the door of the café, flick the sign to 'open' and wait for the day to begin.

I'm coming to the end of my ninth month of running Chocolate Heaven and it's fair to say that I'm totally exhausted. Despite the excitement of putting up the Christmas decorations, today my eyes are gritty from lack of sleep as – in addition to my early start – I was also burning the midnight oil last night trying to keep up with the paperwork. Who knew there'd be so much? It's endless – logging the sales, making sure the orders are being fulfilled, ordering the ingredients, doing tax

2

returns. I am a woman who is more intimate with the art of the spreadsheet than I ever thought I would be. My previous experience with chocolate has been entirely based on consumption rather than the administration thereof. When I was a mere customer of Chocolate Heaven – albeit one of the most fervent ones – I never knew how much work went into simply putting wonderful chocolate yummies on the counter. It's a lot, I can tell you. *A lot*.

My vision of running this – my ideal business – involved me standing languidly savouring my chocolate products in the smugly pouting style of Nigella Lawson, overseeing my newfound empire with a loving eye while retaining a comely size twelve/fourteen figure through the power of positive thinking rather than anything as tawdry or time-consuming as exercise. Fat chance.

Reality check. I'm run off my feet from morning until night and my waistband is getting ever tighter. And I know I'm not pregnant because, frankly, I couldn't tell you the last time Mr Aiden 'Crush' Holby – the love of my life – and I had carnal knowledge of each other. This is due to the fact that I fall into bed every night absolutely knackered and am snoring within about three seconds. He might well have sex with me, but if he does, I don't actually notice.

Nor am I languidly savouring my chocolates in the manner of my fantasy. No, I'm stuffing them in morning, noon and night because I don't have the time or inclination to make myself any other food. Some might say, no change there then.

Perhaps I've got an underactive thyroid. It happens. I'm over thirty now and heading towards That Age. It's a well-known fact that women's bodies start to have minds of their own once we hit middle age. We lay down fat on our hips, tums and bums in case we ever find ourselves in danger of starvation or something. Clearly, I have started already. I could live off my hips alone for weeks. I have another chocolate as now I've depressed myself and chocolate is a most excellent cure for depression. True fact.

Still, I'm not complaining. Not at all. This is my dream gig. All those years of wandering disastrously through the world of temporary office work are behind me now. I've arrived. This is what I was predestined to do. It's my calling. Like becoming a nun or something. Chocolate is my vocation and, for the good of others, I have entered into this life selflessly. I eat another chocolate to celebrate. Yum. Pay's not great, but the perks are unrivalled.

I should point out that it's in my contract that I'm allowed to eat all the chocolate that I want. Oh yes. I think Clive and Tristan thought that after being let loose – literally – in a sweet shop, I'd eventually run out of steam and my consumption would soon wane to the seemly side of moderation. Not a hope. No let up yet. I still can't wait to get here every morning and inhale that heady vanilla scent. Ah, bliss.

Chapter Two

I'm sticking just a few more strategically placed stars and snowflakes on the glass display for good measure when the bell above the shop door dings the arrival of a customer. The first member of my four-strong chocoholic gang – the Chocolate Lovers' Club – lumbers in, puffing heavily.

Our club of chocoholics is formed of my good self – founder member – Nadia Stone, Autumn Fielding and Chantal Hamilton. We're a disparate bunch of women who all met here many moons ago due to our mutual appreciation of all things chocolatey and it still sustains our relationship to this day. We are the best of friends, a family of chocoholics and Chocolate Heaven is our sanctuary, our headquarters.

It's Chantal who's the first to arrive today, wrestling her über-trendy baby carriage through the doorway in her wake. 'My word.' Her mouth drops open. 'This is all a bit Santa's grotto, Lucy.'

'Is it? I thought it was quite restrained.'

Chantal laughs. 'I assumed you were embracing the concept that *more* is more when it comes to Christmas decorations – as it is with chocolate.'

I cast a more critical eye over my efforts. I still don't think it's too bad. 'Do you think I should take some of them down?'

'No.' Chantal kisses me. 'It's perfect. So very you.'

'Let me help you.' I grab the buggy from her and beam at the baby coddled in its depths.

'It's freezing out there,' my friend complains with a shiver. 'I think it could snow heavily again. There's a smattering in the air.'

'Hurrah!'

She shoots me a black look.

'It's Christmas,' I say apologetically. 'Nearly. It *should* snow.'

Chantal rolls her eyes at me and shakes a few flakes of snow from her bobbed dark hair. 'I think slush. I think treacherous pavements. While you're probably fantasising about building a cheery snowman with your loved one and snowball fights that turn into foreplay.'

'I hadn't *actually* thought of that,' I confess, 'but what a lovely idea.' Makes mental note. Snowball fight/foreplay scenario. Excellent.

Chantal's death glare intensifies, so I quickly park the buggy for her while she flops into the nearest sofa with a heartfelt *ouff*. 'Couldn't quite make it to the counter,' she apologises.

I'm not sure that my friend's waddle is entirely down to the fact she's never managed to shift her baby weight – more that she is, in time-honoured tradition, eating enough chocolate for two – or possibly even three. I don't have the heart to tell her that she should probably stop now that dear baby Lana is about five months old. Once she was all designer chic and sharp angles. Now she's more mumsy, gently rounded and into elasticated waists. I think it suits her, but I'm not sure that my friend would agree.

At nearly forty, Chantal is the oldest member of the Chocolate Lovers' Club and I don't think she'd ever really planned on being a mum. Lana was what we might call 'a little surprise'. But now that she has a child, Chantal has taken to the whole motherhood thing like a duck to water.

'The decorations do look lovely.' Chantal takes them in. 'You're right. You can never have enough festive bling. You've been very busy.'

'I was in here at six o'clock this morning.'

'Ha,' Chantal says. 'I should have joined you then. Madam had me up at four. Again. I *long* for the days when I could lie in bed until six o'clock.' Chantal rubs her temples. 'Baby Lana is still working on the theory that night-time is for kicking your heels up and daytime is for sleeping.'

Lana is a little cherub and I coo at her in the manner of a woman besotted. We all adore her. This child has more surrogate aunties than you can shake a stick at and we have all vowed to bring her up to embrace the ethos of the Chocolate Lovers' Club.

'I'm exhausted,' Chantal admits.

'You do look a bit worn out.'

'I think I need a double choc hit. I went down the chamomile tea and boiled egg route, but it didn't even touch my tiredness. Be a love.'

'Can I have a quick cuddle with Lana first? I can't wait.'

'Be my guest.'

Lovely little Lana is swaddled from head to toe against the cold in an adorable pink suit. I lift her up, grunting slightly as I do. Wow, she's a weight. 'Baby Hamilton is getting very big.'

'Tell me about it. Lana is taking after her mummy. I don't think I'm ever going to be able to see my feet again.'

'I thought the weight was supposed to drop off you when you start breastfeeding,' I offer. 'All the celebs say that it does.'

'Yeah? The celebs are liars. Bet they all pay personal trainers

7

to torture them every day and live on nothing but lettuce. I'm permanently hungry, as is this little one.'

Giving Lana a good, squishy cuddle, I goo-goo-gah-gah some more before I reluctantly part with her and head off to make Chantal her drink.

When I'm behind the counter again, I grab some milk and froth it in my whizzy new coffee machine. It looks like the flight deck of some retro spacecraft and I had to go on a course for a whole day just to learn how to drive it. I am a woman who knows her way round a flat white and a hazelnut latte. My caramel macchiato is a thing of beauty.

'How's that chocolate coming along?'

'Be right with you.' There's no packet hot chocolate here. It's all made with real chocolate flakes and I stir plenty in until it's rich and dark just as I know Chantal likes it. Then with a flourish, also learned on my day course, I dust the froth on the top to make a heart in cocoa powder. *Et voila!* I deliver it to Chantal. 'To produce something so wonderful takes a while.'

'Sorry, Lucy,' she sighs. 'I'm sure that time is moving at half its normal pace. The days are stretching out before me interminably. All I do is look after this little one. I love it, but sometimes I do feel like an indentured servant.'

'I think it stops when they get to twenty-one,' I say with a grin.

'I'm not so sure these days. Half of my friends still have children at home in their late twenties. Still, I'm never going to let Lana leave home. I'm going to keep her all to myself for ever.'

With the chocolate, there's a brownie that's so fresh it's still slightly warm from the oven and I've put an extra dollop of whipped cream on the side.

She eyes it longingly. 'What calories?'

I shrug. 'There'll be time enough for dieting. If you can't

over-indulge yourself when you're in the initial stages of motherhood, when can you? If you restrict yourself it might even be dangerous.'

'As if I need any encouragement.' Chantal pats her tummy and bites into the brownie with a grateful sigh. 'Remember the days when I was a groomed, glossy magazine journalist and as thin as a pin?'

'I certainly do.'

'Good. Because I don't. I feel like that was a different person. One that I'm never likely to see again.'

'Don't beat yourself up. It's early days yet. Lana is your priority now. You can't do everything.'

'See this?' Chantal pulls a handful of her short bob. 'I used to get it cut every four weeks without fail at a high-end salon. I did it last night with the kitchen scissors in front of the bathroom mirror. What's happened to me?'

'Your hair looks fine.' Though, if I'm honest, her fringe does look a little bit ragged, now she's pointed it out. 'There's more to life than having the perfect haircut and manicured nails.'

'I'm glad to hear it.' She looks in dismay at the nibbled, varnish-free nails she holds out to me for inspection.

'You'll get back on track. There's no hurry. Just enjoy this little one for now. You're being a great mum to Lana. That's the best job in the world. You have a healthy and happy baby. The cut and thrust of glossy magazines can wait a while.'

'Part of me misses work,' she admits. 'Being at home all the time does make me kind of crazy, but I do love spending my days with Lana, too.' Chantal smiles lovingly at her child.

To me, Chantal still looks amazing, even though – admittedly – she's a slightly larger version of her previous self. Designer tracksuits – loose fitting – have replaced the tight Joseph trousers and fitted Ghost blouses of pre-baby days.

Where once Chantal would never have a hair out of place and her manicure would be perfect in the latest on-trend colour, she definitely now takes a more ... er ... casual approach to her appearance. And nothing wrong with that. If she is packing a few extra pounds, so what? Her smile is warm and contented. What more should we ask of ourselves?

'Some days it does feel as if I'm going out of my mind with boredom.' She tucks into her cream with a spoon. 'On other days I feel that I never want to work again and will spend my whole life just gazing at my little girl.'

'That might be awkward when she gets a boyfriend.'

'She's never going to have one,' Chantal counters. 'We're going to keep you away from all those nasty men, aren't we? We are. You're not going to make the same mistakes that Momma made, are you?'

Lana gurgles happily and we both grin at her, completely smitten.

'How's Ted?' I ask. Chantal and her husband have never had the best of relationships, but it seems to have been very strained of late.

'He's fine. Busy at work. Loving Lana. He's trying very hard to be a good father.' She raises an eyebrow. 'To *both* of his girls.'

I hate to bring this up, but there was a question over the paternity of little Lana when she was born as Chantal enjoyed a fling with our dear friend Jacob Lawson – among others. Ahem. She classes it as her Wild Period.

She wasn't the only one sowing her oats at the time, either. While Chantal was seeing Jacob, Ted fathered another Baby Hamilton too. So now their family arrangements are complicated to say the least. Enough to drive a woman to chocolate. But whose aren't tricky in some way, shape or form these days? This is the age of the extended family. But a swift DNA test proved that Lana is, indeed, one hundred per cent Hamilton baby and, after a shaky time, Ted and Chantal are trying to make things work for the sake of the baby. Which we're all relieved about, not least of all Chantal.

'He adores Lana.'

'Of course he does. She's so cute.' I want to kiss her chubby, pink cheeks. Just looking at her pulls at my heartstrings. Nearly as much as for my beloved Crush and they get pulled for him quite a lot too. 'What's not to love?'

'Think you'd like to join me?' Chantal nods at Lana.

'Me? Have a baby? I don't know. Maybe one day.' I feel a pang of longing. It happens a lot when I look at Lana. I think I would like a baby with Crush as he'd make a wonderful dad. It's all very well being a thrusting, ambitious business-woman, but I have to put everything else on hold for now. I shrug off the question, not trusting my own emotions. 'You know what I'm like. I have trouble keeping my own body and soul together. How could I ever hope to look after someone else without breaking them?'

'Don't leave it as late as me. I'd pretty much accepted that I'd never have children. Once you're over forty and on the downward slide in the fertility stakes, it's not exactly impossible, but it's not that easy either. You're young.'

'I'm in the fresh flush of my thirties. I thought I had years yet.'

'Not necessarily. You need to think about getting on with it.' She gives me a sage stare to reinforce the message. 'I can't say that Lana was actually planned, as you know, but I wouldn't be without her now. I'd love to have another baby, but it needs to be sooner rather than later.'

'What's stopping you?'

'There is the slight issue that Ted and I are not, well . . . you know. *Close* in the bedroom department.'

'Still not?'

Chantal shakes her head. 'No action at all since Lana was born. We've not even held hands.'

We both laugh at that.

'The only thing I want to do in bed now is *sleep*,' she adds.

It's fair to say that Chantal has had a colourful love life. At one point it was the other way round. She was sex-starved and couldn't get Ted interested. How times change! 'It would have saved you a lot of trouble if you'd discovered that some years ago.'

'Ain't that the truth, sister,' she agrees and we have a giggle together.

'You're going to have to do more than *sleep* with Ted if you want Lana to have a sister or brother.'

'I can't keep using Lana as an excuse.' Chantal looks away and sighs. 'Our relationship has changed. I can't quite put my finger on it, but we're not the same together anymore. In many ways we get on better now as we have Lana to focus on, but there's definitely something missing.'

I put my hand on her arm. 'This should be a happy time for you both.'

'Perhaps it just happens when you have a child to consider. The dynamics change. If you're strong, it pulls you together, but if you're on shaky ground, well, maybe the cracks start to show. I keep trying to remember that we're both in uncharted territory and are experiencing a whole new level of exhaustion and commitment.'

'If there's anything I can do, you only have to ask.'

'Thanks. I'm sure we'll work it out,' she says. 'Given time.'

'Pass that delicious baby to me again while you concentrate on your brownie,' I say. 'She needs another cuddle with her Auntie Lucy.'

'She might need her nappy changed too.' Chantal wrinkles her nose.

'Above my pay grade,' I tell my friend. 'Aunties are for playing, talking about boys and educating the next generation in the mysterious ways of chocolate.'

'Are the other Chocolate Lovers' girls coming today?'

'They should be here any minute.'

And, on cue, the door chimes again.

Chapter Three

Nadia Stone and Autumn Fielding sweep in together and, Lana still nestled in my arms, I rush to greet them. 'Hey. Good to see you both.'

Chantal goes to stand to say hello to them and gives up. 'I *so* need to get down to the gym,' she mutters darkly.

'I'll swear this baby gets more beautiful every day,' Autumn says. 'Hand her over.'

I duly give her Lana, who has quickly become accustomed to being passed like a parcel between us. Autumn snuggles her. The baby grabs a fistful of Autumn's flowing auburn curls and sticks it straight into her mouth. My friend's gorgeous green eyes are dull though, and she looks like she needs a cuddle as much as the baby.

Autumn is the youngest of us – a mere twenty-nine years old – but, in some ways, the wisest. She is the one who likes to commune with the earth, can meditate in yoga classes without shouting 'get on with it' – which got me thrown out of mine – and, generally, likes to help make the world a better place. She is the optimist, the glass-half-full person among us. Whereas I am the wine-glass-frequently-half-empty person.

'Congratulate me!' Nadia says, clapping her hands together. 'I've only got a job interview!' She does a little happy dance. 'Yay!'

It makes me smile to see my friend so excited. It's about time that she had something good happen to her as she's had a truly terrible year. 'That's great news. I wondered why you were looking so spruce.'

'Like the suit?' She gives us a twirl.

'You look beautiful. Even more than normal, if that's possible.' Nadia has an Indian heritage, but has lived in England all her life. She's dark-skinned with long, glossy hair that hangs heavily down her back and she regularly turns heads. Until Chantal had Lana, she was the only one who was a mum. Her little boy, Lewis, is four now – a sturdy and demanding chap.

Nadia's been having a tough time recently – understatement. Only a short while ago, her husband died and she's still grieving. Terrible for anyone, but she's only in her early thirties. I know she's trying to hold it all together for Lewis's sake, but it's never going to be easy. I think it's too soon for her, but she's trying to get back to work. Breaking down at interviews, as she did at first, isn't going to go a long way to convince potential employers that she can cope. Yet she needs a job and fast. She's got Lewis to bring up and she's been left by her dear departed Toby in what might be classed as 'difficult circumstances'. Up shit creek, *sans* paddle and with some serious bills to pay.

I give her a hug. 'I'm sure you'll get this one. Have confidence in yourself. You're brilliant, bright and sassy. They'd be mad not to snap you up.'

'Thanks, Lucy,' she says. 'I feel much better, but I could do with a bit of bolstering up. The competition out there is fierce. This is a bit of a McJob in an office and one that I could easily manage, but I'm so nervous. How can I convince them that they need my services more than anyone else's? There are people out there with a dozen degrees doing basic admin work. Lots of them are working as unpaid interns. How can I compete when I actually want a decent salary? It scares me just to think of it. This calls for chocolate, Lucy, and fast.'

I turn up my hands. 'Why is everyone in such a rush today?'

'This is in lieu of breakfast. It took me all of my time to get Lewis ready for nursery.' Nadia scans the counter, homing in like a missile. 'I'll have a cappuccino and a slice of that fabulous-looking coffee and chocolate cake.'

'Coming up.'

'Good grief,' she says with a giggle. 'It still seems really weird that you're on the other side of the counter now. I don't think I'll ever get used to it.'

'Weird in a good way?'

'Yes,' she agrees. 'Poacher turned gamekeeper. Still enjoying it?'

'Loving it.' I stifle an unbidden yawn. 'I'm worn out, though. I feel I have a responsibility to keep the business healthy for when Tristan and Clive return. I'd be mortified if their profits took a nosedive.' I look guiltily at the chocolate that I've just picked up and put it down again. 'Thankfully, you lot are still keeping me busy.'

'The Christmas decorations look great,' she says. 'But that's another thing I could do without.'

'Your first Christmas without Toby is never going to be easy.'

She nods in agreement. 'It will be weird, just me and Lewis.'

'Well, we won't let that happen,' I tell her. We must organise something to take your mind off it. What do you say, Autumn?'

'Of course we must. Addison and I haven't decided what to do either. I know he won't want to go to Mummy and Daddy's house again. Last year was a total disaster.'

If I remember rightly, Autumn's wild-child brother, Richard, turned up drunk and high and did unspeakable things with the turkey.

'Whatever we do, it won't involve my parents.' She shudders at the memory. 'Besides, it's hardly likely that they'll miss me.'

Autumn, at best, has a 'remote' relationship with her folks. 'We'll sort something out. Don't fret. Now, what can I get for you?'

Scanning my lovely range of delights on the counter, she comes to the conclusion, 'I've no idea what I want.' She gives a weary sigh. 'I'll have the same as Nadia.'

Someone else who's too tired to think. 'How are you doing?'

Autumn sighs. 'I'm hanging on.'

She's also still mourning the death of Richard who, tragically, had an addiction to drugs much stronger than chocolate.

Forcing a smile, she juggles taking off her coat while still holding Lana.

'Be kind to yourself.' I look at her with concern. Autumn's fiery hair looks dry and lifeless. Her face looks completely washed out. Even her lovely freckles look faded.

'I'm trying,' she says.

'You need time. It's a great healer.'

'Time and chocolate,' she tries to joke. 'I was going mad staring at my four walls. That's why I desperately need this moment of escape.'

Chocolate Heaven is still a place of refuge to all of us in times of need. A little corner of this earth that wraps us in cosiness, comforts us and feeds us chocolate. Hurrah! Long may it thrive.

I hug Autumn again, and then go to start their order while my friends kiss and fuss over Chantal and Lana. Eventually, they sit themselves down in a huddle around her while I tend to business.

Two more regular customers come in for takeaway orders

and I load them up with goodies. Kick-starting the coffee machine into life again, I set about slicing up the cake. Then I pour the boiling milk onto shots of espresso, sprinkle them with a liberal dusting of chocolate flakes, plate up the cake, add napkins, little forks and, as an extra, take one of those warm brownies for myself. Hmm.

'Here you go,' I say as I cross the floor, tray held high. My waitressing skills have improved vastly in the last few months and I rarely trip over or spill anything on the customers now. 'Let the meeting of the Chocolate Lovers' Club commence.'

I set the tray down on the coffee table in front of my friends and dish out their drinks before sitting myself. I'll have to keep one eye on the counter – as always – but, for now, my best girls are the only customers here.

'News,' I say. 'Tell me *all* the news. Quickly. How are the wedding plans going, Autumn?'

'They've come to a bit of a grinding halt.' Pensively, she twirls one of her curls round her finger. 'I haven't felt much in the mood since Rich died. The last thing I want to do is organise a wedding. I'm not in the right frame of mind. Besides, neither Addison nor I can agree what we want to do.'

'Choices?' Chantal says.

'Addison just wants a quiet register office do. Close friends only. I'm happy with something small, but I want it a little more meaningful than that. I've been looking at something that gets us back to nature. Maybe a beach or woodland wedding.'

'Why on earth you live in London is a mystery,' Chantal says.

Autumn laughs. 'I've never really thought about it. Family ties, I guess. I'm here because that's where Rich is.' She falters slightly as she realises that's no longer the case. 'Was,' she corrects sadly.

18

I squeeze her hand.

'My boarding school was in the country,' she adds, 'and I did love it.'

My dearest Autumn will always be a tree-hugger at heart. That's why she's still attached to tie-dyed material, eats meals involving Quorn and probably should have been a surfer chick in California or a hippy. I think this is why she's also the most socially responsible one among us and works with disadvantaged kids who are trying to get off drugs.

'Why don't you rope in Jacob to help you?' Chantal suggests. 'He made a fabulous job of planning Lucy's wedding.'

'Non-wedding,' I correct.

Let me fill you in. My troublesome ex-fiancé Marcus and I were due to tie the knot on Valentine's Day, but by the time I got to the church, barely a few minutes late, Marcus had changed his mind and done a runner. But all's well that ends well. I consider myself to have had a lucky escape. If Marcus had held his nerve and had waited just five minutes more, I could now have been Mrs Marcus Canning and would be lumbered with Marcus and his Many Women rather than lovely Aiden 'Crush' Holby and his loyalty only to me.

Nadia checks her watch. 'I'd better go. My interview is soon and I've got to get across to Fenchurch Street.'

'Don't worry about rushing back for Lewis,' Autumn says. 'I'll pick him up from nursery for you and take him home.'

'You're an angel.' She kisses Autumn and then stands up. 'Wish me luck, ladies.'

'You don't need it,' Chantal says. 'You'll knock them dead.'

'I've been for a dozen interviews already and I haven't got one offer yet,' she reminds us.

'Don't think about that now,' I tell her. 'Just give it your best shot. You can do no more.'

'I'd better get going too,' Autumn says. 'I said that I'd drop

19

into work for an hour or two today.' Reluctantly, she hands Lana back to Chantal.

'Well, I'm not going anywhere in a rush,' Chantal says. 'I'll have another of your fabulous brownies please, Lucy.'

'Coming right up, madam.' Though I'd like nothing more than to sit with Chantal and have a gossip and another cuddle with Lana, I yawn and heave myself out of an oh-so-comfortable chair which seems intent on dragging me back down. At the risk of being lynched by Chantal, I think I'll put on some Christmas music to get me going.

Chapter Four

It's late when I leave Chocolate Heaven, turning off the Christmas lights as I do. After the girls went, I had a rush of customers for the rest of the day that kept me busy. We're doing some special Christmas cakes to order, decorated with gilded, chocolate holly leaves which are really beautiful. As everyone seems to be getting into the festive mood, they're going great guns. I make sure that I've got all the orders from today collated.

Thankfully, I don't have to make all these delights myself, as my culinary skills lie in the gutter. I don't know what to do with food unless it comes frozen. Very sensibly, Clive and Tristan have employed one of their oldest friends, Alexandra, to do all the baking for me. She's the one who keeps me supplied with all my customers' confectionary requirements and very good she is too. In previous incarnations, she's been a chocolatier and pastry chef at some of the top hotels in the world, but now she has three ankle-biters and has downsized to work from home.

Occasionally, when it all gets too much at her own place, she comes to work in the kitchen here, but mostly she delivers on a daily basis and, conveniently, lives only a few streets away. She's here first thing most mornings to drop off a fresh batch of cakes, cookies, muffins and brownies.

Alexandra is also trialling some mince pies with a sliver of brownie topping for us to sell. I'm hoping they're going to be ready soon. Perhaps she could do us a festive version of the rocky road too, with cranberries, almonds and white chocolate. Christmas is hurtling towards us now like a speeding train and I'd like it to slow down so that I can enjoy it.

Last year my Christmas was totally rubbish. Crush was AWOL in the Australian outback, lost and near death. And, fool that I am, I thought he'd dumped me. Given my history, an easy assumption to make. But, no, he was actually stumbling round the desert without food or water or mobile phone, barely clinging to life. So I spent Christmas Day at a homeless shelter dishing out turkey dinners. Then, to my eternal shame, out of sheer loneliness – nothing else – I shagged my bastard ex-fiancé, Marcus, beneath my Christmas tree. Something I'll regret to the end of my days. I know. Kill me.

Well, this year it's going to be different. This year I am a woman in love and am fully on message with the peace, love, goodwill to all men thing. Except Marcus. Who will never again be getting goodwill from me. Particularly not under a Christmas tree. So there.

I text my darling Crush to tell him I'm leaving. My eyes are heavy with tiredness and I nearly fall asleep on the Tube on the way home. When I get back, jostled and jogged by fellow commuters, I push open the door and go up the stairs to my flat. I haul myself up each one as if I'm climbing a mountain. Slipping my key into the front door lock, I still can hardly believe that Crush will be waiting here for me. We have been living together as grown-up boyfriend and girlfriend in a real, proper relationship for nine months now and it's been more than I could ever have expected. I just wish that we had more quality time together.

There's a wonderful smell wafting from the kitchen and soothing music floats out of the iPod. Home, sweet home. My flat is small, a bit scuffed around the edges. I like to say that I live in Camden High Street as it makes me sound a bit trendy. In reality, it's above a slightly grungy hairdressing salon and I can only afford it because my mum owns the premises and, out of guilt, gives me a cheap deal on the rent. But it's mine and it is a *great* address. I love it even more now that it's full of Crush's man stuff. I hang my coat next to his on the rack and put my shoes neatly alongside his too. There's a car mag discarded on the sofa and a stack of books – mainly crime and thrillers – that he might or might not one day get round to reading. In the bathroom cabinet all my cosmetics are squashed into half the space they used to have. My underarm deodorant nestles side-by-side against Crush's. Our toothbrushes share the same mug. I love it all. Some days I go round and touch all of his possessions, just to make sure that he really is here.

'Perfect timing, Gorgeous,' Crush shouts from the kitchen. 'Supper's just about ready.'

If I'd still been living on my own I would have had a Mars Bar for dinner. Maybe two. Or, if I was on a health kick, a Cup-a-Soup. Now there's something wonderful bubbling on the stove cooked by my lovely partner and I suddenly feel very cared for.

I never get tired of looking at this man. He's tall, as handsome as anyone on telly, and I always feel as if I'm punching above my weight having bagged him for myself. His hair is brown, tousled and his eyes, the colour of chocolate buttons, are permanently warm and smiling. He's kind beyond measure and has the patience of a saint. And he's mine. Mine.

23

'I love you,' I say as I drop my handbag and go to slip my arms round his slim waist while he stirs something in a saucepan. I lay my head on his shoulder and breathe in his scent. 'Do I tell you enough?'

'At least ten times a day.'

'I should say it more. Much more.' Then I burst into tears.

'Whoa. Whoa. Where did that come from?' Crush abandons our dinner and turns round to hold me in his strong arms. 'Lucy, what's wrong?'

'I feel a bit tired and emotional,' I sniff.

'You're working *way* too hard.' He coos as he strokes my hair. 'You're overtired,' he says, as if I'm five.

'I expect so,' I snivel. 'Chantal brought Lana in to see us today.'

'She brings her in pretty much every day,' he points out.

'This felt different.' I gulp back some tears. 'Because I think I might want a baby too.'

'That's fine. Absolutely fine.' Crush pats my back lovingly. 'We can work on that. In fact, we can work on it right after dinner if you like.'

I whack him. 'Not now. One day.' Then I blurt out, 'I realise that we haven't had much . . . you know . . . recently. I've been very busy. You've been busy too. But I'll make it up to you.'

Crush frowns. 'We need to have a talk about that.'

'Really, I'll make it up to you. I promise.' When Crush and I first got together we made love all the time. Daily. More than daily. Now we're lucky if we manage to find time to sleep together once a week and I don't want him to get fed up and start looking elsewhere. Years of being scarred by Marcus's roving eye and wandering hands have left me feeling very insecure. If I don't keep Crush happy in that department then there's always some willing cow who doesn't believe in the sisterhood ready to step into my shoes. 'We can do it with the pink fluffy handcuffs, the nurse's outfit. Whatever you like.'

'It's not about that, you crazy fool.' He chucks me under the chin. 'You're busy, Lucy. Too busy. I know that you love running Chocolate Heaven, but you can't do it single-handedly.'

'I can manage.'

'Barely.'

'I don't want Clive and Tristan to think that I'm not coping.'

'When they were running Chocolate Heaven, they had each other,' Crush points out. 'You haven't got anyone. You've got to take on an extra pair of hands. Someone you can rely on. You've said the business is doing well. They can afford it.'

'I know, I know.' And I do know. I hate to admit this, but I can't limp along by myself. I wanted to prove that I was some sort of chocolate-dealing Superwoman and I am failing. I look up at Crush's concerned countenance. I love this man right down to my fingertips and I'm neglecting him. 'I don't want it to affect our relationship.'

'Neither do I, Gorgeous. But we have to face facts, it's not exactly helping at the moment. I'm working hard to keep my head above water at Targa too. We don't have much quality time.'

'I'm sorry. I've spent too long wishing for a relationship like this to want to mess it up.' Though I have to admit that I've also spent too long wishing for a great job and I don't want to mess that up either.

When I worked as a temporary secretary at Targa all I had to do was sit and look wistfully at my boss all day long – one Mr Aiden Holby – and eat chocolate. Not exactly taxing. Though sometimes my elbows used to hurt from all that leaning on the desk with my chin cupped in my hands. My eyes used to go dry from staring at him. And my cheeks used to ache with longing. Now he's here, I'm in his arms, and I'm too bloody busy and knackered to enjoy it.

'I love you,' he says. 'I'm never going to hurt you. I'm just concerned for you.'

'Thank you.' I cling to him again, grateful.

'I think we should disentangle ourselves, Gorgeous,' Crush suggests as he eases himself gently from my grip. 'The carbonara is starting to burn.'

'It smells divine. You're wonderful.' I am not the one who is the domestic goddess in this partnership. 'I brought a couple of slices of the devil's food cake home as my contribution. Thought that would cheer us up.'

'Perfect.' He kisses me again. 'But I'm not sad, I'm worried about you. That's different.'

I watch Crush dish out our dinner, doing it all with tender attention, and know that I am loved. Truly loved. How many people can say that with absolute certainty? It makes me want to cry again. I spent too long with my ex-boyfriend, Marcus, being treated like dirt to take Crush's love for granted. I'm cherished and I must make Crush feel that he's cherished too. Mr Aiden Holby is absolutely right. He is everything to me. And something has to change.

Chapter Five

Nadia didn't feel that the interview had gone well. She could hear it in her own voice as she answered the questions – she sounded too needy, too desperate, too nervous. They had asked her about childcare arrangements, which she wasn't even sure if they were legally allowed to do, and she'd answered in too much detail, anxiously, making it sound as if it would be a breeze to abandon her son all day to the tender ministrations of other people. Perhaps they could see through her bluster. She didn't necessarily want to work, but she certainly had to. Nadia didn't expect the phone to ring. All in all, another one that would be chalked down to experience.

'Mummy,' Lewis said, exasperated. 'You've read the *same* sentence *two times*.'

'Sorry, sweetheart.' Nadia smiled at his admonishment. She was, indeed, guilty of conducting his nightly bedtime story without concentrating on the job in hand.

'Why are you sad?'

'I'm not sad,' she said. 'I was just thinking.'

Lewis snuggled into her. 'Think *after* you read. When I'm asleep.'

'Yes, of course.' Sensible advice, as it was the evenings that she struggled with. They seemed long, interminably so, now that Toby was gone. During the day she could keep busy. There was housework, Lewis to play with, shopping to be done and, if she was lonely, she could always count on Chocolate Heaven for some solace. When Lewis had gone to bed there was nothing much for her to do but watch television. She couldn't go out or run the Hoover round. Sometimes, she was tempted to keep him up too late just for the company. Other times she went to bed at the same time as Lewis. Better to be asleep than to be alone. But the downside was that she was then wide awake by four in the morning. She'd used to love reading, curled up on the sofa or in bed while Toby was engrossed on the computer – the more romantic the story the better. But she couldn't read a book now as they invariably ended happily and that was a total fairy tale. In real life, shit happened and it stayed shitty.

She was about to regroup and take up the story of *Charlie and the Chocolate Factory* once more, when Lewis said, 'Is Jacob coming to our house?'

Ah, Jacob. There were evenings when she was very grateful for his company. They never did very much – perhaps watched a film together. He seemed to have a never-ending supply of DVDs at his disposal, which was useful. Plus he was easy company. Jacob was articulate and amusing. He was laid back and kind. And he was as happy to sit quietly as to chat. Being with him was infinitely better than sitting alone.

'No,' she told him. 'Not tonight, sweetheart. He's busy with work.' Quite often Jacob's job as an events organiser kept him occupied in the evenings.

Lewis cuddled his teddy to him and his thumb slipped into his mouth – a sure sign that, in a few more pages, he'd be fast asleep. 'I like Jacob.'

'Me too.' He was a good friend and she was very fond of him. Sometimes she wondered whether there would be more between them in the future, but she'd been badly hurt by Toby and it was far too soon to even consider another relationship. She couldn't afford – emotionally or financially – to be burned again.

'Is he going to be my new daddy?'

She laughed. There was nothing like a question from a four-year-old to cut to the chase. 'No, darling. Jacob is just a friend.'

He pondered on that for a moment. 'Like Pasha is my friend?'

'Yes. Exactly like that.'

'Will I ever get a new daddy?'

'I don't know, darling.' She stroked his dark hair. He was changing, looking more and more like Toby as he grew. His mannerisms the same as his father's, down to a T. Sometimes it was difficult to watch. 'Good daddies aren't easy to find.'

'Oh.'

'Do you miss Daddy?'

'Yes,' Lewis said, giving it serious consideration. 'But not so much now.'

She wondered if he could still picture Toby's face, remember what he was like. When he was older would memories of his father remain? They were struggling through it together and Lewis was doing well – better, it seemed, than Nadia was. There were days when she still missed Toby so much, despite the mess he'd left her in. And there was no doubt that she was in a terrible mess. Most of it due to her husband's addiction to online gambling.

It had been an awful time for her – for Lewis too. Even as she was grieving, it was still the betrayal that hurt the most. Toby had been gambling for years but, before his death, it

29

had spiralled out of control and turned him into a man she didn't know.

Perhaps foolishly, she thought that her husband had kicked his habit, but all the time he was sinking them deeper and deeper into debt. Crazily, he went to Vegas for one last make-or-break play – the act of a desperate man. When Nadia found out what he'd done, she'd spent the last of their cash on a plane ticket to follow him out there. She'd hoped that she could find him and stop him from losing all of their money, their future. In the end, she'd got there just too late and, tragically, helplessly, had to watch her husband fall from the top of the Stratosphere Tower to his death. It was heart-breaking.

There were nights when she daren't close her eyes or risk sleep as she'd dream endlessly of his fall through the air, hear his anguished shout. It was something she would never get over.

Needless to say, he'd gambled away everything. She wondered how he'd been able to do that, not only to her, but to Lewis too. Hadn't the thought of leaving their lovely, innocent son without a stable future made any difference to him? Clearly not. She'd forgiven Toby a lot of things over the years, but she could never forgive him that.

To make matters worse, the insurance company were still wrangling over whether it was an accident or intentional and were refusing to pay out on their life insurance policy until they'd made their decision. How long that would take, God only knew.

When the money came through, she wanted to spend it wisely as it would have to last them a long time. But she would spend some of it repairing the house – the one that they'd so nearly lost – it was certainly in need of it. The place looked shabby now and it wasn't in a great area. Perhaps it would be a good time for her and Lewis to move away completely and make a new start somewhere else. She'd love to move out of London, even go to the seaside perhaps. The city was no place to bring up a child. But would she ever have the nerve to leave the friendship of the Chocolate Lovers' Club behind? She relied so heavily on the girls for emotional support that it was hard to envisage. She saw or spoke to one or all of them on a daily basis. At the moment, she couldn't manage without the help that Autumn freely gave to her. Her family had cut her off when she'd married Toby against their wishes. She thought that his death would help to reconcile them, but she'd heard nothing. They hadn't even sent their condolences.

Then, this morning, completely out of the blue, a letter had arrived from her sister, Anita. She wanted them to meet up. Nadia had read the note, in Anita's once-familiar, neat writing, a dozen times. She'd wanted to stay cross at her but, undeniably, there was a chink of happiness that this simple note had created that she couldn't ignore. Anita wanted to see her again and that made Nadia so glad.

'Mummy,' Lewis prompted.

'Sorry, darling.' She pulled her attention back to her son.

'You said that before.' He tucked his teddy under the duvet. 'I'm sleepy now.'

'Can Charlie wait for tomorrow?'

Lewis nodded. So she kissed him and, reluctantly, levered herself from his bed.

'Sleep tight, sweetheart.'

'Night, night, Mummy.'

She turned off the bedside light and, as he settled down and his breathing deepened, tiptoed out of his room. Now she'd sit and watch television, read the letter from Anita again, fret about her interview technique and worry about how she was going to pay the bills.

Chapter Six

Chantal knew that she was spending a lot of time at Chocolate Heaven. Even more than usual. It was doing absolutely nothing to improve her waistline, but it was still preferable to being alone at home all day. Except she wasn't. She'd never be alone again. Now, whatever she did, wherever she went, there was always her daughter to consider.

Since she'd had Lana she felt exhausted, both emotionally and physically. What she needed was an early night. One where she actually slept all the way through from dusk until dawn. No wonder sleep deprivation was used as a means of torture.

Ted had come home late from work and had given her a perfunctory kiss. Not too long ago that would have sent her into a spiral of depression. Now, if she was honest, she was just grateful that he didn't want more from her.

'Hey,' her husband said. 'How's my best girl been today?'

'Wonderful,' Chantal said. 'I took her into Chocolate Heaven. The girls love to see her. I put her down in her cot a little while ago.' There was a snuffle from the baby monitor and they both turned to look at it, breathing again when Lana settled herself and the red lights went out.

'I'll pop up to see her.'

'Don't wake her,' Chantal said. 'It took me an age to get her to sleep.'

'I'll try not to.'

While Ted went upstairs to see his daughter, she plated up some supper for him. A slice of tomato quiche that she'd bought at the nice deli down the road and a green salad. Ted suffered from a surfeit of business lunches and liked to eat lightly in the evening, which was fine by her.

They had become closer as a couple during her pregnancy with Lana, but since the baby had been born, there was precious little time to work on their relationship. At one time, she didn't think that their marriage would survive, but here they still were. They weren't fighting – thank goodness, as she had no energy for that either – but they hadn't exactly resolved their issues. They were living in the same house, sharing a bed, but they were in a celibate relationship, more like brother and sister again than husband and wife – as they had mainly been before Lana was born. The only difference was that this time she didn't see it as a huge problem. On the contrary, she thought it was great. The very last thing on her mind was bouncing around in the bedroom. Plus there was rather more of her to bounce around than there once had been and there was no doubt that was a passion-killer for her. Heaven only knew what Ted thought. To think she'd once been viewed by the girls as man-hungry.

Now Ted had finished his supper and was in the study, catching up with some emails. At the sound of increasingly more determined whimpers from the baby monitor Chantal went upstairs to give Lana her late-night feed.

She was sitting in the rocking chair in Lana's nursery. The light was dimmed and all she could hear was the hum of the television from downstairs playing away to itself and the occasional contented sucking noise from the child at her breast. Despite her tiny daughter being unaware of the impending chaos of Christmas, Chantal had decorated her nursery for her. Lana might be too young to appreciate it, but surely she had to mark her daughter's first Christmas in the world.

Chantal hadn't told any of the girls, but she'd slipped out for an afternoon of shopping with Jacob Lawson and together they'd chosen all of the decorations for Lana's room. It had been great fun, a real tonic and they'd laughed a lot.

She shouldn't see Jacob. It was madness. If she was working on her relationship with Ted, then really Jacob should be out of the picture completely. But she had to admit that he was always a very pleasant distraction.

Also, it was looking increasingly likely that Nadia and Jacob might start a relationship. They'd become very good friends in recent months and Jacob spent a lot of time at her house. Nadia insisted that she still wasn't ready for a relationship and Chantal could well understand that, but she could do worse than hook up with someone like Jacob. Chantal could give him a very good reference as husband material. He was kind, caring, funny and more than a little hot. He was tall, blond, always immaculately dressed and had impeccable manners. She always wondered why he didn't have a string of women on his arm, but that wasn't Jacob's way either. He was loyal, a good friend and unaware of just how attractive he was.

Still, she didn't know how the girls – or, more importantly, Ted – would feel about her seeing Jacob again. So she decided that it would have to remain their secret even though it was entirely platonic.

They'd had a great time. She and Jacob had hit Heals and had splurged on buying Lana some fabulous festive treats.

There was a chubby snowman light standing tall in the corner, giving off a cheery glow. On her dresser there was a contemporary glass vase filled with twinkling pink lights. Next to that was a white Christmas tree hung with pink and silver baubles featuring nursery rhymes. Not only was Jacob good company, but he had excellent taste too. Between them, they would make sure this kid had style.

She looked at the baby nestled against her, felt the warmth of her soft skin. Could it really be her child? Tiny fists worked at the air, opening and closing; she slipped her finger inside one and the perfect fingers closed tightly around hers while dark eyes searched for her face.

'Shush, little one,' she said softly. 'Everything's fine.'

At that the baby hiccupped and Chantal rubbed her back.

'Did you like seeing Lucy, Autumn and Nadia today? They all love you so much. They're going to be such good aunties to you. They're going to teach you so much about great chocolate. Yes, they are. I love them all, Lana, and I hope that you will too. I don't know what I'd do without them.'

Lana's rosebud lips pursed and a frown settled on her brow.

She felt an overwhelming rush of love for her child, a feeling so deep that she had never realised it existed, let alone that she would ever experience it. Chantal knew that from now on she would lay down her life for this little squalling bundle.

'You know, you and I are going to have a lot of fun together.'

Gazing at her baby, Chantal wondered, who exactly *did* Lana take after? Ted was undeniably handsome, but had Lana inherited his good looks? At the moment, Lana certainly didn't bear a strong resemblance to him. Ted's hair was dark, swept back from his face in a classic style. Her darling daughter had fair hair, but, perhaps that would change. At the moment, Lana's features were still predominantly pink and pudgy and Chantal was damn sure she hadn't slept with someone who looked like that during her 'wild period'. Thank goodness for the advances of modern science, otherwise she might have always remained in doubt. She sighed to herself. At the time, it had seemed as if she was having a lot of fun – picking up men in hotels wherever she stayed when she was away on business. It had made her feel empowered. Now she realised how ridiculous and desperate it had all been – not to mention risky. Thankfully, she'd come out the other side of it a wiser woman. She had Lana to thank for that. Chantal was now a responsible mother. She had other people to think about. The family unit had become all-important to her and, from now on, she'd be a one-man woman.

Since then she and Ted had done much to repair their marriage and things were OK between them. In some ways she had a newfound affection for him. However, there was another complication that was going to be more tricky to handle. Ted, too, hadn't been entirely abstemious during their brief separation and now there was another Baby Hamilton waiting in the wings.

Chantal had met Stacey – the mother of Baby Hamilton number two – only a handful of times. She'd answered a few phone calls, enquired about her welfare, and had a couple of fleeting exchanges but not much more. So far she'd managed to keep Ted's other family at arm's length. How long could that last? Stacey lived nearby and Ted went to her house whenever he visited the baby. This Hamilton baby was also a little girl, by Ted's account an adorable bundle called Elsie. Ted always went to see them at least one evening a week and during the weekend. Sometimes he could be gone all day on Saturday and it was strange to know that he'd gone to see his other family. They hadn't discussed what would happen when Elsie got older and he wanted to have her with them for the entire weekend. It was bound to happen.

If she was honest, from what she'd seen of Stacey, the girl seemed nice enough. In other circumstances, who knows, they could even have become friends. The relationship between Stacey and her husband had been brief – over, almost, before it had begun. It was an affair that had started at work while he and Chantal had been temporarily parted. For whatever reason – something else they'd never discussed – their fling hadn't lasted. When Chantal found that she was pregnant, Ted, thankfully, had decided to give their marriage another go.

Now Stacey was the one left holding the baby on her own. There was a part of Chantal that was tremendously grateful Ted had stayed with her. But she also felt awful for Stacey; it must be difficult to be a single mum trying to bring up a child by yourself. Goodness only knew, it was hard enough with two sets of hands to the pump.

What a mess this was. The repercussions of their foolishness would continue for years. Always at the back of her mind were questions and more questions. Would Ted love Lana or the other baby more? Would one of the children look more like him as they grew older? Which of the bonds would be stronger? And how on earth would they cope with their strange little family ties in the future? Chantal sighed to herself. Only time would tell. They had two beautiful babies as a result of their tangled relationships and they were related by blood – half-sisters. The girls should be aware of that.

These were the difficulties that created ripples through the generations, all caused because some stupid grown-ups, after a few badly aimed glasses of wine and a vague sense of entitlement, felt they deserved some 'commitment-free' sex. Chantal sighed to herself. Perhaps that was unnecessarily harsh, but there was no doubt the ramifications were more far-reaching than she'd ever anticipated.

'You've got a half-sister, Lana,' Chantal murmured, stroking

37

the soft hair down on her daughter's head. 'Perhaps we should arrange for some play dates?'

Despite trying to keep the lightness in her voice, she felt a tear spring to her eyes. She didn't want her child's future to be turbulent. She wanted Lana to have a long and happy life, filled with lots of love and a little bit of chocolate.

Chapter Seven

Autumn had been quiet all evening; she was thinking about Rich and it had made her sad. Addison, for once, had seemed keen to discuss the wedding plans, but she couldn't focus. It had caused some tension with him, as it always did. Her fiancé could never be classed as her brother's biggest fan – dead or alive.

'I should go home,' Addison said, somewhat petulantly. There was a scowl marring his handsome, dark face. A scowl that seemed to be there more often than not these days. He ran a hand over his shaved, ebony head.

'Stay,' she said. 'I'm sorry. This is all very raw. I feel so alone without Rich.'

Addison bristled. It was the wrong thing to say. 'You have me.'

'I meant family,' she corrected. 'He's always felt like the only family I have.' She'd hoped that she would have become closer to her parents in the circumstances, but they'd remained as cold and aloof as ever. Her mother had cried at Rich's funeral. It was the first time that Autumn had ever seen her break down. Even then they were controlled, sophisticated tears. No red eyes, dribbling nose or noisy sobbing from her mother. However, her father had resolutely maintained his stiff upper lip throughout. How could someone bury their only son and remain dry-eyed?

She and Addison had watched a film which had slipped past Autumn's eyes without her taking any of it in and, even when she'd laid her head in his lap to cuddle up to him, Addison had remained tense. She hoped that he understood what she was going through. Surely he must have lost a loved one too? Losing someone as close as a brother, particularly one who'd been so very reliant on her, was like losing one of her own limbs. Part of her was missing and she didn't know if, without Rich, she'd ever feel whole again.

Later, she and Addison had gone to bed tetchy with each other and had slept back to back. This morning he'd got up and gone straight into the office. It didn't help that they both worked at the same place. They'd met at the drugs rehabilitation centre, where Addison was much higher up the ladder than she was. He'd started as an enterprise development officer, but had recently been promoted to chief administrator and, all too often, she could see the strain of increased responsibility on his face. All she did was teach classes on stained-glass techniques, which was hardly at the cutting edge of drug treatment, but it did help some of the kids to keep out of trouble. At one time, she was at the centre every day. Now her shifts were being reduced and some weeks she only went in once or twice. The only upside was that it meant there wasn't a problem that she and Addison shared a place of work as she didn't see a great deal of him. Much of Addison's day was now spent on paperwork – but she hoped that his mood would have improved by the time she arrived.

As soon as Addison had left, Autumn sat at the kitchen table and ate a slice of toast. Her appetite had disappeared in the last few months – even for chocolate. Normally, she'd have gone over to Rich's place every day to see how he was, make sure that he was eating and taking his medication and she'd yet to find something to fill that void. Helping out Nadia by looking after Lewis had gone a long way to distracting her from her pain, plus she and Nadia had become closer. They'd both suffered in a way that Lucy and Chantal couldn't fully understand – no one did until it happened to them – and she was so glad of her friendship. She'd hoped that in her grief she would find that closeness and empathy with Addison, but it wasn't to be.

Nadia was desperate for a job and had been called for a second interview by one of the companies she'd seen a couple of weeks ago. Obviously, her friend was keen to go and had called last night to ask if she would look after Lewis for a few hours again today before he went to nursery. Some days he went in the morning, sometimes in the afternoon which could make juggling childcare a little tricky.

Of course, she hadn't hesitated. She adored Lewis and it was never difficult to find the time or inclination to babysit for him. Not that he was a baby anymore; at four years old, he was quite the little man and would soon be going to school all day. Nadia couldn't wait for it to happen as it meant it would be easier for her to go back to work, but it would leave a hole in Autumn's life. She liked the time that she and Lewis spent together. Sometimes it left a longing in her that was hard to ignore.

When she arrived to collect him, Lewis was already buttoned up in his coat.

'It's cold out today,' she warned.

'I don't mind, Auntie Autumn.'

Lewis was an outdoors kind of boy. There was only so

long he could spend with a jigsaw or toy, so there always came a point where she'd take him to the local park to run off some excess energy. It was a bit like taking an exuberant puppy for a walk.

'Good luck with the interview,' she said to Nadia.

'Keep everything crossed for me.' Nadia bent to kiss her son goodbye. 'Love you to the moon and back. Be good for Auntie Autumn. See you both later.'

Then, as Nadia headed towards the Tube, Autumn and Lewis headed for the park. He was holding her hand, rather reluctantly, and skipping along beside her as they went up the road. The snow on the pavement was slushy and Lewis kicked at it in his wellingtons. As soon as they reached the safe area inside the park railings, she could let him off the leash to run wild.

The first port of call was always the swings and today was no different. Lewis dashed towards them, Autumn trailing in his wake, puffing heavily. It was strange how a young child could make you feel both energised and exhausted at the same time.

As the weather was sharp and the sky hanging low, they had very little company. This was usually a very busy play-ground, but the plummeting temperature must have made staying at home to watch television seem very attractive. Autumn clapped her hands together in her gloves to ward off the cold. Lewis had no such issue – he'd already jumped onto the swing and was working his little legs to go higher.

'Auntie Autumn,' he cried. 'Push me. Push me higher!'

She went over to oblige.

On the swing next to Lewis was a little girl of a similar age. At the same time as Autumn took up station behind Lewis's swing, a man came along to push her. Obviously, from the doting look on his face, the child's dad.

'Looks like our duties are required,' he quipped.

'Yes.' He had a nice smile and, though Autumn tried not to look, a few sideways glances told her that he was rather handsome too. He was tall, in need of a shave, and his striped beanie hat hid the colour of his hair, but she suspected it might be chestnut brown as his skin was lightly freckled. He looked muscular too, but that could be due to the bulk of his padded winter coat. Above all he had kind eyes and a sensual mouth that seemed ready to smile. He looked like a man who would be reliable, a good friend.

'This is Florence,' he nodded towards the rosy-cheeked child swinging in front of him.

'And this is Lewis. Say hello.'

'Hello,' Lewis said. 'Enough swings now, Auntie Autumn. Want the see-saw.'

'Me too,' Florence piped up.

'Do you want to share the see-saw with Florence?' Autumn asked. It was never a given. Since he'd lost his dad, Lewis could be prone to a tantrum that came out of nowhere. Sharing could be an issue.

This time Lewis nodded and they all headed to the see-saw together. Florence and Lewis clambered on while Autumn and Florence's dad stood by, observing their charges.

'I was going to ask if you came here often,' the man said, 'but that sounds way too cheesy.'

Autumn laughed. 'I forgive you.'

'It's not a pick-up line, I promise.'

'Then the answer's reasonably often. Probably two or three times a week.'

'I don't know how I haven't seen you and your son before.'

'He's not my boy,' Autumn explained. 'Lewis is my friend's son, but I look after him a couple of times a week for her. She's on her own, so it's hard.'

'I know the feeling.' He held out a hand. 'I'm Miles, by the way. Miles Stratford.'

'Autumn Fielding.'

'Nice to meet you. I'm here virtually every day, but some of the mums still view me with the utmost suspicion. Single man in playground scare.'

'A sign of the times, I guess.'

'Sad though. I work from home, so I'm able to look after Florence in the day and then I work at night when she's gone to bed.'

'That must take a lot of discipline.'

'You do what you have to, don't you? It's not so bad.' He looked down, working at the springy surface of the playground with the toe of his chunky boot. 'Florence's mum and I still live in the same road and we share childcare. Flo has one week with me and one week with my ex. It's not ideal, but what is these days?'

'You've stayed friends?'

He grinned. 'I wouldn't go as far as to say that. But we're not at each other's throats. Not anymore.'

They watched as Florence and Lewis climbed off the see-saw – without accident – and rushed to the shiny spinner. Florence took the seat on it while Lewis leaned on the bar. She and Miles ambled behind them and, when they reached the kids, gave them a gentle spin.

'What sort of work do you do?' She didn't want to pry but, even with this short conversation, he seemed like a very easy guy to talk to. He came across, instantly, as very open and she'd become so used to walking on eggshells with Addison that it was nice to have a conversation with someone who didn't have an agenda.

'Website designer. It's flexible. That's why I can fit my work around Florence. I like to think I do my best work at three in the morning. Though I might be kidding myself.' He smiled. 'Do you work?'

'Part time in a drugs rehabilitation programme called Kick It! It's for young offenders, and we have a drop-in at the Stolford Centre.'

'I know of the place. Worthwhile.'

'I teach stained-glass techniques,' she admitted. 'I'm not exactly at the forefront of the programme, but I think the classes help to take their mind off things and it keeps their hands busy. Even small achievements can do so much for their self-esteem and I do have a few successes. One of my students is running her own jewellery stall in Camden Market.' Then Autumn flushed. 'Now I'm boasting.'

'Not at all. It's interesting to hear.'

Autumn checked her watch. She was reluctant to leave, but it was getting cold standing there.

'Not the day for hanging around,' Miles noted as if reading her mind.

'No. My toes have turned to ice.'

'Let's round up the kids before they freeze to death,' he said. 'If you're not in a rush, we could walk down to the café by the lake.' To close the deal, he added, 'Hot chocolate. My treat.'

Autumn smiled. 'Just what the doctor ordered.' Offering her hot chocolate on their first meeting. She liked that. He sounded like a man after her own heart.

Chapter Eight

'So,' I say to the members of the Chocolate Lovers' Club. 'These are our not-very-long-out-of-the-oven, state-of-the-art mince pie and brownie combos. Let me know what you think.'

I put down the plate with a flourish and they fall on them like vultures. Nice vultures, obvs. It looks like the festive experiments are a big hit.

'Wow,' Nadia says. 'These are amazing. I need the recipe.'

'Like you're ever going to make them when you can buy them from me with your friends and family discount,' I scoff.

'True,' she laughs. 'I don't know what I was thinking of.'

'I'll make you wash your mouth out with wine, if I ever catch you talking like that again.'

'Oh, wine,' Nadia breathes. 'I can't remember when I last had a drink. We *need* a night out. Or I do. I could do with cheering up. I didn't get that job I went for and my second interview came to nothing. I'm beginning to think that I'm unemployable.'

'Something will come along,' Chantal assures her. 'You're fabulous. You'd be an asset to any business. I'll put my feelers out. I'm a bit out of the loop since having Lana, but I can see if any of my old contacts have any openings.'

'Thanks, Chantal. I'd appreciate it,' she says. 'It's not all doom and gloom though. I did have some good news. Completely unexpectedly, I had a letter from my sister, Anita.'

'Oh, Nadia. That's lovely.' The girls knew that when she married Toby, Nadia had become estranged from her family as he wasn't their choice of husband. They thought that he was unsuitable marriage material and it turns out that they might have been right.

'The letter didn't say much,' Nadia continues, 'but she asked if we could meet up. So I rang her straight away and we're arranging to get together.'

I know that Nadia would dearly love to be back in the bosom of her family. We, the Chocolate Lovers' Club, do all we can for her, but there are some roles that can't be filled by anyone other than blood family and I know that she particularly misses her sister.

'I thought I might bring her here. What do you think, Lucy?'

'If you let me know when, I could put a reserved sign by the sofa over in the corner, so that you'd have a bit of privacy.'

'Sounds great. I'll see what she wants to do. I feel like I'm walking a bit of a tightrope. I can't assume anything.'

'It's a start,' I say encouragingly. 'That can only be a good thing.'

Chocolate Heaven is busy today. Extra busy. So busy that I haven't even had a minute for my usual daydreams about Crush. The weather's bright and crisp, so the sprinkling of snow hasn't stopped play. As we're nearly in December, I've risked putting a festive playlist on my iPod as background music in the café. No one's complained yet, which has to be a good thing.

'I've been thinking that I should have a night out with Ted,' Chantal says. 'Lana's nearly six months old and we haven't had a single date night yet. Could you babysit for us, Autumn?'

'Yes, of course.'

'It's his birthday later in the week. Would that suit you?'

'I've got nothing planned. Addison is very busy with work at the moment, so I'm not seeing much of him.' Autumn shrugs. 'I'm all yours. Just let me know.'

'Great,' Chantal says. 'Not sure what we'll do yet. Probably go for a meal somewhere nearby. I don't think we'll be painting the town red. My days of that are definitely over, but I'll ask Ted to clear the evening in his diary.'

I flop down in the chair next to them for a second, eye still on the counter in case anyone comes in. 'Is that what it comes down to? Clearing space in the diary for each other?'

Chantal nods at me. 'It's hard to be spontaneous with a kid on your hip.'

'It's hard to be spontaneous without one,' I admit. Then, when they all stare at me, expecting further information, I offer, 'Crush and I rarely seem to have any time together now. I'm so busy here; all I want to do is fall into a heap when I get home.'

'Ask Clive and Tristan to provide some help for you,' is Chantal's solution.

'I don't like to bother them.'

'It's their business. They should know that you're run ragged.'

'It's probably just the build up to Christmas. I'm expecting it to be quieter in January.'

'You should do something nice for Crush,' Autumn suggests. 'It doesn't have to be an expensive gesture. Cook him a romantic dinner.'

'I might poison him.'

'Go and get a ready meal from Marks and Sparks,' she suggests. 'Even you couldn't make a mess of that, Lucy.'

I chew my lip. 'Do you think? He's always cooking for me.'

'Then, surely, it would be a nice surprise.'

'It's a plan,' I say. 'To be honest, I'll do whatever it takes.

Having found someone as lovely as Crush, I don't want him to fall out of love with me.'

'He worships you, Lucy,' Chantal tuts. 'You know he does.'

'I don't want to take it for granted.'

'He's not Marcus,' she reiterates.

'I know, but I still want to look after him.'

'Why don't you take a dessert home from here?' Nadia adds. 'You know the way to a man's heart is with chocolate cake.'

It's certainly the way to Crush's heart. I high-five Nadia.

'What?' she says.

'You, my dear and inspired friend, have just given me the most excellent idea.'

'I did?'

I can feel myself beaming widely.

'Don't over-reach yourself, Lucy.' Autumn looks worried. 'You know what happens when you do.'

'This will be a breeze,' I say. 'Trust me. I have to do nothing but be fabulous.'

Now they *all* look worried.

'Trust me. I will *so* rock this.'

Then the door opens and I'll swear it's a coach party. A dozen people crowd round the counter. Perhaps word is spreading about Alexandra's fabulous chocolate cakes as business is booming. I box up half a dozen for customers to take home with them and, when I've taken their orders, the rest settle themselves at tables or on the available sofas. Chantal's right. I should speak to Clive and Tristan. I'm exhausted. This place is getting very popular and I can't run it single-handed even though I am a Superman-type woman, if you know what I mean.

Still, I throw back my shoulders, pin on my smile and, while I set to making the orders, I turn up the Christmas songs a little and think about the night to come.

Chapter Nine

As Autumn suggested, I pushed my way through the crowds of cranky Christmas shoppers to good old Marks and Sparks on the way home and bought multiple boxes of delicious and, more importantly, ready-made food. All I have to do is ping them or throw them in the oven when Crush arrives. Miraculous! What did we ever do without mobile phones, microwaves and ready meals?

For dessert, I've brought home two individual chocolate mousse cakes. Heart-shaped. Romantic, eh?

But, enough of food. That is all going to be the After-Show Party. I have something much more exciting planned for the Main Event for Crush beforehand. I've texted him and asked him not to be late. I didn't like to tell him that I was cooking dinner as he'd then dread coming home, thus defeating the objective of my cunning plan.

I'm so tired that, as soon as I've piled up all my goodies in the kitchen and have put the mousse cakes in the fridge, I go and have a lovely soak in the bath.

While I'm reclining in the bubbles, I look at the jar that I've placed on the side of the bath. There was one other shop

I called at on my way home and the fruit of my labours is now staring back at me. Chocolate body paint. A great big tub of it. I grin to myself. Oh, what fun Crush and I are going to have with that!

Here's my plan. When I'm lovely and clean, I'm going to prostrate myself on the rug in the living room, smother myself in chocolate body paint and wait for my loved one to come home. Upon which, he'll be so overcome with lust for me that he'll fall on my chocolate-coated body, lick me all over until we're both in a frenzy of lust and then we'll make mad passionate love. It will be a night to remember all round. Even though we might well have to throw the rug out.

Once he's satisfied by my body, I will then ping him M&S delights and sate his other appetites. Job done, walk away! What could possibly go wrong?

I'm feeling very relaxed when I get out of the bath. I yawn and blink my eyes awake. I think I might have even fallen asleep in there for a few seconds.

I dry myself, wrap a fluffy towel around me and pad to the living room. It's looking lovely and Christmassy in here. I've gone to town a bit this year after my miserable effort last December.

There's a mammoth tree in the corner which Crush did have to wrestle through the door. He was very kind about it all, though. It's decorated with a heart theme as befitting our loved-up state and is covered with the little beggars in every shade that I could find them. While I've gone for tasteful restraint at Chocolate Heaven, the same can't be said of my home. Pink and glitter both feature heavily.

On the fireplace, there's a large singing and dancing reindeer which belts out 'Rudolph the Red-Nosed Reindeer' and 'Jingle Bells' with very little encouragement. I give his button a push and he serenades me, ending with a cheery 'Ho-ho-ho'. That doesn't stop me from stifling another yawn.

I spread my towel on the rug and lie down. I've brought a pillow for our heads, too. No need to be uncomfortable while being passionate, I feel. Then I realise how chilly it is being in the living room in the nip, so I haul myself from the floor and crank up the central heating. The gas fire goes on too for good measure and I have a brief moment of regret that my flat doesn't come with a roaring open fire, which would be perfect for this lovemaking scenario. The steady blue glow of a gas fire just isn't the same, but it will have to suffice. I don't forget the seductive music either. Crush should be home from work very soon, so I shouldn't have to wait for too long for our chocolate-assisted shag fest to begin.

Back on my strategically placed towel, I open my jar of chocolate body paint. The plan is to be covered in this and striking a seductive pose the minute he comes through the door. I have a quick glance at my watch. Yep. Better get slapping it on. I have a quick tester taste – yum, yum – and it smells wonderful too. What an excellent erotic aid for the modern relationship. How will Crush be able to resist me?

Tentatively, I rub some on my arms. Feels a bit strange. And, potentially, a waste of good chocolate. I lick my fingers. Hmm. I'm quite tasty too. Carrying on, I smear it liberally over my chest, breasts, stomach and thighs. With my skin still pink from the bath I'm looking slightly like a chocolate-covered jelly baby. Not exactly what I was aiming for, but I'll have to make the best of what I've got.

The fire is making the room very warm now and, having coated myself in delicious chocolate, I lie down again. Because of the heat, I'm quite a bit more melty than I'd planned, but I drape myself in a seductive manner. Oh, my eyes are heavy. I think I'll close them for five minutes while I'm waiting. That can't do any harm. I haven't been to my yoga class for ages, so I could try some rhythmic breathing. That way I will not only be delicious but also relaxed. So, trying not to get chocolate everywhere, I let myself sink into the pillow. And, of course, that's the last thing I remember.

Chapter Ten

The next thing I know is that I hear the sound of a key in the lock and I start awake. For a moment I wonder what I'm doing naked on the rug covered in brown stuff and then it all comes back to me in a rush. Mission Make Love to Crush.

Quickly, I shake myself awake and arrange myself in a more suitable pose, checking there's no dribble on the towel. Never a good look. But when I glance properly at the chocolate, it's dried to a crust now and no longer looks glossy and delicious. I look more like I'm having a dirty protest. Hmm. Perhaps Crush will be so overcome by my womanly sexiness that he won't even notice.

The door opens and I pop on my most seductive pout.

'Hey, Lucy,' he shouts. 'Guess who I brought ho— *whoa!*' He pulls up short in the doorway and spreads his arms wide. '*Whoa! Whoa!*'

'*Aarrgh!*' That's from me.

'Back up, back up!' he cries. 'Back up *right* now.'

But it's too late. The two salesmen he's brought home from Targa are staring straight at me wide-eyed, mouths agape.

'Out, out!' Crush reiterates and turns to hustle them out of the door.

'Bye, Lucy,' one of them shouts. 'Nice seeing you.'

Crush closes the door while I scrabble for my towel. When I'm safely swaddled again, I risk looking at him.

He stares at me, aghast. 'What are you doing?'

My lower lip trembles. 'I thought we'd have some grown-up fun with chocolate body paint.'

At that, he laughs out loud. 'Well, I guess we have had a bit of fun, but not quite in the way you imagined.'

'That was Greg and Steve, wasn't it?' I recognised them instantly.

'Yes. It's been a while since you were the talk of Targa, Gorgeous,' Crush notes. 'I'm thinking that will change by tomorrow.'

'You have to swear them to secrecy.'

'Not a hope,' he says. 'They've both probably sent texts already.'

'I hated working there,' I say as crossly as I can.

'You didn't,' Crush says. 'You used to love staring at me all day.'

'Only a bit.' Then I sigh. 'Now I feel foolish and I wanted you to be blown away by my temptress ways and make mad passionate love to me in front of the fire like they do in movies.'

'And I've spoiled it.'

'You weren't to know,' I relent. That's the snag with surprises, I suppose; they're so often a surprise. I should have known no good could come of it.

'I'd give you a cuddle, you crazy woman, but I'll end up covered in chocolate and I only popped home to tell you that I'm taking Greg and Steve for a Chinese meal. We've got an important meeting tomorrow that we need to prepare for and we simply ran out of time at the office. I thought I'd stand them dinner while we talk about our strategy.'

Strategy, schmategy.

'I won't be long,' Crush promises. 'An hour and a half at the most.'

I feel my heart sink. Crush obviously reads my disappointment.

'Come with us, if you like.'

'I'll never be able to look either of them in the eye again,' I say sulkily. That's the Targa Christmas party off limits for me as well.

Making sure he doesn't get too close in his smart business suit, Crush bends down and kisses me.

'I love you,' he says. 'It was a really nice thought. I'll be back as soon as I can and I'll be sure to make it up to you.' He wiggles his eyebrows in an encouraging manner. 'Go and get into bed, you dirty girl, and wait for me there.'

Despite my deep disappointment and humiliation, I manage a smile. Perhaps my plans for a night of passion are not yet thwarted.

Chapter Eleven

Jumping in the shower, I wash all the luscious chocolate body paint down the drain, regretting that my plan wasn't better executed. Clearly, I am much more suited to masterminding criminal activities – as I have proved in the past – than seduction scenarios.

When I'm all clean again, I put on my snuggly pink pyjamas and burrow down under the duvet. I think I'll read until Crush comes home. I've had a book on my bedside table for months now that I haven't even glanced at. The night is still young. Maybe we could salvage some romance from the evening. Then my eyes close again and I know it's futile to fight sleep. Perhaps if I just have a little doze, then I'll wake up and be ready and raring to go.

Moments later Crush is gently shaking me awake. 'Hey, sleepy head.'

When my eyes finally focus, I realise that he's naked except for his boxer shorts, toned abs very much on show. I didn't hear him come back. I look at the alarm clock, but can't make my eyes focus on the numbers. How long has he been home?

He picks up a plate of toast from the tray on the floor and places it on the bed next me. 'Breakfast.'

All night, it seems.

Crush also puts a cup of coffee on the bedside table. 'I made it strong,' he says. 'Looks like you might need it. You were out for the count when I came home.'

'I didn't even hear you.'

'It would have been difficult above the snoring.'

I whack him. 'I do *not* snore.'

'I'd better get a move on or I'm going to be late for work,' Crush says. 'We'll have some time together tonight, Gorgeous.'

Grabbing his hand, I say, 'Stay. For just a few minutes.'

'I know you've got evil on your mind, young woman,' he counters. 'Much as I'd love to, I have a meeting with the directors at nine o'clock. Can't be late for that.'

'And I've got a date with some chocolate,' I sigh.

'Another one? Hope you're going to be wearing more clothes in Chocolate Heaven than you were last night.'

'I'm so embarrassed.'

He grins at me. 'Greg and Steve couldn't believe their eyes. Neither could I, for that matter. You were the talk of the Hong Kong restaurant last night, you hussy.'

I give him a dark look. 'I bet I was.'

Crush laughs and crosses to the wardrobe and pulls out a shirt and his suit. I love him in a suit; he looks so sexy. However, I have to say that he's looking mighty fine without his suit too.

I'm filled with a rush of love and lust for him.

Even though he's doing the reverse of a strip – A Getting Dressed, I suppose – he's making me feel all hot and bothered. No one has ever looked sexier putting trousers on.

'Let's have a romantic weekend away,' I suggest. 'Soon. We could spend all weekend having rampant sex.'

'We could stay here and do that,' he points out as he buttons his shirt.

'I know. But we never seem to get round to it. We could go somewhere snowy and really get in the mood for Christmas.' I'm warming to my theme now. 'We could perhaps take in a Christmas market.'

'Deep joy.' Crush knots his tie. 'What do you want, sex or shopping?'

'Maybe a bit of both.'

'If it will keep you happy, we can do that. Could you get the time away from Chocolate Heaven? It's surely your busiest time of the year?'

'Oh, yeah.' Another ill-considered plan bites the dust.

'Maybe one of the girls could hold the fort for a couple of days,' he puts forward. 'Would Nadia be glad of the extra money? Perhaps Autumn could do a few hours too.'

'A brilliant idea!' Now I know why Mr Aiden Holby was my boss and I was the lowly temporary secretary who could never find the filing. 'It's the perfect solution.' I jump out of bed and fling my arms round Crush. 'I love you,' I say.

He grins at me indulgently when he answers, 'I love you, too.'

Chapter Twelve

Nadia arrived at Chocolate Heaven ahead of her sister. 'I'm nervous, Lucy,' she said. Lewis had caught her anxious mood and had been particularly fractious this morning. It was becoming increasingly difficult to be spending so much time away from her son but, for once, she was relieved to be dropping him off at the nursery.

'Don't be,' Lucy said, kindly. 'Remember, Anita was the one who contacted you. She's the one who offered the olive branch. Surely she must be looking for reconciliation.'

'You're right.' Nadia tried to stop wringing her hands. 'What's the worst that can happen?'

'You'll be fine,' Lucy assured her. 'If you start coming to blows, I'll be sure to step in. But, before she gets here, I wanted to ask you a favour.'

'Ask away.'

'Crush and I were thinking about going away on a romantic weekend somewhere. Preferably before Christmas if we can squeeze it in. Do you think that you could look after Chocolate Heaven for me for the weekend so we could sneak off? I know it's a lot to ask.'

'As long as Autumn can help me with babysitting, I'd love to.'

Lucy kissed her. 'You're a star.'

'You haven't negotiated rates yet,' Nadia laughed. 'You might not be able to afford me.'

'I know you,' Lucy countered. 'Will work for chocolate.'

'So true.'

Lucy handed over her cup of espresso and a chunk of the delicious rocky road that was her current favourite. It was rich, dark chocolate and loaded with pistachio nuts and squishy marshmallows. Every bite was pure heaven. What could be better to calm her nerves?

Nadia made her way to the leather sofas in the far corner of the café and settled down. Lucy had put a reserved sign on the coffee table as she'd promised, but there was no need as Chocolate Heaven was unusually quiet this morning. Though it rarely stayed that way for long.

Nadia had only taken the first sip of her coffee when the doorbell chimed and she saw Anita come through the door. Her sister was older than Nadia by two years, but it was like looking at her twin. They had the same long black hair. The same nose. The same dark, almond-shaped eyes. It was only when she saw Anita that she realised how very much she'd missed her these past years. She was a part of her and not seeing Anita had left a hole inside her.

Standing up, Nadia waved and, as she did, noticed that her hands were trembling. Anita saw her and made her way towards the back of the café. Nadia stood awkwardly as she waited, not sure what to do. Anita did the same. They stood and looked at each other, a whole raft of emotions clear on their faces.

'Are we both going to stand here all day?' Anita said, voice husky.

Nadia stepped forward and Anita threw her arms round

her sister, hugging her tightly. When they pulled apart, there were tears in their eyes and they both felt self-conscious.

'This is a nice place,' Anita said, trying to regain her composure. She glanced around at their surroundings. 'Christmassy.'

'It's a bit of a home from home for me.'

'I can see why.'

'The girls I meet here are great.' It was sad to think that her sister didn't even know who her closest friends were. In fact, she didn't know what she would have done without them in recent times. When her family had deserted her, the girls of the Chocolate Lovers' Club had stepped in to take their place. Lucy in particular had been like a sister to her but, obviously, telling Anita that would be like rubbing salt in wounds.

Nadia sat down again and her sister sat opposite.

Lucy came over to them, pad in hand. 'Hi.'

'This is Lucy,' Nadia said. 'She's one of my best friends.'

'Pleased to meet you, Anita,' Lucy said, brightly. 'I've heard a lot about you and it's so lovely to see you here. Welcome to Chocolate Heaven. Now, ladies, what can I get for you?'

'I recommend the brownies,' Nadia said.

'The brownies are fresh this morning and we've also got a lovely tiramisu cake today,' Lucy added.

'I'll have a brownie and a black coffee please,' Anita said.

Nadia remembered that her sister was a chocolate fiend too.

'Anything else for you, Nadia?'

'Just another coffee please, Lucy.'

Lucy went off to get their drinks.

It was obvious they were skirting round the main reason why they were here, but it had been a long time and wounds couldn't instantly be healed. This would take time and effort on both sides. Nadia searched her brain, struggling for the best thing to say to span the breach.

'I'm sorry,' Anita said, pre-empting her. She reached out to clasp Nadia's hand. 'I should have contacted you before now.'

'I'm just glad that you did,' Nadia said. 'Nothing else matters.'

'It's been too long.'

Six or more years. Yet there was still a pain in her chest when she thought about how easily her sister had seemed to turn from her.

'I missed my little sister too much. I had to see you.'

'I was so pleased to get your letter. But, I have to ask, why now after all this time? What made you get in touch again?'

'It was coming up to Christmas that made me start to think of you. The boys are getting older and it made me wish that you could see them and that I could see my only nephew. I looked out some of our old photographs. We used to be a happy family, close. Didn't we?'

Nadia felt a tight ball of emotion close her throat. Her family had cut her dead when she'd announced that she was marrying Toby. They weren't a very traditional family, but there was still the hope that she'd marry a nice Indian boy. They'd found Toby too brash, too loud. They thought he was flighty. Sadly, he'd proved them right.

All the time, Nadia had hoped that her sister would defy her parents and keep up a relationship with her but, sadly, that hadn't been the case. Anita hadn't liked Toby either and, in the face of all the opposition, their relationship had fractured too. Nadia had missed her. She'd missed them all. None of her family had ever even met Lewis. She thought that after his birth, her parents would come round, thrilled by the prospect of a new grandchild, but they'd all become too entrenched in their positions. Nadia regretted that now.

'I couldn't let another year pass,' Anita said, a tear squeezing from her eye. 'I only hope that you'll forgive me.'

'Of course I will.' They hugged again. It was easy to say,

63

but the sense of betrayal and abandonment ran deep. She was going to have to work on that.

Lucy brought their order and they distracted themselves, exchanging pleasantries about the brownies, stirring the coffee, adding sugar.

'How are the boys?' Nadia asked. Anita's sons, Mani and Daman, were both a few years older than Lewis and she hadn't seen them since they were toddlers.

'A handful,' Anita admitted with a laugh. 'They're growing at a rate of knots. It won't be long before they are teenagers. I think they'll be much taller than me and Tarak when they grow up. Whatever I feed them, they can always eat more. They must have hollow legs. You and Lewis should both come to the house for dinner.' Anita's eyes filled with tears again. 'I dearly hope you will, sister. They'd love to see you.'

Nadia wondered if her nephews would even remember her after all this time.

'Tarak says that he can't wait for them to start work.'

Ah. Her dear brother-in-law. That was one member of her family whom she hadn't missed at all. It had always been a more difficult relationship and if she never saw Tarak again, it would be too soon. He was an unsuitable husband too and yet her family thought the sun shone out of him.

'How is Tarak?' she asked, dutifully, keeping her tone neutral.

'He's fine. The shops are doing really well. He has a chain of them now. Four in all.' Anita glowed with pride. 'They keep him very busy. He's always there, working late.'

When they were last in touch, Tarak had just the one shop. A place called TD Fashions which sold cheap, high-fashion clothes on Brick Lane. She should have known that his ambition would have led him to open more.

Her brother-in-law was a handsome man, always a little too smarmy for Nadia's liking. Even when he'd first married

Anita, his eyes had always lingered on Nadia for too long, his comments had been a bit too personal. He was always too keen to touch her if he passed her in the kitchen, his hands warm, damp. He gave her the creeps.

He'd tried to kiss her once at a family party when he'd caught her by herself on the landing as she went to retrieve the coat of one of their many aunties. He'd grabbed her wrist and pulled her into the spare bedroom at her parents' house, where he'd pushed her up against the wall, crushing his mouth against hers. It was really unpleasant and she'd kicked him in the shin before bolting for the door. She'd never told anyone but, after that, she'd made sure she was never, ever alone with him and their relationship afterwards had been strained. They maintained a cool civility, but no more. Thankfully, her sister, smitten as she was with Tarak, had never noticed.

Still, despite his flaws, on the surface he seemed to be a reasonably good husband to Anita. They lived in a nice home and, as far as she knew, still took holidays abroad every year. Money had never seemed to be a problem – even when he'd had one shop – and, from the way Anita was dressed and the jewellery she wore, it didn't appear to be now. Her sister gave every impression that she was very happy and she certainly looked as if life was treating her well.

'How are you coping?' Anita asked. 'Without Toby.'

Nadia hugged herself. 'I've been better.' There had been times in the last few years when she'd needed her family around her so much, and never more so since Toby died. 'The insurance company are still dragging their heels about paying out and I feel as if I'm in limbo until then.'

'I should have been there for you,' Anita said.

She should have. So should her mother and father. The fact that they'd left her floundering alone cut deep and there was nothing that Nadia could say that would smooth that over. Her friends had been the ones to step in and hold her up. She would never have managed without them. They were the ones who made sure that she was never alone for too long, that there was food in the cupboards, that Lewis was kept occupied when she had days so dark that she could hardly get out of bed.

With a skill that had been born of practice, she pushed the memories to the back of her mind. 'Thankfully, after a long wrangle, they've decreed that Toby's death was accidental.'

'That must be good news.'

'Of course,' Nadia agreed. 'As soon as I have the settlement cheque from them that will make life a lot easier, but we're managing. I only wish that they'd hurry up.'

However, the bank and credit card companies were still in dispute with Nadia about what she had to pay back from their credit cards, so she wasn't yet out of the woods. She needed to get on the phone to them again this afternoon. All the paperwork had been exhausting and she seemed to be forever chasing, chasing, chasing.

'I need to get a job now that Lewis is at nursery. But it's not easy fitting around his hours.'

'Have you had any luck?'

'No,' Nadia admitted. 'I've had several interviews, but they've all come to nothing. It's tough out there.'

'What sort of thing are you looking for?'

'Anything,' Nadia said. 'I've worked mostly in PR, but I've stopped setting my sights too high. To be honest, I'm applying for anything going. Beggars can't be choosers. I've been unemployed for a while and my confidence is at rock bottom.'

'I work for Tarak, in the original Brick Lane shop. Only a few days a week, but it keeps me out of mischief. I was bored at home now that the boys don't need me so much.'

If only she had the luxury of whether to choose to work or not, Nadia thought.

Anita's eyes lit up. 'Why don't you come and work for us too? Tarak's looking for someone else to help out. He'd be thrilled. You know what we're like. We want to keep everything in the family.'

Her blood chilled. 'I'm not so sure.' A long time had passed but she still wasn't sure that she wanted to spend her days in close proximity to her brother-in-law.

'You must,' her sister insisted. 'How wonderful would it be for us to work together? We have lost too much time, Nadia.' Her eyes brimmed with tears. 'We could gossip all day!'

'I'm sure Tarak would love that.'

'He would,' Anita said, firmly. 'He only ever wants to see me happy. What would delight me more than working with my baby sister?'

'What would you say to Mum and Dad?'

'They'll come round,' Anita assured her. 'Let me talk to them. It's time that rift was healed. I've made the first step. We can only go forward.'

It was tempting. The thought of spending more time with her sister was very appealing and there was no doubt that she needed a job – and quickly. Tarak was older – as they all were – and hopefully wiser. Perhaps he wasn't the same man that he used to be.

'I'm sure Tarak would want to help you too,' Anita pressed on, animated by her idea. 'I know that we've been estranged, but I want to make amends for that. Please let me. We're family, Nadia. That's all that matters.'

There was something in the back of her brain that said she should turn this down, it was foolish to think that it could work. Her relationship with Anita was still on a tentative footing and she didn't want to upset her again.

Yet, despite all her misgivings, she heard herself saying, 'If Tarak says that it's OK, then I'd love to.'

Chapter Thirteen

Chantal gave up trying to struggle into the little black sequined number that she'd chosen and tossed it onto the bedroom chair.

'Another one for the charity shop,' she muttered as she delved back into her wardrobe again. 'Come here, comfy pants. You are now officially my best friend.'

She slipped on the black trousers – now one of the few things left that actually fitted her increased girth. Sadly, they were maternity trousers. Chantal huffed at herself and idly wondered whether she'd ever regain her pre-baby figure. Part of her admitted that she didn't really care. As far as she was concerned, her days of being a sex siren were long behind her. Ted might feel differently, though.

Autumn was babysitting for them so that they could have a date night. The first one since Lana had been born. If she was honest, she'd prefer to be sitting at home in front of the television with Lana nestled against her and a bar of good chocolate. Ted hadn't been hinting either. In fact, he seemed surprisingly relaxed about their current situation but, as it was his birthday, she felt as if she should make some small effort.

She'd put on nice underwear. They hadn't slept together since Lana's birth, but perhaps tonight would be the night. It was Ted's birthday, after all. The thought didn't exactly fill her with joy. At the moment she felt that if she never had sex again, it might be too soon.

They weren't going far for dinner. Just to the little Italian place that they both liked a few streets away. Sequins would have been way too much for it, anyway. Chantal consoled herself with that thought. Their risotto was heavenly and they made a great double chocolate espresso torte – a rich creamy ganache on a chocolate biscuit base. She could almost taste it. Perhaps she could persuade Lucy to add it to the menu at Chocolate Heaven. Was it wrong that she was looking forward more to the dessert than the actual night out with her husband?

As she slipped on her boots, the doorbell rang and she knew that it would be Autumn – punctual as usual. Ted opened the door, so she popped into the nursery to see Lana before she left. Her daughter was sleeping soundly and Chantal hoped that it would last. She knew that they wouldn't linger long at the restaurant, but she'd expressed plenty of milk just in case Lana was ready for another feed before they were home. Of course, Autumn would be itching to give her a bottle. Autumn was the one who was the natural earth mother among them all.

No one had been more surprised when her own nurturing instinct had kicked in the minute she'd laid eyes on Lana. She stroked her daughter's downy head, felt the usual rush of love and whispered, 'Sleep tight, sweetheart.'

Then she ran down the stairs to greet her friend. Ted was already taking Autumn's coat.

'Hey,' Chantal hugged her. 'The fridge is stocked. There's wine. Some treats from the deli and plenty of chocolate.'

'I should babysit more often,' Autumn joked.

Chantal glanced at her watch. 'Our table is in ten minutes. We'd better get a move on.'

'I'm ready,' Ted said.

As her husband hung up Autumn's coat with one hand, he passed Chantal's to her with the other and she shrugged it on.

'We won't be long,' she said to Autumn.

'I'm not going anywhere,' Autumn said. 'I'm yours for the evening. Take as long as you like.'

'Call me if you need to. Don't hesitate.' It was the first time she'd left Lana and she knew that she was panicking unnecessarily.

'Everything will be fine. Go.' Autumn shooed them towards the door.

'She's fast asleep.'

'Then I'll resist the urge to wake her up for a cuddle as soon as you're gone.'

'There's a bottle ready to warm in the kitchen if she does wake up.'

'Get out of here,' Autumn said, waving towards the door. 'Don't fuss.'

Chantal kissed Autumn's cheek. 'I love you.'

'I love you, too. Have a lovely evening. Relax. Drink wine.'

'We will if we ever get out of the house,' Ted said.

Chantal held up her hands. 'I'm outta here.'

A few seconds later, Ted ushered her out onto the street. The wind was biting and the weather forecast was for a dusting of snow again. It was looking more and more likely that a white Christmas was on the cards.

'Cold?' Ted asked.

'Freezing. Let's hurry.'

He tucked her arm into his and together they set off at a good pace. That would soon get them warm. A hard frost was settling on the trees along their street.

When they reached the restaurant, it looked inviting with candles flickering in the window. As they opened the door, the scents of garlic and herbs wafting towards them were equally appealing. It was warm inside, slumber-inducingly so. It was a long time since she'd had an unbroken night's sleep and she wondered if they had a couch in here that they'd mind her using for a pre-dinner nap. Holly and mistletoe hung from the beams in the ceiling and a Christmas tree that was really too large for the space was crammed in the corner. She remembered why she'd loved this cosy place.

As it was a week night, the restaurant was relatively quiet with only a few other couples already seated. Thankfully, it was too small to host the office parties that normally started with a vengeance at the beginning of December. They were fussed over by the owner and shown to what had once been their regular favourite table. It felt as if they were turning back the clock.

'This is nice,' Chantal said.

'We should do it more often,' Ted agreed.

'Once a month. Without fail.' They both knew that it was highly unlikely, but the sentiment was there and that was a good start.

When they'd ordered, she and Ted chatted about nothing in particular until their food came. Her husband had two glasses of Prosecco, which she eschewed as she was mostly still breastfeeding Lana and no one liked a drunk baby.

She toasted her husband's birthday with a Diet Coke. 'Happy birthday, darling.'

They clinked glasses.

As she tucked into her pumpkin risotto topped with crispy sage, Chantal broached the subject that always hung between them when they were alone now and asked, 'How are Stacey and Elsie?'

Most of the time she could simply blank out the fact that her husband had another child. He disappeared during the day on Saturday to visit them and, a couple of nights of the week, called at Stacey's house on the way home from work. On Wednesday evenings, he tended to stay late and surely it must be time spent alone with Stacey as Elsie, presumably, would be long in bed. She wondered what they talked about, what they did. Perhaps the reason she and Ted weren't sleeping together was that he was still actually having a relationship with Stacey. The thought had crossed her mind more than once, but she really tried not to dwell on it. Was there still more between them than Ted admitted to? Somehow, it was only when she and Ted were sitting quietly together that she felt she had to face it.

The fork he was holding stalled on its way to his mouth and Ted cleared his throat. He dropped his food back to his plate. 'It's something I've been meaning to talk to you about.'

Chantal felt her stomach clench. She tried to be cool about this. Families took many different shapes and forms these days. Blended. Wasn't that the word? Besides, she could hardly blame Ted for this. Her own copy book was hardly blot-free. Shouldn't she embrace the other half of the Hamilton family as best she could?

'Shoot,' she said as calmly as she could.

'It's Stacey, really.' He faltered slightly as he said her name. It wasn't often that they spoke of her. Their conversations, when they had them, tended to focus more on Elsie.

She waited, silently, until he found the words to continue.

'I'm worried about her.' Ted pursed his lips. 'She has very little help with Elsie. There's no family nearby to pop in as Stacey's folks live in Scotland. And Elsie seems to be a bit more . . . demanding . . . than Lana. She doesn't sleep all that well. So I believe.'

Chantal tried to remain impartial, but it was at times like this when she couldn't help but feel a pang of jealousy. 'Doesn't she have any friends?' The first people she'd turn to in a similar situation would be the girls of the Chocolate Lovers' Club.

'Most of her friends are high-fliers,' he said. 'I'm not sure that they empathise with her current situation. I can't quite put my finger on it, but I feel as if Stacey's going downhill.' Ted avoided her eyes. 'She cries a lot.'

'That doesn't sound good.' Yet Chantal wondered whether she wouldn't cry herself in the same situation. 'Has she spoken to her doctor or the health visitor?'

'I don't think so.' Ted sighed heavily. 'I have a big favour to ask you, Chantal, and I could fully understand it if you said no.'

'You want me to go and see her?' It wasn't hard to work that out.

Ted's face sagged with relief. 'Would you? I don't know what else to do. I thought if you could find out what's wrong it might help?'

Perhaps it was simply because she was on her own with a baby, and the man she loved – even if it was as briefly as Ted insisted – is now back with his wife. That was never going to be easy.

'It's a big ask, Ted.'

'I appreciate that. If you don't want to . . .' He looked as if he had no idea what else he would do if she said no.

Chantal sighed to herself. 'Will Stacey even want to speak to me?' She wasn't sure how she'd feel in Stacey's situation.

'I think so. I'll ask her to. She needs someone and I'm completely useless.'

Chantal tried a smile as she teased her husband. 'You're a guy. Of course you are.'

Ted laughed, the tension dissipating. 'I knew you'd help.'

'I can't promise to make things any better,' Chantal said, 'but I'll do what I can.'

He reached across the table and squeezed her hand. 'Thank you.'

So she'd agreed to a face-to-face with Stacey. Who'd have imagined it? And, though she managed to smile and chat throughout the rest of the meal, there was a tight knot of anxiety in her stomach.

Chapter Fourteen

Autumn noted that it was still early when Chantal and Ted returned from the restaurant – not yet ten o'clock. She knew that their relationship was still on a shaky footing, though Ted had his arm round her shoulder, so that had to be a good sign.

Chantal came in and threw her handbag down. 'How has my little angel been?'

'Disappointingly well-behaved,' Autumn said. 'I thought about prodding her awake just so that I could have a cuddle.'

'Oh, bless,' Chantal said. 'It probably means that she'll be bright-eyed and bouncy for half the night, though.'

Autumn stood up and stretched. 'I'll leave you to get to your bed then.'

'Stay,' Chantal urged. 'At least have a cup of tea with us.'

Autumn shook her head. 'I should go.' She punched a number into her phone and requested a cab. 'They'll be here in five minutes.'

'Perfect.'

'Goodnight, Ted,' Autumn said and headed for the hall. Chantal followed her and closed the living-room door behind her. She lifted Autumn's coat from the rack and helped her to shrug it on.

'Did you have a good evening?' Autumn asked, raising an eyebrow.

'Yes,' Chantal said, but there was a noticeable hesitation. 'Sort of.' She pursed her lips and then lowered her voice. 'Ted asked me to go round and visit Stacey.'

'Wow,' Autumn said, matching her tone. 'For any particular reason?'

Chantal looked to check that the door was fully closed and dropped her voice further to a hushed whisper. 'He said he thought that she was struggling. It sounds like she's depressed.'

'Baby blues?'

'Maybe. Apparently she has no family locally and all her friends are high-powered businesswomen who don't seem particularly interested in her predicament. I think she's a bit out on a limb.'

'That must be hard with a new baby. Perhaps she'd be glad of a visit then?'

'And perhaps she'll want to stab me in both eyes. It could go either way.'

'Maybe she'll be too exhausted to launch a physical attack.'

Chantal smiled. 'Ah. So true. You think I should go?'

'If Ted has asked you to, then it would be nice to find a way to reach out to her.'

Her friend tutted. 'Has anyone ever told you that you're far too nice for your own good, Autumn Fielding?'

'I could come with you.'

'If she'll agree to see me then I should do it one-on-one. I couldn't cope if she rocked up here with a mate for back-up.'

'If she had someone like that to call on then I don't think Ted would be asking you to go and see her.'

'True enough. Maybe I should sleep on it.' Chantal kissed her cheek. 'I'll see you tomorrow? Chocolate Heaven?'

'I'm sure. Text me what time you'll be there.'

'I love you,' Chantal said. 'Thanks for looking after Lana for us.'

'I did nothing except watch *Notting Hill* and eat all your chocolate.'

'That's what babysitters are supposed to do.'

A text pinged in to let her know that her cab had arrived and Chantal opened the front door. A few flakes of snow fluttered in the air.

'Don't wave me goodbye, go inside and close the door,' she said to Chantal. 'It's really cold. Give Lana a kiss for me.'

Autumn knew that she should ring Addison. He was at a conference tonight in Brighton but, for some reason, she didn't want to call. She'd told him that she was babysitting for Chantal and would be late home. If it was anything like the conferences he usually went on then he'd be in the bar at this hour, 'networking'. Probably better not to disturb him.

Then she was gripped by a need so visceral that it startled her. She didn't want to be alone tonight. She missed Rich desperately and had to find some way to be close to him. So Autumn knocked on the glass partition and, when the taxi driver slid the window open, she gave him Rich's address.

The traffic was light, the streets of London quiet as the cab made its way to her brother's apartment instead of her own. The windscreen wipers swatted the snow away lazily and she let her eyes close, allowing the cabbie's chatter about the state of the weather drift over her.

A few minutes later he dropped her off. She stood on the pavement, watching him drive away and, as the cold crept up her legs, she wished that she'd worn boots instead of shoes.

Rich's apartment was in a salubrious area of London. It

had been funded partly by him – though she had never wanted to acknowledge exactly where his money came from – but mostly by their parents. What their mother and father lacked in emotional support for their offspring, they made up for by throwing wads of cash at them. They'd known that Rich had been seriously ill, his immune system compromised by years of drug abuse. They'd also known that when he returned home he still wasn't out of the woods, but they weren't so interested in that. They'd made a few hospital visits and stumped up some money. As far as they were concerned, that was all their involvement needed to be. Though they were prepared to pay the bills, she didn't think they'd even been to this apartment since he'd moved in. And now it was too late.

If they hadn't paid for Rich's accommodation, then he might have been forced to return home and, quite frankly, they wouldn't have been able to cope with that. As children, both of them had been shipped off to boarding school as soon as humanly possible, so they hadn't lived permanently at home with their parents since they were about eight years old.

Perhaps that's why Autumn felt that she needed to over-compensate. Every transgression from Rich had felt like a failure on her own part. He'd been her responsibility. She'd been more like a mother to him than their real mother and she'd let him down. Now he was gone and it was as if her own reason for being here had disappeared along with him.

Rich's apartment was on the ground floor. It was small, one bedroom, but this was London and a good area, so it was ruinously expensive nevertheless. The snow was coming down heavier now. She wondered what she'd do for Christmas this year. Addison had made it clear that he wouldn't want to go to her parents' house again after last year's disaster. Rich had turned up drunk and high and had behaved very badly. They'd all ended up wearing Christmas dinner rather than eating it after Rich created a scene at the table. Now she'd brought it to mind, she wouldn't be that keen herself. She wondered whether her parents would insist on seeing her, but it was unlikely. She realised that, no doubt, her parents would prefer to be at one of their many homes in the sunshine or at their ski lodge. They never had been the biggest fans of Christmas or of family get-togethers.

It was late and she was doing no good standing here getting chilled down to the bone. She should go home. Yet, despite her logical reasoning, she still took the key out of her pocket, punched in the code to allow her access to the building and, with a deep breath, went inside. Rich's apartment was the first door on the right. Her heart had started to bang in her chest now. There was still a feeling that she would open the door and he'd be there sitting waiting for her or, worse, with the motley crew of druggie friends that he gathered around him.

When she let herself inside, the apartment was still exactly the same as it had been on the night of Rich's death. Of course it was. What else had she expected? Yet it broke her heart to see it. She wandered through the rooms, all of them empty, untouched, a shrine to Rich. If her parents wanted to sell this place then they hadn't mentioned it.

In the bedroom, his medication still stood on his bedside table. Along with his watch, his phone, some change in a shallow dish, a half-read novel. This was where he'd died. Quietly slipping away in his sleep, all alone. Why hadn't he waited for her to say goodbye? She'd forgiven him for all that he'd done in the past, but she felt that she'd never forgive him for that. He'd seemed fine when she'd left him a few hours earlier. Weak, tired, but not close to death. His heart had just given up, the doctor said. The effort of keeping Rich's damaged body alive proving far too difficult a task. She would have given her own heart to him if that's what it would have taken to keep him alive.

Autumn picked up the book, a crime thriller by a writer she'd never heard of. Rich had never been much of a reader. It was only since he'd been sick and frail, spending most of his days in bed, that he'd seen it as a worthwhile pastime. She turned the book in her hands, wondering if he'd ever managed to finish it, whether this story ended as badly as Rich's own had. As she did so, she caught a small packet of marijuana as it fell out from between the leaves of the book. She stared down at the drug in her hand. This inoffensive-looking packet of dried leaves had been the thing that had caused all of the disruption and pain in Rich's life. If she'd put it in her tea caddy you'd barely be able to tell it apart from her green tea.

Autumn slipped it into her cardigan pocket, cleared a space on Rich's bed and lay down. She hoped that the covers might still smell of him and that it would help her to feel closer to her missing brother. She buried her face in the pillow, but it just smelled fusty and unwashed. Soon she'd clean the apartment from top to bottom, strip the bed, dispose of Rich's possessions. Soon, but not yet.

She had good friends, a job, no money worries, all of her life before her, yet she'd never felt so depressed. It was as if the darkness was coming to consume her and the tears flowed.

'I miss you, Rich,' she said into the silence. 'I don't know what to do without you. Why did you leave me?'

But her words hung, unanswered, in the air.

Chapter Fifteen

Nadia and Jacob were watching a film. She wasn't even sure what it was. A thriller – supposedly – of some kind. She'd long since lost her grip on the plot, but Jacob still seemed pretty enthralled. However, Nadia was aware that she'd become more conscious of Jacob sitting close to her on the sofa than the action on the screen.

They'd been out a few times together in the daytime over the last few months. Nothing very exciting. A handful of trips to the park or to McDonald's and always accompanied by Lewis. Jacob seemed to be really good with her son and was always up for a kick-about with the football. That was something that Lewis really missed Toby for. Apparently, it simply wasn't the same playing football with his mum.

Jacob had been all-round brilliant with her since Toby had died. He'd really been there for her, keen to help with any of the small jobs that were more traditionally done by men. He'd taken her car to the garage for her when it needed new tyres. Sorted out the computer printer for her when it had decided, without warning, to stop working. It wasn't that she couldn't handle these things if she had to, but it was sometimes nice not to have to deal with them. There was something comforting about knowing there was someone there who'd got your back.

But was that all there was to it? There was a certain chemistry between her and Jacob – she was sure – but it hadn't progressed beyond a certain level. They were, perhaps, a little more than friends now, but it had never moved to anything more intimate between them. She wondered if he was deliberately taking it slowly. Certainly, if he'd tried to rush her into anything then that would have sent her running for the hills. Jacob was a sensitive man and he couldn't fail to be aware of that. Was he simply sitting back, biding his time and waiting for her to make the first move?

How hard this all was. With the supposed wisdom of age you would have thought that this dating business would become easier. But the older you got there seemed to be even more complications.

She didn't want to be alone for the rest of her days, but it would also be difficult to let another man into her life after what had happened with Toby. He'd been so secretive and his gambling addiction had brought them to the brink of destruction. It would have to be a very special man to persuade her to let her guard down again. There had been so many lies in her marriage that it had soured her outlook. Plus she had Lewis to consider. He was four now and becoming increasingly aware of his surroundings. Lewis adored Jacob, but she couldn't risk getting close to another man unless she was absolutely sure that he was going to stay around. Lewis had suffered one major loss in his little life; she couldn't risk bringing another one to his door.

She glanced across at Jacob, curled up on the sofa next to her, a bowl of Kettle Chips forming a barrier between them. He was a handsome man with his fair hair and striking blue eyes. He had a strong, straight nose, high cheekbones and a fine jaw. He was wearing a black shirt and jeans – both expensive-looking, classy. Jacob was always beautifully groomed. He was the sort of man that advertising agencies chose for aftershave campaigns. He was kind, too, and easy company. No wonder Chantal had carried a torch for him.

Perhaps that was also part of the problem. Chantal had enjoyed a close relationship with him. A fling they both said, but she knew it was more than that. There had been strong feelings between them and there were occasions when she couldn't help but think that there was still something between them. Sometimes she caught Chantal looking at him or vice-versa and wondered if it was all as in the past as they insisted. There was a warmth and an affection in both of their faces when they looked at each other that they clearly found hard to hide. It worried her. If they became more than friends would she always be thinking of what he'd had with Chantal?

He sensed her staring at him and turned towards her. 'What?'

'Nothing,' she said.

'You're not enjoying the film?' He looked concerned. Possibly because it was his choice.

In her opinion he'd picked wisely. It was a non-committal thriller. No warnings at the beginning for sex, violence or swearing. That suited her fine. Generally, she preferred a nice rom-com, but hadn't been able to face watching them since Toby died. She certainly wasn't at the stage with Jacob where she would have felt comfortable crying at a film in front of him.

'I've kind of lost track of it,' she admitted.

'Do you want me to rewind it?'

She shook her head. To be honest, she was tired now. Lewis had been in bed for hours and she very much wanted to be in her bed too. Alone.

'I can stop it,' Jacob said. 'I've seen it before, anyway. I know how it ends.'

'Oh.' She smiled at that. 'If you don't mind.'

'I'll leave the DVD with you. It's a good film. You might feel more like watching it another day.'

'Thanks, Jacob. You're very sweet.'

'No worries,' he said. 'I'll make a move.'

It was dark out there, cold and possibly snowing. It seemed cruel to turn Jacob out into the night. He'd have to walk up to the Tube, which was quite a hike and he lived several stops away from her. Should she offer him the sofa to stay over? Would that take them another step further towards a relationship? Would she really be able to go upstairs and leave him down here with nothing but a blanket and a pillow for company?

Jacob stood and stretched. Then, while she wrestled with her indecision, he found his boots and slipped them back on.

'I'll call you later in the week,' he said, heading towards the door.

'Thanks, Jacob,' she said. 'Sorry that I've not been brilliant company tonight. I've been thinking about the job at my brother-in-law's shop and other stuff.'

'That's OK,' he said. 'I understand.'

And that was the problem with Jacob; he always was so nice, so very understanding.

'You've got a lot to think about. But I'm glad that you're in touch with your family again.'

'Me too,' she confessed. Jacob wasn't to know the complications that lurked within.

She followed him to the door and, when he opened it a flurry of snow blew in.

'Wow,' he said, closing it quickly. 'It's getting a bit wild out there. I'll say goodnight here and then make a break for it.' He put his hands on her arms and, maybe it was just her imagination, but she felt as if they lingered there for a second or two longer than usual. His touch was strong, comforting. What would it feel like, she wondered, to be held in those arms? Properly held. Like a woman once more.

She hadn't missed sex as such, but she'd sorely missed the warmth of a man's embrace. If she asked, she knew that Jacob would just spend the night holding her. Could she risk opening herself up to that?

He kissed her forehead, his lips warm.

It was on the tip of her tongue to ask him to stay, not to go home.

Then her phone rang and, flustered, she fumbled for it. Jacob let his arms fall. When she saw the display, she frowned. 'It's Autumn. It's unlike her to call so late.'

Chapter Sixteen

I leave the warmth of Crush's side to dash over to Autumn's flat. Nadia's already with Autumn and Chantal turns up in a taxi right behind me. We stand together, grim-faced and worried, as I press the intercom.

'Autumn's in a terrible state,' Nadia whispers when she opens the door to us. 'She rang me from Rich's flat and I dashed straight over there. She shouldn't have gone there by herself. It took me ages to get her to stop crying and coax her back here. I didn't want to leave her alone.' She lowers her voice further. 'I was afraid she might do something stupid or harm herself.'

We all exchange a worried glance. We all know that Autumn is struggling, but I don't think we realised quite how bad she is.

'I'm glad you rang us,' Chantal says.

'I didn't know what else to do,' Nadia admits. 'When I was at my blackest after Toby died it was only the fact that I had to be there for Lewis which got me through it. Autumn doesn't have that.'

'Oh, baby.' I sit next to Autumn on the sofa where she's

curled up into the cushions and hug her. Her eyes are swollen, her face blotchy from weeping. 'Don't cry. Don't cry.' I wipe the tears from her cheeks with the end of my sleeve.

Autumn cries some more and I hold on as tight as I can.

'I don't know what to do,' she says, tearfully. 'What can I do? He's gone and he'll never come back.'

'We're here now,' I soothe her. 'We'll look after you.'

'I shouldn't have dragged you all out in the middle of the night,' she sobs.

'That's what friends are for.' Nadia puts her arm round Autumn.

'Hot chocolate,' I suggest. 'It's the only remedy. I'll do the honours.'

I don't even need to ask if Autumn has any; it's a given.

'Come on.' Nadia gently leads Autumn into her bedroom. 'I'll help you into your pyjamas.'

In the kitchen cupboard Autumn – as I knew she would – has a selection of Prestat hot chocolate. I choose the box of spicy cinnamon flakes and set a pan of milk on the hob. Soon the warming aroma is filling the place. In the living room, Chantal has switched on the gas fire and it's feeling much more cosy. Autumn and Nadia come back and Autumn is looking much better now that she's wrapped in her fluffy dressing gown and slippers. We all snuggle down on the sofas together, nursing our chocolate.

'Have you called Addison?' I ask.

Autumn shakes her head. 'I can't tell him that I went to Rich's apartment. Addison hates me even talking about him. He may be gone, but he's my brother. What else can I do? Addison will only start ranting about what a loser he was. I can understand that. I know only too well what he was like, but that doesn't stop me missing him like crazy and I can't bear to hear it about him.'

Chantal and I exchange a worried glance. I'm not sure that Autumn and Addison are getting along all that well at the moment. There's very little talk of any upcoming wedding plans. She looks very forlorn and I think it's telling that she's turned to us first.

'He has to do a presentation in the morning,' she adds. 'There's no point in disturbing him. I knew you'd be here for me.'

'Of course we are,' Nadia says.

'This isn't the end to your romantic evening that you envisaged, Chantal,' Autumn apologises. 'I'm sorry.'

'Ha,' Chantal laughs. 'I certainly don't think that it's the ending *Ted* had in mind. I think the fact that I haven't had my bikini line waxed since Lana has been born tells you what is or *isn't* on my mind! I'm rocking the eighties vibe, if you know what I mean.'

'Crush and I haven't made love for weeks,' I confess. 'We're just too busy. But I have tried. I lay on the living-room floor covered in nothing but chocolate body paint.'

Nadia laughs out loud. 'Lucy, you didn't!'

'I did.'

'What happened?'

'I fell asleep waiting for him and then he brought two of his sales reps home, who got an eyeful. That didn't turn out to be quite the night of passion I had planned, either.'

At least my confession brings a smile to Autumn's weary face. Then she stifles a yawn.

'You should go to bed,' I say. 'You look worn out, but I don't want to leave you on your own. Shall I stay with you?'

'Would you mind, Lucy?'

'Of course not.' I push away the vision of Crush – naked and warm – waiting in bed for me. He'll understand that I have to be here for my friend in her hour of need.

'I should get back to my baby boy,' Nadia says. 'You don't mind me going?'

Autumn shakes her head. 'I'm feeling much better now. Really.'

'Who's looking after Lewis?' I ask.

Nadia looks more than a little coy when she says, 'Jacob was at my place, watching a film. He was just about to go home when Autumn called. He's staying over now.'

Chantal and I raise our eyebrows.

'On the sofa.'

Our eyebrows rise further.

'*Sofa*,' she stresses. 'Nothing more.'

'You must have a will of iron,' Chantal notes. 'There was a time when I couldn't have said no to Jacob.'

'I'm not you,' Nadia says crisply. 'And there was a time when you couldn't say no to *anyone*.'

Chantal doesn't take offence, but merely laughs. 'So true. My, how times change.'

'Autumn's exhausted, poor love.' I give her a sympathetic look. Her face is pale with tiredness. 'She doesn't need all of us here. It's late. I'll stay. You should both head home.'

I text Crush and let him know what's happening. He wanted to come over with me too to make sure that Autumn was all right, but he has a busy day at work tomorrow and I knew that the other girls would be here.

He texts back: *I luv u. Take care. xx*

In spite of it being cold and the seriousness of the situation, it gives me a warm glow to know that he's there for me.

'We can make up the spare bed,' Autumn says, wearily.

'Just give me a blanket, I'll take the sofa. I'm so tired that I could sleep on a clothes line.' I'll miss snuggling up to Crush, putting my cold feet on him. When I get out of the bed in the night, he rolls over to keep my side warm until I get back in. How caring is that? But my friend needs one of us here and Chantal and Nadia have more pressing commitments than me.

So the other girls kiss us both and hug Autumn to bits, then they leave and I rummage in the airing cupboard until I find some spare blankets. I usher Autumn from the sofa, helping her to the bedroom before tucking her into bed. When she's snuggled down, I stroke her hair and kiss her cheek as if she's a child.

'Thanks, Lucy,' she says. 'I don't know what I'd do without you all.'

'We're always here for you. Get some sleep.' I turn off the light and head to the sofa. 'You'll feel better in the morning.'

Then I head back to the sofa and curl up under the blankets, groaning as I realise that I have to be up in a few short hours. I pull the blankets around me and try to imagine that they're Crush's arms.

Chapter Seventeen

Crush and I have already spoken this morning, but before I head into the Tube, I send him a sex text. This is how modern I am.

Missing you, big boy! I can't wait until I see you tonight. Perhaps we can get naked and naughty in the shower??? L :) xx

Ha! Let him think about that for the rest of today.

The Underground from Autumn's place to Chocolate Heaven is hell on earth. Damp, sweaty bodies all pressed up against each other. But I cheer up my journey by imagining what Crush and I could be doing if we were in bed and not on separate journeys on our way to work. I'm one of the lucky ones who's managed to get a seat and I let my eyes close for a second. And, of course, almost miss my stop.

At the other end, I bolt out of the station hurrying along towards Chocolate Heaven to open up. As I get my key in the lock, my phone pings.

I take it that text wasn't for me, Lucy. Your father.

Gah.

Still, it could have been worse. I should have known that

anything remotely sexy would only end up going to Crush's mother or the CEO of Targa or someone. At least it was only Dad and he can't really take the moral high ground with me right now. My mother and he were briefly reconciled after my non-wedding. It was a difficult time, but she abandoned her millionaire boyfriend in Spain and her lavish lifestyle and came home to Dad – forgetting in that second flush of love that he is tighter than two coats of paint. It was never going to last. He only had to start to query the amount my mother was spending, look askance at every new carrier bag that entered the house and she wanted to run for the hills. My mother, given very little encouragement, could turn a failing economy round single-handedly while my father makes Scrooge look profligate. Inevitably, they've parted – once again. Mum has moved to Brighton, joined a dating agency for elderly millionaires and is steadily working her way through the ones who live on the south coast. Dad has fallen for another woman who is barely older than me. Last time it was The Hairdresser. This time she is a thirty-five-year-old Pilates instructor and has the figure of a pencil.

Still, while I know more than I need to about my parents' relationships, they need to know nothing about my own. So it's probably best in future that I don't commit what I'd like to be doing with my loved one to any electronic device.

As it's still early, Chocolate Heaven won't be busy for a little while, so I have a short time to gather my thoughts and eat breakfast. There is a *pain au chocolat* and a double espresso with my name on it. I take them to one of the sofas and rest for a minute. I was so tired that I did manage to sleep on Autumn's sofa last night, but my back's aching and there's a crick in my neck.

There's also been a fresh fall of sleety snow this morning and I think that's keeping people indoors for the time being.

If I didn't have to be here, I'd be reluctant to go out too. The roads are clearer now as it never lasts that long in London, but the pavements are still lethal. I didn't even go home, but ran round the shower at Autumn's this morning and borrowed some clean knickers and a flowery shirt.

She seems to be holding up OK this morning. It's coming up to Christmas and that always seems to make these things worse, doesn't it? The other thing that worries me is that by the time I left, she still hadn't spoken to Addison. Not good.

My eyes are gritty and my lids feel as if they're sandpapering my eyeballs. I might have managed a few hours of sleep, but it clearly wasn't enough. Obviously more sugar is required.

Now, I'm propping up the counter and trying not to slide into a deep sleep. I'm on my third cup of strong coffee and my second *pain au chocolat*, but they are failing to provide the energy I need. I've had a little rush of customers and it's a good job that the sofas are now fully occupied as I'd be tempted to shut up shop and lie down for a little while. In an attempt at revitalisation, I turn up the volume of the Christmas songs and help myself to a single-origin truffle, dusted with cocoa powder to try to boost my vitamin levels. It's a well-known fact that chocolate is, in fact, medicine. It's packed with vitamin wotsit and anti-oxidant thingies. All very good for you. Essential. Chocolate is better for you than red wine. True fact. Of course, if you opt for the chocolate/red wine combo then it's practically the same as going to a health spa.

Other upside is that you don't usually end up going to bed with someone unsuitable as a result of an excess of chocolate, whereas an excess of red wine is, as proven on many occasions, the proverbial minefield.

Chantal barges through the door with the buggy. Here is my friend who is living proof of that.

'Wow,' I say. 'This is early for you.'

'I know.' She looks very harried. 'How's Autumn?'

'OK. Tired. Still a bit emotional. Nadia's going over there today.'

'I'm off to see Stacey,' she explains. 'Ted told me that she's struggling and asked me to see what I could do. Me?'

'Wow.'

'Exactly. Like a crazy fool, I agreed.' Chantal shakes her head, perplexed. 'He called her last night while I was at Autumn's and has arranged for me to see her *now*.' She rolls her eyes.

'Nothing like striking while the iron's hot.'

'Tell me about it.' Chantal grimaces. 'I was thinking next week, maybe next month. I don't feel in the slightest bit prepared for it at all. Give me some chocolate. Anything. Do I look a complete state?'

It's fair to say that it's a little while since Chantal has been her usual groomed self. Since around the same time that Lana shot out into the delivery room, to be precise.

'Well . . .'

'Like I give a damn,' Chantal says. 'I'm *only* going to see the mother of my husband's other child. My former love rival.'

I box her some chocolates. Nice ones.

'Thanks,' she says. 'I'll be back later to tell you how I got on. Get the other girls in. Wish me luck.'

'OK. Good luck,' I say as she crashes her way out again. I didn't even get to see Lana.

It all goes quiet again for a while. I wipe the tables, fluff my Christmas decorations, and eat one of the gold-wrapped chocolates off the tree. Then I go to lean on the counter again while I wait for some more intrepid customers to make it through the snow.

I should enjoy this lull while I can, as I know it won't last.

Later I've got a Chocolate Ecstasy Tour dropping in. They're run by my lovely new friend, Jennifer, who I've met since becoming manager here. Jen takes small groups round the chocolate emporiums of London to delight and educate them in the ways of the world's finest foodstuff. She's so knowledgeable and eats so much chocolate that she could almost be an honorary member of our club. Today she's bringing ten clients for a special chocolate tasting of some of our finer offerings – another little innovation by me – and that will keep me busy for an hour or so. Until then, I can drift off for a minute or two to recharge my sadly depleted batteries.

Just as I think I'm about to slip into a coma, there's a terrible roaring noise outside and I stare out of the window. A sleek red Ferrari screeches to a halt outside the window of Chocolate Heaven. Oh my, very smart. And very reckless to be risking the snowy conditions in such a gleaming, sleek machine. We have a lot of posh customers here. Some very well-known names send minions to collect chocolates for them every week. If this was my business, I might well instigate a delivery service – at a premium price. I stand and stare at the Ferrari in a slightly drooly manner. It could be a member of a boy band or a soap-opera star. My heart lifts a little.

Then I see who it is and my momentarily lifted heart lurches.

Oh, flipping, no.

It's Marcus Canning. My bastard ex-boyfriend, one-time fiancé and nearly husband.

What on earth is he doing here?

Chapter Eighteen

Marcus blips the lock on the Ferrari and turns to stride towards the door. Without meaning to, I stand more upright, straighten my blouse and smooth my hair. I wish Marcus had chosen to pop in on a day that I wasn't looking quite so rancid. I'm shallow and I hate myself.

He opens the door and a few snowflakes dust his fair hair. He's fit and tanned and is wearing a very sharp grey suit. Despite me wishing that he'd turned into a toad, he is still blond and movie star beautiful. I'd like to tell you that I'm indifferent to his charms, but it has never been that way with Marcus. Somewhere deep in my ridiculous core I'm drawn to this man however badly he treats me. There is still something that pulls inside me whenever I'm near him.

It's been months now. Lots of them. That doesn't make this any easier. The last time I saw Marcus he was walking away from our wedding venue – alone. He went on our honeymoon – alone. And sent me a postcard to say he was missing me. Despite trying to convince myself that frankly I don't give a damn, I find myself wondering where he's been and with whom. If fate hadn't intervened and Marcus hadn't been a cruel-hearted commitment-phobe, I'd have been Mrs Canning by now. It wouldn't be that long off our first anniversary. Gah. I don't even want to think about that.

'Hey,' Marcus says in a charming manner as he reaches the counter. 'How are you doing, Lucy?'

'Fine,' I say and my voice sounds pleasingly normal. It's a good job that the other members of the Chocolate Lovers' Club aren't here to see Marcus rock up or they'd run him out of town. They think that I'm weak-willed when it comes to Marcus and, if I'm being truthful, I've never done anything to prove otherwise. But times change. I think the experiences that Marcus and I have been through together have, hopefully, made us just that little bit wiser.

'I had no idea that you were working here.'

'Really?'

'Well,' he says, 'I called your mobile and your landline, but you've changed your numbers.'

Oh, yeah. Clever me. I thought that would *absolutely* stop Marcus from getting in touch. Maybe I've not wised up as much as I think.

'Then I rang Targa and they said you were working here now.'

'I've been here since . . .' Since you jilted me, if you want to know. 'Well . . . a while. Clive and Tristan went for an extended break to the south of France. I'm the manager in the meantime.'

'Your dream job.'

'Yes. I love it.' Then I move into business mode. 'Anyway, I can't stand here chatting. What can I get for you, Marcus?'

'It would be optimistic of me to ask for another chance with you, wouldn't it?'

I laugh. It's tinkling and light. As if what Marcus has said is the best joke on earth. 'I think we're both beyond that point. But I can offer you an excellent cappuccino and a brownie-topped mince pie.'

'Just the coffee will be fine,' Marcus says.

He never was as fond of chocolate as I am. Marcus could exist purely on testosterone, whereas Toblerone would be all I'd need. Another reason why we were completely incompatible. That and his inability to stay faithful for more than ten minutes, of course.

'You're looking good, Lucy.'

Fat. He means I'm looking fat. I'm not fat, I'm just chocolate enriched.

'Thanks.' Tomorrow, I am *so* starting a diet. I push the tray of double choc muffins away from me. See? Easy.

'I've heard that you're still with that other guy?'

'Aiden? Of course.' I think I should tell Marcus that I spent what was destined to be our wedding night with Mr Aiden Holby. That might well change his opinion of me. He would know for sure that I have Moved On. But, of course, I'm too cowardly. 'We're *very* happy together.'

'Then I'm happy for you too,' Marcus says and he actually sounds sincere. 'I'm sorry for running out on you, Lucy. Truly I am. It was the biggest mistake of my life. If I could have my time over again—'

'Well, you can't.' I hold up a hand. 'It's all water under the bridge now. No hard feelings. You probably did us both a favour. I don't think we were ever really suited.'

'I'd beg to differ,' Marcus notes smoothly.

The coffee machine hisses that it's ready and I'm glad of the distraction.

'Looks as if you're doing well.' I hand over his cappuccino without sprinkling the usual cocoa heart on top. That's how over Marcus I am. 'Flash car.'

Marcus laughs. 'A little indulgence.'

I'd like to tell you that he's only got a big fuck-off car because he has Small Penis Syndrome, except I know from personal experience that in Marcus's case it isn't . . . ahem . . . true.

He gives me a self-satisfied smile and I wonder if he's able to read my thoughts. He always could. My cheeks flush.

'I had a huge bonus at work, Lucy. I've bought a new place too. I have more money than I know what to do with.'

'Nice,' I say. 'Send some my way. I always have less than I can manage on.'

'You know that you'd only have to ask.'

I would rather live a life without chocolate than ever ask Marcus for money. Ooo. Did I actually just say that? It made me feel a bit wobbly just processing the thought.

'Are you OK?' Marcus asks.

'Fine. Yeah. Fine.'

Marcus checks that there are no customers in earshot and lowers his voice. 'Look, Lucy,' his face is earnest, 'I know that we ended on bad terms.'

You could say that.

'But I still . . . I still love you.'

At that I burst out laughing and frighten the couple sitting on the nearest sofa.

Marcus looks wounded. 'I do.'

'Those were two words that you *couldn't* manage to say,' I remind him. 'The only person that you love, Marcus Canning, is yourself.'

His lips tighten. 'I wouldn't be so sure about that, Lucy Lombard.'

Chapter Nineteen

Marcus sits and drinks his coffee, staring wistfully out of the window. I, in turn, try not to stare at him. I am *so* not going over to talk to him. I am playing it cool, cool, cool. So cool that I actually shiver. Brrrr. I pretend to organise things on the counter and catch Marcus sneaking a peek at me. I make myself even more busy.

He looks great, though. Not as great as Crush, obviously. But great, nevertheless. It's no wonder legions of impressionable women fall at his feet. I often used to wonder what he was doing with me at all. Unfortunately, it seemed as if Marcus did too. It would bode me well to remember that.

As an antidote, I text my lovely, loyal Crush. *Hello, you sexy beast. Still up for some hot sex later? L :) xx*

Ping. A text comes right back. Which makes me smile.

Wrong person again. Your father.

Pfft.

Sorry, Dad. Tired.

Probably too much hot sex, my dad texts back. And not in a good way.

I sigh to myself. I wish.

Despite not wanting to, I glance up at Marcus again. I wonder if he's a little lonely. Why would he be looking me up, if all was as right in his world as he's making out? It's all very well having a swanky car, pots of money and some young floozy on your arm, but does that make you happy? I think in Marcus's case, probably yes. But, somehow, there doesn't seem to be the same sparkle in those dark cornflower blue eyes of his as when we were together.

He brings his empty cup back to the counter. 'That was good.'

'My speciality,' I quip. Despite the lack of the cocoa heart. I hope he noticed that.

'It's been good seeing you and chatting like this. But, I did come in with a purpose, you know,' he says.

'Oh, yeah?'

'I'm doing some research into chocolate as a commodity on the stock market. It's becoming big business. Very investable.'

'I always knew I was a trendsetter.'

Marcus laughs. 'There's a huge chocolate festival coming up in Bruges. Why don't you go along? It would give you some great ideas for how to grow the business. There are loads of new product launches too. This might be Chocolate Heaven, but that's chocolate paradise.'

'I don't think Clive and Tristan would give me the time off.'

'You'd only need a few days. Bruges is just a couple of hours by train from London.'

'Really?' Geography has never been my strong point.

'It's a beautiful city and the Christmas fair will be on, too. Hot chocolate, ice sculptures, fairy lights.'

Oh, I'd thought about going to a Christmas market with Crush. I can feel myself weakening.

Marcus clearly senses it. 'If you want a reason to do it, I could get you a gig. Give a talk about Chocolate Heaven – a new breed of café or something.' He shrugs as if he doesn't care one way or the other.

'Sounds great,' I admit. If I dwell on it too much, I might hyperventilate. I've heard so much about Bruges being the epicentre of chocolate that, of course, I'd love to go. Add to that a Christmas market and it's fair to say that I'm on the point of spontaneously combusting. But I am a different woman now and Marcus would have to get up early to catch me out. He *must* have an ulterior motive.

I narrow my eyes. 'Are you going?'

'No.' He shakes his head sadly. 'Why? Would you let me take you?'

'Certainly not!'

'I'd love to go,' he says, 'but I'm *way* too busy. I just thought it was something that you'd enjoy.'

I'd love it and Marcus knows that.

'You know, it does sound good. *Aiden* and I have been promising ourselves a romantic weekend away. We could combine it with a bit of work.' Take that, Marcus, I think. 'You've got me sold.'

'Perfect.' He pulls out his phone. 'I'll set it up for you and send the details through. What's your new mobile number?'

I rattle it off, before I realise what Marcus has just so suavely done. Now, with very little effort, he has my new number.

He grins at me and pockets his phone.

Bastard.

'I'll speak to you soon.' He gives me a cheeky wink and I note that the sparkle is back in his eyes.

I sigh with resignation as he heads for the door. 'Bye, Marcus.'

He jumps into the splendid Ferrari, guns the engine and screeches off down the road. The equivalent, if you ask me, of waving your willy as you leave.

Chapter Twenty

Chantal stood on the pavement outside Stacey's house, the buggy bearing Lana positioned like a barrier. She was clutching a box of chocolates from Chocolate Heaven as if her life depended on it. If she was going to turn and run for it, now was the moment.

She hadn't specifically avoided Stacey since their babies had been born, but she hadn't exactly gone out of her way to involve the woman in their lives either. Ted had decided to stay with Chantal but always at the back of her mind was the feeling that it was a tenuous arrangement. Part of her strategy was that if Stacey was out of sight, then she was out of mind, too.

Stacey's home was modest, but on a smart street not very far from Chantal and Ted's own house. Convenient. Maybe a little too much so. But, at least it meant that it was easy for Ted to pop in and see Elsie when he could. It was a white-painted, Georgian terrace, neatly kept. For the festive season, fairy lights framed the inside of the windows and a holly wreath with a red velvet bow graced the front door. The day was grey with a few flurries of snow, so the lights were shining out hopefully already.

Chantal sighed. She'd come this far. Ted had asked her to visit and, if she was honest, Ted rarely asked her to do anything. It couldn't hurt to see how Stacey was doing. Could it?

Now she was getting cold, so she inched the buggy towards the door and rang the bell. She hoped that Elsie wasn't having her morning nap. A few moments later and Stacey opened the door. 'Hi,' she said, not quite managing to pull off the smile she tried. The result was forced, brittle. 'Come in. The buggy will fit in the hall.'

Chantal eased her way inside. She'd become a lot more adept with her buggy-manoeuvring skills, but sometimes it still felt as if she was trying to park a double-decker bus – particularly if there was someone watching her intently. She wished she'd brought the car and just had Lana's portable car seat to deal with. But walking everywhere was, supposedly, part of her health kick. It barely lasted more than a few days at a time before she gave into exhaustion and the comfort of a warm car with heated seats. She put the chocolates in the top of her bag for safekeeping. If this didn't go well, she might hang onto them herself.

Stacey stood with her arms folded across her chest, protective, defensive. What on earth was she doing here? How had she let Ted convince her to come? It was clear that it was a bad, bad idea. But what could she do? Now she was here she'd have to tough it out. She could hardly turn tail and run when she was barely through the door. This woman was in her life whether she liked it or not.

Surreptitiously, Chantal looked her rival up and down. She was beautiful, there was no doubt. And younger. Stacey had ten years on her, at least. And she wondered, not for the first time, if Stacey was still in love with her husband and if her husband was in love with her. She could hardly blame Ted if he was.

'It's terrible weather,' Stacey said, trying in the typically British way to fill the awkward silence between them.

'I hate to admit it, but I'm growing to like snow,' Chantal said. 'It's making me feel grudgingly festive.'

'Yes, Christmas will soon be here.' More strained small talk. This was going to be a tricky hour or so. As soon as she could, she'd make her excuses and leave. It was obvious that Stacey didn't want her in her house any more than Chantal wanted to be here.

It had been a while since she'd seen Stacey but, unlike herself, she still looked like the glossy woman she remembered. Her long chestnut hair was pulled back into a high ponytail and her face was immaculate in full make-up. OK, so there were dark shadows circling her eyes which matched Chantal's, but what mother of a new baby didn't have those? She was wearing a lilac cashmere sweater and grey trousers. Expensive, chic. Her clothes weren't covered in baby sick and Chantal quickly checked her own. Plus it looked as if Stacey's figure had snapped back into shape after the birth. Chantal wished she'd put on her squash-it-all-in underwear and something that wasn't a shapeless jumpsuit. What on earth was Ted worried about? She looked fine. More than that. This woman was clearly the Martha Stewart of new motherhood.

'Let me take your coat,' Stacey said, coolly polite.

Chantal slipped off her damp, snow-flecked coat and handed it to Stacey. Then she unstrapped Lana and hoisted her from the buggy.

'She's growing fast.'

'Yes. Bigger every day.'

'Hello, Lana,' Stacey said.

Obligingly, Lana grasped the finger that was proffered and pulled it towards her mouth.

Stacey laughed. 'She's strong!'

'Takes after her mother,' Chantal joked.

They relaxed slightly with each other as they moved onto an area of common ground.

'The kettle's just boiled,' Stacey said. 'Tea or coffee?'

'Tea, please. Black, no sugar.'

'Go into the living room. Elsie's in there. She's a bit dazed as she's just woken up, but she's not grizzling yet.'

So, while Stacey went to make the tea, Chantal headed into the living room. It was a small space but nicely furnished. There was a brown, squishy sofa and the ubiquitous pile of children's toys. There was a basket of fir cones with red bows tied to them in the hearth, and in the corner was a real Christmas tree, sweetly scented and decorated in red tartan. On the mantelpiece there were a handful of cards. Chantal noted that she still needed to write hers, but then she also needed to buy them and pretty much everything else to do with Christmas. Her efforts with Lana's room had been as far as she'd got. As time was pressing on, perhaps she'd get Jacob to lend a hand.

But, most importantly, sitting quietly in her chair trying to focus on the room was Elsie. The little girl, the reason she was joined to this woman, was dressed in a pretty Christmassy dress and red leggings. Chantal's breath caught in her throat. The child looked exactly like Ted – a mini-me if ever there was one. He could never question the paternity of this baby, that was for sure.

'Hey, Elsie,' Chantal said and she knelt on the floor in front of her chair. 'This is Lana. She's your half-sister.'

The baby gurgled contentedly.

Stacey came back with a tray which bore two cups and a bottle. 'She'll want feeding in a minute,' Stacey said as she put the tray down on a side table. 'I'm only surprised that she's not screaming the place down already.'

Chantal wasn't sure what Ted had been worried about; Stacey seemed perfectly in control. The house was immaculate, and so was she.

'Have a seat.'

She and Lana made themselves comfortable on the sofa. 'You have a lovely place.'

'Thank you.' Handing over a cup of tea to Chantal, she placed two chocolate biscuits on a plate next to her, then sat on the seat opposite, perched on the edge, back poker straight.

'What was it that you wanted to see me about?' Stacey asked as she sipped her tea.

'Er . . .' Wow. This was awkward. She'd assumed that Ted had told her he was concerned about her. It seemed not. 'I'm not quite sure what to say,' she admitted.

Stacey waited patiently for her to explain.

'I . . . er . . . I think Ted was worried,' Chantal began.

'Worried?' Stacey raised a perfectly shaped eyebrow, making Chantal wonder when she'd last plucked hers. 'What about?'

'You,' she said frankly. There was really no point beating about the bush – Stacey knew this wasn't likely to be a social call.

Stacey gave a perplexed laugh. 'Me?'

'He thought that you might need a friend. An ear to bend. A shoulder to cry on.'

The girl looked at her blankly.

'Maybe he's got it all wrong.' Chantal waved a hand dismissively. 'You know what men are like. If there's a wrong end of the stick to grasp, they'll hold onto it.' She would *kill* him when she got home. Fancy putting her in this position. Awkward! She distracted herself with a bite of a chocolate biscuit. 'These are good.'

'I'd like to be able to say that I baked them myself,' Stacey said. 'But they're out of a packet.'

'Look,' Chantal said. 'This isn't easy for either of us. I'll hold up my hands, say that I made a mistake. I'll finish my tea and leave you alone.'

Stacey nodded. Her expression was unreadable. 'That's probably a good idea.'

Right, Chantal thought. She had told Ted she would try and she had failed. There's no way that she'd meddle in someone else's business again.

Chapter Twenty-One

Nadia made sure that she arrived at Autumn's apartment as soon as she could, so that her friend wouldn't be on her own for long after Lucy left for Chocolate Heaven. They'd spent the morning chatting and drinking coffee across the kitchen table from each other and Autumn had seemed much more settled after a good night's sleep. Then, together, they'd picked up Lewis from the nursery. After a grey and snowy start to the day, the sun had eventually peeped out and the sky was a pale winter blue.

'I want to pop into work quickly and then we'll go to the park for an hour while you get off to work,' Autumn said.

'This is a bit of a tester session. I haven't got the job yet,' she reminded her friend.

'It's a given,' Autumn assured her. 'You've nothing to worry about.'

Autumn didn't know about her strained relationship with her brother-in-law and now wasn't the time to explain her fears. Nadia had her fingers and everything else crossed in the hope that over the years things had changed. 'I hope you're right.'

'I'll take Lewis home after we're finished in the park. I think there could be a jigsaw challenge on the cards.' She looked at Lewis for approval and he nodded his head enthusiastically. 'Can I get something started for dinner?'

'You're an angel,' Nadia said. 'Lucy called and I said that we'd pop into Chocolate Heaven later on our way home.' Lewis beamed at that. He was always spoiled with little treats when she took him there. 'There's some chicken in the fridge. I was just going to make a curry. Not from scratch tonight. There's a jar of jalfrezi sauce next to the cooker.'

'You had me worried there for a minute.' Autumn looked relieved.

'If you put it in the slow cooker then it will look after itself while we go to Chocolate Heaven. Stay and have some dinner with us. I don't want you going home to an empty flat.'

'I will. That would be nice.'

Nadia bent down to kiss Lewis. 'Be good for Auntie Autumn. I'll see you later.'

Her son wiped the kiss away and Nadia smiled to herself. She hoped he would be about fifteen before he got fed up of her overt displays of affection but it seemed that it was coming far too soon. Leaving him in the care of others was the hardest part about having to go back to work. It was something that all working mums struggled with, so she'd simply have to learn to get on with it.

'I'd better get going. I'm meeting my sister at the shop. She's going to show me the ropes and see if I like it. Then it's down to Tarak to decide if I can stay.' It was only a few stops from here to Aldgate East Underground station, but she didn't want to be late. If she did get the job then she'd have to do this commute on a regular basis.

'Good luck.' Autumn hugged her tightly. 'I hope it goes well. Thanks for being there for me last night and this morning.'

'I couldn't leave you alone. This is all part of the grieving process. I know what you're going through. You *will* feel like yourself again, I promise. But you can't hurry it.'

'I know.'

'See you later.'

Nadia strode away from them both, heading to the Tube and waving over her shoulder as she did. It broke her heart to leave Lewis, even though he seemed to be quite happy with Autumn as a surrogate mum. Perhaps that hurt a bit too. Fortunately for her, Autumn did a great job of looking after her son. She was a natural mother and Nadia wondered, not for the first time, whether Autumn would be keen to start a family as soon as it was feasible.

A short time later she was making her way up Brick Lane and towards her brother-in-law's shop. If he had a chain of them now, perhaps she'd see very little of him. She could only hope so, as she really wanted this chance to spend time with Anita again.

The shop, when she saw it, looked much as she'd remembered it from years ago. It was sandwiched between a slightly seedy bar and what looked like a relatively new bakery. There was a functional black and white sign, plus a rather plain window featuring two mannequins wearing cheap-looking short skirts and cropped tops. The floor area of the window display was covered with a random range of handbags and shoes. It wasn't exactly enticing and she wondered why Anita hadn't done more to spruce up their image. Nadia considered whether she would actually enjoy working here. It was pretty downmarket and quite depressing. TD Fashions could hardly be classed as competition for Harvey Nicks.

As soon as she stepped inside, Anita rushed to greet her warmly. 'I was worried that you'd change your mind.'

'No. Of course not.'

'I've had to stop myself from pestering you with texts.'

Nadia laughed. It felt good to be wanted.

'You'll love it here,' Anita gushed. 'We have our regular ladies and they're such characters.'

'And Tarak doesn't mind?'

At that moment, her brother-in-law stepped through a beaded curtain and came into the shop. 'I don't mind at all, Nadia,' he said with a broad smile. 'It's lovely to see you after all this time. Nice to have you back in the family.'

It was hardly that when her parents still refused to acknowledge her, but it was a start and his welcome was much warmer than she'd anticipated. Perhaps, after all, she could relax and enjoy this.

She grinned at them both. 'Well, now I'm here, what would you like me to do?'

'I'll leave you in Anita's capable hands,' Tarak said. 'I have to go to one of the other shops. There'll be some new stock arriving soon. You could both sort that out and price it up.'

'Will you be home for dinner tonight, Tarak?' Anita asked.

'I'll text you. I may have a late business meeting,' her husband said. 'Good to see you again, Nadia.'

She checked his parting smile for signs of sarcasm or smarminess there, but saw none. Perhaps age had mellowed Tarak. She hoped so.

Anita showed her how to work the till in lulls between customers and it seemed straightforward enough. Then the delivery arrived and, when it was unloaded, they sorted through the rails of dresses and marked them up. They were all the height of fashion, but cheaply made and would look great for a couple of washes. Yet that's what people wanted – everything disposable. In fairness to Tarak, there were some nice dresses and separates for very reasonable prices.

'We could vamp up the window display, if you like,' Nadia suggested. She was itching to get at it with some window cleaner and a duster.

'I've never done that,' Anita admitted. 'But we could try. Should I check with Tarak first?'

'We could give him a surprise. If he doesn't like it, we can put it back how it was. But it's up to you.'

Her sister nodded her consent. 'OK. Let's do it. Do you have some ideas?'

'Loads!'

Anita laughed at the twinkle in her eye.

So they stripped out the mannequins and the mounds of handbags and dusty footwear. Nadia kicked off her shoes and climbed into the window, setting to with the duster and cleaning spray, which earned her a few wolf whistles from van drivers as they passed by.

She and Anita picked out festive colours from the latest arrivals and redressed the mannequins in their new Christmassy clothes. Nadia found some white cardboard in the stockroom and, with the help of Google Translate, wrote out signs in her best handwriting with Christmas greetings in different languages – *joyeux Noël*, *feliz Navidad*, *Честита Коледа*, *Boldog karácsonyt*. In the stock room she found some discarded white boxes of differing sizes and they used those, in the most artistic manner she could muster, to create a display of the handbags and shoes. She propped up the Christmas greetings against them while Anita dashed to one of the pound shops down the road and picked up some red tinsel and baubles to add to their creation.

While they worked, they also managed to catch up on gossip about the family and mutual friends and Nadia realised that she really enjoyed being with her sister again. They could have fun together and there was plenty of scope for increasing

113

the business here. It was obvious that Tarak was letting it just coast along, but there was a lot of untapped potential. Perhaps they could have girly evenings and get in someone doing manicures or hair extensions. Maybe they could even do something with Chocolate Heaven. A choc and shop night. The premises might look a little run down, but it wouldn't take much to spruce it up and Brick Lane was a prime location. Nadia felt quite excited about the possibilities.

'Wow,' Anita said when they'd finished. 'That looks fabulous. Tarak will be pleased.'

Nadia stood back and admired their handiwork. It looked great. She only hoped that Anita was right and that Tarak would like it too, as she was suddenly very keen for this job to work out.

Chapter Twenty-Two

Autumn and Lewis had jumped on the Tube too, but going in the opposite direction from Nadia. Addison would be back from his conference now, but he'd gone straight to work at the Stolford Centre. His new job there kept him more than busy. She hadn't called him and neither had he called her. Had she missed him while he'd been away? She wasn't sure. She'd *needed* him. But that was a different thing altogether.

The centre was in an old school and it badly wanted money spending on it. Many of the windows were cracked, the gutters leaked and the boiler was on its last legs. Still, inside it was a relaxed, comfortable place with free coffee and biscuits on tap; a lot of their clients were homeless and glad of any place with a warm welcome.

With funding cuts, she now only worked sporadically and, at most, three afternoons each week. It wasn't enough and she knew that she had to do something more with her days. At the moment, it was convenient as she was able to look after Lewis for Nadia and she loved spending time with her little charge. However, she was relying on trust money from her mother and father to keep her going and that was what she hated. She was nearly thirty years old and it was time – more than time – that she stood on her own two feet. Addison had told her that more than once.

Perhaps that was part of the difficulty. Maybe they *were* just too different. Addison was streetwise; his family had come here as immigrants from the Caribbean when he was a boy. They'd arrived with nothing and had lived in one of the rougher areas of London. Whereas Autumn's family were old money. Her grandparents had inherited a large estate in the Home Counties and both of her parents were barristers. Addison, all credit to him, had pulled himself up by his boot-straps and had been the first in his family to go to university. He was a striver, whereas Autumn had never really had to work for anything. That didn't make her a bad person, just lucky. Yet the longer they were together, the more she felt as if he resented her well-heeled, privileged background. He wouldn't be the first.

She held Lewis by the hand as they walked through the corridors.

'Is this where you work, Auntie Autumn?'

'Yes, sweetheart.' However, she wondered for how long. She loved it here and wished that there was a way she could make this into a full-time job. The kids who came through their doors generally just needed a bit of love and attention and someone to talk to. It didn't really matter whether they showed any aptitude or real interest in stained glass. Even if they were just fiddling about with the glass, it enabled her to get alongside and chat with them. If their hands were occupied, they seemed to be able to talk more openly about the things that bothered them. That had to be worthwhile.

When she came to Addison's office, she poked her head round the door and wasn't entirely surprised to see him perched on his desk talking to a colleague.

'Hi,' she said, cautiously. 'I just came to say hello. I can go again if you're busy.'

'No,' Addison said. 'We'd just finished.'

The woman was new to the centre and worked more on the funding side. Autumn had been introduced to her, but couldn't remember her name.

'See you later,' the woman said and left, smiling at Autumn.

'Who is she again?'

'Monica Desmond. The person who now holds our purse strings.' Addison nodded after her, an admiring expression on his face. 'She's going places.'

'Hmm. Perhaps you could persuade her to give me a few days' extra work.'

Addison shrugged. 'You know what it's like.'

Only too well. Teaching arts and crafts to drug addicts was never going to be high on the list of priorities. Despite the budget constraints they'd recently introduced street-dance lessons and music sessions, which were infinitely more popular.

'How did the conference go?'

'Brilliant.' His chest puffed up. 'My presentation was really well received.'

'That's good. Let's walk down to the craft room. I was going to let Lewis play with some of the coloured paper for a while. You can tell me all about it.'

Addison looked as if he was about to decline her invitation, but he tidied some papers on his desk and came to join her. Then they fell into step together as they walked along the corridor. She noticed that he didn't take her hand, nor did he seem particularly pleased to see her, but then he could be distracted when he was at work. The thought made her feel even more empty inside.

When they reached the craft room – Autumn's usual domain – she settled Lewis with a pencil and some scraps of paper.

117

'Draw me a dinosaur,' she said.

Lewis chewed the end of the pencil, contemplating his task. 'A scary one or a friendly one?'

She ruffled his hair. 'Why not do both?'

Addison leaned against the work bench. He was tall, handsome and his dark chocolate eyes still made her heart flip.

'I missed you,' she said. Yet even as she spoke the words, she wondered if it was really true.

'Me too,' he admitted. 'What did you do last night?'

She didn't want to tell Addison what had happened, but she couldn't lie to him either. Moving away from Lewis, she lowered her voice so that he couldn't overhear their conversation. 'I babysat for Chantal while she went out with Ted. Then, later on, I went over to Rich's apartment.'

Addison rolled his eyes and she ignored it.

'I needed to be close to him.'

'And an empty apartment did that for you?' Addison said.

'No. I thought it would, but it didn't.'

'Are you ever going to be able to let go of him?'

'He was my only brother. My closest family.' She felt on the verge of tears. How could the girls always support her and yet the man she loved couldn't offer her even a word of sympathy?

'Look,' Lewis said, from across the room. He held up the two dinosaurs he'd drawn.

'Wow,' Autumn said, shakily. 'How clever are you?'

'I've got to get back to work,' Addison said, taking his chance to escape. 'I've a million reports to write after the conference.'

Perhaps that was another problem. Addison was now so bogged down with paperwork and meetings and committees that he was weary and disillusioned. Maybe he'd lost sight of what they were actually trying to do here. Help drug addicts. Help people like Richard before it was too late.

'I'll swing by your place later.'

'I promised I'd have dinner with Nadia and Lewis,' she said. 'I won't be back until about ten.'

Addison looked quite put out.

Autumn relented. They wouldn't get anywhere if they were both being stubborn. 'I could call Nadia and cancel.'

'Don't bother,' Addison said coolly. 'There are things I can do. You enjoy your dinner. I'll see you tomorrow or sometime.'

Autumn found herself sighing inside as he walked away. She loved him. She was sure she did. It was just sometimes recently she found it quite hard to like him.

Chapter Twenty-Three

Chantal sipped the last of her tea. Now she couldn't wait to leave. This was beyond awkward. She didn't really know what she'd hoped for with this meeting, but maybe she'd wished that they could at least rub along together for the sake of their girls. Seemed as if that wasn't to be. Years of strained relationships loomed ahead of them. Marvellous.

'Thank you,' Chantal said politely. 'That was very nice.' She stood to leave. 'Oh, before I go, I bought you some chocolates.' She delved into her bag, glad to be back on a safer subject. 'They're from my favourite place. At least accept these. Peace offering.'

Chantal handed her the gift and Stacey took it politely.

'Thank you. That's very kind,' she said, stilted. Then Stacey noticed the label. 'Oh, I love Chocolate Heaven. I don't get there much, particularly not recently, but I've been a couple of times in the past.'

'You have? It's my favourite place. My spiritual home. My friend Lucy is running it at the moment, while the owners are away.'

'What a great job.' Stacey gazed at the chocolates longingly.

'This is really very thoughtful of you and I don't think I can resist these.' She looked up at Chantal and her face was anxious, uncertain. 'Shall we open them now?'

'You want me to stay?' Chantal said.

'Yes.' She risked a warmer smile. 'If you would.'

Stacey tore off the lid and then gasped with delight. 'Gorgeous.' She went to hand them over to Chantal. 'You first.'

'No, no, no,' Chantal said. 'They're yours.'

Picking one, she then passed them to Chantal. She chose one without even needing to refer to the menu that Lucy had popped inside. She knew her way round these chocolates as well as she knew the back of her hand.

'Chocolate is my new best friend,' Stacey said, savouring every bite. 'These are delicious.'

Chantal laughed. 'Why would we ever need men in our lives when we can have these bad boys?'

After a few minutes they were both more at ease and Chantal risked saying, 'I should talk to you more about why I'm here.' She took a deep breath. 'This is difficult for me to say as I'm not sure it's my business, but Ted has made it so.'

Stacey visibly tensed.

'He really *is* worried about you,' she said before her courage deserted her. 'And you know Ted, he never notices anything.' She tried a laugh again, but this time Stacey didn't join in. Her mouth was dry as she continued, 'I think it concerns him that you don't have any friends or family locally to help you. That must be tough. We all need our friends around us.'

Stacey's voice was suddenly serious. 'I'm fine,' she said, tightly. 'Really. Everything's fine.'

Though her jaw had set in a determined line, Chantal noted that the other woman's eyes had also filled with tears.

'This is a difficult time,' Chantal said softly. 'Having a new

121

baby is incredibly testing. If anyone can empathise with that it's me. I adore Lana, but I seem to be veering between ecstasy and despair every five minutes. There are some days when I feel like death warmed up and no matter what I do she won't stop screaming.' Chantal shrugged. 'I wouldn't change it for the world, but no one told me it would be this hard.'

Stacey said nothing. It would be simpler in many ways to get up and leave, to pretend this wasn't her problem, but their futures were entwined now. That couldn't be avoided.

'We can't undo the past, but we could make it easier going forward,' Chantal pressed on. 'We're in each other's lives now whether we like it or not. We might as well be frank with each other. If you want me to mind my own business and leave, then just tell me to clear off and I'll go. But if you want me to do anything to help, if I can, I'll do it. Though I have to say, it looks as if you're doing a really great job.'

Stacey's chin jutted. 'I don't need any help.'

Chantal held up her hands. 'I'll say goodbye then.' She was so crap at this sort of thing. Lucy would have been so much better. The sooner she could gather up Lana and her stuff and get out of here, the better for both of them. 'I hope we'll be civilised when our paths cross, as they inevitably will. I hope our girls will become friends in the future, but I promise that I won't interfere again.'

At that, Stacey promptly burst into tears. She dropped her head into her hands and sobbed her heart out.

Chantal stood frozen for a moment. Well, she hadn't seen that coming. As soon as she gathered herself, she went to hug the weeping woman.

'Hey,' Chantal cooed. 'Nothing can be that bad.'

Stacey cried harder.

Chantal patted her back. 'What can I do?' she murmured. 'How can I help?'

'Ted's right,' Stacey sniffed. 'I've no one. My family are scattered all over the place. Mum and Dad are up in Scotland and they still have busy jobs. My brother and sister live overseas and they haven't even seen Elsie yet. My friends are all high-fliers and they're not interested in baby talk. They all came to see me when she was first born, brought ridiculously expensive and impractical gifts, then promptly disappeared.'

'No wonder you're struggling.'

Her sobbing renewed. 'I've never felt so alone.'

What remained unspoken was, added to that, the father of her child lived with another woman. Chantal genuinely felt sorry for her.

She handed Stacey the cup of tea. 'Here. Sip this.'

Stacey took it, gratefully.

'A double brandy might be better.'

'It's a nice thought, but that might finish me off completely.' Stacey sighed wearily. 'I've been up all night,' she admitted tearfully. 'You should have seen the state of the house yesterday. When Ted said that you wanted to come round, I was up and cleaning until three o'clock this morning.' The laugh she gave sounded slightly unhinged. 'Then I was ironing until four. I had a backlog that looked like Mount Everest.'

'You mad thing,' Chantal chided.

'I know. Then I washed my hair and put my make-up on so that you wouldn't see how I normally look. I slept upright in the chair for an hour so that it wouldn't smudge.' She tried to push back the tears that trickled over her lashes. 'I feel as if I've hardly been out of the house since Elsie was born.'

Chantal frowned. She had to admit that she'd seen this woman as competition, but now she was sad for her. It could equally have been her in this position.

'I'm used to running a multi-million-pound financial desk, for heaven's sake,' Stacey said. 'Yet I can't cope with a small baby. I love Elsie so much, but it's so hard. I've been trying to stay strong and I simply can't anymore.'

'I know,' Chantal soothed. 'I know.'

'Do you? Ted makes you sound perfect. How do you do it, Chantal?'

'He does?' She laughed out loud. 'Oh, if only you knew.'

Stacey smiled despite her obvious distress.

'I should have given you more notice or maybe just popped in on spec. But, to be honest, I was terrified of even coming to see you.'

'That would have been much worse,' Stacey admitted. 'Now, at least, the house is tidy.'

They laughed together.

Chantal grasped her hand. 'How silly we are.'

'Thank you for coming, Chantal. I know our situation is difficult, but I do appreciate it.'

'I only wish I'd known sooner. I admit that I've kind of been avoiding you.' Chantal grimaced an apology. 'We should try for our children's sake to be friends.'

Stacey gulped back her tears. 'I'd like that.'

'It's settled then.' She felt relieved, too. 'Friends?'

'Friends,' Stacey agreed.

'Now, we can do one of two things. You can either go and have a lovely sleep while I look after this delicious little bundle for you. Or you can put your coat on and we can walk down to Chocolate Heaven and come up with a master plan.'

'I've learned how to exist without sleep, so another few hours won't kill me,' Stacey said, brushing away her tears and pinning on a smile. 'I could do with getting out of the house. Chocolate and master plan, please.'

Chantal squeezed her hand. 'I have some lovely friends at Chocolate Heaven, Stacey, and I think you're going to fit in just fine.'

Chapter Twenty-Four

Autumn and Lewis stayed for a while longer at the centre and then they walked down to the park. The sun was high in the sky, milky. There was little warmth from it, but it was nice to know it was there and trying its best, nonetheless.

As usual, the chilliness of the weather didn't trouble Lewis and, as soon as they hit the gates, he raced off towards the swings. They were occupied again by the nice man and his daughter she'd met the other day, Miles Stratford and Florence. She felt cheered to see them.

Lewis made a bee-line straight for Florence and Autumn ambled up behind him.

'Hey,' Miles said when she approached. 'We thought we were going to be on our own today. Only the most hardy souls are out in this weather.'

'I don't think four-year-old boys feel the cold,' she said. 'I have the devil's own job getting Lewis to keep his coat on.'

'I must have become soft in my old age,' he said. 'I'm freezing.'

'Me too.'

'What say we whizz them round the playground and then

tempt them into the café with sugary treats? They'll never know it's a ploy.'

Autumn grinned at him. 'Good idea. Let's exploit them while we can.'

They duly went and pushed the children on the swings and then there was the obligatory go on every single piece of equipment, no matter how cursory. They were still done in under half an hour.

'Excellent work,' Miles said as they walked down towards the café again. 'You're brilliant with kids. Never thought to have any of your own?'

The question stabbed Autumn in the heart.

'Sorry,' he said. '*Way* too nosy.'

She shrugged. 'That's OK.'

There were very few others there and they got a table by the window overlooking the water. In the summer they had boats to rent and it would be nice to bring Lewis down here to row around the lake. She wondered if Miles and Florence would like to accompany them, ostensibly because Miles could do the rowing. Then she realised how far ahead she was thinking and flushed.

Miles whipped off his beanie hat to reveal his mop of chestnut hair. Autumn resisted the urge to tidy it for him. He went straight to the counter while she settled the children and, minutes later, returned with the drinks.

'I'll pay,' Autumn said and handed over the money.

'There's really no need.'

'I'd like to,' she insisted.

The children tucked in to hot chocolate, both getting a blob of whipped cream on their noses.

'You seem quiet,' Miles said. 'Distracted. Everything all right?'

Autumn sighed and it sounded shuddery and tired.

'Not that it's my business.' Miles held up a hand. 'That's the second inappropriate thing I've asked you in ten minutes. Tell me to back off, if you like.'

Yet, for some reason, she felt like opening up to this kind and friendly man. He seemed to be someone who didn't harbour dark secrets. A man who wore his heart on his sleeve.

'It's my brother, Richard,' Autumn said. 'He's recently died and sometimes it just hits me all over again, like someone punching me in the stomach.'

'I'm sorry to hear that. Were you close to each other?'

'Very. My mother and father are still around, but I think it's telling that I've barely spoken to them since Rich has been gone.'

'That's sad.'

'Yes.'

'And you've no one else?'

'I rely very heavily on my friends. Lucy, Chantal and Nadia. They're brilliant. We call ourselves the Chocolate Lovers' Club.' It sounded a bit silly, childish when she said it. 'We're very close.'

'But there's no other family?'

Autumn's mouth went dry. She hadn't said this out loud ever. Not to anyone. Not even to the Chocolate Lovers' Club. For fourteen long years it had been her secret. She'd buried it deep down inside her but, since Rich had gone, it had been a pain that had become harder to ignore.

She took a deep breath. 'Actually,' she said, 'I do have a daughter.'

Chapter Twenty-Five

I have been mad busy all day at Chocolate Heaven. We're selling a range of upmarket Christmas novelties that I've bought in. There's a big, fat Santa Claus, a white chocolate snowman – particularly tasty – some chocolate baubles with swirls of milk and dark chocolate, plus lots of other festive treats which are going down a storm. We're really getting in the Christmas mood now. Alexandra has also made a nice reindeer chocolate cupcake complete with glittery red nose, and some gingerbread stars iced and studded with silver dragées. Delicious. I have fully embraced the arduous task of tasting them all for consumer research purposes. I can safely say that, at this rate, Clive and Tristan will be able to retire permanently to the south of France. Leaving me, Lucy Lombard, as permanent business manager and chief taster. It's a plan.

I help myself to a hazelnut latte and a slice of coffee and walnut cake – lunch. Which I'm counting as at least two of my five a day. Walnuts are healthy, right? Though it's no wonder I'm becoming decidedly more curvy. I can only hope that Crush proves to be a secret chubby chaser and likes the more Rubenesque woman. Ahem.

Just for five minutes, I sit at one of the tables in the window and breathe. Crush is right; I can't keep going at this pace alone. I'm going to need some help. And soon. It's something I'm going to have to address with Clive and Tristan. Yet I don't like to bother them. I want them to think I'm capable and coping. To be honest, this is the first time in my life that I've been good at anything.

As the coffee kicks in and I'm starting to chill, the door opens and Chantal enters, followed by another woman also pushing a buggy. This can only be Stacey.

'Hey,' Chantal says. 'Don't get up. Looks like you need to sit for a while. It will take us ages to get these two organised.' She nods at the babies in their prams.

'I'm just having lunch.' I nod towards my coffee cake.

'I could be tempted myself,' Chantal says. 'This is Stacey.'

I thought as much. 'Lovely to meet you. Make yourself at home.' I pat the chair next to me and budge up so that they can squeeze round the table.

'She's in need of some *serious* TLC.'

'Then you've come to the right place. TLC is our speciality.'

Stacey sags with relief. She's looking red-eyed and a little weary, but she's quite a glamorous woman. 'It's nice to meet you.'

She holds out a hand for me to shake, but I stand up and hug her instead. There's nothing of her. This woman definitely needs her chocolate and cake levels addressed. 'I'm Lucy. Haven't I seen you in here before?'

She nods. 'I've been in a few times. It's lovely.'

'Thanks.' Had no idea that this was *the* Stacey, though.

'This woman needs chocolate and comfort immediately,' Chantal says. 'She's been struggling on her own, but that all ends today.'

Stacey looks as if she might weep with gratitude.

Chantal heaves Lana out of her buggy and plonks her in my arms. 'Take her coat off, Lucy. I'll help Stacey.'

So I do as I'm told and Lana bears my inept ministrations with her usual good humour.

'This is Elsie.' Chantal holds up the new baby for inspection. 'Is she not totally gorgeous?'

'Very beautiful,' I concur. And a lot like Ted.

Chantal settles Stacey and Elsie, then retrieves Lana.

'Right,' I say in a very determined manner for someone who would be quite happy to sink back into that comfy armchair. 'I'm back on café duty. What can I get you guys?'

They reel off their orders and I make them as quickly as I can so that I can return to the gossip.

'We need to get you some help. As soon as possible,' Chantal says to Stacey in a voice that will brook no argument. 'I'm going to organise a cleaner for you. That's just for starters. Ted can pay up.'

'He won't mind?' Stacey looks anxious.

'Of course not,' Chantal says. 'Besides, it's the least he can do. I only wish he'd told me earlier that you had no one to help you.'

'My family all live a long way from here,' Stacey says to me by way of explanation.

'As well as fine chocolate, we provide an excellent surrogate family service,' I tell her. 'There's no need to be on your own now.'

At that moment, Autumn arrives with Lewis. 'Here's another of our girls.'

They're both shivering and have bright red noses. I jump up to meet them. 'You look frozen through to the bone. What do you want to drink?'

'Hot chocolate for Lewis,' Autumn says. 'I'll just have tea, but we'll have a couple of chocolate-chip cookies too. Though we'd better not tell Mummy just how much chocolate you've had today. It will be our secret.' She winks at Lewis. 'You'd better promise me that you'll eat all of your dinner.'

'I will, Auntie Autumn.'

'How are you doing?' I ask Autumn quietly.

'I'm OK,' Autumn says, but she looks very pensive. Then a text pings in and she checks her phone. 'It's Nadia. She'll be here in two minutes and she's a woman in need of sustenance in the form of a caramel latte.'

'I'll get to it then.' I take Autumn's hand and lead her to the table. 'Come and meet Stacey,' I say. 'And this is Elsie.'

'Oh, she's lovely. Hi, Stacey.' Autumn and Lewis sit down with them. 'Can I have a cuddle?'

Elsie is handed over and looks slightly more surprised by it than Lana usually does.

A moment later Nadia joins us. A blast of cold air comes through the door with her and I'm pleased to see that there's a smile on her face.

'How did your first day at work go?' I ask her.

'Not too bad. I think. It was lovely to spend some time with Anita. It was as if we'd never fallen out at all. The shop, however, has got quite run down. There's a lot I could do to make it look better.'

'So you're going back tomorrow?'

'Yeah,' she says, pulling a face that might be a little bit excited, a little bit frightened. 'I am. I've re-joined the world of work. I feel really nervous, but I'm looking forward to it too.'

'Good for you.' I give her a hug. 'I knew you could do it. Now, go and sit with the others. Stacey has joined us.'

Nadia raises an eyebrow in question.

'She seems lovely. And in need of some friendship,' I fill in.

'We can do that,' Nadia concedes.

'I got your text order. I'll be right with you.'

Nadia goes over to the girls and throws off her coat. She introduces herself to Stacey and then hugs Lewis. He slides on to her lap and she holds him tightly, kissing him even though he tries to wriggle away. 'I've missed you today.'

'Stop it, Mummy!'

'Have you been good while I've been at work?'

'He's been brilliant,' Autumn says.

When I take over the drinks, I say, 'I think we'll have to start a crèche corner if we produce any more babies.'

'I've no plans for another,' Chantal holds up her hand. 'Much as I adore Lana, one is hard enough work.'

'We should celebrate their arrival though.' I hand round the cakes and cookies. 'We haven't really done that yet.'

'Any excuse for a get-together,' Nadia agrees.

'We should have a joint naming party,' Chantal suggests. 'Have you made any plans yet, Stacey?'

'No,' she admits. 'It was just one more thing that seemed too difficult to organise.'

'You could have it here,' I offer. 'Alexandra could make a cake.'

'I like the sound of that,' Stacey says.

'Then let's do it. Soon, too,' Chantal says. 'We have to get Clive and Tristan back from the wilds of France. They'd love to see what you've done to this place for Christmas.'

'It would be great to see them,' I agree.

'I'll text them and find out if they're planning to come back at all.' Chantal pulls out her phone. 'I haven't spoken to them for weeks. Surely they must be planning a festive jaunt back to London.'

Suddenly, I feel quite buzzy about the idea and then I remember that I'm supposed to be trotting off to Bruges for the chocolate festival for a romantic weekend.

'Oh,' I say. 'You'll never guess who came in here this morning.'

'Marcus!' The girls say in unison. They don't even hesitate.

I frown at them. 'How did you know that?'

'Because only Marcus can bring that stupid look to your face,' Chantal says.

'He does not.' I try to make my face look less stupid.

'Oh, Lucy,' Autumn says. 'Not Marcus again.'

'It was nice to see him. Well, quite nice.'

'So, tell us. What does that low-life want from you now?' Chantal asks.

'Nothing.' They're all wearing sceptical faces. 'Really. He just came to say hello for old time's sake.'

Much tutting.

'He told me about this fantastic chocolate festival in Bruges. Marcus said that if I wanted to go he could get me a slot to do a talk or something.'

'I knew there'd be some scheme,' Chantal says. 'What's Marcus got to do with a chocolate festival?'

'He's investing in it or something.'

'He's trying to worm his way back into your life more like it.'

'I don't think so. Not this time. He knows it's over. Really he does.'

Much disbelieving snorting.

'I thought it would be a brilliant idea. Crush and I were talking about going away for a romantic weekend. I've neglected him so much recently because of this place. We need to reconnect on a deeper level.'

'You mean that you need to spend the weekend shagging like rabbits,' is Chantal's assessment.

I choose to ignore the comment even though it may be close to the mark.

133

'Oh, Lucy,' Autumn sighs. 'Anything to do with Marcus makes me nervous. He wouldn't happen to be going along too?'

'No!' I laugh at the very thought. 'At least, I don't think so.'

'You know Marcus, Lucy,' Nadia warns. 'How many times has he let you down? You shouldn't trust him as far as you can throw him.'

'I think he's changed.'

They all guffaw at that.

'He has,' I insist. 'Marcus has learned his lesson. He knows that I'm with Aiden now and that's how it's going to stay.'

'I hope you're right, darling,' Chantal says. 'For your sake, I really hope so.'

'You're too trusting of him, Lucy,' Nadia agrees.

Sometimes, I can't believe how little faith they have in my ability to stay strong in the face of Marcus's charms. Admittedly, I've given them plenty of reason in the past. But that is the past. Since he dumped me at the altar, I have grown up and so has Marcus. We were together for a long time and it would be nice if we could salvage a friendship from the wreckage. Surely that's the mature thing to do?

'Be careful,' Chantal advises. 'Marcus is one slippery bastard. None of us want to see you in pieces again because of him.'

'You won't,' I assure them. 'This time it will be different.' And I'm really determined that it will be.

'Right. We have just one thing left to do before we get stuck into this chocolate,' Chantal announces. She raises her cup. 'Ladies, are we willing to embrace another member of the Chocolate Lovers' Club?'

'We are!' we all say.

'Will we support and love her through thick and thin?'

'We will!' we all say.

'Will we eat chocolate with her on a ridiculously regular basis?'

'We will!'

'Then all that remains for me to say is welcome, Stacey.'

'Thank you.' Our new friend, tears in her eyes, smiles gratefully. 'You don't know what this means to me.'

'It's good to have you on board.' I squeeze her hand.

Then we all lift our drinks in a toast. 'To the Chocolate Lovers' Club.'

Chapter Twenty-Six

I'm laying full length on the sofa with Crush watching *Chocolat* and, even though it's my very favourite film, my poor eyes are rolling with tiredness. It's been yet another busy day at Chocolate Heaven. But how lucky am I that I have someone wonderful to come home to – even if it is just to collapse on the couch with. I nestle further into him, which is potentially dangerous as I might well nod off.

'Do we have to watch *Chocolat* again, Lucy?' Crush murmurs against my neck. 'You play it, on average, once a week.'

'It's not that often.' Surely.

'Can't we watch something with car crashes and gratuitous violence? Something with Jason Statham kicking in baddies?'

'*Chocolat* is a lovely film. Besides, this is really work. Research,' I tell him. 'If you ask me, there aren't enough chocolate-based films in the world. It's an untapped market. It's nothing to do with Johnny Depp at all.'

'Pull the other one,' he says. 'That's got bells on it.'

I pop a Malteser into his mouth. And mine, of course. You have to watch a film with a bag of Maltesers. It's the rules.

A little yawn escapes, despite the fact that it's at my favourite bit, where Vianne and Roux finally get down to it after the lovely party.

'Come on,' Crush says. 'We should head to bed.'

'I like the sound of that.'

'To *sleep*,' Crush adds. 'You know how the film ends, anyway. You're dead on your feet, Lucy. I feel we're both just surviving from week to week. The sooner we book up that romantic getaway the better.'

'Oh.' I sit upright. 'I don't know how this went out of my head. You'll never guess who came into Chocolate Heaven today.'

'Marcus,' Crush says wearily.

'How did you know that?'

'He's been gone for too long. Like every bad penny, he had to turn up at some point.'

'I think he's changed,' I say and now it's Crush's turn to roll his eyes just as the girls did. 'No, really.'

Crush gets up and turns off the television.

'Marcus suggested that we go to Bruges for our romantic weekend. There's a chocolate festival on and a Christmas market. It sounded absolutely perfect.'

'It's Marcus. There has to be a catch.'

'I don't think so. He said that he could fix me up with a talk or something, then I can justify it as work, too.'

'I thought the idea was to get completely away from work?'

'It is, but a tiny little bit of work wouldn't hurt, would it? How long can a talk last? An hour? I might get a fee, too, which would pay for the trip.'

Crush looks resigned. 'I haven't been to Bruges. It looks great. Though I'd much rather organise it ourselves.'

'But if Marcus can swing this for me, it might be a great opportunity.'

Crush sighs. 'Well, if you think he isn't up to his old skul-duggery, then we should do it.' He frowns. 'Marcus isn't going to be there too, is he? I couldn't stand that.'

'No, of course not.' Yet I admit that there's a little moment of panic that crosses my mind, as it's the second time it's been raised. He wouldn't do that. Would he?

Crush pulls me up and throws his arms around me. 'All I want is for you to be happy, Gorgeous. If that means taking you on a trip to Bruges, then let's do it.'

'You'll be able to get the time off before Christmas?'

'It'll be tight,' Crush admits. 'We've got a lot on at the moment. Targa is the company that never sleeps. Or expects its employees to. I've got meetings, targets, deadlines, blah, blah, right up until Christmas. But I've actually got two weeks' worth of holiday to take before then, so surely they can't deny me a couple of days of that? How will you get away?'

'I'm hoping that Nadia and Autumn might manage it between them. I wanted to confirm that you were up for it before I checked with them. It will take a bit of childcare juggling for Nadia, so I need to sort out the details as soon as possible.'

'What did *they* say about Marcus?'

'Much the same as you,' I admit.

'You're too soft, Lucy.' Crush shakes his head. 'Be careful when it comes to your ex. You know only too well what he's like. Give Marcus an inch and he'll take a mile.'

'I won't let him,' I promise. 'I can't just cut him out of my life, though. We have a lot of shared history.' I very nearly married the man, for heaven's sake. 'I'd like it if we could be friends.'

'Would Marcus accept that?'

'Yes.' I'm convinced he would. 'This time things will be on a very different footing.'

'I wish I could believe that.'

'I love you,' I tell him. 'You've nothing to worry about. I would never let Marcus come between us again. The minute he steps out of line, he's gone. I swear. And, if you want him out of our lives now, this minute, then you only have to say.'

'That's your call, Lucy. He treats you terribly. I don't want him taking advantage of your good nature.'

'He won't.' I wrap my arms round Crush's neck.

He grins down at me.

'It's not that late,' I coo. '*You* could take advantage of my good nature, if you like.' I lie down on the rug in front of the fire.

Crush pulls the cushions from the sofa and puts one under my head. He lays down beside me and takes me in his strong arms. 'As if I'm going to turn down an offer like that.'

And we make love bathed in the light of the fire and the sparkly Christmas tree. In the heat of passion I kick the reindeer on the hearth and it belts out 'Rudolph the Red-Nosed Reindeer' while doing a little dance, but even that can't distract me. I think of no one but Crush. All my attention is focused on him and him alone. Marcus doesn't come to mind once.

Chapter Twenty-Seven

Another day in paradise. Sometimes I look around Chocolate Heaven and can't believe that I actually work here. I am the most lucky Lucy in the entire world. I celebrate my good fortune by eating two hazelnut praline chocolates. And then have a third for good measure. There is no such thing in this world as too much pleasure. Chocolate releases all your endolphins or something like that and makes you feel fabulous.

Also, I am still luxuriating in the pleasure that occurred on my living-room rug last night. Sex is also quite good for the endolphin thing too. I would text Crush and tell him so, but would probably get my father instead and I'm not sure his heart could stand it.

Alexandra's car pulls up outside and she opens her boot and lifts out a couple of boxes. Our cake here gets eaten at an alarming rate and Alexandra is having a job keeping up with it all, particularly with the extra pressure of the Christmas orders.

'Hey, Lucy,' she says as she swings in.

'Hey, yourself.'

'How's it going?'

'Mad busy. You?'

'Same. I'll be glad to see the back of these chocolate reindeer cupcakes.'

'They're our most popular seller.'

'I'm seeing shiny red noses in my sleep now.'

Alexandra is younger than me and prettier with longer, blonder hair. Despite her complaints she looks as if she has time to wash and style it. Already, she has it all – thriving business, fab husband and a brood of sweet-faced children. She's as slender as a reed and looks as if she never eats any of the delicious cakes she bakes or the yummy chocolates she makes. I think running round after her kids must keep her trim. Perhaps Chantal will find it easier to lose her baby weight when she starts chasing Lana about. Or Ted.

Today Alexandra is wearing tight jeans tucked into UGG boots and a cable sweater. It makes her look as if she's stepped right out of a Boden catalogue. I never look quite so good when I do casual. My attempts at casual end up looking like bag-lady chic. If she wasn't so very nice it would be easy to dislike her.

'Just a few more boxes and then I'm out of your hair.'

'Excellent. I paid your invoices last night.' As I'm in Chocolate Heaven by myself all day, I have to do the paperwork at night, which is not an inconsiderable amount. I really must speak to Clive and Tristan about the workload, but I hate to make a fuss. In fact, since they've been gone, I've hardly heard from them at all. They've very much taken a hands-off approach to my supervision. I could have simply shut up shop and they'd be none the wiser. As it is, I think they'll be surprised by how well we've been doing.

Alexandra puts the last two boxes on the counter. 'That should keep you going for the rest of the day.'

'Thanks,' I say. 'I don't know what I'd do without you.'

'It works both ways,' Alexandra says. 'You're paying for my kids' toys this Christmas.'

Then as she turns to leave, Marcus's Ferrari pulls up outside.

'Wow,' she says. 'Cool car.'

'It's my ex-boyfriend,' I tell her.

'Your ex?'

'Long story.' But not one that I'm going to tell her now as Marcus is already out of his swishy car and at the door. He's also rocking the casual look today in black jeans and leather jacket. Even though the entire cityscape is a slate-grey colour, Marcus is wearing aviator shades.

Alexandra winks at me. 'I'll leave you to it.'

'Hi,' he says as he comes in. Then, as Alexandra leaves, his head swivels after her.

I purse my lips. Perhaps Crush is right after all. Leopards never change their spots.

His gaze lingers as she bends over to put her handbag on the passenger seat of her car.

'What can I do for you, Marcus?' I say loudly.

His attention snaps back to me. 'Oh, hi.'

'We already did that bit.'

'Who's that woman?'

'Alexandra. She makes our cakes.' I keep the sigh from my voice and my heart. 'She's happily married with three kids.'

'I thought I recognised her from somewhere,' he says defensively. 'That's all.'

Yeah, right.

'Can I get you something?'

'I'm not staying,' Marcus says. 'Unfortunately.'

Now his charm is turned back to me.

'I hope you're still up for the weekend in Bruges.' Marcus holds up two tickets. 'I've got you a gig booked. Friday afternoon you're to talk about the UK chocolate market to the delegates.'

'Me? What do I know about that?'

'You keep it afloat single-handedly,' Marcus points out. 'I'll send you some figures and stuff through. It's only for half an hour. You can blag that.'

'OK.' Is it OK? I feel anxious already.

'I've also got you two tickets for the ball on the same night. I take it you're still planning to go with . . . what's his name?'

'*Aiden*,' I fill in. As if Marcus has really forgotten. 'Yes, we're still going to have a blissful *romantic* weekend together.'

'Perfect.'

'Just one thing, Marcus. You're *definitely* not going to be there as well, are you?'

'Me?' He looks taken aback at the very suggestion. 'No. I've already told you. Why, do you want me there to hold your hand?'

'I do not. The further away you are, the better.'

He laughs at that. 'Then you're in luck. I have an important meeting in Scotland that weekend that I can't get out of.'

Perhaps he sees the relief on my face as he says, 'I've accepted that I've missed my chance with you, Lucy. I had you and I let you go. More fool me.'

I feel my cheeks burn.

'But I can see that you're happy with . . .'

'*Aiden*.'

'I wouldn't want to do anything to spoil that.'

'The girls think that I'm mad having anything to do with you.'

'They were never my biggest fans.'

With good reason, I think. They were the ones who had to scrape me off the floor and put me back together again after every one of Marcus's dastardly deeds. And there were plenty. Remember that, Lucy Lombard. Remember that.

'Anyway, here are your tickets for the ball, Cinderella.' He hands over some gold embossed cards. Fancy. 'With my compliments. It's a black tie and evening-gown kind of do. You both need to scrub up.'

'We can do that.' I can see it now. Crush in his tuxedo looking all suave. Me in a slinky evening gown. I've only got one posh frock and Marcus bought that for me – too many memories – so I might have to see if I can borrow something from Chantal. There'll be more chocolate than we can shake a stick at and a Christmas market to boot. Woo-hoo! It's all I can do to stop myself from clapping my hands with glee.

'There's no fee for the talk, but your hotel is all paid for and it's a beautiful, top-notch place alongside one of the canals. I guarantee that you won't be disappointed.'

Sounds like heaven. It also sounds as if Marcus has been there before and I wonder who with.

I fold my arms, frown my darkest frown and fix him with a stare. 'Why are you doing this for me, Marcus?'

'Because I've treated you badly, Lucy. I know that. I'm never going to make it up to you, but you can let me do little things for you. I want to show you that I'm not a total bastard.'

I cave. As I always do with Marcus. 'I do appreciate it. Thank you, Marcus.'

He shrugs. 'Think nothing of it. If you and . . .'

'*Aiden.*'

'. . . have a great time, that would make me really happy.'

'That's very kind of you.' Then, before I can think better of it, I say, 'If you stay, you can have one of my special lattes on me.'

He grins at me. 'Then it would be churlish to refuse.'

Chapter Twenty-Eight

Nadia was back for her second day at TD Fashions and this time she was in the shop alone as her sister only worked part time. Nadia had always wanted to be a stay-at-home mum, but so few women had that luxury these days. Without Toby, it fell to her to be the sole breadwinner, so she had no choice. Like it or lump it, she had to go back to work. Yet she was a lot luckier than most women who spent a huge amount of their earnings on childcare. Her dear friend looked after Lewis for nothing but a few shared dinners and she was so grateful to her. As soon as she had her first wage packet, then she'd treat Autumn to something nice in return for her unstinting kindness.

The morning had gone quickly, with a number of customers coming in and buying up the new stock. It was nearly noon before Tarak showed up and she felt herself tense as he arrived. There was no reason to, she convinced herself – he'd been perfectly civil yesterday. They might never be best friends, but there was no reason why they couldn't have a good working relationship.

Her brother-in-law tossed his car keys onto the counter.

'The window looks great,' he said. 'Your handiwork, I assume.'

'Yes,' Nadia said. 'Mine and Anita's. We hoped you'd approve.'

'Very much so,' Tarak said. 'You always did have a good eye for clothes. You know how to put together an outfit.'

His eyes raked her body and it made her feel uncomfortable, but they were talking about fashion and she wondered if she was being over-sensitive.

'Let's have a look at the takings for yesterday.' Tarak came and squeezed past her in the small space, resting his hands lightly on her hips as he did so.

There was nothing lascivious in it, not really, nothing too suggestive at all, but still it made her flesh crawl.

'Shall I make you some coffee?'

'Yeah,' Tarak said. 'That would be great.'

In the slightly grubby kitchen, she made some instant coffee. A cheap supermarket brand. This would be the next place to be given a Nadia Clean. She wondered at Anita letting it look so neglected, as she was always so house proud. Perhaps this was Tarak's domain and she hadn't liked to mess too much with it. Well, that would change. Nadia wanted to work somewhere nice and not a place that constituted a health risk. The toilet was sorely in want of some strong bleach, too.

Still, it didn't do to march straight in and stamp all over someone else's turf. She'd have to tread carefully but, hopefully, when Tarak saw some increased sales, then he'd leave them alone to look after the place.

She took Tarak his coffee.

'It was a good day yesterday,' he said, nodding approvingly at the receipts on the computer in front of him. 'Obviously the new stock is going down well with the punters.'

And the fact that the window display no longer looked like the bottom end of the charity shop market would surely have helped too, but Nadia thought it best not to point that out.

Tarak sat on the stool behind the desk and folded his arms. Nadia stood and tidied the rack of dresses nearest to her. It would be nice if they had an iron or steamer in here; the clothes would look so much better with a little presentation.

'You're still a good-looking woman, Nadia,' he said.

She chose to ignore the comment.

'How are you managing without Toby?'

'Lewis and I are getting along just fine,' she said. Though it wasn't strictly true. There were some days that she felt she was barely hanging on by her fingertips. It was only with the help of the Chocolate Lovers' Club and dear Jacob that she coped at all.

'You must miss having a man in your life.'

'No,' she said, firmly. 'I'm afraid having a man in my life caused me nothing but pain, Tarak. I wouldn't be in a rush to do that again.'

'But those long, lonely nights?'

'I have a stash of chick flicks and an even bigger stash of Dairy Milk. Who needs love when you've got chocolate? That's all I need for company these days.' He didn't need to know that it wasn't strictly true. There were days when she missed Toby desperately, despite his faults.

If she was honest with herself, she quite liked having Jacob there for company, too. She wondered what would have happened the other night if Autumn hadn't called at a critical moment. Would she have kissed Jacob? Would she have asked him to spend the night with her? She didn't think so. That was a step too far. The truth of the matter was that she was still too bruised to consider a relationship and she was sure that there was unfinished business between Jacob and Chantal. She didn't need to find herself in the middle of that.

Anyway, it was immaterial now as, at the critical moment,

she'd had to dash off to help Autumn, and Jacob had been pressed into babysitting for Lewis. And, of course, he hadn't complained. Jacob was always willing to step in and help her. He was an all-round good guy and, if she'd been considering another relationship, that was exactly the type of man she needed in her life.

Could she risk letting her guard down again though? She'd been so traumatised by Toby and all his deceit, and Jacob might be lovely, but it wasn't as if he came *entirely* without baggage. Did she want another woman in the equation? Even if it was one of her dearest friends, she'd be there lurking in the background.

'Perhaps you need a real man.' Tarak's voice interrupted her thoughts.

She snapped her attention back to her brother-in-law. There was a smarmy look on Tarak's face now.

'Perhaps I do. But, at my age, all the good ones are already happily married and are faithful to their wives,' she said pointedly. 'I wouldn't touch another cheating bastard with a bargepole.'

Tarak looked stung.

Perhaps she'd overstepped the mark. He might be family, but he was also her boss. He was flirting with her, though. She was sure of it. Although it was a long time since a man had done that and she might be reading this wrongly. Perhaps Tarak was simply indulging in some banter. They were both older and, supposedly, wiser now; surely he realised that he couldn't treat her like the gauche teenager she had been?

She liked the fact that Jacob didn't flirt. He never said anything inappropriate or that made her feel uncomfortable. He didn't push her or press her to do anything that she didn't want to. If he did have any ideas of starting a romantic relationship with her, then it was clear that he was leaving her

148

to do the running and she liked that. But, he was a red-blooded man after all, and she wondered just how long he'd be content to have a purely platonic relationship. He never mentioned that he was seeing other women and, whenever she called, he seemed to be available. Yet, surely, he couldn't be happy living as a monk.

'You and Anita are lucky to have had such a long and happy marriage,' she said in a placating tone. Tarak had given her this job and she was grateful for it. What was the point in antagonising him? It had taken a long time for her family to make an attempt to bring her back into the fold. She loved spending time with Anita again and being prickly with Tarak was only going to put that in jeopardy. She had to tread carefully. 'It's rare these days. You should both cherish that.'

'Humph,' Tarak said. He put down his coffee cup, still half-drunk. 'I'm going to the other shop. I'll be back later to lock up.'

Arms folded across her chest, she watched him stomp out of the door and go to his van, relieved that he was leaving her alone.

Chapter Twenty-Nine

Miles had called Autumn, as she'd hoped he would. After their last meeting in the park, it seemed only right that they should swap telephone numbers.

'It's too cold to go to the park today,' he said. 'If you're not busy, why don't we take Lewis and Florence up to the Winter Wonderland in Hyde Park? There are a few more things to do indoors there and it's quite sheltered. Flo and I went last year and it was great fun.'

'I'm sure Lewis would love it,' she said. 'I'll just check that Nadia is OK with me taking him there.'

When she hung up she thought that it was nice he was thinking ahead about them meeting in the park, and she realised that she'd been looking forward to their regular get-together. Autumn was sure Nadia wouldn't mind, but she'd text her before she mentioned it to Lewis.

A moment later, a text pinged back. *Of course it's OK. Have fun. Tell Lewis I miss him loads. N xx*

So Autumn called Miles back and arranged to meet him at the entrance to Winter Wonderland.

Only a short while later she and Lewis were both standing

under the glitzy sign decorated with smiling Santas, reindeers and idyllic snow scenes. They were flanked by two huge Christmas trees laden with twinkling lights and Lewis looked up at them in awe. Cheery Christmas songs in German filled the air and the welcome scents of baking and spices floated towards them. They were both bundled up in scarves and hats against the cold and even Lewis hadn't protested when she'd zipped him into his thick coat. He'd even managed to keep his gloves on.

It must be hard for Nadia to be away from him while she was at work and have someone else doing all the fun stuff with him. Even though she wasn't working full-time, the hours were long enough. By the time Nadia got home from the shop, there seemed to be precious little of the evening left. When she'd cooked dinner and they'd played with Lewis's Lego for a bit, it was just about time for Lewis's bath and bedtime. He adored his nightly story, so that had to be squeezed in too. Nadia would have to make sure that they caught up on quality time together at the weekends if she could. But then there was all the house-work to keep on top of. It made Autumn realise that life as a single parent wasn't easy and she wondered how she would have managed in the same situation. Yet every fibre of her wished that she'd been able to bring up her own daughter, no matter how difficult. They'd have coped. She was sure of it.

But how? She had been little more than a child when she fell pregnant. A teenager who'd never really had to fend for herself. Her parents would have cut her off, so how would she have managed? They'd have made sure she saw none of their money. How would she have looked after them both? She saw how Nadia was struggling – and she was older, experienced in the ways of the world. She'd had a husband, a roof over her head. Autumn would have been cast adrift with nothing. It didn't bear thinking about.

She made sure Lewis's little scarf was tucked up round his

neck so he wouldn't get a draught inside his coat. Autumn's fingers trembled as she wondered who had done this for her daughter when she was this age. Had the people who'd adopted her only child cared for her and kept her warm in the winter? Had she enjoyed the love of a good mother? All Autumn could do was pray that her child was happy. Now that she'd finally spoken of her to Miles, the little girl was never far from her mind and an ache that had always been buried deep in her heart had pushed itself to the surface once more.

Her daughter would be fourteen now. Only a little younger than Autumn when she'd given birth to her. What did she look like? If she was in this crowd, would Autumn even know her? Perhaps she'd walked past her in the street and hadn't recognised her own flesh and blood. She'd called her Willow, but that probably wasn't her name anymore. Her new parents could have called her something else. Something that didn't suit her nearly so well.

Autumn was barely fifteen herself when she'd had Willow. That seemed a terrifying thought. She'd believed at the time that she was so grown up, able to cope with a baby. Her parents, of course, had felt differently. The child was the result of a few stolen nights spent with one of the young gardeners who tended the grounds of her boarding school. All the girls fancied him. Probably because he was the only male for miles who wasn't a teacher. She'd found out afterwards that she wasn't, as he'd told her, the only girl that he'd taken to his sparse room in the cottage by the woods, but she was the only one foolish enough to get pregnant. He had been kind, funny and tender. He was called Finn and she really thought she was in love with him. As soon as she found out she was pregnant, he was fired from his job and the little cottage in the woods stood empty. She never saw him again. Probably just as well. After all these years, Autumn could hardly remember what he looked like.

Autumn had been dispatched, instantly, to a finishing school in Switzerland – well out of the way of anyone who knew the family. There, she'd had the baby in an immaculate and soulless clinic among strangers. When Willow was born, she looked exactly like Autumn. The fine down of her hair shone like gold. Her skin was such a delicate pink it was like mother-of-pearl and she could have gazed for hours at her perfect little fingers and toes. That wasn't to be, either. Would she still look like Autumn now? Would that delicate golden down have morphed into the same mad auburn curls her mother had? Would she spend most of her life trying to do something to tame them? Did Willow ever look in the mirror and wonder if she looked like her birth mother?

The baby was taken from her as soon as she came back to England. Her mother saw to everything. She dealt with Social Services and all Autumn had been required to do was sign the necessary papers. Her parents insisted that it would be better if she didn't have any further contact with Willow for the sake of the child. She'd agreed. It seemed too heart-breaking to know where her child was and not be able to see her. Put her out of your mind, her mother advised. Get on with your life. Pretend it never happened. It was the worst possible thing she could have done. She should have taken advice from the experts, had independent counselling and, most of all, not listened to her mother. But she didn't and was railroaded into accepting her mother's agenda. It still made her sick to think of her complicity.

She never knew who'd adopted her child, only that it was a nice, middle-class family from a good area. That would matter to her mother. All she did was write a letter to Willow, apologising for what she'd done and telling her how very much she loved her. Her mother wouldn't agree to deliver it and so it had stayed in a little box of keepsakes that she'd secreted away – a lock of Willow's hair, a pair of her tiny bootees, the hospital identification band with her name on it, the letter she'd written. Not much to show for Willow's time with her, but so very precious. There was many a time when just looking at them, holding the lock of hair to her cheek, had kept Autumn sane.

From that day to this, she and her parents had never spoken of it, but there'd been a hole in Autumn's heart ever since. It was probably one of the reasons why she'd stepped in to be a surrogate mother to her brother. That had helped to ease the pain.

Only Richard had known about Willow and now Miles did, too. She could talk to Rich about anything and now he was gone. Who else would fill that void? She'd never even told Addison or the girls of the Chocolate Lovers' Club about her daughter as she felt ashamed that she had let her child go, if not lightly, then too easily. She should have fought for her more. But how could she? She had nothing, was entirely reliant on her parents and they were holding all the cards. Like a good daughter, she had bent to their will.

If Autumn was being charitable, she would have liked to say that they were only doing their best for her, but she knew in her heart that they were doing what was best for themselves. A teenage daughter with a baby would have hampered their lifestyle; it would have shown a chink in their perfect facade. No, her parents did what they did purely for themselves. Her wishes were never even taken into account. No one had ever sat her down and asked what she wanted.

When they took Willow from her arms, she heard a terrible, inhuman, keening sound. It took a moment to realise that it was coming from inside her. It felt as if her heart was being wrenched from her. She couldn't think, couldn't eat, could hardly breathe for weeks, months, years afterwards. But, eventually, faced with the constant disapproval of her parents and with the threat of anti-depressants and counselling hanging over her, she'd battened it all down, hid all the hurt as deep as she could and had got on with her life. Now it felt as if the floodgates had been opened again and all she could think of was Willow.

She gazed at the gaudy but warming Christmas scene around her. How she would have loved to have been doing this with her own daughter. Children were so precious and she'd learned that the hard way. She was only glad that she could look after Nadia's little boy for her. That helped to stop the ache. Sometimes. She hugged Lewis tightly to her.

'Auntie Autumn,' he complained. 'Don't squish me.'

'Sorry.'

He righted his hat and she laughed at him.

Then she saw Miles and Florence walking towards them and felt her spirits lift. After all the worry, sorrow and not getting along well with Addison, she needed a day to have some fun.

'Hello,' Miles said, slightly breathlessly. 'Glad you could both come.'

'It's a great idea,' Autumn said. 'Thanks for asking us.'

'I brought plenty of cash,' Miles said. 'So let's go crazy.'

'That sounds perfect.'

They headed into the melee. Although it was early in the day, the tourists were already out in force and Winter Wonderland was bustling. She didn't much feel like Christmas this year. How could she contemplate celebrating anything? What would it be like without Rich? She'd never go to her parents again – it was just too traumatic. It could simply be her and Addison alone. At one time, the thought of that would have filled her with joy, but not today.

The four of them made their way through the lane of market

stalls selling fluffy hats that looked like animal heads, Christmas decorations, sweets, marshmallows, delicious-smelling pretzels and roasting nuts. There were chocolate fountains and cabins selling all manner of chocolatey delights. Lucy would be in her element here.

There wasn't an inch of the Wonderland that wasn't covered with pictures and statues of Santa or snowmen. There were stars, holly wreaths, Christmas trees galore, candy canes, bells, baubles, mistletoe and snowflakes in abundance. If you didn't feel festive when you arrived, then you couldn't help getting into the mood by the time you left.

They came to a children's ride with a big snowman in the middle and carriages that looked like penguins wrapped up in stripy scarves. Miles paid for the kids and, bursting with excitement, they climbed into one of the penguins together.

Autumn and Miles stood together and watched Lewis and Florence as they were twirled and whirled on the ride, shrieking with joy.

'That looks great fun.' Autumn nodded towards the ride. 'I wouldn't mind a go myself. I haven't been on a carousel in years. It looks amazing.'

'We can take a turn if you like,' Miles said, his eyes offering a challenge. 'That wouldn't compromise my manliness too much. It's great what you can get away with when you've got a kid with you.'

'I'll buy us some hot chocolate,' Autumn said. 'They'll be glad of it when they get off.'

So she went to the nearest stall and ordered four cups of chocolate all topped with whipped cream, marshmallows and chocolate sprinkles. It smelled sweet, comforting.

By the time she returned, Miles was helping the children to climb out of the penguin carriages. She ushered them to a bench nearby and handed out the chocolate. The last one she gave to Miles and their fingers touched. He looked at her and held her eyes.

'This is lovely, Daddy,' Florence said. 'What can we go on next?'

It broke the moment and Miles turned away. 'Carousel. Autumn's request.'

'Yay.'

So they drank their chocolate and headed further into Wonderland, passing Santa's Hall of Mirrors, the ten-foot-tall singing Christmas tree and the balloon sellers holding bunches of helium balloons the size of a bus. The children were enraptured.

Eventually, they came to the carousel and climbed on board. Miles took Lewis with him on one of the colourful horses. Florence picked a pink one with flowers on its mane and Autumn lifted the little girl to sit in front of her. She felt so tiny and delicate compared to the boyish sturdiness of Lewis. She had missed this, all of this, with her own child.

The carousel started up, turning faster and faster. The horses galloped round and round. Autumn took off her hat, letting her hair stream behind her and she opened her mouth in a laugh. The gust of cold air sharpened her senses. It was good to be doing this. She felt light and free.

When the music stopped, she felt almost giddy, as if she'd had a double sugar rush. Miles lifted her down from the platform, hands on her waist and, once again, their eyes met. Her heart was beating too fast and her mouth was dry. His arms felt strong. His touch reliable, steadfast. It was good to be held by Miles. Too good.

'I'm with someone else,' she said softly.

'I know.'

Yet when Miles let his hands fall to his sides, she desperately missed his touch.

Chapter Thirty

Chantal thought that shopping with Jacob was *the* best thing. Who better to draft in to help her with her Christmas shopping? He was an honorary girl when it came to retail therapy. He absolutely got the whole being-laden-down-with-carrier-bags thing and they'd both been giving Regent Street their best shot all morning.

Despite vowing to stay away from Jacob, she had to admit to herself that it was nice to have an excuse to spend some time with him. With Lana and everything else, she saw so little of him these days. She could rationalise that she had to keep him at arm's length, yet something inside her didn't want to lose the friendship that they had. Being with Jacob made her feel special, wanted. He gave her a warm glow when he was around. She liked him a lot, he was fun, easy company and more than a little handsome to boot. What's not to love? But they were friends now, nothing more. Above all else, she had to remember that. She was a mother, a married woman. A *faithful* married woman. She could do nothing to rock the boat. For Lana's sake, she was working hard on her relationship with Ted.

They'd had a great morning of bending plastic. With his usual impeccable taste, Jacob had chosen a great black cashmere sweater for Ted and a Paul Smith scarf in Liberty's. She'd then picked up some chocolates in Godiva for her husband – a lavish box of their signature truffles. Well, more for herself really. It was a shame, but Ted wasn't exactly crazy about Christmas at all. Maybe it would be different now that they had Lana. There would be more point to it.

After that they'd headed straight to Hamleys – the oldest toy shop in the world – which had come in for a particular hammering. She'd loaded up with toys for Lana and Elsie – which she'd put on Ted's credit card – while Jacob had bought a couple of dream boy-toys for Lewis.

They swung out of the shop and headed out into the crowds. Regent Street was bustling with shoppers getting their festive fix of commercialism. Just as they were. The street looked amazing in its Christmas garb. Strings of lights like frosted branches hung from side to side and there were tableaus of the twelve days of Christmas in gold in the middle, running the length of the street. As usual, all the shops had gone to town with their decorations and the whole street felt magical.

'I need a chocolate hit,' Chantal said. 'I'm flagging.'

'You can't be,' Jacob said. 'We've barely started.'

'I'm not the woman I once was. I'm out of training,' she admitted. 'I've let my shopping muscles go to waste along with the rest of them. I have to pace myself until I'm back to full retail fitness.'

'Lightweight,' he teased.

Chantal patted her tummy. 'Not these days. I'm more heavy-weight.'

'You look as great as you ever did,' Jacob said. 'A more curvy shape suits you.'

'That is *so* the wrong thing to say to a woman.'

159

He laughed at that and his eyes sparkled in the way she really liked.

'I haven't even had breakfast yet,' he said. 'I'll buy you *pain au chocolat* and then you'll forgive me. Let's go to The Gallery. We're only round the corner.'

It had once been their favourite place for quiet assignations. 'Lovely. It's been a long time.'

So they swung out of the crowds and into a side street. The Gallery was a mad place, part café, part art gallery, part fashion boutique – but, somehow, it worked. She and Jacob used to sneak off here and hold hands over the table together. The memories were still so clear for her and she wondered if Jacob was thinking the same thing.

They were shown to a secluded corner and Jacob ordered coffee and chocolate croissants for them both while she admired the new additions to the artwork and trendy furniture. He was easy company to be with. So easy.

She glanced at him under her eyelashes as he arranged their stash of carrier bags around their table. It was effortless to love a man like Jacob. With Ted, she always seemed to be walking on eggshells. It had always been difficult for them to be in love, even before their current issues. They weren't great communicators and she always felt that so much between them remained unspoken. Ted was never good at discussing his feelings and that's why she'd been so surprised that he'd asked her to visit Stacey; it wasn't like her husband to admit that there was anything wrong.

When she'd broached it with Ted after her visit, he'd been more than happy to agree to fund a cleaner for Stacey's house. Just as she knew he would. If Ted could throw money at it rather than get emotionally involved, then it was fine by him. He'd even suggested a nanny to help Stacey, which was great. Chantal thought it sounded like a damn good idea for her

160

too, though she didn't voice that. Perhaps it was something to address in the new year.

Stacey was proving to be an eye-opener, too. Since she'd been round to see her, they'd got along just fine. Chantal could see that they could actually be good friends, which was such a relief. It was also especially good for the babies and she felt a real connection to Elsie. It was clear that Stacey felt the same about Lana when, so easily, there could have been jealousy there.

This morning, Stacey had kindly volunteered to babysit for Lana while she went out. All Chantal had said was that she was going Christmas shopping. She might be classed as a friend now, but they weren't quite bosom buddies yet and Stacey didn't need to know all the details right now. The newest member of the Chocolate Lovers' Club still had to meet Jacob and she certainly didn't know their history. Chantal viewed that as a good thing.

The waitress brought their coffee and a plate of warm chocolate croissants for them. She glanced at Jacob again while she enjoyed her coffee. He was relaxed, laid back – her own stress levels subsided when Jacob was around. It didn't help that she had intimate knowledge of him. She knew that underneath that well-fitted white shirt and jeans, there was a tight and toned body. She also knew exactly what he could do with that body and it was more than impressive. He had been a good lover, there was no doubt. The best. Chantal felt quite warm thinking about it and that had been the last thing on her mind for a good while.

'Are you OK?' Jacob asked. 'You're looking a bit pink in the cheeks.'

'I'm fine,' Chantal said. He was solicitous too. The thing she loved most about Jacob was that he loved women. He was definitely a woman's man rather than a man's man. 'I'm probably heading for hot flush territory.'

He laughed. 'Stop putting yourself down. You're fabulous, Chantal.'

She felt her colour deepen.

'There's plenty of life in you yet,' he teased.

'I'd call that damning with faint praise.' Chantal rested her head back and sighed. 'It's nice that we're doing this.'

'Yes,' Jacob agreed. 'It's been too long.'

She pursed her lips. 'I didn't tell Nadia that we were going Christmas shopping together.'

'Me neither,' he confessed.

'Why is that?'

'I like her,' Jacob said. 'I know she worries that we have shared history.'

'I paid dearly for that "shared history".'

Jacob laughed. 'You're never going to let me forget it, are you?'

'Of course I'm not.' She'd first met Jacob when she'd used his services as a male escort and his rates had been eye-wateringly expensive. 'Though you were worth every penny,' she added mischievously.

His eyes twinkled. 'I'm glad you thought so.'

Then she was suddenly serious. 'I know that it's all water under the bridge now, but I won't ever forget what we did.'

Jacob took her hand and gave it a squeeze. 'No. Me neither.'

'It was good,' she said. 'I can't deny that.'

She was glad that Jacob had come into her life, even if it was through slightly unconventional circumstances. There were times when she missed him more than she cared to admit. There were also times when she looked at Lana and wondered how things would have turned out if Jacob had been her father rather than Ted. Would Jacob have been keen to embrace a parental role? Knowing Jacob as she did, she was sure that he would have very much wanted to be a hands-on dad. He obviously loved kids and was great with Lewis.

Chantal wondered what Jacob really thought about Nadia, but couldn't even bring herself to ask the question. She knew that her friend *liked* Jacob, but did it go further than that? What if it did? Would it ruin their friendship if Jacob and Nadia became a couple? There was no doubt that they would be good together. Yet there was also a small nagging part of her that was jealous of Nadia getting so close to Jacob. Chantal knew that they shared cosy film nights in and regular outings with Lewis. She knew that it shouldn't bother her; after all, didn't Nadia deserve a little happiness considering what she'd been through? But it was there nipping at her – green-eyed and insistent – and she couldn't deny it.

'We should drink up and get back to the shopping,' Jacob said into her musing.

'I still have the ladies of the Chocolate Lovers' Club to buy for.'

He laughed. 'Well, at least that won't be difficult.'

'No. We should wander across to Carnaby Street. There are a few great chocolate emporiums round. I haven't seen what their Christmas offerings are yet, but I'm sure we'll get their presents there.'

'Buying from Lucy's rivals?'

'She won't mind eating the competition, I'm sure. You know Lucy. Chocolate is chocolate is chocolate.'

'She's certainly doing a great job with Chocolate Heaven.'

'Yes. She has a real flair for the business and she deserves some luck. I'm just worried that Marcus seems to have reared his ugly head again.'

Jacob raised an eyebrow.

'I know. He dropped in the other day, out of the blue, and has persuaded her to go to a chocolate festival or something

163

in Bruges.' Chantal shook her head. 'He's bad news, that one. I hope he hasn't got some trick up his sleeve. It would be just like Marcus. She can never say no to that man. You know how soft she is.'

'I do. But she's got you ladies to look out for her. She'll not come to much harm while you're around. It would take a braver man than me to cross the Chocolate Lovers' Club.'

Chantal laughed. 'Don't you forget it.'

'I'll pop by and see Lucy this week too. It's been a while.' He drained his cup and signalled for the bill. 'In the meantime, you have my undivided attention. Where shall we head to first?'

She stood up as Jacob did and, with a sudden rush of affection for him, she hugged him tightly. It was wrong, but she still loved the feel of his body against hers. She'd had a lot of men – too many – but none of them had moved her like Jacob. There was a comfort in clinging onto him like this that she hadn't realised she'd missed. It felt good, so good. Chantal pressed her face against his neck and he stroked her back. But he was a free agent and she wasn't. She was a married woman, with a child, and had sworn to make her marriage work. She mustn't take her eye off that ball.

When, eventually, she pulled away Jacob gazed at her, his expression gentle. 'What was that for?'

'I like having you in my life,' Chantal said, earnestly. There was a lump in her throat, tears behind her eyes. 'I don't tell you enough. You're a good friend, Jacob.'

'And that's all I'm ever destined to be?'

She nodded.

Jacob smiled at her sadly. 'I can live with that.'

They would have to.

Chapter Thirty-One

What I'd like to know is, if carbon offsetting is supposed to work then why can't we have calorie offsetting? I like the idea of me stuffing my face with chocolate and some skinny bitch on the other side of the world bloating up. Any politician who introduced that would certainly get my vote.

As it is, I have to bear my own carb-loading, but that's not stopping me from trying these delicious Christmas cupcakes that Alexandra has brought in. Hmm. Her creativity knows no bounds and, despite her protesting that she can't wait for it all to be over, I think she's really getting into the festive groove. Spread in front of me are cupcakes galore – gingerbread latte, pink ones topped with a stripy candy cane, some flavoured with eggnog; others have a green swirl of icing for a Christmas tree and there's an almond cupcake with an angel piped on top in pale apricot frosting. But my favourite of all is the mince pie cupcake, baked with mincemeat in the sponge and topped with brandy-flavoured buttercream. These babies are going to be gone in sixty seconds.

I'm licking the crumbs from my fingers – essential quality

control – as Chantal arrives. She breezes in with an excess of carrier bags.

'I don't need to ask where you've been.' I nod at her stash of shopping.

'It's only however-many-shopping-days-it-is until Christmas,' Chantal informs me. 'Thought I'd better make a bit of a dent in it.'

'Looks like you've done a sterling job. I haven't seen you laden down with bags like that for a good while.'

'Hasn't been done in a while. More's the pity.'

'No baby girl today?'

'Stacey's been looking after her, but I've just texted them. I caught her mid-feed so, as soon as she's done, she'll be coming along in a minute.'

'She's nice, isn't she?'

'Lovely,' Chantal agrees. 'It's funny how things work out. Who'd have thought that we would become friends? But I'm glad that we're trying to make it work.'

'What does Ted think about that?'

Chantal laughs. 'On the one hand he seems quite relieved but, on the other, I'm sure it makes him quite nervous. He'll simply have to live with that. Better that the two women in his life are mates than at each other's throats, surely?'

'I'll second that.' Then, 'What can I get for you?'

'I don't care,' Chantal says. 'Just load me up with as much sugar as possible, I'm exhausted.'

'A caffeine hit too?'

'Whatever you say.' She flops into the sofa by the window and sighs.

A moment later, Autumn arrives with Lewis. I'm still thinking a crèche corner would be a good idea. Get them started on chocolate young and these are my customers of the future.

'Usual?' I ask.

'You're a lifesaver, Lucy.'

'You're looking very flush-faced,' I note.

'We've been to the Winter Wonderland in Hyde Park. Haven't we, Lewis?'

He nods. 'It was fun. We went on the carousel and skating on ice and on a ride with penguins.'

'Fabulous. Are you any good at skating?'

'The best,' he says modestly. 'Miles said so.'

'He did?' I give Autumn a knowing glance. 'Good for you. You can have a chocolate-chip cookie as a reward.'

Lewis's eyes widen. 'Thank you, Auntie Lucy.'

As casually as I can manage, I say to Autumn, 'So, it wasn't just the two of you?'

'No.' She grins at me. 'Lewis and I were with Miles and Florence.'

'Hmm,' I say. 'This Miles, his name is getting dropped into the conversation quite regularly.'

'He's nice,' Autumn admits, flushing a little more. 'I like being with him.'

I know that things aren't going well with her and Addison at the moment, but I don't know how bad they are. It seems that this Miles is quietly edging into the picture, though.

Just as I've got one lot of drinks ready, both Nadia and Stacey arrive at the same time. Stacey has the two babies tucked tightly into the buggy together like two peas in a pod. They look like twins rather than half-sisters.

I hand the tray over to Autumn. 'Be a love and take these to Chantal and Nadia. I'll bring yours in a sec. What can I get you, Stacey?'

She gives me her order and Chantal comes over. 'Let me give you a hand with these lovely girls.'

'They're both fast asleep,' Stacey says. 'Shall I bring them over in the buggy?'

'Sure. We'll park it right here.' Chantal laughs. 'I used to hate the yummy mummies taking up all the room in cafés with their baby paraphernalia and now I'm the worst of them.'

It's so very tempting to put up the closed sign on the door so that I can have some quality time with my best girls, but I daren't. As I predicted, Alexandra's cupcakes are proving to be a huge hit and nearly every customer who's come in today has taken some away with them or has placed an order in time for Christmas. I'll have to keep running backwards and forwards so that I can keep up with the gossip.

After I've dealt with the little rush, everyone in the café seems happy for a few minutes so, when I take over the rest of the order, I sit down for five minutes. I've got a cuppa and a slice of coffee cake for myself – which is, technically, lunch.

Nadia pulls Lewis onto her lap and gives him a cookie. 'Did you have a nice time today?'

'We saw Father Christmas and everything,' he answers, chocolate round his mouth already.

'She went with *Miles*,' I say and flutter my eyelashes.

Autumn blushes furiously. 'Stop it, Lucy. There's nothing in it,' she insists. 'He's just a nice man.'

'Well, I think romance is in the air,' I declare. 'It's Christmas and that is the perfect time for lurve.'

'I do *actually* have a fiancé,' Autumn retorts.

'Whatever.' I make a W sign just to tease her a bit more.

'Lucy, how are your plans for your romantic weekend coming on?' Nadia asks.

'I booked my tickets for Bruges in a brief lull between customers this morning,' I tell them excitedly. 'We're all set to go. I can't wait to tell Crush this evening. It will be wonderful. A chocolate festival *and* a Christmas market.'

'You'll think that you've died and gone to heaven.'

'And Marcus is definitely *not* going to be there?' Chantal, probably with good reason, has a very suspicious nature.

'Absolutely not.' I texted him this morning to let him know that I've booked my tickets and all I got back was one saying *Great*. Nothing more. No declarations of love. No kisses. Nothing.

And I, for one, am pleased that Marcus and I can remain friends.

'I promise to bring you home some fabulous Belgian choccy treats.'

'You and I can manage between us, can't we, Autumn?' Nadia says.

'Definitely.'

I kiss them both. 'I love you,' I say. 'And not just for Christmas.'

'Nadia bites into a double choc cookie. 'I'll make sure it's in the diary. Tarak hasn't asked me to work weekends yet, so I'm sure it will be all right.'

'How's it going in the heady world of fashion?' Chantal asks.

'Tricky,' Nadia admits. 'I like the job well enough and it's great being with Anita again, but my brother-in-law and I have a difficult relationship. He likes me a bit more than he maybe should.'

'Awkward.' That's Chantal again.

'Yeah. But I'll deal with it. Somehow.'

She does look worried, though. 'Statistically, you're more likely to run off with your brother-in-law than anyone else,' I say to lighten the mood.

'I suspect that only works if your brother-in-law is George Clooney,' Autumn counters.

Which, at least, has the desired effect of making Nadia laugh.

'I take it that Tarak's certainly no Gorgeous George?'

'No,' she laughs. 'I guess that makes him a lot easier to resist.'

'We could put a date for our naming party in the diary too,' Chantal suggests. 'Clive and Tristan are coming back this weekend. I know it's a rush, Lucy, but could we do it then?'

'Sure. We can do it after the shop shuts on Sunday. Would that work for everyone?'

'I don't see why not,' Chantal says. 'Does that suit you, Stacey?'

'Yes,' she says. 'I'm going nowhere else.'

'Do you want to check with your family before I book it in?' I ask her.

'No,' she says. 'They won't travel for this. The snow's quite bad where they are and they wouldn't view it as a proper christening.'

Chantal gives her a hug. 'We'll make it a lovely party.'

'How are you feeling?' I venture. She certainly looks a bit brighter than when she first came in with Chantal.

'I'm hoping to get a cleaner in place soon,' she says. 'Perhaps later this week. Even that makes me feel better. And I know that there's somewhere I can go if I feel lonely.'

'I always have tea, sympathy and chocolate available here,' I assure her. 'There's nothing else you need in the world.'

'Thanks,' she says shyly. 'You've all made me feel very welcome.'

'Sunday it is then,' Chantal says. 'I'll phone Clive and Tristan and confirm it with them.'

'I'll get Alexandra to sort out some cakes for Lana and Elsie.' I can also get some balloons and decorations online. I can't wait already. Oh, I do love a party.

Chapter Thirty-Two

Crush and I are lying in the bath together being all romantic. My back is against his chest, his arms round my waist. I've poured us both a glass of wine and there's a row of chocolates lined up along the edge of the bath. My smoochy Christmas songs playlist is serenading us. Our favourite Elvis rubber duck bobs around my nether regions. We are covered in bubbles and bathed in the light of a dozen candles. I could lie here for ever and never get bored. This is the life.

'Put some more hot water in, Gorgeous,' Crush says languidly.

I am Keeper of the Taps and with that job comes great responsibility. With a skill that has been honed over many years, I move the tap lever with my big toe and, lo, hot water gushes in. Elvis bobs in the torrent.

When the temperature has risen sufficiently we snuggle down again. I sip my wine.

'Oh, good news,' I say. 'I managed to book for Bruges today and, considering it's coming up to Christmas I got a good deal, too. It wasn't cheap, but it wasn't hideously expensive either. We go out by Eurostar from St Pancras on the Friday morning and we'll be back by Monday lunchtime. Sorted.'

'Ah,' Crush says.

And not in a good way.

I twist in the bath to look at him. 'Tell me you can get the time off work.'

He shakes his head. 'I can't, Lucy. I meant to call you this morning and I was so busy that I clean forgot. I was all set to go and an important job came in at the last minute. It's a potential multi-million-pound contract and I just can't risk letting my sales team go on their own. I'm the manager. It's my neck on the block. I need to be there.'

'Aiden.' I try my most whiny voice. 'We *need* this break.'

His arms tighten around me. 'We do. You're right. I really hate to let you down. Believe me, it's the last thing on earth that I want. But, if I can get this in the bag, then next year will be a lot easier for me. You know what it's like at Targa – we're being pushed to bring in more revenue all the time and this would take me a long way towards my target. It might even get me a big, fat bonus. Who knows what fun we could have with that?'

'What sort of fun?'

'I'm thinking sparkly rings kind of fun.'

'Really?' I want to stay sulky, yet I can't help but grin. 'You're not just saying that because I'm sulking?'

'No,' he laughs. 'Let's not get *too* far ahead of ourselves, but I don't think it would be premature for us to become engaged people next year.'

'Engaged!' Wait until I tell the girls. Finally, I have bagged my man, the man of my dreams nonetheless. 'I'd like that,' I say. My little, loved-up heart beats erratically. 'I'd like that very much.'

He kisses me long and hard. There's something else bobbing

around my nether regions and I don't think that it's Elvis the duck.

When we break apart again, Crush looks at me earnestly. 'So you see why I need to go to Scotland?'

'Scotland?' I can't help but let my face fall.

'Edinburgh. I'm going up there next Friday morning and I have to take the clients out to dinner that night, but I'll be back by Saturday afternoon. Couldn't we go to Bruges then?'

'It would hardly be worth it,' I say. 'Besides, I can't change it now. The reason I got a great price is that it's fixed. I've paid for it up front.'

'I'm sorry, Gorgeous.'

I know that Crush wouldn't let me down unless he absolutely had to. He is kind and reliable. Earnest. He's nothing like Marcus.

'I'll still have to go. Marcus has arranged for me to give a talk about the chocolate market in the UK on the afternoon we'd arrive. Plus he'd got tickets for us to go to the ball the same evening. I can't let him down.'

Crush frowns.

'Marcus won't be there,' I reassure him. 'I'm just worried about going alone.'

'Would one of the girls go with you?'

'I've already roped in Nadia and Autumn to look after Chocolate Heaven in my absence, so they can't. Maybe Chantal would come with me.'

I pout at him.

'I know it's not the romantic weekend that you had all mapped out for us.'

'I had all manner of *very* kinky sexual treats planned for you. Lots of them involving chocolate.'

'You did?' He raises an eyebrow at that.

I didn't really, but I'm sure I could conjure something up if push came to shove – as it were.

'I hate to remind you, but it didn't go all that well last time you combined chocolate with foreplay.'

Oh, crap. Hoped he'd forgotten about the Dirty Protest Incident. Clearly, he is as scarred by it as I am. It will be a long time before I consider smearing chocolate on my breasts again. Or anywhere else for that matter.

'I'm sorry, Gorgeous. What can I do to make it up to you?'

'Oh, I don't know,' I murmur as he pulls me close and his lips find mine again. I knock all the chocolates off the side of the bath and into the water, but I don't care. Elvis gives a squeaky quack in protest as he's squashed in the tangle of our limbs. 'I'm sure I'll think of something.'

Chapter Thirty-Three

Autumn didn't know what was wrong with her. She normally wasn't the kind of person to feel down in the dumps, but she was more depressed than she'd ever been before. She felt as if her life was crumbling apart at the moment, as if it had all become too much to take.

Autumn had left Chocolate Heaven with Nadia and Lewis and had gone back to their house to eat the dinner that she'd prepared earlier. As always, it was lovely to spend time with them, but now she had to go home by herself and she felt as if she'd put on a layer of loneliness along with her coat. If she was honest, she was beginning to feel a little outside of the group of friends, too.

She loved Lewis to pieces and it was getting harder to fill the hours when she wasn't looking after him. Nadia always thought that it was Autumn who was doing the favour in babysitting her son, but Autumn didn't know what she would have done without those hours with her small charge.

Chantal and Stacey had their babies to keep them fully occupied and perhaps she was dwelling on that too much. Sometimes she ached so much with the need to hold Lana or

Elsie that it made her feel nauseous. Sometimes she could almost feel the essence of her own child in her arms and Autumn wondered how much longer she could keep her secret from the other girls. She'd told Miles about her daughter, but still hadn't mentioned it to the Chocolate Lovers' Club, who'd been her best buddies and confidantes for years. Why was that? Wouldn't it be better if it was all out in the open?

Sadness overwhelmed her and her head seemed to be filled with regrets. Regrets that she'd been compelled to give Willow away. Regrets that she hadn't been able to keep her brother on the straight and narrow. Regrets that she had no relationship with her parents to speak of. She thought she was a good, caring person, so why was it that all her relationships were so difficult? Had she done something really terrible in a former life and her punishment was to see everything that she loved taken away from her?

Lucy was completely besotted with Crush and he with her. That's how it should be. But who did Autumn have? She hadn't heard from Addison all day. Again. She'd sent a couple of texts, but hadn't received a reply. It seemed as if their relationship had cooled and she didn't really understand why. They needed some time to sit down and discuss what was going wrong with them and whether it could be fixed. She'd been avoiding talking to him, partly because she knew he wasn't supportive of her feelings about Rich and, right now, she needed someone to care.

Autumn stayed at Nadia's house into the evening, lingering until she couldn't put off going home any longer. She left Nadia curled up reading Lewis a bedtime story and took a cab back to her own place. The central heating had gone off and it was cold and unwelcoming. Christmas was only a few weeks away and yet she'd never felt less festive. She didn't even think that she'd bother with a tree this year. If she needed a Christmas fix then all she had to do was pop to Chocolate Heaven, as Lucy had done a great job in there.

Reluctant to take her coat off, she turned on the gas fire and flicked up the thermostat. Still, the flat was small and would soon warm up. In the meantime, she went through to the kitchen to put the kettle on. When she opened the drawer to find a spoon, there was a packet of cigarette papers there and a lighter that Rich had left behind. She'd thrown the weed that she'd brought from his flat in there and now she took it out and slipped it into the pocket of her cardigan.

When the tea was brewed, she came back and curled up on the sofa, hugging her knees to her, sipping from her mug. She sat there staring at the flickering blue flame of the gas fire and, without really knowing what she was doing, drew out the contents of her pocket. She stared at the small packet in her hand and, for want of something else to occupy her, she rolled herself a joint. It was years since she'd smoked anything at all. Probably at university. Even then, she hadn't been that interested. The effect that it had on Rich and the destruction it had wrought on his life had made her very anti-drugs. She never usually even touched a cigarette. It held no appeal for her whatsoever.

But now she lit it up and held the roll-up to her lips, taking a deep toke. It was ridiculous, desperate even, but this made her seem closer to Rich, feeling as he felt. What was it about the pull of this drug that made him put everything else on the line for it until it had, ultimately, cost him his life? She simply didn't know. If she'd had the answer to that maybe she'd have been able to help Rich more.

Autumn sat mesmerised by the glowing tip. Her working day was taken up by people whose lives had been blighted by this. She took the smoke deep into her lungs. Did it make her feel relaxed, mellow, any more together as a human being? No. It did nothing for her. She could take it or leave it. Were some people simply destined to be addicted to any form of drug more than others? Did Rich always have that kind of personality? He certainly seemed to be attracted to anything that was dangerous and illegal. Rich had also drunk heavily, whereas a glass of wine was enough for Autumn. Did the two things go hand in hand?

She'd nearly finished the joint and her eyes were heavy. Perhaps it would help her to get a good night's sleep. It was then that there was a knock at her door.

It was late and her heart lifted. For a few moments before reality hit again, she thought it might be Rich. He was the one who normally turned up late at night, unannounced. Sometimes it was so very easy to forget that he was gone.

'Hey.' Instead, it was Addison who stood there. 'I just finished at a meeting and thought I'd say hi. I didn't have a minute all day to return your texts.'

It was really lovely to see him as she hadn't expected him to call round this evening. She went to hug him and then realised that she still had the joint between her fingers.

'Oh,' she said. 'Let me get rid of this.'

She turned back into her living room, looking for her saucer or something to put it out in.

Addison followed her and when she looked at him again, he was frowning. 'Is that what I think it is?' He sniffed the air. 'Christ, Autumn, it is.'

'I know,' she said, both of them aware of the remains of the packet on the coffee table. 'It was stupid of me. I brought it back from Rich's place. I know I shouldn't have, but . . .'

Her boyfriend's face darkened. 'I might have known that your bloody brother would have something to do with this.'

Addison was barely over the doorstep and yet, already, they were arguing.

'I'm too tired for this,' she said. 'It was silly of me. I won't do it again. Let it go at that.'

'I work for a drug rehabilitation unit,' he said, unnecessarily. 'We both do. Why do you think that is?'

'I'm not a child,' Autumn said. 'You don't need to speak to me as if I'm five years old.'

'You seem to have no concept of the real world. You think you're somehow immune to the effects of drugs here in your little ivory tower.'

'How can you say that when I've had to deal with all the trouble it's brought into our lives through Rich? Is *still* bringing into our lives.'

'We could go round in circles about Rich,' Addison said harshly. 'If it hadn't been for your parents funding him, he might still be around today. Think about that.'

It stung. Because, at the end of the day, there was a grain of truth in it. 'So I'm from a privileged background. Everything we argue about comes back to Rich or to that. I can't change how I've been brought up. What's done is done. It's history. *My* history. Just because you've had to struggle more than me, it doesn't mean that you're a better person.'

Autumn was reeling. Addison had launched into a full-on verbal attack and he hadn't even sat on the sofa yet. It was as if he'd been looking for an excuse.

'I could have you sacked for smoking dope,' he said. 'Instead, I'll accept your resignation.'

'That's ridiculous.'

'No, it isn't. It's real life, Autumn. Not even your parents can buy you out of this one.'

'This is the first time I've smoked dope in years and I've had a few puffs. That's all. And, believe me, I have my reasons.'

How could she really explain that she'd wanted to smoke because for one silly moment she thought that it would bring Rich close to her once more? 'We should talk about this.'

'There's nothing to say. I'm not having one of my workers smoking weed.'

'Worker?' Autumn said. 'Is that *all* I am to you?'

Addison sagged for a moment. Then he sighed and said, 'Yes.' His eyes were cold when he looked at her. 'We should have talked about this, I suppose, but I don't think things are right between us. They haven't been for a while. We're too different. We want different things from life.'

Did they? At one time, in the early days, it hadn't seemed so.

'As far as I'm concerned,' he added, 'we've reached the end of our relationship.'

Autumn's mouth gaped, but before she even had time to answer, Addison turned on his heel and left.

Chapter Thirty-Four

I try very hard not to rush the last of the dawdling customers out of Chocolate Heaven when, quite frankly, I want to shout at them, 'GET A MOVE ON! GO HOME!'

Don't they know I have Things To Do?

Of course they don't. But today's the day of Lana and Elsie's naming party and I want to start prettifying Chocolate Heaven as soon as I can. In fact, I've been itching to do it all day. I have cake. I have helium balloons. I have party bags. I have pink flower arrangements courtesy of the florist two doors down. I have sparkly pink champagne. I'm glad that the babies aren't boys as blue drinks are just WRONG.

Now, all I need to do is run round for half an hour and set up the tables ready for the guests to arrive. It's a select little gathering, but none the worse for it. I'm so pleased that Clive and Tristan will be here too as I want them to see how well I've been doing with the business. It's all present and correct, just as they left it. The ceiling hasn't fallen in. A gas main hasn't exploded underneath it. A plane hasn't landed on it. Nothing.

Eventually, Chocolate Heaven is empty and, with a relieved

sigh, I turn the sign to 'Closed'. Now it's dark the fairy lights shine out and the Christmas tree looks especially twinkly.

Without further ado, I set to. I push two long tables together to make up the cake buffet. At each end there's a single-tier cake for the babies – one chocolate, one vanilla. They're pink and white striped, trimmed with flowers and both iced with their names. I put out the cupcakes that Alexandra has decorated in a baby theme too and, once the sugar base layer has been sorted, I add a selection of savouries – little quiches, sandwiches, some flaky sausage rolls – all bought from the local deli. After that, it's all a blur as I hurriedly make preparations.

In the nick of time, it's all ready and I'm just popping the cork on the first bottle of pink champagne when Chantal and Ted arrive with Lana in her buggy. Seconds later they're followed by Stacey and Elsie and it's clear that they've all walked down here together, which is nice.

I pour them all champagne while they fuss with unbundling the girls from their many layers of clothing.

'The cakes look beautiful, Lucy,' Stacey says. 'Thanks so much for organising this.'

'You're welcome. I hope Alexandra is going to find time to join us for a drink, so you can tell her that you like them. Can I hold Elsie for a minute?'

She passes the baby over, which leaves her free to stand and talk to Ted.

Nadia and Lewis arrive. Then, shortly afterwards, Jacob. It's been a while since I've seen him and it's great that he's able to come along. I know that it's a bit premature to be saying this as Nadia insists that they're just good friends, but I think he and Nadia would make a lovely couple.

Jacob comes to hug me and takes Elsie into the embrace too.

'Long time, no see,' I say.

'Too long. You're looking great, though. Love clearly suits you.'

I flush at that.

Jacob laughs. 'Now I've embarrassed you.'

'No, not really. But you're right. I'm very much in love and deliriously happy.'

'Good to hear it. Will you want my wedding-planning services again soon?'

'I might well do,' I say in the most enigmatic way I can manage.

'Oh, really?'

'It's a bit early for a formal announcement, but I have high hopes.'

'I'll come in again next week and we can catch up properly. Clearly you have a lot to tell me.'

'Nothing else has changed,' I shrug. 'Working too hard. Barely keeping my head above water.'

'It seems as if you're making a good job of it. This all looks great.'

'Thanks, Jacob.'

'Hey.' Autumn comes through the door with a man and a little girl in tow. 'I hope you don't mind some extra guests?'

'Of course not,' I say. 'This must be the much-talked-about Miles.' The man behind her is tall, more than a little good-looking and seems quite bashful.

He takes off his beanie hat. 'Hi, Lucy. I've heard a lot about you, too.'

'Glad you could come.'

I bend down to the little girl. 'You must be Florence.' She clings to her father's leg, suddenly shy. 'This is Elsie.' I give a wave with Elsie's hand and Florence smiles timidly.

'Let's take your coat off, Flo.' Miles bends to assist her and

I like the way that he gently and patiently unpeels his daughter from her layers of outdoor clothing.

I nudge Autumn. 'This is a turn-up for the books,' I whisper.

'Addison and I had a terrible row last night,' she murmurs back.

'What about?'

'Long story,' she says. 'One that will require a lot of chocolate and cake. I'm pretty sure it's over between us. It certainly seems that way. Addison said a lot of hurtful things.'

'Wow. I'm sorry to hear it. Why didn't you call me?'

'It was late and I went straight to bed. Weirdly, I don't even feel that upset. I've not quite processed it yet, but I think it's been on the cards for a while.' She sighs. 'He couldn't come today, anyway. He's going up to Manchester with a colleague for a Think Tank day. The dreaded Monica Desmond.' She rolls her eyes.

Ah, yes. Autumn has told us all about the new dragon in her workplace.

'He caught the train with her this morning,' she continues, 'and I just didn't want to come alone today. You really don't mind?'

'Of course not. And he's *hot*!'

'I'd noticed that,' Autumn admits, pink-cheeked. 'I wanted you to meet him. He's a lovely guy. Bit of a baptism of fire for him, though. He won't know what's hit him.'

'Looks as if he's coping all right.' Miles has already moved on to chat to Jacob and they seem to be getting along famously. I also spot that Jacob is shooting surreptitious glances in Chantal's direction.

'You'd better go and catch up with your guests.' I give Autumn an encouraging wink and, smiling anxiously, she heads off towards Miles and Florence.

I've returned Elsie to her mum and am opening the second bottle when Crush arrives.

'Hi, Gorgeous.' He's breathless and a bit harried. His face is pink from the cold, his hair a tangled mess when he pulls off his hat. 'How are you coping?'

'Just fine.' I kiss his chilled cheek and my lips feel hot against it.

'I meant to come a bit earlier and give you a hand, but my paperwork took longer than I thought.'

It's bad that even Sunday isn't a day of rest for us.

'You're here now. That's all that matters.'

'I need a drink.' I hand him a glass of champagne and he takes a good gulp. 'That's better. Shall I take the bottle round for you and top up everyone?'

I kiss him again. 'You're my hero.'

He grins at that and disappears with the bottle. I realise that I'm the only one without a drink, so I open another bottle and help myself. As long as I stay one drink behind my guests then all should be fine.

Fashionably late, Clive and Tristan arrive too. They're both looking fabulously tanned, healthy and considerably more slender than when they ran Chocolate Heaven. Tristan's blond hair has lightened in the sun over the summer in the south of France and he's looking very French in his black shirt and skinny jeans. Clive, the older of the two, looks more relaxed than he has in years and is embracing his feminine side in a pink shirt and sweater. Clearly life in La Belle France is suiting them. Instantly, we mob them, swamping them with a group hug.

'You guys,' they say. 'We've missed you.'

'Look at you,' I cry. 'You both look like you haven't a care in the world.'

'We haven't,' Clive admits. 'Our biggest stress is deciding who is going to walk down to the *boulangerie* to buy our baguette for the day. A lot of that's down to you, Lucy. You're doing a great job. We're delighted to see that Chocolate Heaven is still standing.'

'Not only that, but thriving,' Tristan adds.

I feel myself glow with pride. 'I've turned over a new leaf,' I tell Clive. 'Honestly, I have. I no longer destroy everything I touch.'

'You're doing a great job,' he says. 'I've been keeping an eye on the books. Well done.'

'I've got some new ideas,' I confide. 'If you've got a bit of time later.'

'Yeah.' A slightly troubled frown settles on the brow that appeared so carefree just a moment ago. 'I want a quiet word with you, too.'

That makes me panic a bit. Much as I'd love them to come home, in the back of my mind I'd also like them to stay away because if they do return then they'll probably give me the boot. And nothing on this earth would make me go back to being a temporary secretary. I'd rather give up chocolate for the rest of my life.

Then I think, even for me, that was a very foolish thought.

Chapter Thirty-Five

The party is in full swing. Chantal and Stacey have read out poems for the little girls. I put candles on the cakes which Chantal and Stacey blow out. Then we toast the babies, wishing them good health and happy lives.

I take the cakes into the kitchen to cut them up and then, when I'm handing round the slices, I notice that Ted and Stacey seem to be getting on very well. *Very well*. There's a definite chemistry between them. Oh dear.

I'm handing some cake to Chantal when she says, 'You noticed it too.' She inclines her head towards her husband and his one-time lover. 'There's still a spark there.'

I don't think she's wrong.

Chantal sighs and bites into her chocolate cake. 'It's hard to watch. He doesn't look at me like that anymore.'

'But you've been together a long time.'

'Ted and I rub along well enough. He's made a surprisingly good father, but I don't know if we'll ever get our relationship back to what it once was. At the moment, due to this demanding young lady,' she gazes lovingly at the baby in her arms, 'we can just ignore it, but there'll come a time when we need to address the issue.'

I kiss Chantal's cheek. 'I hate to see you so worried. If you and Ted love each other enough, then I'm sure it will all work itself out.'

My friend laughs. 'That's because you are the eternal optimist, Lucy Lombard. Sometimes love isn't enough, or it takes different forms. I'm only just learning that. You have to work hard at relationships and I've been guilty of not doing that. Take advice from your Auntie Chantal: put that man of yours at the top of the list.'

'Ah, it's a good thing you said that. I've got a favour to ask you. A big one.'

Chantal looks intrigued.

'Crush isn't going to be able to make the trip to Bruges with me. Pressure at work.'

'That's a shame.'

'I'm gutted, but it's something important that he can't cancel. Would you come with me? I know it's a big ask, but it's all booked and paid for. There'll be lots of chocolate and a Christmas market.'

'Try to keep me away. I'll just have to make sure that Ted can look after Lana for a few days without me.'

'You don't know how relieved I am. Call me a wuss, but I didn't want to go on my own.'

'We'll have a lovely time. I know it's not what you planned, but it will be nice to have a few girly days to ourselves.'

Checking to see where Crush is, I see that he's being regaled with tales by Clive and Tristan. This might only be a small gathering, but I don't feel as if I've had a minute to myself yet and I certainly haven't had a chance to catch up with my bosses yet. But it looks as if they're being their usual entertaining selves. They look happy with each other too and that's a bonus. When they scuttled away to the continent their relationship was at breaking point.

I move on to Nadia, who's at the other side of the room. 'You look a bit glum. Everything OK?'

She shrugs. 'Have you seen the way Jacob is looking at Chantal?'

He does keep glancing across at her. 'Maybe he's just looking for a chance to go across and chat to her while Ted's otherwise engaged.' I don't want a punch-up between them at the party. 'There's a lot of history there, Nadia. They'll always be good friends.'

'Where does that leave me?'

'You're holding him at arm's length, Nadia, and Jacob is being respectful of that. He's such a gentleman. If you do want to take things further with him then you'll probably have to make the first move.'

'I don't know if that's what I do want.' Nadia frowns. 'Now Chantal is ogling Jacob.'

I try to laugh it off. 'I don't think she's really *ogling* as such.' Maybe looking a little too longingly, though. Not good.

'Perhaps you and Chantal need to sit down together and have a chat to clear the air. I'm sure she'd be delighted if you and Jacob get together. Just don't rush things. Go over there now and have a snuggle with lovely Lana. That'll make you feel better. I don't want you two to be bad friends.'

'We're not,' Nadia says. 'It's just that my head feels a bit messed up at the moment. It's probably better that I don't try to force things while I'm feeling like this.'

'Good idea.' I put my hand under Nadia's arm and steer her towards Chantal. 'It's probably starting work again and all that goes with it. Don't put yourself under too much pressure. You've been through a lot. Small steps.'

Thankfully, Nadia breaks into a smile as we approach

189

Chantal. As we get closer, Lana spits out her dummy and, with amazing skill, Nadia catches it just before it hits the floor. She takes a tissue from her bag and wipes it.

'Thanks,' Chantal says. 'You've got better reflexes than me.'

'Once a mother, always a mother,' Nadia quips.

'I hate using these things, but needs must. Lana loves it.'

'Lewis did too, but they grow out of it.'

'Yeah,' Chantal says. 'You don't see many eighteen-year-olds with pacifiers.'

'Hand over that delicious bundle,' Nadia says.

'Glad to.' Chantal places Lana into her arms. 'She's getting heavier every day. Just like her mummy.'

'I've never seen you look sexier,' I say to Chantal, who's looking very curvaceous in a form-fitting dress. 'You're rocking the Nigella vibe. Do you need another drink?'

'No,' Chantal says. 'But now that my hands are free, I might well work on my curves and hit the cake buffet again. Can I leave you with Lana for five?'

Nadia nods and Chantal heads across the room, zooming in on the cake.

'Did she just snub me?' Nadia asks.

'Of course she didn't, darling.'

'Sorry, Lucy. I'm being paranoid. I don't know what's wrong with me.'

Then Jacob leaves Autumn and Miles and goes across to chat to Chantal. Last time Ted, Jacob and Chantal were together – at my non-wedding – Ted found out that Jacob had been sleeping with his wife and punched him. A good right hook to the jaw. I hold my breath for a moment but Ted doesn't even notice. He has Elsie in his arms and is far too engrossed in what Stacey's saying.

Nadia notices though and her lips tighten.

'You have to clear the air. Otherwise you'll drive yourself

completely potty,' I advise. 'But now's not the time. Let's just enjoy the evening. We're all friends together.'

I take a swig from the champagne bottle. Flipping heck, there are more underlying tensions here than at the Annual Ewing Barbecue at Southfork.

Chapter Thirty-Six

It's late. The babies are overtired, so are taken home and everyone else has left except Clive and Tristan. Crush has gone home ahead of me to start making dinner. Otherwise we'll be eating Kit-Kats and toast at midnight. Again.

Clive and Tristan have been great, helping me to tidy up – now Chocolate Heaven is all back to normal and ready for me to open up in the morning.

We all flop onto the sofas together. 'Great job, guys,' I say. 'Couldn't have managed without you.'

'We've realised how difficult it is for you to be running this place single-handedly,' Clive admits. 'It was OK for a short time, but we know it can't go on.'

'I did want to talk to you about that,' I admit.

Tristan stands up again. 'I think we need a caffeine hit. I'm going to make us all a cappuccino. If I can work out how to operate that fancy machine.'

'I have loads of plans,' I say excitedly to Clive. 'We're on the route now for Chocolate Ecstasy Tours which bring in new customers and they come nearly every day. Jen, who runs them, is great and we could do a lot more with her.'

Clive raises his eyebrows in approval.

'I'd like to start doing chocolate-tasting events, too. Maybe the occasional supper or special chocolate cocktail evenings. I couldn't manage that alone, though. I'd need to get in some help.'

'It all sounds great, but there's something I need to tell you first, Lucy,' Clive starts. 'There's no easy way of saying this.' He glances anxiously at me. 'Tris and I have decided to stay in France. We love it there. The pace of life suits us both so much better and we've got time for each other in a way that we never had here. This is a great business, but it sucks the life out of you.'

Don't I know it.

'If you want me to keep on running it, then I'm more than happy to,' I jump in. 'I could just do with some help. Aiden and I hardly see each other.'

'The thing is . . .' Clive looks uncomfortable. 'We've decided to sell Chocolate Heaven. We need to move on and there's a little place we've seen in our village that we'd like to buy. We can't do it without the money from here.'

'Oh.' Hadn't seen that one coming. I had an inkling that they might not return, but I never thought they'd be able to let Chocolate Heaven go.

'That's why we're over here this week. Why we were able to come to the party. And it was a great get-together.'

'Yes.' We got through it without bloodshed, I think. Though I fear it might have been a close-run thing. I hate to acknowledge that there are undercurrents in our friendships – we have all been so steadfast and true, always there for each other. Friendships like that don't often come along in a lifetime and we should cherish that.

'We're going to get the place valued and it will go on the market straight away.'

'Wow,' is all I can manage.

Tristan comes back with our cappuccinos. He doesn't make them as well as I do. There's no heart in cocoa powder on the top and the froth isn't as frothy as mine. It's clear that he's out of practice.

'I know it's a bit of a surprise,' Clive continues.

Too damn right. And I'm not sure that 'surprise' quite covers it. Body blow, more like.

'We wanted you to be the first to know.'

I gulp at my coffee, even though it burns my throat. I think I'm in shock.

'If you want to buy the business, we'd give you first refusal, Lucy. I was looking at the books with the accountant yesterday and the takings are up massively since you've been managing it.'

'Really?'

'You're our rightful heir. We'd love you to have this place.'

'I'd love it too,' I manage to say. 'But I've absolutely no idea how I'd raise the money.'

I've nothing. No collateral. No deposit. Not even a pot to piss in. I'm wishing that my mother was still in Spain with The Millionaire, as I might be able to tap them for a few bob. My dad is now impoverished too, as he spent most of his money on The Hairdresser and now The Pilates Instructor. Damn them and their University of the Third Age libidos.

'I can't see anything much happening before Christmas,' Clive says. 'You've got a few weeks at least.'

A few weeks. My heart plunges to the doldrums.

'We know that you're a resourceful woman, Lucy. You'll come up with something.'

He smiles at me in an encouraging manner and I want to weep. I'm glad Clive thinks I'm resourceful because, frankly, I feel as if I'm floundering. A few short weeks and I could lose Chocolate Heaven. There could be a new owner who boots me out onto the street. What will I do?

Right now the only thing I can think of is writing a begging letter to Santa asking for a Christmas miracle.

Chapter Thirty-Seven

It was late when the taxi dropped off Nadia and Lewis at their little house. Her son was tired after the excitement of the afternoon and it wouldn't have been fair to drag him across London on the Tube, so she'd splashed out to travel in comfort. Well, if you could call a London minicab that looked as if it hadn't been near a car wash or an MOT station in recent years, comfort.

She paid the driver. A man who didn't seem to have the best grasp of the English language or, even, the geography of the area. Still, it meant that he hadn't talked to her all the way home and Lewis had been free to doze on her shoulder. He'd been eating chocolate and cake to his heart's content this afternoon and, after his sugar rush, now came the inevitable sugar slump. Tomorrow she'd make up for it with a surfeit of carrot snacks and an ultra-healthy packed lunch.

Rousing her son, she ushered him towards the front door. This wasn't the best area to live in and she was getting to hate going out at night by herself. Perhaps if her job worked out, she might be able to move somewhere a little nicer in years to come. She'd certainly like to get Lewis out of this environment. Somewhere nearer to Chocolate Heaven and the other girls might be nice, though she imagined that the property prices would be prohibitively expensive. Anywhere decent in London was extortionate these days.

She fumbled with her key in the lock and, as she did, a man stepped out of the shadows by her wall, making her jump.

'Nadia,' he said and, of course, she recognised his voice instantly.

'Tarak?' Her heart was banging loudly in her chest. 'What are you doing here?'

'I came to talk to you about a few things for work,' he said. 'I'm not going to be in the shop tomorrow and I wanted to catch you.'

'You could have called me.'

'I was just passing.'

'How do you even know where I live?'

'From Anita, of course.' Her brother-in-law looked offended, as if it was perfectly reasonable for him to be lurking in the bushes next to her house late at night. She wondered exactly how long he'd been waiting for her to return and the thought creeped her out.

'It's late, Tarak. I need to get Lewis into his bed. We've had a busy day and he's falling asleep on his feet.'

'I can come in and wait.' Tarak was undeterred. 'I'll put the kettle on or pour us a drink.'

'I've had enough to drink today.' But, as it looked as if she wasn't going to get rid of him otherwise, against her better judgement she said, 'You can make us a *quick* cup of tea.' Emphasis very much on the quick part of it.

She was tired herself and the thought of a long bath and an early night was very appealing.

They'd been stood on the doorstep for too long, so she let

them in, Tarak following close behind. She wondered if Anita really knew that he was here.

'Go right through to the kitchen,' she said, pointing the way. 'You'll see where everything is. I'll take Lewis straight up to bed.'

She steered her son to the stairs and up to his room. As she helped him to undress, Lewis asked, 'Who's that man?'

It was telling that her son didn't even recognise his uncle. 'Your Uncle Tarak,' she told him. 'That's who I work for now.'

'I don't think that I like him.'

She felt much the same. 'He's family,' she said, avoiding agreeing with him.

In the bathroom, Lewis cleaned his teeth. 'I like Jacob better.' Toothpaste spluttered out of his mouth.

Me too.

She thought about ringing Jacob and asking him to come over. That way Tarak was sure to leave. However, it wasn't exactly fair to use Jacob like that. Instead, she pulled out her phone and texted him.

Can u ring me in 10 mins, she typed. *Unwanted visitor*. She could hear Tarak moving around downstairs, opening and closing her cupboards, rummaging through her belongings. Goosebumps prickled her skin.

Who? Want me to come over?

That was just like him and a sense of relief washed over her. He was the best friend she could have, always at the other end of the phone.

No. Only Tarak. Jacob knew full well what she thought of her brother-in-law and her difficulties with him.

Sure, came the reply.

Ur a pal. xx

When Lewis had finished his ablutions, she tucked him into bed. 'No story tonight. Straight to sleep. Uncle Tarak wants to talk about work. I'll come and kiss you before I go to bed.' Though most nights Lewis seemed to find his way out of his own bed and into hers. She didn't usually have the heart to take him back.

Downstairs and Tarak was waiting in the living room. There was a cup of tea on the coffee table and he was holding a mug in his hands.

'He's getting to be a big boy,' he said to her.

'Yes.'

'Man of the house.' Said in a way that implied he was aware she was alone.

Everything about him made her want to shudder. How had her sister stayed married to him for so long? Did she not see what he was like? She wondered if there had been other staff in the shop who'd refused to stay for long due to his attitude and constant innuendo. She thought this sort of sexual harassment had gone out of fashion in the workplace in the seventies.

She took her tea and went to sit in the armchair as far away from him as possible. 'What was it that you wanted, Tarak?'

'I thought we should get to know each other all over again.' He made himself comfortable on the sofa, his stomach, soft now, spilling over the waistband of his trousers.

'You said it was about work.'

'I think good staff relations are very important.'

'I'm too tired for this now,' she said. 'I can't play games, Tarak. I'd be really glad if you could just drink up and leave.'

'That's not very nice.' His voice became even more smarmy. 'We're family. I'm not going anywhere, Nadia. It would pay you to treat me well.'

'I like my job, Tarak. I like working with my sister. If you and I have a good relationship, it's a bonus, but it's not my priority.'

His smile faded. 'Maybe it should be.'

'If my job depends on it, then maybe I should resign straight away. I'll leave you to explain it to Anita.'

Her phone rang. Not a moment too soon. When she answered it was, of course, Jacob.

'Hi,' she said. 'Yes, I'm still awake. Excellent. It would be good to see you.'

She tried to pretend that she was ignoring Tarak, but she could see that his face had darkened.

'I'll look forward to it.' She hung up and turned to her brother-in-law. 'I'm expecting someone. Perhaps you should go home to your wife.'

Tarak put his mug down. 'Booty call?'

'I don't think that's any of your business.'

She stood up and walked to the door. Somewhat reluctantly Tarak followed her lead.

In the cramped hallway, he stood close to her. Too close.

'We could be good for each other,' he said. 'Remember that.'

'All I want from you is a job. Nothing more.'

'You may come to regret that,' Tarak said.

'I don't think so.'

His smile was oily. 'I'll see you in the shop then. There are times when it'll be just the two of us. We should make the most of it.'

Nadia shut the door behind him and listened until his car roared away into the night. Only then could she breathe easy. Creep.

A second later her phone rang again, startling her. It was Jacob.

'Hi.'

'Has he gone?'

'Yes,' she said. 'Just. He's such a sleazebag.'

200

There was a pause before Jacob said, 'This might be completely the wrong thing to say.' He hesitated again. 'But do you want me to come over anyway?'

Nadia hesitated, heart still pounding. Were Jacob's words loaded? If so, it was more than she could deal with right now.

'Not tonight,' she said, managing to keep her tone neutral. 'I'm going to go straight to bed.'

'OK. Night then, Nadia.'

Was that disappointment she could hear in his voice or was he simply worried about her? 'Night, Jacob.'

Hanging up, she felt a hot tear squeeze out of her eye and roll down her cheek. Did she want to get involved with Jacob? Did she want to get involved with any man? There was so much at stake.

Nadia was jaded, weary and, despite not wanting to cry, she let the tears flow. It was so difficult. She was tired of being alone and yet terrified of getting involved again.

Chapter Thirty-Eight

Chantal lay in bed, Lana nestled at her breast. It had been a nice naming party. Lucy had pulled out all the stops for them and, other than a little tension with Nadia, everyone had got along brilliantly.

She listened to Ted in the en-suite bathroom. He'd been in the shower and now he was shaving to save a few precious moments in the morning. He was humming tunelessly but happily. Her husband wasn't a great one for social gatherings these days, but he seemed to have enjoyed himself. A few glasses of champagne had certainly helped to relax him; he seemed uptight so often these days. She guessed that he had a lot on his plate with two families to juggle now.

She'd seen him looking at Stacey and remembered that, once upon a time, before life got in the way, he had looked at her like that, too. If she was going to keep this marriage together, then she was going to have to get him to look at her like that again.

Since Lana had come along, Chantal felt that her love for Ted had, if anything, deepened. Sometimes she watched him caring for Lana, the love shining in his eyes, and her heart felt full of love for them both. She was eternally grateful that he'd turned out to be such a good dad. OK, so he might not be at the front of the queue when it came to volunteering for nappy-changing duty, but he was a world expert when it came to winding.

Yet she couldn't ignore the fact that it was a more platonic love she held for Ted now, rather than the passion they had once shared. Something had shifted. The early chemistry they'd had wasn't there anymore. There was no passion. There was, however, a mellow respect and affection. She wondered if he felt the same. Was that how all relationships ended up – particularly after you introduced children into the mix? No one wanted to frolic around the bedroom when they had a new baby, did they? She should talk to Ted about it, but how to broach it?

Ted came out of the bedroom, towel slung round his waist. When he dried himself he'd put on a clean T-shirt. No longer did they sleep naked together, bodies entwined, as they had in the early days of their love.

'Hey,' he said softly. 'How are my best girls?'

'One of us is nearly asleep in her supper,' Chantal said and nodded towards Lana, who was struggling to keep her eyes open.

He sat on the bed next to them both. His daughter clutched at his proffered little finger, grasping it with her fist.

'Lucy asked me to go on a trip to Bruges with her on Friday,' she said. 'A chocolate festival and the Christmas market.'

'That sounds like your version of heaven,' Ted noted. 'I take it you said yes.'

'I'd love to go,' she said. 'But only if you're happy looking after Lana for a few days.'

'Won't you be taking her food supply with you?'

Chantal laughed. 'She'll be fine on formula milk for a few days. She takes it quite happily. I'll express some milk, too.'

'We'll manage, won't we, Lana?' Ted glanced away from her. 'I'm sure Stacey will help.'

'Yes,' Chantal said, feeling a nip of unease.

Ted frowned at her. 'What's wrong? I thought you two were getting on great.'

'We are,' she said, pushing down any doubts. Stacey was a nice woman. They'd be fine here on their own. What could they really get up to with two demanding little girls in tow? After all, he usually spent one day of the weekend with them anyway.

'It would be good for you to have a break,' he added.

'Lucy really needs me there.'

'It's fine by me.'

Had he agreed to her absence too readily? Was there any subtext there? This would be a good time to talk, but she was tired after the party. Chantal put a hand on Ted's arm. His skin was damp, warm from the shower. Once, something as simple as that would have sent a thrill through her. Now there was nothing more than affection for this man. Would that come back in time?

'I love you,' she said. 'Are we going to be OK?'

'I don't know what you're talking about,' Ted said with a shrug. 'We're fine, aren't we?'

'Yes. I hope we go on being fine.'

'I want to be here for you and Lana. I told you that.'

'But being here for us means that Stacey and Elsie have to struggle.'

'No one said that this would be easy.' He let out a tired sigh. 'We're managing quite well, though. All things considered. I don't think Stacey feels quite so alone now that you've taken her under your wing. Thank you for that, Chantal.'

'She's a lovely woman.' Too lovely? In trying to be kind, understanding, grown up, modern, had she simply stirred the hornet's nest? 'I didn't know if you wanted to keep the two parts of your life separate.'

Ted ran his hand through his hair. 'I don't know what the best way is to deal with our situation,' he admitted. 'There's no manual on fatherhood and certainly not one that has a chapter on our set-up.'

'No.' She smiled wearily at that. 'We can only do our best. But we're in for a lifetime of this, Ted, and we both deserve to be happy.'

'You're not happy with me?'

'I didn't say that.' Chantal bit the bullet. It might as well be out in the open. 'But if you felt that you needed to be with her, you would tell me?'

Ted tutted. 'You're being ridiculous. I'm here and this is where I'm staying.'

He stood up and crossed to the wardrobe. He pulled out clean underwear and slipped the boxer shorts on beneath his towel – as you would if you were getting changed on a beach in public. Only when he was covered again did he peel off his towel. Was this normal behaviour between a man and his wife?

'I'm not trying to push you away, Ted,' she assured him. 'I *really* want this marriage to work. For our sake and for Lana's sake. I'm trying to be practical. I want to consider what's going to be best in the long term for all of us.'

The truth of the matter, too, was that she couldn't stop thinking about Jacob. She liked being with him. They shared the same interests, the same sense of humour. And, of course, Jacob was always easy on the eye. The only glimmer of sexual frisson that she experienced these days was when she was thinking about Jacob or was with him. She loved his strong, straight nose, the way he laughed, the sparkle of mischief that was always in his eyes when he talked to her. Oh, there was a lot that she liked about Jacob Lawson. Too much. She had to stop thinking about him, stop seeing him. It was the only way. He should be with Nadia. It was clear that he liked her and, no doubt, he adored Lewis. He'd make a great dad, too. They'd had their time together and it had passed. It was history.

Lana was asleep in her arms now and Chantal pulled down her top. A few more minutes and she'd take her through into the nursery. She smiled down at her sleeping child and kissed the silky down on her forehead. Just a few minutes more.

Ted slipped into the bed next to her. 'We're fine,' he said, decisively. 'Everything's fine.'

Chantal wasn't so sure, but neither was she prepared to argue. Whatever happened though, it had to be the best for Lana.

Chapter Thirty-Nine

Crush and I are curled up together in bed, watching Davina's *High Energy Five* fitness DVD on my tiny telly and we have a bowl of Maltesers between us. I've done this DVD a hundred times before and it's brilliant. But tonight it's going past my eyes without even registering as my brain is trying, in vain, to pull together the scrambled thoughts of my conversation about the uncertain future of Chocolate Heaven.

'I'm not sure that lying in bed *watching* a fitness DVD with a bowl of Maltesers is the way that God intended exercise to work,' Crush says.

'When do I have time to exercise? I'm too tired to jump up and down,' I say grumpily. 'I'm hoping to absorb it by osmosis or something.'

'Good luck with that one.'

'I have to do something otherwise I'll be as fat as an elephant by Christmas.' I have another Malteser for comfort and watch Davina leap about more intently.

'Cheer up, Gorgeous. It's not like you to be down in the dumps.' He chucks me under the chin. 'We've had a great day. The party was a resounding success.'

'I know, but it was a *big* shocker from Clive and Tristan. I didn't see that one coming.'

'They might not sell it. You never know.'

I feel sick just talking about it. 'I'm so worried. I have the best job in the world,' I remind him. 'The *entire* world. And I might lose it. Very soon. What can I do?'

'I don't know, Gorgeous,' he says with a frown. 'You'll have to wait and see what happens. Fretting about it won't make any difference. Perhaps the new owner will keep you on as the manager. You're an asset to any business. Why wouldn't they?'

Clearly, he has forgotten my time at Targa.

'But he or she could close it down and turn it into a shop that cuts keys or sells wellingtons,' I point out. 'Or make it a bog-standard café with only a modicum of chocolate.' I can hear my voice wavering and I feel like weeping.

Crush puts his arm round me and pulls me closer. He pops a Malteser in my mouth. 'We'll work something out.'

But it's only a platitude. 'Isn't there something more proactive I can do? How much money would I need to raise to try to buy it?'

'I've no idea,' Crush says. 'Though I think it's safe to assume that it's beyond our reach. It's in a prime area of London. Property doesn't come cheap anywhere in the capital.'

'You should see how much cash Chocolate Heaven pulls in during a week. It's a little goldmine and I have so many more plans for it.' That does actually make me have a weep.

Crush kisses my forehead, tender butterfly kisses to try to ease my pain.

'Let's see how much Clive and Tristan want for the business,' he says. 'We can do nothing until we know that.'

'Everything was so lovely for a brief while,' I simper in a way that sounds ridiculously pathetic, even to me. But I've found the one thing in my life that I'm good at and now it's going to end. 'Why does it always have to change?'

'You've got your trip to Bruges to look forward to,' Crush says. 'That might bring some opportunities.'

'Without you.'

'I know. I'm sorry. It can't be helped this time. My meeting's shaping up nicely and if I get this deal it will be a big feather in my cap. I promise that I'll make it up to you at Christmas. We can do whatever you like. Long walks in the snow, toasting marshmallows by the fire, any gushy romantic stuff that you can dream up.'

'Sounds lovely. I can't wait.' I wrap my arms round him and lay my head on his chest. 'This will be our first proper Christmas together. But I'll still miss you in Bruges.'

'You did ask Chantal to go with you?'

'Yes.' I sniff back my tears. 'She's going to come.'

'There.' He gently thumbs my damp cheek. 'You'll have a fabulous time. It's a shame that you can't all go together. I'd like to be a fly on the wall with the Chocolate Lovers' Club let loose in Bruges.'

I sigh. 'Things are so complicated now.' There are jobs and babies to consider, tricky relationships to negotiate, tensions that have never been there before. 'It's not as simple as it used to be. The days of us all being able to rock up and eat chocolate at a moment's notice have gone.'

'It's part of growing up,' Crush says, as if I'm still a child. 'I hate to see you sad, Gorgeous.' He flicks the remote and turns off Davina. 'What can I do to take your mind off things?'

That makes me smile. 'I can't possibly think.'

He moves the bowl of Maltesers and then eases me down in the bed, so that I'm lying beneath him. 'I think we should have a Malteser treasure hunt. That would burn off some calories.'

'Would it?'

'I have no idea, but it would be fun finding out.'

Crush eases down my pyjama bottoms and I kick them away. He slides up my top and I wrestle the rest of it off. When I'm naked and a bit squirmy, he places a Malteser in my belly button, which makes me giggle. He kisses all round it before he eats it.

The next one goes between my breasts. 'Don't move,' he instructs, 'or you'll make it roll away and then what will we do?'

I stay as still as I can while he inches his way up my stomach, nibbling and kissing as he goes.

'What happens when all the Maltesers are gone?'

'Ah,' Crush says, popping another one in my mouth. 'You'll have to wait and see.'

And indulging in this little bit of chocolate heaven manages to take my mind completely off what's going to become of the other one.

Chapter Forty

It was Autumn's first shift back at the Stolford Centre since she'd rowed with Addison, and, for the first time since she'd started there, she was dreading going to work. To prove that she could be every bit as stubborn as he was, she hadn't phoned Addison. Her head was so messed up that she needed to find time to discuss the situation with the girls. They'd know what to do. She didn't know whether he was serious about ending it all between them or whether he'd simply been blowing off steam. Well, she'd find out soon enough. Whatever happened in their personal life she had no intention of handing in her resignation. She loved this job; if he wanted her gone from here as well as from his life, then he'd have to fire her.

Nevertheless, despite her fighting talk, she made her way timidly down the corridor, taking off her woollen hat and unbuttoning her coat. It was freezing out today, too cold for the park. She was picking up Lewis from his nursery later for Nadia and she'd arranged to take him to the cinema with Miles and Florence to see something made by Pixar. She was looking forward to that infinitely more.

Both she and Nadia were going to work in Chocolate Heaven

over the weekend to cover for Lucy. Lewis would have to be juggled between them but, somehow, they'd work it out. Lucy so seldom asked for help that Autumn felt they needed to step up to the plate when she did. Not that it would exactly be a hardship working at Chocolate Heaven. In fact, she was really looking forward to it.

Addison, thankfully, was out of his office as she passed it and she walked more purposefully to the art studio. Any confrontation would wait until later. She wondered if it was really over between them and there was a numb feeling in her heart whenever she tried to think about it. It was sad as, at the beginning, they'd been good together.

The studio was sweltering hot this morning. There might be cutbacks looming, but it never seemed to occur to anyone to turn down the ancient, chugging central heating. Even in the height of summer it was often blazing out. A few days ago she'd brought in a jazzy white artificial tree and had decorated it with some of the stained-glass bits and bobs that students had left behind over the years – colourful Santas, snowmen, snowflakes and a sprinkling of stars. It was a bit of a token effort, but it brightened it up a little and, sadly, this was the only glimpse of Christmas that some of the visitors here would get. Autumn turned on the Christmas lights and brought a bit of festive cheer to the room. While she waited for her students to arrive, Autumn warmed her hands on one of the radiators for a few minutes and then tore herself away from the comforting heat to prepare the room for the session.

They were making Christmas decorations again – the schedule never varied much. Valentine's hearts, Mother's Day flowers, Easter eggs, summer suncatchers, Halloween ghosts and Christmas baubles. It was best to keep it simple. Plus she never saw the same students for a whole year round, so they didn't mind. It depended how long they were clients of the

Stolford Centre as to how long they stayed with her. Sometimes they only came along to one class and decided that stained glass was something they could live without.

She laid out boxes of coloured glass in festive shades of green, red and white. At the moment, there were only six students taking the stained-glass classes and that was also part of the problem. The numbers for her course were dwindling as their clients chose the sexier options of music production, film editing and street dance that had been newly introduced into the programme during the winter months. And who could blame them? It gave them much more street cred to be involved in those activities. Yet were they any more likely to be able to get a job with such skills?

'Hey.' The door opened and a girl with pink hair and coal-black eyeliner tentatively stuck her head inside. 'Thought I'd try to catch you before class.'

This was one of her success stories. The best one. A dream outcome. And the one thing that kept Autumn's hopes high that she wasn't simply wasting her time here.

'Tasmin.' Autumn went to hug her warmly. 'What a lovely surprise. I didn't expect to see you here.'

'I dropped by to bring you a little Christmas pressie.' She looked awkward, shy and pulled at her worn, oversized coat. A least she now had a coat, Autumn thought; only a short time ago it had been so very different for Tasmin.

The girl offered her a small, beautifully wrapped box.

'That's so kind of you.' Autumn felt her throat tighten. 'I didn't expect a gift.'

'It's nothing. Really. You turned my life around, Autumn,' she said. 'How can I ever repay that?'

Tasmin had been living on the streets, using heroin for years and it had broken Autumn's heart to see her malnourished frame, scarred with needle marks, as she laboured over her glass work. Autumn discovered, after many painful weeks of trying to draw her in, that the girl possessed a real talent for jewellery-making and had done her very best to nurture it. It had all been worthwhile. Autumn had given her a helping hand to get her started and now Tasmin had a successful stall on Camden Market selling her own jewellery and was settled with her partner, Fraser. Autumn smiled to herself as she remembered Fraser, too. He was a love-lorn young man who only used to come to the classes so that he could gaze adoringly at Tasmin. He was clean now too and, historically not the most reliable of characters, was managing to hold down a regular job as a courier. They had a council flat together and were doing well. A happy ending and so deserved. Autumn found it touching that they wanted to remain close to her.

'Is Fraser well?'

The girl nodded. 'He's fine. Working hard.'

'That's good to hear.'

'We're both looking forward to our first Christmas together. You'll have to come up to the flat and see us.' Tasmin scuffed the floor with her Doc Martin. 'We've got it nice. We could have a Christmas drink or something. Get a pizza in.'

'I'd really like that. My treat.'

Tasmin shrugged. 'OK.'

Autumn opened the box and inside was a ruby glass droplet contained by a twist of silver wire. 'Oh, Tasmin, it's beautiful. Very festive too. I'll swear that you're getting more and more talented. I'll wear it with pride.'

Tasmin grinned at her, cheeks pink, bashful.

Autumn's eyes welled with tears. 'You've no idea how much I need this today.' She kissed Tasmin and held her again.

The girl frowned. 'Everything all right?'

'Yes, yes,' Autumn assured her. 'Don't mind me. Just feeling a bit weepy. Hormones. The time of the year. Not enough chocolate.' It was so good to see that Tasmin had turned out all right. All she'd needed was someone to care about her. She was older than Willow would be, but she hoped that her daughter hadn't needed to go through some of the pain and trials that Tasmin had in her young life. She'd seen too much, experienced too much. Autumn could only hope that Willow had been taken in by a family who adored her and cared for her, and that she hadn't had to struggle for her place in society.

'I have to go,' Tasmin said, apologetically. 'I need to open up the stall. I'm mad busy for Christmas.'

'I'm so delighted to hear that. I'll come down and have a look. I need to do some Christmas shopping with you.'

'I'll give you mates' rates,' Tasmin teased.

Autumn resisted the urge to hug the girl again. She felt a rush of affection and love for her and wondered what it would feel like to be so proud of your own child. The thought nearly had her undone. 'Thanks for stopping by.'

Tasmin held up a hand in a wave and turned for the door. 'Catch you later. Merry Christmas.'

Autumn watched her go and then she turned the ruby glass pendant in her hand. It caught the wintery sun from the window and glowed. Sometimes Tasmin felt like a daughter to her and it was wonderful and painful at the same time. Then she let the tears flow; she cried for the thoughtfulness of the gift, for the joy of seeing a life turned around and for the shame of not being able to help her own daughter in the same way.

Chapter Forty-One

A short and busy week later and I'm standing waiting at St Pancras Station. I check my watch. Chantal should be here by now and she's not. I'm watching the departures board and the time of our train is getting perilously near the top of the list. I've texted her a couple of times but there's been no response. I'm hoping that the lack of replies from Chantal means she's in the Tube or has accidentally packed her phone in her suitcase.

On one side I'm being jostled by hordes of French teenagers wearing navy blue jumpers, skinny jeans and talking loudly. On the other there are parties of tourists, mainly elderly, pushing and shoving their way to the front in a determined and slightly bad-tempered manner. Relaxing, this is not. I had envisaged Crush and I sitting in the champagne bar on the platform before departure, sipping fizz – even at this hour – and looking longingly into each other's eyes. Fat chance.

Every time the phone tings I get a rush of hopefulness, but it's always Crush wishing me luck, telling me he's so sorry that he's not with me. Which is lovely, but it's still not Chantal. As I headed to St Pancras Station this morning, Crush jumped on the Heathrow Express to catch his plane up to bonnie Scotland.

Just as I've bitten my fingernails down to the quick with worry, my phone rings. Again, it's not Chantal. It's Marcus. I get elbowed in the back by a pesky pensioner as I pick up and have to bite down my weary sigh.

'Just wanting to wish you the very best for your trip to Bruges,' he says smoothly. 'You must be about to leave.'

'Yes. I'm at the station now.'

'Well, you and . . .'

'*Aiden.*'

'You and Aiden have a great time.'

'He's not coming.' I blurt out my confession. I never could lie to Marcus. 'He had to go up to Scotland for an important meeting.'

'Oh,' Marcus says. 'That's a terrible shame.'

He doesn't sound like he thinks it's a terrible shame at all. 'Chantal's coming with me instead.'

'She is? Oh. Great. Good plan.' He doesn't sound like he thinks that's a good plan either. 'Except that she's not here. And now I'm worrying.'

'You'll be fine, Lucy,' he says. 'Open yourself to new experiences. Embrace all that might happen in Bruges.'

'I'll give it a go,' I tell him. 'And thanks, Marcus. Thanks for setting it up for me.'

As soon as I've hung up, my phone rings again. This time it *is* Chantal.

'Where on earth are you?' I ask. 'I was starting to panic.'

'With a sick child. I've been up with her half of the night, Lucy.'

'Oh, no.'

'I'm really sorry, but I'm not going to make it. I can't leave Ted on his own to cope with this. This baby is making her

217

own version of *The Exorcist*. There are unspeakable things coming from both ends of her body.'

'Oh, man. Too much information!'

'I know. I hate to let you down. If she'd been showing any signs of picking up then I'd come. But I'm thinking this might involve a trip to A and E rather than Bruges.'

'It can't be helped,' I say while my heart is plummeting to my boots. 'Lana must be your priority.'

'You'll still go?'

That's currently under debate. I look anxiously at the departure board. I only have a few minutes in which to make up my mind.

'You'll be absolutely fine, Lucy,' Chantal assures me. 'Remember you're a rufty-tufty businesswoman bringing them knowledge of British chocolate. Go and kick their asses.'

I should go alone. I so should.

'I'm frightened,' I admit.

'Feel the fear and do it anyway,' she advises. 'Remember there'll be chocolate waiting for you at the other end.'

That convinces me. 'I'll go.'

'That's my girl.'

'I'd better dash,' I say. 'This train will wait for no man.'

'Be bold. Be ballsy.'

Bold. Ballsy.

'Ring me as soon as you get there,' Chantal urges. 'I'm with you all the way.'

'Thank you. I hope Lana gets better soon. Give her a kiss from me.'

'I am holding that stinky child at arm's length,' she says.

'I'd better go, Chantal. The train's due to leave soon.'

'Take care. I love you. Have a great time. Bring us back some fabulous chocolate.'

'I will.'

So I hang up and, taking coals to Newcastle, I wheel my suitcase filled with chocolate supplies towards the security scanner and the Eurostar train to Bruges.

It's a sad indictment of my life that I've hardly travelled anywhere alone. That's not very Modern Day Woman, is it? I find my seat and pretend that I'm being very cool as I settle myself, but my knees are shaking.

I have a Wispa or two to calm my nerves. I'm quite disappointed when we go through the actual tunnel as I thought it would be more exciting to be under the sea on my way to France. But I can see nothing. At all. Nothing. I thought there might be fishes or something.

So I have nothing to distract me from what lies ahead and my anxiety level inches ever upwards. At this moment, I'd even be happy to see Marcus on the train.

Chapter Forty-Two

Nadia was on tenterhooks all day at work in case Tarak came in and she was by herself. The last thing she wanted was another awkward situation. But she needn't have worried. Thankfully, Tarak had been busy at the other shops. She wasn't sure whether he was deliberately avoiding her or whether it was a welcome coincidence. Either way, it made her life easier.

She and Anita worked together all morning, selling several dresses and a few handbags that they had to get out of the window. As Christmas was looming large, Anita had brought in some strings of fairy lights and a big carrier bag full of decorations that she'd retrieved from her loft so they could give the inside of the shop a festive air. They gave the whole place a good clean, Anita dusting vigorously while Nadia vacuumed every nook and cranny. After that, they'd dressed the ends of the racks with baubles and put a little tinsel round the counter. After lunch Anita had gone home and had left Nadia happily adding to their Christmassy window display.

The fairy lights her sister brought in stretched far enough to go all round the edge of the window and Nadia had woven some in and out of the handbags on the floor. She'd strung baubles together and had hung them from the fingers of the mannequins. Tinsel was draped around their necks like feather boas. It was cheap and cheerful, but it had lifted the window display considerably.

It was late afternoon now and she was just taking a five-minute breather before putting the finishing touches to it. She made a cup of tea in the small kitchen at the back of the shop and was looking forward to a small bar of chocolate that she'd grabbed from the Co-op as a much-needed pick-me-up. She hadn't slept very well last night, tossing and turning, thinking about her brother-in-law. She hoped that he wouldn't become a problem, as she liked this job. It didn't exactly pay the best rates but, much to her own surprise, she really enjoyed the bright lighting, the racks of dresses – more neatly presented since she'd arrived – and the regular flurries of chatty customers.

She heard the bell at the shop door ding an arrival and hoped that it wasn't Tarak at this late stage. When she took her tea back through to the shop, she was relieved and delighted to see that it was Jacob who was standing there.

'Surprise,' he said.

'Jacob!' Nadia grinned at him. 'What are you doing here?'

'Just passing. I had a meeting in the next street and thought I'd come to see how you are.' He nodded back towards the front of the shop. 'The window looks great, by the way. Your handiwork?'

'Yes. Glad you like it. I've nearly finished. You can give it the once over with your stylist's hat on.'

'Looks good enough to me exactly as it is.' Jacob glanced up and down the shop, and then lowered his voice. 'Are you alone here?'

She nodded.

'To be honest, I was worried about you after your call the

other night. I was in two minds whether to get dressed and come straight round.'

'That's really kind, but I'm fine,' she assured him. 'Tarak is being such a pest, but there's been no sign of him all day. Thank goodness.'

'I don't want this to be a problem for you.'

'I think I put him right. I've made it very clear that I'm not interested in him. He's my sister's husband, for heaven's sake. But it might help if you can carry on being my imaginary boyfriend.'

Jacob pursed his lips and looked as if he was about to say something more, then stopped himself.

Nadia flushed. Why did she say that? It was stupid of her. She hid her discomfort by rushing out, 'I can make you a cup of tea, if you've got time?'

Jacob checked his watch. 'My next appointment isn't for an hour. That would be great.'

'I'll even let you share my bar of chocolate.' She pushed it towards him across the counter.

'Wow,' he said. 'I *am* honoured. However, I can do better than that.'

He put down the brown paper bag that he was carrying and Nadia saw that it bore the name of one of her favourite bakeries. 'One of the lessons that I've learned in life is that you never approach a member of the Chocolate Lovers' Club without being suitably armed.'

Nadia laughed and then peeked inside the bag. There were two double choc chip muffins nestled inside. 'Excellent choice. We should make you an honorary member, Jacob. I think you've earned your stripes by now.'

'I'm not worthy,' he teased.

'Don't dare start eating these until I get back.' She disappeared into the back and made him a cup of tea.

When she returned, Jacob had pulled a tall stool up to the counter.

'Come to the house tonight,' she said. 'There's plenty of extra for supper and then we can watch a film together. If you're not doing anything else.'

'I can't tonight.' He looked disappointed. 'I have an event on. A new idea at a big hotel. They're hosting their first literary salon. That's where I'm heading next. I've set it all up, so I can't miss it.'

'Oh. Never mind.'

'What about tomorrow?'

'I'm going to be busy all weekend,' she rushed on. 'Autumn and I are looking after Chocolate Heaven for Lucy. She's gone off to a chocolate festival and the Christmas market in Bruges. Crush was supposed to be going too, but he had to work.'

'Poor Lucy.'

'Chantal stepped into the breach but she called me earlier to say that Lucy's gone on her own. She had to pull out because Lana has been taken poorly.'

A worried frown creased his brow. 'Nothing serious?'

'No, no. Usual kiddie things. It's probably a twenty-four-hour bug, but she couldn't leave Ted to manage by himself.'

'She's such a little beauty,' Jacob said wistfully.

'Just like her mum,' Nadia added.

'Yeah. Well . . .'

She noted that Jacob flushed. 'I hadn't planned on cooking tomorrow,' Nadia said. 'I was going to pick up a takeaway on the way home.'

'Let me cook something for you and Lewis,' Jacob offered. 'I'm always ligging on your hospitality.'

'I never mind.'

'Perhaps I can take my turn, though,' he said. 'I'll get a Disney movie in. We'll watch something early.'

'That would be nice,' she conceded. If she was honest, the last thing she'd want to be doing was going straight home to an empty house after her working day. The thought of Jacob, in his apron with a hot meal ready for her, was very appealing indeed.

'Great. I'll do it.'

Nadia smiled. 'It's a date.' Then she flushed furiously again. It wasn't a date. It most definitely wasn't a date.

Chapter Forty-Three

Bruges looks flipping fabulous in its festive garb. The medieval buildings, the narrow streets, the canals are all clothed in a sprinkling of snow, just as they should be. The main square, the Markt, is host to the Christmas fair and I've just got time to have a quick look around before I have to head to the convention centre for my talk.

It's mid-afternoon, getting dark now, and all the buildings have their crenulations picked out in fairy lights, making them look magical. There's a huge Christmas tree covered with myriad white lights shining out in the dusk. A few delicate flakes of snow flutter in the air. Overlooked by the towering belfry, there's an ice rink in the middle, busy with families and couples skating. Even standing to watch them, I can feel the chill rising from the ice. Though the happy shouts from the skaters tell me that it's not bothering them too much. There's a host of wooden chalets around the borders of the square selling Christmas decorations and a mouth-watering range of foods, including the ubiquitous Belgian *frietkoten*, scalding hot chips with mayonnaise. Yum. I can feel Christmas seeping into my pores.

To my delight, chocolate abounds too and I can't believe that I haven't visited here before. As Marcus promised, this isn't just chocolate heaven, this truly is chocolate paradise. It's really beautiful and I wish with all my heart that Crush was here to enjoy it with me. I work my way along the stalls, weaving through the crowds and sampling some of the wonderful chocolates on offer. I'll have to take some of these back for the ladies of the Chocolate Lovers' Club.

I rush back to the hotel, vowing to come and spend more time here tomorrow when my brief stint of work at the chocolate festival is done. As he said, Marcus has booked me into the most beautiful hotel. It's a quaint, old-fashioned and half-timbered building with leaded windows overlooking the prettiest bit of the canal. This is possibly the most romantic place I've ever seen and is the best hotel in Bruges, by all accounts. It's stunning and I can't believe how lucky I am being able to stay here. The reception is decked with garlands and a pretty Christmas tree fills the space by the roaring fire.

As I retrieve my key from the receptionist, she hands me an envelope. 'A message for you,' she says.

'Thanks.'

I nip up to my room, in a hurry to get changed now. The room is also wonderful. Marcus might have a lot of faults, but his taste in hotels is impeccable. My bedroom is up on the top floor and the view over the canal is spectacular. It has a vaulted ceiling and is heavily beamed. The wallpaper is pale blue, adorned with cherubs; the bed linen is cream and a deep shade of blue. Above the ornate headboard there's an elaborate lamp in the style of a candelabra. There's also a gold chaise longue and a small writing desk beneath the window. If I were ever going to write a novel, I would want to do it here in this very room.

On the desk there's a box of chocolates, a bottle of champagne on ice and a lavish bouquet of red roses which have been delivered while I've been out. These can only be from Crush. How very thoughtful of him. Even though he's miles away, it makes me feel close to him.

Bouncing onto the bed, the covers cradle me with comforting softness in the absence of my lover's arms. Ahhhh.

I rip open the envelope in my hand. *My dear Lucy*, it says. *Hope you like the room and your welcome gifts. I hope your stay in Bruges is wonderful. Your talk has been moved to tomorrow morning. Details to follow. Have a wonderful time at the ball tonight. Marcus xx*

My heart sinks. My talk has been shifted and these lovely flowers, chocs and booze aren't from Crush after all. Bloody Marcus. Why does he always have to be such a smoothie?

I send him a text. *Thank you, Marcus. That was very kind of you.* No kisses or anything.

I don't want to go to the ball alone. I'll be Mrs No Mates. I'd hoped that during my scheduled session this afternoon, I'd meet some friendly faces who I could perhaps join up with. Fellow comrades in chocolate. What exactly does one do at a ball by yourself?

I could simply not turn up and stay in this room all night. Or go back down to the Markt and have a skate. Skating on your tod isn't such a bad prospect, is it? But that seems madness. I went to extraordinary lengths to get my best dress here without too much crumpling and I also have totally bling-di-bling jewellery borrowed from Chantal and everything. I have to go, don't I? Besides, Chantal would kill me if I didn't. I could ring one of the girls for a pep talk, but I know exactly what they'd say. They'd tell me to man up, get my gladrags on and go to the party. Of course, I must. It would be a wasted opportunity otherwise.

However, I have plenty of time now, so I pop open the

champagne, aiming the bottle out of the open window so that I don't take out one of the medieval windows. The cork shoots out in a pleasing arc and lands straight in one of the tourist canal boats sailing beneath, causing them all to shriek. I hold up a hand in apology. 'Sorry. Very sorry!'

Pouring myself a fulsome glass, I swig it back. Wish I'd had some chips now as I'm a bit hungry. Instead, resourceful as ever, I open the box of chocolates and tuck in. The cherry liqueur is the first to bite the dust. Oh, yeah.

I can also now take time to avail myself of the deep double bath amid the acres of marble in the bathroom. I go for the works. Why not? Someone else is paying for it all. I'm lavish with the bubble bath, and then I pour myself another glass of fizz and sink into the water.

Arranging the bubbles in a pleasing manner, leaving my boobs bare above them, I take a selfie, smiling seductively. Then, before I can think better of it, I send it to Crush with the message, *Missing u big boy!*

That should cheer up his meeting.

Straight away, a message pings back. *Txs, Lucy. Nice to see so much of you. Love Marcus. xxxxxxx*

Doh! I am so terminally unsuited to technology. I'm going to throw this phone in the bin as I'm a liability with it. I'm so mortified that I can't even bring myself to reply. At least I didn't send a picture of my boobs to my dad. A small crumb of comfort.

Not daring to risk another seductive text, I try ringing Crush's number instead, but it goes straight to voicemail.

'Hey,' I say. 'My talk's been cancelled until tomorrow and I'm now getting ready to go to the ball alone. I feel like Cinderella.' Aiden should be here with me, then we'd be having a lot more fun. As it is, I've inadvertently sent Marcus a picture of my tits. Stupid, stupid me. I sigh down the phone.

'I miss you. Bruges is fabulous. The hotel is amazing. I hope your meeting has gone well.' I'm reluctant to hang up, but what else can I do? 'Love you.'

I have some more champagne to cheer me up and sink into the soothing bubbles to contemplate the night ahead.

Some time later, I emerge from the bath, pink-cheeked and sleepy. I might have even dozed off for a little while. I check my phone, but still no text or call from Crush.

In the bedroom, I lift my long black evening dress out of my wheelie case. I was going to borrow something from Chantal but nothing was quite right. This dress Holds Memories. I've had this for a long time as Marcus bought it for me, at great expense, for one of the Christmas parties at his firm. It's so posh that it rarely gets an outing but, despite the memories, it's actually really nice to be wearing it again. It squishes everything in and holds it in just the right places.

I feel a bit squiffy as I ease myself into the slinky gown. Hmm. I might have put on a few pounds since I last wore it. Quite a few. It takes a bit of huffing and puffing to get the zip done up. Maybe I should have tried it on before I left home. I might have to ration my breathing a bit.

Before I leave the room, I check myself in the mirror. Looking hot, Lucy Lombard. It's just a shame that I'm a boyfriend-free, friend-free zone. To bolster my confidence, I pick another treat from the box that Marcus sent. That makes me smile. At least I have chocolate. That never lets you down.

Chapter Forty-Four

I stand at the top of the staircase to the grand ballroom, acutely aware that I'm alone. Below me there's an ocean of people, a cacophony of noise. My instinct is to turn tail now, just run away, back to my hotel room to lick my wounds. What am I going to do here by myself?

I should return to the big comfy bed, get in my jim-jams, make use of their fluffy dressing gown and branded slippers. I could ring Crush, find out how his day has gone as I've heard nothing from him yet. Perhaps we could even have phone sex, as that's the only action I'm likely to be getting tonight.

The Master of Ceremonies announces my name. 'Ms Lucy Lombard, Chocolate Heaven.'

No one even looks up. That's how important I am.

Then, in the sea of anonymous faces, I see one person staring intently at me. He's over by the bar where they're serving champagne and he's looking so very terribly suave. My heart, momentarily forgetting that it shouldn't, does a couple of somersaults and throws in a back flip for good measure. I can't believe that he's here, as large as life.

Marcus.

I shouldn't feel relieved either, but I am. He's making his way towards me now with two glasses in his hands. Slowly, but not so terrified as I was a moment ago, I descend the stairs. I know someone. I know someone here. And I'm almost giddy with the knowledge. Even though it's Marcus.

'Hey,' he says when I reach him.

'Hey to you.'

He smiles more than a little smugly as he hands over a glass. 'Did you know that the shape of a champagne bowl was modelled on Marie Antoinette's breasts?'

'No, Marcus. I did not.'

'Things you didn't know, eh?' He raises an eyebrow. 'Thanks for the text, by the way.'

'It was a mistake. Obviously. The least said about that the better.'

'I thought you were grateful for the arrival gifts.'

'I am,' I hiss. 'But not *that* grateful.'

Marcus is completely unfazed.

'I didn't know that you were going to be here, Marcus. You *specifically* said that you weren't.' I lower my voice even though there's no one listening. 'What on earth brought you here? And if you say the Eurostar, I might have to punch you.'

'I got an opportunity to come along at the last minute,' Marcus says smoothly. 'My meeting was cancelled. I thought I might come and give you moral support. That sort of thing. As friends do.' He's looking at me over the top of his glass as he drinks and his eyes twinkle in the light of the dozens of fabulously ornate chandeliers. 'I thought you might even be pleased to see me.'

I can't deny that I am. 'I was scared to death,' I admit, clutching his arm. 'I'm on my own and my knees are shaking.'

'I thought you were coming with Chantal?'

231

'Sick baby,' I explain. 'Getting dumped seems to be my fall-back plan.'

'Sorry to hear that.' Marcus looks at me sadly. 'I want to make sure that you have a good time. Bruges is fabulous and this ball is one of the highlights. Everyone who's anyone is here. Can I ride in on my trusty white charger and be your knight in shining armour?'

'It would be a first.' I shouldn't let Marcus know just how very grateful I am to see him. That way danger lies.

He looks suitably chastened and I relent. Marcus has actually set all this up for me and the ball does look fabulous.

'Maybe you can be my knight in shining armour just for tonight while Aiden isn't here,' I offer. 'I *am* glad that you're here. Really. I was so scared that I was about to turn and flee back to the hotel.'

He frowns. 'Surely not?'

'All these people seem so well to do. Look at them. There's not a single person here who is not "labelled" up to the hilt.'

'You look as beautiful as any of them. More so.'

'Thanks.' I pull in my stomach. 'Remember when you bought me this dress?'

Marcus nods. 'Of course I do. And you still look fabulous in it.'

I get a flashback to Marcus slowly taking me out of the dress after the party, and damp it down. It was the one thing in our relationship that Marcus was very, very good at. It was also a shame that he felt the need to practise his skills with every other woman who crossed his path. It would bode me well to keep that to the front of my mind.

'Come on,' Marcus says. 'We'll do the rounds. I'll introduce you to some of them.'

'You know people here?'

'Quite a few,' he admits. 'And there's a sprinkling of celebrities too. We can do a bit of star-spotting.'

'Wow.' Marcus never ceases to amaze me. 'I thought I might be able to home in on a few friendly faces at my talk. By the way, how come it was moved?'

'Ah,' Marcus says. 'Bad news. It's been cancelled. Pressure of suitable space.'

'Really? How do you know?'

'Er . . . Checked in with the festival office when I got here.'

Why didn't I think to do that? But then it said nothing about it on my information pack, such as it was.

Marcus tucks my arm in his and steers me into the crowd. 'We ought to have more champagne in commiseration.'

He stops the passing waiter and changes our empty glasses for full ones.

'I've already had a shed load of this,' I confess as I drink it down. 'I cracked open the bottle you sent me and drank half of it in the bath.'

'That's an image I like,' Marcus says with a smug smile. 'Was it before or after you sent me that charming text?'

'Stop it,' I tell him. 'You have to forget you ever saw that.'

'Of course,' he grins. 'I'll do my very best.'

'This is business,' I remind him. 'I'm here to do networking and stuff.'

'Of course. Hungry?'

'Starving.'

'Let's have something to eat first before we do the rounds. Essential networking should never be done on an empty stomach.'

Perhaps we might even bump into someone who is rich enough to lend me the dosh to buy Chocolate Heaven from Clive and Tristan. I should tell Marcus about that, but I don't want my bad news to spoil the evening. This is a very lovely place. It's not often I get to rub shoulders with the rich and famous. I'm more of a hoi-polloi kinda gal.

Marcus takes my hand and looks at me with such sincerity in his eyes that it takes my breath away. 'Tell me you're happy that you came.'

'Yes,' I confess, 'I am.'

'Let's get stuck in then.' He claps his hands together. 'Some of the chocolate here is amazing. You'll be bowled over.'

Chocolate. And that, of course, is the magic word as I suddenly start to relax.

Chapter Forty-Five

Autumn had been busy all day at Chocolate Heaven, but she'd really enjoyed herself. Thankfully, Stacey had stepped into the breach and had looked after Lewis to help out Nadia. Lucy's festive offerings had kept the till ringing all day, but now the customers were starting to tail off as it was nearly time for mums to collect their children from school. Autumn realised that her feet were hurting and she'd be more than ready to slump on the sofa this evening.

It helped that she'd sneaked a few of her favourite treats during small lulls between serving customers to keep her going. No wonder Lucy liked working here. If she was out of a job at the Stolford Centre, she wouldn't mind it on a more permanent basis herself and she knew that Lucy could do with an extra hand. Most days she was run ragged.

It was nice that Lucy had finally managed to get away for a break, even though it wasn't quite the romantic weekend she'd envisaged. She hoped that Lucy and Chantal were having a great time in Bruges. Perhaps it was something they could all do next Christmas. A chocolate festival *and* a Christmas market. In the next quiet moment, she should find time to text them both and see how they were getting on.

Then half a dozen customers arrived in quick succession and she was busy heaping their plates with brownies, tiramisu cake and chocolates. The coffee machine was, once again, on overdrive.

The next time she glanced up Chantal was coming through the door.

'I thought you were in Bruges with Lucy?'

'Lana was too ill for me to risk leaving her this morning,' Chantal answered wearily. 'I've been up half the night with her. My child is a puking and pooing machine. She finally went to sleep about half an hour ago, so I scrubbed myself down with disinfectant and made my escape. I've left her with Ted for an hour.'

'You look worn out.'

'That doesn't begin to describe how I feel.' She rolled her eyes. 'Hit me with whatever you've got to make me feel human again.'

'Go and find a comfy seat. We have some lovely, fresh double vanilla muffins piped with buttercream and topped with strawberries. They look like Santa's hats.'

'Who cares what they look like? Bring me one.'

Autumn laughed. 'I think I'd better fix you some double-strength coffee too.'

'That's more like it.' Chantal lets out a long, heartfelt sigh. 'Sounds like bliss.'

As she headed towards the vacant sofa in the window, Autumn bustled about making the order, added a latte for herself and then took it over to her friend.

A weak shaft of sunlight coming through the window fell on Chantal's face, and her friend had her eyes closed, enjoying the warmth. As there were no customers at the counter, Autumn sat down next to her for a well-earned break.

'How's Lana now?'

'Exhausted and looking very pale. But at least she's stopped ejecting bodily fluids from every orifice.'

Autumn grimaced.

'It scared me to death, I can tell you. Whoever said that having kids was fun is a complete idiot.'

'But you wouldn't be without her now?'

Chantal's face softened. 'I'd lay down my life for her. Who wouldn't do that for their child?'

Autumn felt her heart racing. 'I have something to tell you.' Her palms were all sweaty. 'I have to get it off my chest or I think I'll go mad.'

Her friend raised an eyebrow.

'I have a daughter,' Autumn said.

At that, Chantal sat bolt upright. 'What?'

'A daughter,' Autumn repeated. It still sounded unreal, even to her own ears. 'I had her when I was a teenager and was made to give her away.' Hot tears prickled her eyes. 'She'll be a teenager herself now.'

'Wow.' Chantal looked as if she'd been sucker-punched. 'I'm guessing that none of the other girls know?'

Autumn shook her head. 'I've never told anyone. Until last week. It's not an easy thing to admit to. I've always felt so ashamed that I let her go up for adoption.'

Chantal put an arm round her and hugged her. 'Why didn't you tell us?'

'I'd never really come to terms with it. Not even after all these years. You just cope, don't you? Mostly. Now it all seems to have come to the surface again. I don't know whether it's because I'm spending so much time with Lewis or if it's due to Lana and Elsie being around, but I'm suddenly unable to push it to the back of my mind anymore.' Autumn let out a weary sigh. 'They may have taken the baby out of my arms, but they've never taken the love for her out of my heart.'

'Oh, sweetheart.' Chantal wiped a tear from her eye.

'All I've done is squash it down. That's been my coping mechanism for all these years.'

'I never knew.' Chantal looked at her coffee. 'I think I could do with a double brandy in this. You probably need one, too.'

Autumn gave a teary laugh. 'Doesn't Lucy have a secret stash here?'

'She should.'

'With Rich having gone, too, it suddenly made me realise that I've got family out there, my own flesh and blood. A daughter.'

'Wow.' Chantal still looked stunned. 'What are you going to do? What *can* you do?'

'I don't know yet. I've started to look online at what my options are. I want her to know that I didn't give her up lightly. At the time, I felt that I had no choice. You know what my parents are like.'

'It sounds like something they made people do in the sixties, not when you were a teenager.'

'It was terrible and I felt powerless.'

'I'm not surprised. How cruel of them.'

'All I can hope now is that I'll have a chance to put it right. At least explain to Willow what happened. She should know. Yet without the permission of her adopted parents, she can only look for me in a few years when she turns eighteen. But I can put my name out there to say that I'm looking for her. That's what I'm going to do. I want it to be on every adoption reunion site available. If she does ever decide to look for me then I want it to be very easy for her to find me.' Autumn pressed her lips together to stop herself from crying.

'We can help you,' Chantal said. 'Whatever it takes, we'll be there for you.'

Tears squeezed out of her eyes. 'I want my baby back,' Autumn said bleakly. 'I know nothing about her and that's gnawing at me. Has she been looked after well when she's been sick? What kind of girl is she now? I would so love to know.'

Chantal soothed her, rocking her as she would Lana. 'My poor love.'

'When I think of all those years I've been without her, it breaks my heart. I want all that time with her back. And that's something that can never happen.'

Chapter Forty-Six

Chantal texted Ted to find out how he was coping. Lana, he told her, was still fast asleep and her temperature seemed to be coming down nicely. It meant that she had time to snatch another much-needed coffee. She was still deep in thought about Autumn's situation. If only she'd told them before, maybe they could have helped her or been more sensitive. How awful to have all these babies waved in your face when you were feeling bereft.

Fancy having to hold in a secret like that. It wasn't right. Poor Autumn. Chantal only hoped that there would, eventually, be a good resolution to this. Perhaps now that it was out in the open it would be easier for her to talk about. She loved Lana so much she couldn't even begin to imagine how hard that must have been for Autumn.

Now her friend was busy with customers again and their conversation had come to a halt, so it was lovely when the door to Chocolate Heaven swung open and Stacey came in, loaded with shopping.

Chantal stood up to kiss her. 'How nice to see you.'

Stacey frowned. 'I thought you were going away with Lucy?'

'Change of plan. Lana's poorly.'

'Oh no. I'm sorry to hear that.'

'It was such a worry, but she seems a bit brighter now. I'm not staying for long as I left Ted on duty for an hour and he'll be panicking.'

'I wondered why he hadn't called me,' Stacey mused and Chantal felt a nip of jealousy. She wondered if Ted and Stacey had made plans for the weekend while she was away. Plans that would now have to be cancelled. Ted hadn't said anything and it looked as if Stacey wasn't going to enlighten her further.

'I just checked in with Ted, but Lana's still fast asleep. I'm hoping that doesn't mean she'll be awake all night again.'

'Poor lamb.' Stacey dropped her carrier bags by the sofa and then sank into it with a welcome sigh.

'How are things with you?'

'Better. I think.'

She was looking brighter, more vivacious, that was for sure, Chantal thought. There was a glow to her skin, a pinkness to her cheeks that hadn't been there when they'd first met. There was no doubt that Stacey looked a lot happier with her life.

'I spoke to an agency about a part-time nanny and they set me up with a lady yesterday for a trial period. She came and spent the day with me and Elsie and seemed really great. So this afternoon I've left her looking after Elsie for the first time by herself.' Stacey fanned her face. 'I'm glad that I had Lewis to take to nursery. I was so anxious about leaving Elsie that she had to practically push me out of the door. When I'd dropped him off, I really didn't know what to do with myself, so I thought I'd take the opportunity to head to the supermarket and stock up the cupboards.'

'Rock 'n' roll,' Chantal said.

Stacey laughed. It was tinkling, light. 'Well, it did help to take my mind off it.'

241

'Do you think it will work out?'

'I hope so.'

'Great. Sounds as if you're sorted.' Something acidy ground away in her stomach.

'It's lovely having help, Chantal. Thanks for arranging that for me.'

Her smile was sincere and Chantal felt bad for harbouring mean thoughts. 'No problem. I just said a word in the right ear.' They both knew who she meant. 'You're looking much better in yourself.'

'It's all these visits to Chocolate Heaven,' Stacey grinned. 'I'm sure that's putting the colour back in my cheeks. I've just got time for a quick coffee and some sustenance before I have to dash back to collect Lewis. It's all go.'

Autumn came over. 'Hi Stacey.' She kissed her. 'How's it going with Lewis?'

'He's been as good as gold. What a sweetie. I'll have him anytime. I'm glad of a breather though.'

'What can I get for you?'

'I'll have a hazelnut latte and a piece of millionaire's short-bread,' Stacey said.

While Autumn jotted down the order, Chantal put her head in her hands. 'I can't believe I've let Lucy go to a foreign country on her own. There's bound to be an international incident, at least. We'd better watch the six o'clock news.'

'I hope she's doing nothing silly.' Autumn chewed her lip anxiously.

'I wouldn't stake my life savings on it,' Chantal noted. 'There's more than a whiff of Marcus's machinations behind this and that's never good.'

'Who's Marcus?' Stacey asked.

'Lucy's ex-boyfriend. He's trouble with a capital T. Whenever Lucy pulls away from him, he reels her right back in.'

'I love all these little secrets between us,' Stacey said, hugging herself.

Chantal and Autumn exchanged a wary glance.

'Marcus isn't a secret,' Chantal said. 'He's a festering boil.'

'I hope she'll be OK. All I can do is make sure I look after this place while she's gone,' Autumn said.

When Autumn headed back to the counter, Chantal picked at the crumbs on her plate. 'Did you enjoy the naming party last Sunday?'

'Yes, it was really lovely. That's one of the reasons I popped in today. I wanted to thank Lucy. I've bought a little gift for her.'

'That's kind.'

'I got her a little trinket box that looks like a box of chocolates.' Stacey took it out of her bag and showed it to Chantal. 'Do you think she'll like it?'

'It's perfect. She'll love it.'

When Autumn had delivered Stacey's order, Chantal said, 'I've been wanting to talk to you about the party.' She pursed her lips. 'This is tricky.' She avoided Stacey's eyes. 'You and Ted looked as if you were getting on really well. I mean *really* well.'

Stacey flushed. 'I don't know what you mean.'

'Is it really over between you? There's nothing happening that I should know about?'

'No.' She looked aghast. 'Nothing. I swear. I wouldn't want anything to come between us, Chantal. You and the girls here have been my lifeline. This is a difficult situation and I thought we were all making the best of it. I suppose this sounds silly, but I felt like we were becoming a family.'

'We do have to make the best of this situation and I think we're doing a pretty decent job.' Chantal paused, her mouth dry. 'But I have to ask you this question: do you still love him?'

Stacey hung her head, raked her fingers through her glossy hair.

243

'You might as well be honest with me,' Chantal said. 'If we're going to make this work, then we have to have the girls' interests at heart.'

'Of course I still have feelings for him. He's the father of my child.'

'Ted and I are probably getting along better than we have in a long time and I'm trying very hard to make our marriage work.'

'And you don't want me interfering?'

'I just want to know what I'm dealing with, where you two stand. I've tried to talk to Ted, but he has a great capacity for burying his head in the sand.'

'He's your husband, Chantal. I respect that. I know what we did before was wrong . . .'

'You know, that's all in the past. What happened, happened. It's how we move forward that counts now.'

'I'd love for our girls to be brought up together, like sisters. I'll do whatever it takes to make that work.'

'We should make sure that we all sit down regularly and have a good heart-to-heart,' Chantal said. 'It's the only way we can manage our situation.'

Stacey nodded. 'We have to be really honest with each other and upfront. Do what's best for the girls.'

Chantal reached across and squeezed Stacey's hand. 'Now I feel terrible for even raising it.'

'I hope this has cleared the air between us.'

'Ted always said that I'd like you, but who'd have thought it would turn out like this?'

'I'm glad it has,' Stacey said.

'No secrets between us,' Chantal stressed.

'No secrets,' Stacey agreed.

Chapter Forty-Seven

Marcus and I take a turn of the grand ballroom, arm in arm. He's at his most sparkling and charming. He points out a couple of top chocolatiers – people I've heard of but have never seen in real life. There are also a few minor film stars and a French singer who looks rather like Johnny Depp. Marcus has gossip on them all and he regales me with some juicy anecdotes until we're chuckling together like schoolchildren. He really can be the most delightful company when he tries.

I'm glad we're on a tasting mission as I realise that the best part of a bottle of fizz on an empty stomach is a Really Bad Idea. There's definitely a bit more squiffiness in my demeanour than I'd like and my giggling is way too loud.

In the centre of the room is a towering glass stand laden with strawberries all dipped in white or dark chocolate and then piped with a rainbow of colours. I look back at it long-ingly as we skirt round it to go towards the savouries first.

'Taste this.' Marcus brings us to a halt at one of the many buffet tables laid out along one side of the vast room and hands me a tiny cone made from a tortilla that's filled with delicious chicken mole, flavoured with dark chilli chocolate.

'That's amazing.' I sample another one – or two – before we move on.

The next table and I'm offered a bite-sized chocolate choux bun filled with smoked ham.

'Ooo.'

'Good, eh?' Marcus agrees.

He proffers another feather-light choux bun, holding it to my lips. I duly eat it. Marcus gently wipes a crumb from my lip with his fingertip. Our eyes meet.

'Stop it, Marcus,' I say. 'Stop it now.'

'What?' He looks at me, completely guileless.

'I might be drunk, but I'm not *that* drunk.'

He grins at me. 'I could never fool you, Lucy.'

If I wasn't quite so tiddly, I would remember that he did fool me – quite a lot and quite often.

'I need more food and less drink,' I tell him.

Yet, foolishly, I don't resist when the passing waiter tops up my glass.

We move on and Marcus selects baby back ribs from the next buffet station. They're spiced with cinnamon, allspice and ginger. When I bite into the succulent meat, I get a depth charge from a coating of cocoa powder and a blast of heat from fiery mustard. Wowsers. My tongue is on fire and I glug my champagne to quell it.

Then we try a spoonful of *Chile Ancho Sopa de Chocolate* – a smooth and fiery soup made with blackened peppers, enriched with a 70 per cent Peruvian chocolate and topped with a slice of avocado and a swirl of sour cream. Wonderful. That's followed by a white chocolate *baba ghanoush*, a smoky Middle Eastern dish of aubergine puree and white chocolate shavings that's topped with pomegranate seeds. Divine.

'Perhaps you could put some savouries on the menu at

Chocolate Heaven,' Marcus suggests. 'They're certainly different and could work well.'

'It's a great idea,' I say. I could see my customers going for a chocolate chilli or this amazing soup. 'There's only one problem.' I'm going to spill the beans when I hadn't meant to. 'Clive and Tristan are planning to sell up. The shop is going on the market now. There could be no more Chocolate Heaven after Christmas.'

'Why?' Marcus looks taken aback. 'Doesn't the current arrangement work well for them?'

'I thought so, but they've decided that they want to be in France on a permanent basis. They've seen a bar or bistro or something that they want to buy.'

'Where does that leave you?'

'In limbo, at the moment. I'd love to be able to snap up the place, but that's not going to happen unless I win the lottery in the next few weeks.'

'Something might turn up.'

'That's what Aiden said, too.'

Marcus, for the first time this evening, looks a bit shifty. 'Heard anything from lover boy?'

'No,' I admit. 'I thought he would have called me by now.' And it's true. I'm really surprised that Crush hasn't tried to contact me. Perhaps this meeting has kept him tied up all day. I know that it's a crucial one for him.

Once again, I think that I'm really glad Marcus is here. Truly, I am. It's so much more fun to be with someone who knows the ropes rather than being a Billy No Mates, but I do miss Aiden. He really would have loved this.

'Ah, well,' Marcus says. 'He doesn't know what he's missing. Ready to hit the dessert tables?'

'Absolutely.'

The counters are dressed like ice-cream carts and the

pâtissiers are preparing hand-created desserts on chilled marble slabs. They pipe and work the chocolate into twirls, fans and musical notes which are then used to dress magnificent sundaes made to your own design.

Marcus chooses scoops of chocolate and blood-orange ice-cream topped with chocolate sauce. The chef fashions him a decoration for the top in a dollar sign which makes us laugh.

I opt for Madagascar vanilla and chocolate ice-cream drizzled with salted caramel sauce. My decoration is shaped like an engagement ring, which makes me flush. If only they knew.

Finally, to my relief, we head to the splendid tower of chocolate-dipped strawberries and thoroughly check those out too. Despite thinking that I couldn't swallow another thing, I manage to guzzle some down.

After we've eaten I'm buzzing with a combination of too much champagne and sugar. I think we should have done networking first because, of course, now I'm completely incapable.

The band has started and the dance floor has a smattering of couples moving around.

'Dance with me,' Marcus says. 'I know how you love to.'

I do and I get very little opportunity to do so now – only if I get invited to a wedding or something. Then I remember that thinking about anything to do with weddings in connection with Marcus is another Bad Idea.

We move onto the dance floor and Marcus cocks an ear. 'Isn't this our song?'

'We didn't have a *song*, Marcus.'

'We didn't?' he coos. 'We should have.'

He smiles at me in a slightly indulgent way and takes me in his arms. It feels so familiar and so wrong at the same time. I try to keep some space between us.

'No funny business,' I slur.

Marcus laughs. 'Am I such a threat, Lucy? Does it really worry you so much to be so close to me?' The space between us disappears and Marcus holds me tightly. 'Do you think you might like it too much?'

'No. I am completely immune to your charms.'

'That's a shame,' he murmurs against my hair. 'We were once so very good together.'

'And you blew it,' I remind him.

'Ah, yes.' His hand strokes the small of my back and he sways me slowly in time to the music. 'The biggest mistake of my life.'

'It wasn't, Marcus. It was simply another indiscretion in a long line of them.'

'We *were* good together,' he purrs, mouth close to my ear. 'So good.'

'Are you drunk?' I know that I am.

'Only from being near you again.'

Cheesy. With extra cheese.

He takes my hand and turns the palm towards him, planting a lingering kiss in the centre. 'We should have been married now.'

'But we're not.' I put my hand on Marcus's chest and ease him away from me. 'I love Aiden. He's the man I want to be with.'

'But he isn't here, is he?' Marcus's arms tighten around me. 'And I am.'

Chapter Forty-Eight

I have a few more dances with Marcus and then my head starts to spin. Too much champagne. Waaaay too much champagne. Plus my resistance to Marcus has been stretched to its limit and I don't want to push it any further.

'I need to go now,' I tell him. 'I'm very tired.'

'Me too,' he agrees. 'I'll see you back to your hotel.'

I hold up a hand. 'I'm fine. I can find it.'

'No you can't, Lucy,' he insists. 'Pound to a penny that you haven't a bloody clue where you are now.'

I frown. Actually, he could be right.

'Bruges is beautiful at night,' he continues. 'It's a five-minute walk. Ten at the most. Can you manage that?'

I look down at my insubstantial shoes. It was snowing out there when I arrived and I was brought here in a taxi.

Marcus grins. 'I can carry you.'

'I'd rather get a cab.'

'Where's your spirit of adventure gone, Lucy Lombard? Has Whatshisname "crushed" it out of you?'

'No,' I say. 'He has not.'

Marcus capitulates. He holds up a hand. 'OK. I'll phone

for a cab.' He takes out his phone, taps in a number and requests our pick-up. When he hangs up, he says to me, 'They'll be here in five minutes.'

'I'll get my coat.'

So we head towards the cloakroom, leaving behind the grand ballroom and all that wonderful chocolate.

Marcus helps me to slip on my coat and we head out into the fresh night air. It's still snowing, flakes drifting to the ground as if they have all the time in the world. There's no sign of a cab.

'You don't have to come with me, Marcus. Stay and enjoy yourself. There are lots of pretty girls in there.'

He refuses to acknowledge the dig. 'I want to make sure that you get back safely.' Casually slinging an arm round my shoulder, he draws me in.

That feels nice as he shelters me from the breeze and I shiver against him.

'What can we do to keep warm while we wait for our transport?'

My eyes are heavy with sleep, I feel my lids lower and I lean against Marcus. Then, suddenly, his mouth is close to mine, so close.

Immediately, I snap out of my champagne haze. 'You're not really going to try to kiss me, are you?'

'Well . . .'

At that moment, an elegant black carriage drawn by a beautiful white horse comes clippety-clopping round the corner and stops in front of us.

I look at Marcus, open-mouthed. 'Tell me you didn't order this.'

He does his cutest smile. 'I thought it would be fun.'

'Romantic is what you thought it would be, Marcus. *Romantic*.'

He shrugs his shoulders. Guilty as charged. 'Isn't it?'

'You are absolutely insufferable, Marcus Canning. I'm not getting into that thing.'

Marcus grabs my hand and urges me towards the carriage. 'Please, Lucy. You know you want to.'

'I don't!'

'It is a beautiful city to fall in love, lady,' the carriage driver says dreamily.

'That's not exactly helping,' I retort and the driver looks stung. 'I was due to marry this man and he ran out on me. It's going to take more than a naffing horse to make me forget that.'

'Lucy . . .' Marcus cajoles as he gestures towards the carriage. 'What's not to love?'

'I'm not getting in there. I'd rather freeze to death.'

'Oh, Lucy. Don't be a spoilsport.'

'You've gone too far, Marcus. We had a lovely evening and now you've pushed it beyond that. You've completely ruined it. Why couldn't you be happy for us to be just friends?'

Hitching up my gown, I start to stamp away, feet already soaked by the snowy pavements.

'Lucy.' He comes after me, grabbing my arm.

I shake him off.

'Hey, friend,' the driver shouts – not so dreamy now – 'you owe me some euros.'

'What?' Marcus turns back, torn.

'You have booked for the moonlight tour. Now I need to be paid.'

'*Moonlight tour?*' If I wasn't seeing red already, then the mist descends. Moonlight tour, indeed. Is that how easy Marcus Canning thinks I am?

Don't answer that.

'I need to be paid,' the driver shouts again – this time more aggressively – and jumps down from his carriage.

'Keep your hair on,' I hear Marcus say. He turns back, taking his wallet out of his jacket pocket. 'Lucy, wait!'

But I see this as my chance to bolt and I dash down the nearest alley as fast as my inappropriately clad feet will carry me, slithering and skidding in the snow and ice. I turn this way and that, running along past canals, pretty statues, quaint shops lit brightly for Christmas.

I don't know where I'm going. Not a clue. I just know that I need to be away from Marcus Canning.

I hear him shouting after me, his footsteps on the cobbles. But, eventually, I must manage to lose him as soon I can't hear him anymore. I stop and lean against a wall under a bridge, catching my breath. It billows out in front of me in a cloud of steam. I'm wearing a low-cut evening gown, ridiculous stiletto heels and the temperature must be below zero. I can't believe I've let myself get into this stupid situation.

The Chocolate Lovers' Club would have seen this coming. But I like to think the best of Marcus. It seems, as ever, my trust was misplaced. Where are my best girls when I need them? Where is Aiden now?

Of course, within minutes, I'm hopelessly lost. And the helpful tourist map given to me by the receptionist? On the pretty little writing desk in my bedroom. I put my head in my hands. Think, Lucy. Think.

I can't stay here all night and I don't know which way to go. Then I hear Marcus's voice again.

'Lucy!' He sounds very worried. 'Lucy! Where are you? Lucy!'

Well, let him sweat. This is all his stupid fault.

The cobbled streets are deserted and, in the still of the night, I hear footsteps on a bridge further down the canal coming towards me. There's no way that I want Marcus to find me.

So I dash out of my hiding place, hitching up my long skirt and running on tiptoes along the edge of the canal. In some places the path is very narrow and icy and I am in silly shoes when I should be wearing boots. Big, sturdy boots.

I'm looking over my shoulder, seeing all kinds of dangers in the stretching shadows, when suddenly my shoes lose what little grip they have. My heel goes into a dip between the cobbles and I feel it snap. Then I teeter and totter and topple, clutching at something to support me and finding nothing. I lurch forward into space and I'm falling, falling, falling. The pavement is above me and my arms windmill uselessly in the air. The dark water of the canal is looming towards me.

I'm going to die, I reflect calmly. But at least my last night on earth has been filled with chocolate. I think of Crush and how much I love him.

Then I hit the freezing water and all the breath is knocked from my body.

Chapter Forty-Nine

In my panic I gulp in a mouthful of foul water and sink under the surface. I've never been the strongest of swimmers. In my view, the water is best viewed from a sun-lounger on the beach, but now I seem to have forgotten how to do it at all. I flail my arms around, but all it seems to do is drag me further under.

'Help!' I scream. 'Help!'

Then I remember that I'm in Belgium and no one will understand me. I have no idea what the Belgian word for 'Help' is. God, I wish I'd embraced being European more fully.

I do my best and dig up my schoolgirl French. Surely that's quite like Belgian. They're next-door neighbours, for heaven's sake. Aren't they? '*Au secours*,' I cry, swallowing even more stinking canal water. '*Au secours*.' What's 'I'm drowning' in French? '*J'ai faim! J'ai faim!*'

I go under one more time and when I bob up again I realise it's true that you see your life pass before your eyes; when I surface I imagine that I see Crush standing there on the bank. He's the love of my life and it's only right that I have a vision of him in my last moments. He is standing there looking so very handsome in a tuxedo. My eyes go cloudy.

'Help!' I shout again, more weakly now. '*J'ai faim!*'

'Stand up, Gorgeous,' my vision advises.

'*J'ai faim!*' I offer with faint hope. '*J'ai faim!*'

'Lucy, you're telling half of Bruges that you're hungry. In French. Just stand up.'

Spluttering some more water, I clutch at the air. Oblivion is coming. Goodbye cruel world.

This is all Marcus's fault. It's his fault that I won't grow old with Aiden, that I won't marry him, that I won't have his children. His fault that I will end my life in a watery grave in Bruges, the home of some very excellent chocolate.

'Lucy!'

My vision sounds quite a bit more exasperated than he should. I flounder about some more and the water closes over me. Who knew that it would take so long to drown?

'Oh, for heaven's sake.' There is much tutting.

My vision walks down three steps that I hadn't actually noticed before. I gasp as I surface again. 'You've come to save me!'

I hear a heartfelt sigh. Still in his full evening dress, Crush wades into the water and comes towards me.

'Stand up, Gorgeous,' he instructs as he towers above me.

I can't quite stop splashing around. So he grasps me, rather roughly, by the front of my evening gown and yanks me out of the water.

Crush sets me upright and I sink up to my ankles into thick mud on the bottom of the canal. It's really disgusting. *Really* disgusting. Think of the most disgusting thing you can imagine and then double it. Yet, even in my shell-shocked, half-drowned state, I notice that the water only comes up to my waist.

'Oh.'

With a weary laugh, Crush sweeps me into his arms. 'Trust you, Gorgeous.' He shakes his head. '*I'm* the one supposed to be giving *you* a surprise.'

'I'm not dead?'

'Not yet,' he says candidly.

He carries me out of the canal and back onto dry land. My knight in a slightly sodden tuxedo. My heart swells and not just because it's water-logged. He's come to save me from a fate not worse than death, but *actual* death, in the very nick of time. I couldn't possibly love him anymore.

I'm soaked through the skin and shivering now. I also seem to be covered in slime and weed and unspeakable goo from the canal. Can you get any deadly diseases from canal water? I bet you bloody can. My shoes have disappeared, probably eaten by the mud.

'I thought you were a mirage or something,' I confess, dazed. 'But you're not, are you?' Tentatively, I stroke his rather soggy lapel.

'No,' he says flatly.

'I thought you were in Glasgow or somewhere. What are you doing here?'

'Apart from saving you?' He shakes his head again. 'My mysterious client never turned up for the meeting. If I'm not very much mistaken, I think the whole thing was a big hoax. So I jumped on the first plane that would get me here. My idea was that we could still salvage a romantic Christmas weekend.' He looks at me sideways. 'Now I realise that you're actually not safe to be left alone for five minutes. What on earth were you doing in the canal?'

I fling myself into Crush's arms and wail. 'Oh, it's all Marcus's fault.'

His face darkens. 'Marcus?'

'He was chasing me and I was running away from him and

hiding under the bridge.' I hang my head in shame and humiliation. 'It all went a bit blurry after that.'

Crush puffs out a very cross-sounding huff. 'I bet it did.'
He tsks. 'Bloody Marcus Canning. I might have known he'd
be behind this.'

'What do you mean?'

'I bet your talk's been cancelled, hasn't it?'

'Yes.' I'm still puzzled.

'There never was a talk, Lucy. Exactly like there never really
was a client with a multi-million-pound contract on offer for
me. We've both been duped by him.'

'No!'

'When will you learn, Gorgeous? All he wanted was to get
you here alone.' He shakes his fist in a very manly way. 'Just
wait until I get my hands on him.'

I think that's probably best avoided. My heart sinks. Am
I really that gullible? I thought Marcus was trying to do his
best by me – until the bit with the dancing and the attempted
kiss and the romantic horse interlude. Probably best if I don't
actually mention all that.

'Can we just go back to the hotel?' I'm on the verge of
tears, the slime is freezing to my skin and my feet are about
to drop off with the cold. I don't feel the slightest bit fucking
festive or romantic. This was all a very stupid idea. And now
I want a hot bath and hot chocolate and to curl up next to
my hot man who has just rescued me from what I was convinced
was certain death. 'Have you any idea where it is?'

Crush turns round and nods. Behind us the hotel sign swings
slightly in the breeze.

'Oh.'

It's a good job that they have excellent chocolate in Bruges,
otherwise I think I might just hate it.

Chapter Fifty

Fucking Bruges. Crush carries me back to the hotel, dripping wet. He still holds me in his arms while I shiver and shake as we go up to my bedroom in the lift.

When we're inside, he turns on the bedside lamps so that the light in the room is subtle – in different circumstances, it might be classed as romantic. Then he starts to run me a bath while I stand here and look suitably pathetic and ashamed. If Crush notices the nearly empty bottle of champagne on the desk and the half-eaten box of chocolates or, indeed, the monster bouquet of red roses, then he doesn't mention them. But I grit my teeth together and think, bloody Marcus. He planned this all along. I realise that now. There was no presentation on British chocolate, blah blah blah, no networking. He just wanted to get me here all for himself.

I wonder what he'd have done if Chantal had come along. That would have thwarted his plans. Would Marcus have contrived to lock her in a cupboard or something while he tried to have his wicked way with me? I wouldn't put it past him. I wish she had been here; Chantal's so much sharper than me and would have seen through his ruse right away.

It's only me who's completely stupid when it comes to Marcus.

While all this is going through my mind, Crush is very patiently picking bits of slime and weed and smelly goo off me. I catch sight of myself in the mirror. My hair seems to have a million snakes coming out of it. I look like something out of *Pirates of the Caribbean*. That green, barnacled bloke that's encrusted with all sorts of sea crap who emerges from the walls of the ship. Him. That's who I look like. It's not what I was aiming for when I set out this evening.

As Crush tenderly slips the shoulder straps down from my dress, I start to well up.

'Thank you,' I say. 'Thank you for coming to Bruges to save me.'

He smiles at me, indulgently. 'Glad to be of service. I'm just relieved to have got here in time. Otherwise the whole of Belgium would have been rushing out with food for you.'

Shit. Must look up what 'help' is in Belgian for future emergency occasions – as there are sure to be some.

'Thank you for loving me even though I'm an idiot.'

Crush sighs. 'We have to talk about Marcus. You have to cut him out of your life, Gorgeous.'

'I know.'

'He seems to have a hold over you, Lucy, and that worries me.'

'I was only trying to be friends with him.'

'Men like Marcus can't do that.' He moves to undo my zip. 'He won't be happy until he's ruined our relationship.'

I throw my slimy arms around him and hold on tightly. 'Tell me that won't happen. I couldn't bear to lose you.'

'Of course it won't. But it would certainly help if I didn't always feel that I had to watch out for a knife in my back.'

'I've learned my lesson,' I swear. 'Marcus is history. Total history.'

My phone tings. I'm surprised that it even works, having had a thorough soaking in the canal. I reach into my handbag for it. Brown water pours out. I look at the sodden phone. A text from Marcus.

Ru OK? It says. *I love u.*

I show it to Crush.

'Exactly,' he says.

'I'll get a new phone.' I'm probably going to need one so it's not the grand gesture it might be. 'I'll change my number.'

Crush strips off my dress. My underwear looks as if it's gone mouldy. There's the tail of a little fish sticking out of my bra, still flapping.

'Aaaargh!'

Crush picks it out with his fingers, takes it to the window and returns it, still flapping, to the canal.

'I hate Bruges,' I whimper. 'Especially the wet bits.'

If I was mayor or whatever, I'd fill the canals in with concrete. They are dangerous, dangerous things.

'We'll have a lovely time, Gorgeous,' he assures me. 'Now get into the nice, hot bath before you catch your death of cold.'

'Are you going to join me too?' I look at his ruined tuxedo.

'Of course. Do you think I'd risk leaving you in water alone?'

I'm grateful that he's still smiling. Another, less tolerant man, would be fed up of me acting like a twat all the time. Even though I never mean to.

Crush starts to undress. He, unlike me, is still managing to look suave. Canal chic suits him. I feel a rush of love and lust for him.

When he's naked and in my arms, I say huskily, 'Have you ever made love to a slime-covered woman?'

'No.' He takes my hand and leads me to the bathroom. 'And I'm not about to start now, Gorgeous.'

'Oh.'

'I am, however, going to scrub you from head to toe with a loofah.' He grins at me. 'Roughly.'

I grin back. 'How roughly?'

He gives the matter some consideration and settles on, 'Quite roughly.'

I guess tonight I'm going to have to take my pleasure where I can.

Chapter Fifty-One

They say that you can't catch a cold by getting wet. It's a virus, they say. Well, *they* can't have had an encounter with the bottom of a Belgian canal.

I have a cold. A streaming one. But that doesn't stop me and Crush from wrapping up warm and heading out to explore the delights of Bruges for the rest of the weekend. The non-wet ones. Marcus will *not* spoil this for me.

Despite having snot dripping from my nose it will be ROMANTIC if it kills me. So there.

Once Crush had loofahed all the slime off me, obviously, and shortly before my cold came on, we made love a million times last night. Over and over again until we were sated. Well, maybe not a million times, but four. At least. Certainly three. But that's bloody brilliant, right?

So, all loved up like the lovers we are, we set out to explore all that Bruges has to offer. Arm in arm we go to the exhibition of ice sculptures and wander through the freezing halls of carved ice statues, marvelling at them even though we haven't a clue who some of them are. Clearly big in Belgium.

Then we trawl the stalls of the Christmas market for

unnecessary festive tat and buy some baubles for our tree at home. I select some chocolates to take home for the girls – having duly sampled them first, of course. I can hardly take them substandard chocolates, right? When we're laden with carrier bags, we drink hot chocolate in steamy cafés and stuff ourselves with delicious fresh cream Belgian chocolates until we're fit to burst.

We have a traditional lunch of *moules-frites* and sit in the warmth of the crowded café for too long, trying different flavours of Belgian beer. After lunch – a bit squiffy from the beer – we climb aboard the carousel in the Markt. The snowflakes land on our faces as we canter round on our brightly painted horses, holding hands as we rise and fall. Christmas is the most magical time of the year and it's even better when you have someone you adore to share it with. I gaze into Crush's eyes and grin at him.

'Hold on, Lucy,' he says. 'Don't fall off.'

'I'm fine, really.'

And when the ride ends, without incident, he helps me down from my horse.

Then we skate at the ice rink beneath the magnificent Bell Tower and Christmas tree. The sound of festive songs fills the square. Holding tightly onto Crush, I find my feet, and we might not be the most elegant couple on the ice, but at least we stay upright. Every time I start to scrabble, he catches me and holds me steady. Much like he does in the rest of my life. Breathing in ice-cold air and giggling like loons we while away the time and, leaving the pressures of Chocolate Heaven behind, I think of nothing but having fun. I feel like I'm cocooned in a beautiful snowy bubble and I never want this day to end.

I do another quick bit of teetering and tottering. Crush clamps his arm around me. 'You're not planning on falling and breaking an ankle, are you?' Crush asks, as we glide together across the ice. 'This is all going too well at the moment.'

'No. This is the all-new, sensible Lucy,' I assure him, slightly breathlessly. 'The era of pratfalls and unadulterated idiocy is officially over. I'm a grown-up now and I'm going to behave like one.'

Crush doesn't look overly convinced.

'You will never have to fish me out of a canal again. Or anything else.'

'I have to say I'm slightly relieved about that.'

'I love you more than I ever have,' I tell him. 'Nothing is more important to me than this relationship.'

'I'm glad to hear it.' Skilfully, he steers me round a kid clinging onto a plastic penguin.

I've been slightly worried that Marcus would stalk us, popping up at inopportune moments behind an ice carving of Snow White or the Taj Mahal. But I haven't seen hide nor hair of him. Perhaps he's given up graciously. I wonder if he saw me take a bath in the canal. It was all *his* fault and yet it would be all *my* fault if I let him come between me and Crush.

The ice is getting busy now and I'm not sure that I have the required skill to cope with a crowd.

'Shall we quit while we're ahead?' Crush says.

'Yes, good idea.'

'Besides, it must be nearly an hour since you've been topped up with hot chocolate.'

I look up at him and feel a rush of love and possessiveness. The other skaters bustle around us but I can see only him. 'You will love me for always, won't you?'

He smiles down at me. 'To the moon and back.'

How lucky I am to love and to be loved in return.

'I don't want to go home,' I tell him. 'I want to stay here

in Bruges for ever and not think about what might happen to Chocolate Heaven.'

'It will be fine,' he assures me. 'Don't spoil Christmas by worrying yourself sick about it. What will be will be.'

I wish that I could be so philosophical, but I am struggling. This is the one thing – the *only* thing – that I'm good at.

If only I could keep Marcus out of my life and keep Chocolate Heaven in it, then everything would be perfect in my world.

Chapter Fifty-Two

It was only being at this side of the counter that made Nadia appreciate just how hard Lucy had to work and she was grateful that she'd arranged to go to Jacob's house for dinner this evening. She was so tired and foot-sore that she'd never have had the wherewithal to cook for her and Lewis after this.

It had been non-stop all day and Nadia didn't even like to think how many shopping days were left before the twenty-fifth of December. But, there was no denying it, the Christmas rush had begun in earnest.

Thankfully, Autumn had been working alongside her this afternoon. The festive treats that Lucy had brought in were flying off the shelves again today. Nadia had lost track of just how many chocolate Santas and reindeers she'd wrapped. It had made her feel quite in the Christmas mood and it seemed as if their customers felt much the same. Lucy, who could get herself into trouble alone in a locked room, clearly had a flair for this business.

Finally, Autumn turned the sign on the door to closed as the last of the customers left. She breathed a sigh of relief and leaned against the glass. 'We survived.'

'It's been like a mad scrum,' Nadia agreed. 'It's a good job it's not like this every Saturday. I don't know how Lucy does it. The rag trade certainly isn't this busy. It's positively genteel at Tarak's shop in comparison.'

'All going well there?'

'It would be if my brother-in-law would back off.' She told Autumn about him turning up at her house unexpectedly.

'Not good.' Autumn moved to tidy and restock the retail shelves before they went home, so that they were ready for another onslaught tomorrow. The reindeers were looking very ravaged.

'I don't know what to do about it,' Nadia admitted. 'I don't want to rock the boat with Anita, especially as we've only recently got our relationship back on track.'

'Maybe he'll get bored when he sees that you're really not interested, and leave you alone.'

'I hope so,' Nadia said. 'Men like Tarak don't seem to be easily dissuaded. I think I might just drop Jacob's name into the conversation more often.'

'How's it going there?'

'Fine.' But there was a niggling worry in her mind that it wasn't fine. If only she could get the vision of Jacob and Chantal together out of her head then that would help. 'I'm going to his place for dinner tonight. I'm so grateful, as I couldn't have faced cooking.'

'He's very kind.'

'He is,' Nadia agreed. The nicest of men. So why couldn't she quite take a step forward into a relationship with him? If she couldn't make a go of it with Jacob, would she ever find anyone she could trust? Toby, with his gambling and lying, had really dented her faith in men. She glanced at her watch. 'Right, we'd better go now. Lewis, gather your toys together. We're heading to Jacob's house and we don't want to be late.'

That would make sure he didn't dawdle – her son adored Jacob. Another thing to consider.

'Have a lovely time,' Autumn said over her shoulder.

'Are you doing anything tonight?'

'Addison texted and asked if he could take me to dinner.' Autumn shrugged. 'I thought it was over between us. He said as much and he hasn't contacted me at all before now. I haven't even seen him at work. Yet now he's booked a table at that new chocolate restaurant that's opened in town. What should I make of that?'

'I'm not sure,' Nadia admitted.

'Well, I'm taking it as an olive branch. I hope I'm right.'

'It's supposed to be a great restaurant. I'd love to try there.'

'That's partly why I've agreed,' Autumn laughed.

'It seems as if Addison's making an effort. I hope it works out with you guys. You make a great couple.'

Autumn pulled a face. 'You wouldn't take someone to a really nice restaurant unless you wanted to get back together, would you?'

Nadia laughed. 'I don't think so. No man would spend money on a good meal pointlessly.'

Her friend joined in and they giggled together. 'You're probably right.'

Lewis came over, toys all packed away in his backpack as requested.

'Good boy. You've played really nicely. For that, you can pick a treat from the counter.'

Lewis homed in on a chocolate snowman. 'That, please.'

'I'll put it in a bag and you can have it after dinner. Jacob's making us lasagne and we don't want to spoil your appetite.'

Nadia wrapped it and that went into Lewis's backpack too. 'I'd better take some chocolates for Jacob as well, or I won't hear the last of it.'

She selected a box of six of his favourites and sat the package carefully in the top of her handbag.

'You go,' Autumn said. 'I'll tidy up the last bits here. There's not much to do.'

'You'd better order some more cakes from Alexandra. Lucy's got a big Chocolate Ecstasy Tour coming in next week and we don't want to run out of treats for them.'

'I'll give her a call.'

Nadia slipped on Lewis's coat and then her own. She kissed her friend. 'I'll see you tomorrow. I'll be here in time to open up and you can take over for the afternoon shift. Though I don't mind staying on if we're busy again.'

'Let's see how it goes.'

'Have a good time tonight. Don't do anything I wouldn't do,' she teased.

'I wish it was Chantal saying that,' Autumn countered. 'That would give me a *lot* more leeway!'

It was snowing again and Nadia and Lewis huddled together as they headed from the Tube towards Jacob's house, sleet stinging their faces. Then they stood on the doorstep, playing a game of stamping their feet, until Jacob opened the door.

A warm, mellow glow greeted them and the scent of herbs coming from the kitchen was tantalising. It was very nice being able to pick at chocolate at will all day long, but now she did need something more substantial to eat.

'Hey.' Jacob was wearing an apron and brandishing a wooden spoon. His cheeks were pink from the heat and he looked sweeter than she'd ever seen him. 'Come on in. Take your coats off. It looks bitterly cold out there.'

'It is,' Nadia said as they hurried into the hallway. She stripped Lewis out of his coat, scarf and hat, shaking the flakes of snow from them.

'Put them here on this hook, right near the radiator.' Jacob nodded towards it. 'Then they'll be nice and warm for when you go home.'

She took off her own coat and arranged their outer clothes on Jacob's coat rack so that they'd dry out. Smoothing a hand through her long, dark hair, she tried to tame the ravages of the weather. While she did, Jacob held out his arms and Lewis ran into them.

'Mind my spoon,' Jacob warned with a laugh. 'I don't want your mum telling me off for putting tomato sauce in your hair.'

'I've got a chocolate snowman.' Lewis pulled it out of his backpack and proudly showed it off.

'Wow.' Jacob looked suitably impressed. 'You must have been a *very* good boy.'

'I have,' he said proudly. 'All day while Mummy worked.'

'He's been great,' Nadia confirmed. 'No trouble at all.'

'I could share it if you like,' Lewis offered.

'I'd very much like that.' Jacob ruffled her son's hair. 'But I'm warning you, I can eat a *lot* of chocolate.'

'*After* dinner,' Nadia reminded them both.

They followed Jacob through to the kitchen. She didn't come here very often, mainly due to the complexities of babysitting, as she tried very hard not to put upon Autumn too much. Jacob's home was a smart terraced house and, although very much a bachelor pad it still managed to be homely.

'No Christmas decorations?'

'I'm a last-minute merchant,' he admitted. 'My tree usually goes up on Christmas Eve and it's down again by the second of January.'

'Don't tell Lucy that. We've had to stop her from decorating Chocolate Heaven in August.'

'I can imagine. I think she loves Christmas nearly as much as she loves chocolate.'

'It's a close-run thing,' Nadia agreed.

'How's she getting on in Bruges?'

'None of us have heard from her, so I think that's a good thing.'

'Let's hope she leaves Bruges in one piece.'

'It's never a given with our Lucy.'

Lewis tugged at her arm. 'Can I watch television, please?'

'It's already on in the living room,' Jacob said. 'You know where the remote is, champ.'

Lewis wandered off, leaving them alone.

'Right.' Jacob clapped his hands. 'The lasagne's in the oven.' He crouched down to look at it. 'It'll be about twenty minutes or so. There's also a glass of passable red already poured for madam.'

'Much needed.'

He handed Nadia the glass and she sipped the wine gratefully. 'I bought you a little gift.' She dipped into her handbag and then gave him the chocolates.

Jacob grinned at her. 'I must have been a good boy, too.'

She was filled with a sudden rush of affection for him. He was so kind and caring. 'You're always wonderful.'

Before she knew what she was doing, she'd stepped forward and kissed him softly, warmly on the lips. Instinctively, her hand reached up to his hair and her fingers twined in it, surprising both her and Jacob.

'Sorry,' she said, flustered when their mouths parted. 'I don't know why I did that.'

'I hadn't expected it,' he admitted.

'I don't want to give you the wrong impression.' Her heart

was pounding wildly, but there was no way that she was ready for this. The shaking of her legs was, she was sure, more down to terror than elation. Wasn't it? The last thing she should do was rush into anything. Particularly with Jacob. She needed to be sure that there was nothing going on between him and Chantal. There needed to be clear water between them and she had to be in no doubt that there was. It all seemed still quite murky. There were a couple of pertinent questions that needed asking and she wasn't ready to do that. There was no way she could risk starting a relationship until she was absolutely certain.

'It's OK. Really. We're friends. Don't think about it.' Jacob stroked her arms. Kindly rather than erotically, but it still sent a shiver through her. 'It never happened.' He stepped away from her. 'I'd better check on the food.'

What was the expression on Jacob's face? She couldn't read it. After the initial surprise was he pleased or simply puzzled? If he'd wanted to start something with her, then would he have responded differently? Or did she really just take him so much by surprise that it had been awkward? Damn, she was so out of practice and it wasn't like her to do this kind of thing. She could have kicked herself for being so impulsive. Now where did she stand?

Chapter Fifty-Three

Addison was waiting at the table when Autumn arrived. He kissed her warmly, if a little formally, and held out a red rose.

'Thank you.' Self-consciously, Autumn took the rose and sat down opposite him. 'This looks lovely.'

'I wanted to apologise for my behaviour the other night. It was out of order.'

'It was a silly mistake on my part.' She lowered her voice. 'You know how I feel about drugs, Addison. It was a moment of madness. A one-off. I did try to explain.'

'I know.' Addison hushed her. 'It doesn't matter. I've said I'm sorry and I hope you accept that I messed up. Shall we try to put it behind us and have a nice evening together? It's a long time since we've done this.'

He'd certainly pushed out the boat, there was no doubt about that. This place was beautiful. It had only recently opened and was modelled on an old plantation house; it was all stripped wood and, owing to the chocolate theme, sump-tuous cocoa-coloured furnishings. The menu, when it came, was impressive too. Expensive. And Addison didn't really do expensive.

'Order whatever you like,' he said, expansively. 'Shall we have a glass of champagne?'

'Wine's fine. Honestly.'

'Nothing's too good for you, Autumn.' His hand covered hers. 'I mean that.'

This was a sharp turnaround, Autumn thought, and she wondered what had happened to make Addison change his mind. Was it simply the thought of life without her that had made him backtrack like this?

They ordered from a selection of dishes that all featured chocolate in some shape or form. She chose bitter chocolate pasta filled with ricotta cheese, spinach, and portobello mushrooms, while Addison opted for a rack of lamb rubbed with cocoa, basted with chocolate balsamic vinegar and served with horseradish mash.

They chatted about nothing in particular while they waited for their meals. She told him that Lucy was in Bruges and that she and Nadia were looking after Chocolate Heaven in her absence. She thought that Addison's attentiveness seemed a little forced. It was probably better to get him onto a subject he was more keen on.

'How was your Think Tank day in Manchester?'

'Good, good,' he said, animated now. 'We came away with some great ideas. The trouble is, all of these things come down to funding and, as you know, we're looking at cuts rather than an extra input.'

'You said that my classes might be for the chop.' That would be a hard one to forgive and forget.

He waved a hand dismissively. 'We can talk about that.'

Their food arrived and it tasted as good as it looked.

'We could think about changing to a charitable status,' he said. 'That's one option. Monica is very keen.'

'Oh,' Autumn said, trying to keep her voice non-committal.

Monica, she mimicked in her head. There was something about Monica Desmond she didn't like. The woman was a bully, a player. The atmosphere at the Stolford Centre had been completely different from the minute she'd joined.

'We could look to companies for donations, private individuals,' Addison continued.

'Sounds like you've done a lot of thinking about it.'

'Monica suggested that you might be the perfect person to help spearhead the fundraising. After all, you're very well connected.'

'Not me,' she protested. 'Beyond the girls of the Chocolate Lovers' Club, my circle of friends is mainly made up of impoverished artists and musicians. It's my parents who mix in the higher echelons.'

'Perhaps they'd like to become involved? It would be the ideal cause for them – what with Rich and everything.'

'I'm not sure they'd see it that way. They rather like to hide their heads in the sand when it comes to Rich.'

'You could get them to change their minds. You're very persuasive when you need to be. They could do it in memory of him.'

'I'm not sure.' Autumn fiddled with her hair, uncomfortable. She felt as if she was being chugged. 'My parents are of the school that believes charity begins at home. They like to pretend that unfortunates don't exist. Now that their son has gone, they can completely ignore it.'

It seemed that now Rich was out of sight, he was very much out of mind.

'It would really help us out,' Addison pressed on. 'If they could only donate a bit of money. A hundred grand would secure our future for the year.'

'A hundred grand?' Autumn spluttered out a laugh. 'That's hardly a "bit" of money.'

Addison frowned. 'I thought they were rolling in it.'

'They are.' She sighed. 'But they also rather like to keep it for themselves.'

'It's only a thought,' he said more brusquely. 'Promise me that you'll think about approaching them. For me.'

'Of course I will. But I wouldn't get your hopes up, Addison. My parents would rather invest in property or fine wines than disadvantaged children.'

He snapped open the menu. 'Are you ready to order dessert now?'

'Yes.' Once again the food was sublime. The Chocolate Evolution she tried featured chocolate-coated cocoa beans, a shot glass of liquid chocolate and a selection of truffle mousses.

Addison tucked into a white chocolate mascarpone cheese-cake topped with mango jelly and drizzled with a rich chocolate sauce. It looked divine and she was happy to taste the proffered spoonful.

After coffee and another glass of wine, Addison insisted on paying the not inconsiderable bill. He did so without flinching. Mostly. Outside, in the frosty night, he hailed a cab and climbed in with her.

As they headed through the brightly lit city streets towards her apartment, he took her in his arms. 'Can I stay tonight?'

If she was honest, Autumn wasn't sure that she wanted him to, but heard herself saying, 'Yes. Of course.'

For the first time in weeks, he kissed her deeply and her head started to spin. There were times when they could be very good together.

In her apartment, they didn't even turn on the lights, but went straight to the bedroom. They made love, swiftly, silently and her primary emotion was for some reason bordering on regret rather than enthusiasm. Somehow it felt perfunctory,

277

as if they were going through the motions. The connection they'd once had simply didn't seem to be there.

Afterwards, she lay in Addison's arms and wondered why she didn't feel content anymore. Was it the fact that she couldn't help thinking about Miles – at times that it really wasn't appropriate to? The light of the moon coming through the window caught her engagement ring, making it shine. She hadn't taken it off when Addison had told her it was over between them and she wondered why. Neither of them had mentioned the still unplanned wedding at all.

Addison threw his arm over her, his breathing heavy. 'Think about what I said,' he murmured, sleepily. 'See if your parents will stump up some money for the centre.'

'I told you that I will.'

'Good girl.' He sighed contentedly in the darkness.

While he slept, Autumn lay there, gritty-eyed, wide awake. She couldn't help feeling that she was being played.

Chapter Fifty-Four

So my lovely little trip to Belgium ends and I'm back at Chocolate Heaven. I haven't heard anything from Marcus at all. But it's good to know that his dastardly little plan back-fired, as Crush and I are more loved up than we have ever been.

I have turned over a new leaf and will now, from this day forward, be improved, sensible and grown-up Lucy Lombard.

So na-na na-na-nah to Marcus!

Autumn and Nadia have done the most fabulous job holding the fort while I've been away. In fact I think that Autumn is a bit disappointed not to be carrying on until Christmas.

I've had a mad busy day – all thoughts of my romantic trip forgotten. Well, almost. I still have a little glow of warmth when I think about it. Apart from the Marcus-based trickery and my canal dunking, of course.

The last of the customers leave and I turn the sign to closed. Now only the members of the Chocolate Lovers' Club remain and it seems ages since we've had a proper pow-wow. Even the children of the Chocolate Lovers are out in force, which is lovely.

Chantal, Nadia, Autumn and Stacey are all settled on the best sofa in the window. Lewis has carved himself out a play corner, which I'm definitely going to make a permanent feature. Then I remember nothing here is permanent now, which puts a little shadow on my sunshine. There's a letter here from Clive and Tristan which I've been staring at all day. I hardly dare open it.

I make drinks for all of us, pile a plate with cookies, cakes and some of the chocolates I brought back from Bruges. Then, glad to take the weight off my feet, I go to join the girls.

'It seems like so long since we've done this,' I say as I put the tray down.

Everyone falls on the goodies.

'I hope you had a fabulous time while I was stuck at home with a sicky-icky baby,' Chantal says, handing Lana over to me for a cuddle. 'We want to hear all about your trip to Bruges.'

'You don't,' I counter, snuggling the wriggly baby on my lap. 'Really, you don't.'

'Blow by blow,' she insists.

So I fill her in on all the details. The non-existent talk. The surprise appearance at the ball by Marcus. The attempted kiss. The romantic horse-drawn carriage. The impromptu swim in the canal. And my ultimate rescue by the world's best boyfriend.

When I finish, they're all sitting looking at me, slightly agog. 'What?'

'That's mind-numbing even by your standards.'

'I've learned my lesson,' I say. 'No more foolishness for me. From now on I'm going to be wise, considered Lucy.'

That causes a good five minutes of unbridled laughter.

'I knew that Marcus would have something up his sleeve,' Chantal says, when she's stopped giggling. 'I'm so sorry I couldn't make it. I feel terrible for letting you go on your own. Really I do.'

'I missed you,' I admit. 'But it all worked out well in the end. Crush came as soon as he could, thank goodness, and we had a wonderful romantic time.'

'That's good to hear,' Chantal says.

'Let me take Elsie from you, Stacey,' Autumn offers. 'I could do with a cuddle and you can then give your full attention to your cake.'

Stacey duly hands her baby over. It's amazing how easily she's slotted into our select little group. Even more amazing given the circumstances. The slight frostiness that seemed to have developed between her and Chantal at the naming party seems to have thawed, thank goodness.

'How was your dinner with Addison?' Nadia asks Autumn. Then to us, 'He took her to that fab new chocolate restaurant that's just opened.'

'Jealous.' I savour a little taste of Bruges with a dark chocolate filled with lemon cream.

'It's lovely,' Autumn admits.

'We'll have to have a girly night out there,' I suggest. 'For research purposes. Everything okay between you and Addison now?'

'I think so,' she says.

'You don't sound so sure,' I venture.

She frowns. 'He wants my parents to donate some money to the centre where we work. Addison has hopes of setting it up as a charity and securing the future of the Kick It! programme.' Autumn stirs her chocolate thoughtfully. 'It seems like a good idea. On paper. I just can't understand why I feel so hesitant.'

'It sounds like a plan to me,' I admit.

'Yes, but you don't know my parents.'

Which is true enough. From what Autumn says about them, I imagine them as the Rockefellas or the Rothschilds – that ilk.

'I've also realised that, if my relationship with Addison is to survive, I need to stop seeing Miles.'

'Oh,' Nadia says. 'But Florence and Lewis play so nicely together. And you like him so much.'

Autumn grimaces. 'That's part of the problem. Miles is such great company and is so easy to be with, I start to doubt what I want when he's around. I'm engaged to Addison. I need to remember that.'

'Are you going to share your other news?' Chantal asks her.

Now our friend flushes. 'Should I?'

'We share everything, Autumn,' Chantal says. 'A problem shared is a problem halved.'

Our friend takes a deep breath and tucks her auburn curls behind her ears. 'I have a daughter,' she says with a shy smile. 'I bet none of you were expecting that?'

'Not me,' I confirm.

Nadia looks stunned. 'And you've somehow kept this to yourself?'

'I felt as if I had to,' she confesses. 'It's only now – since Rich has gone – that I feel I can talk about it. I had her as a teenager and she was adopted straight away. I hardly got to know her, but that doesn't stop me thinking about her every day. She's my flesh and blood. I want to know where she is.'

'Oh, Autumn.' Nadia's eyes fill with tears.

'I'm going to try to find her,' Autumn continues. 'I've only just been able to admit to myself how much I miss her. All I want to know is that she's all right, that she's been happy with her new family.'

At that, she starts to cry quietly.

I throw my arms round her. 'What can we do? How can we help?'

'I can't look for her,' she says. 'But I've put my name on some agency sites. If she looks for me, then I want to make it easy for her to find me.'

'How old is she now?'

'A teenager. And I don't even know what she looks like.'

Nadia joins in the hug.

'You have to find her,' Nadia says. 'You'd make a great mum. No wonder you're so fabulous with Lewis.'

'She might want nothing to do with me,' Autumn points out. 'I'd so love to be in her life, but I have to be prepared for my heart to be broken all over again.'

Chapter Fifty-Five

We are all reeling so much from Autumn's revelation that we need extra chocolate supplies. When we've all finished bombarding her with questions about Willow, I hurriedly go to stock up for us.

During a lull in the conversation, I turn to Nadia and ask, 'How are you getting on at work?'

'OK,' she says. 'I love the job and it's great to be with Anita again. I've still got problems with Tarak, though. He turned up at my house the other night and just this morning he asked me to meet him at a hotel.'

'Cheeky bugger. Did he think you were going to say yes?'

'Clearly.'

I shake my head. 'You need to nip this in the bud.'

'I don't know how.' She looks crestfallen. 'I've tried saying no and he just ignores me. I wish he'd back off.'

'We need a cunning plan.' I do my best thinking expression. 'I'll come up with something.'

Everyone groans.

'What?'

'Your plans are always completely bonkers,' Chantal points

out. 'I thought you'd turned over a new leaf and were becoming Mrs Sensible?'

'You are forgetting that in our recent past I have pulled off two marvellous coups. The Great Jewellery Heist and the Slightly Dodgy Bridesmaids' Drug Drop both worked perfectly well. Thank you very much.'

My best girls all give me a sideways glance.

'They did! You got all your jewellery back, Chantal. And Autumn got a holdall full of dirty cash that we didn't quite know what to do with.' Though both of those things do seem like a lifetime away now.

'Don't be too hard on Lucy,' Autumn chides. 'Against all the odds, they *did* actually both work.'

'Beautifully,' I add.

'Though we could just as easily have ended up in jail,' Chantal feels the need to note.

'But we didn't,' I point out. 'I think I'm just the person to hatch a master plan to solve Nadia's pressing brother-in-law problem.' Another collective groan, but I'm on the case now. I can feel the cogs in my borderline criminal mind whirring. 'Leave it with me.'

'What's in the letter?' Chantal nods at the envelope on my tray.

'It's from Clive and Tristan,' I tell them. 'Brace yourselves.' It makes me weary of heart even to say this. 'They've decided to sell Chocolate Heaven.'

There's a disbelieving gasp.

'I know. It's awful.'

'Why?' Chantal wants to know. 'Why the hell would they do that?'

'They've decided that they're going to stay in France for ever and run a bar or something.' I sound quite reasonable when inside I feel like I'm dying. 'They've had Chocolate

Heaven valued. I'm guessing that this includes the estate agent's details.'

'Come on, then,' Nadia urges. 'Tell us the worst.'

I can hardly bring myself to look at it but, bravely, I put my finger in the top of the envelope and inch it open.

Sure enough, inside is a bundle of sheets giving the particulars of Chocolate Heaven. I smooth them flat, giving myself time to absorb the details. There's the price for the leasehold of the premises and the cost of buying the business. At best, they're shocking. There seem to be far too many noughts on the end. Needless to say, it adds up to a figure that I could never, ever, not in a million years, afford.

'We could be on the verge of having our last cappuccino, chocolate and cake at this fine emporium, ladies.' With trembling fingers, I show them the letter.

'Wow,' Nadia says. Her eyes look as if they may pop out of her head. 'That's a serious amount of money.'

'Tell me about it.' I put my head in my hands. 'I'd love to be able to take over this place, but there's no way I can raise that.'

'It seems such a shame,' Autumn says. 'You're a natural.'

'No one loves chocolate more than me,' I agree disconsolately.

'There's nothing for it,' Chantal says. 'We need wine to go with this very fine chocolate.'

'I can do that.' And, of course, I brighten immediately.

'You never know what might happen between now and then, Lucy,' Autumn tries. 'There may be hope yet.'

Everyone keeps saying this, but I don't know what form this hope might take. 'I've asked Santa for a million quid for Christmas. That should sort it.'

'We haven't even talked about what we're going to do for Christmas yet and it's just around the corner,' Chantal says. 'We should all go away together.'

'I'd really like that,' Stacey says. 'I was going to be at home alone with Elsie.'

'Well, we can't have that. Would everyone be up for a cottage somewhere?'

Much nodding around the group.

Nadia nibbles a fingernail and says, 'It would depend on the price. I'm a bit stretched at the moment. Christmas seems to cost a small fortune these days and I haven't got one.'

'Let me worry about that,' Chantal says, dismissively. 'This can be my treat to us all. Shall I do some research?'

We agree that she should.

'It could be a blast.' Chantal clearly has her festive head on now. 'Thinking about it has got me in the Christmas mood. We need some of those fab festive cupcakes that Alexandra bakes, Lucy. Have you got any?'

'Coming up.' I stand to get them. 'I can do better than the wine, too. They'd go down seriously well with a glass of bubbles and I have just the thing secreted away in the kitchen.'

'We can't let anyone else take over here, Lucy,' Chantal says. 'How would we cope?'

I don't want to put a spoiler on things as we're all getting in the Christmas spirit, but this place won't stay on the market for too long. I think we'll find out sooner rather than later that Chocolate Heaven has a new owner.

Chapter Fifty-Six

'I don't like this playground, Auntie Autumn,' Lewis complained as he worked his sturdy legs through the air.

'It's nice,' Autumn countered. 'There are different things to play on.'

Lewis sighed wearily as she pushed him on the swing. 'But it hasn't got *Florence* in it.'

'I thought we'd have a little change.'

'Can we have a change again tomorrow and go back to the other one?'

It was difficult logic to argue with. How could she explain to a four-year-old that it wasn't Florence she was trying to avoid, but Florence's dad?

'We'll see,' Autumn said.

'That's what grown-ups say when they mean no,' Lewis said astutely.

'We can still go for hot chocolate,' she said as a diversionary tactic. 'There's a café here, too.'

She hoped that might mollify her small charge.

'And a chocolate-chip muffin?'

She laughed. Four years old and already a smooth negotiator.

'Yes. If you're good.' At least that made him smile. Lewis was also very much his mother's son when it came to his appreciation of cake and chocolate. 'One more push and we're done.'

'A big one!'

'OK. Hold on tight.'

His chubby fingers gripped the chains of the swing and, as instructed, Autumn pushed him higher.

It had been a week now since they'd visited the playground they usually frequented, the one where they'd got into the habit of meeting with Miles and Florence virtually every day.

Autumn had stopped texting Miles with their plans and hadn't responded to the dozens of texts he'd sent her. He'd called her a few times too but, when she'd seen his number come up, she'd let the call go straight to voicemail.

Things between her and Addison were difficult, but she was sure that it was only a phase. She couldn't give up on their relationship without a fight. All that was needed was for them to get back on track. For that, she should focus entirely on their relationship and nothing else. She was hardly likely to be able to do that when it was Miles who always seemed to be at the forefront of her mind.

When he'd finished on the swings, as promised, she took Lewis to the café in the park. He was a little tetchy today, not only missing his playmate Florence but also his mother. It wasn't easy for either of them being apart so much now. But the warmth of the café cheered him immensely and, as he tucked into his treat, his constant chirpy chatter resumed and Autumn let it wash over her.

Later, she dropped him off at Nadia's house and he ran into his mother's arms. They hugged each other tightly as if they'd been parted for years and there was always a little bit of Autumn that felt bereft.

As she finished cuddling her son, Nadia asked, 'Has he been good today?'

'Yes. As always.' Lewis grinned at her and her heart melted. What would this feel like if it was ever her own child?

Nadia frowned at her. 'You look a bit subdued today. Everything OK?'

'I'm going to see my parents now,' Autumn said. 'I know it's wrong, but I never really look forward to it. As Addison wanted me to, I'm going to ask them if they'd like to donate some money towards the Stolford Centre, which could be a tricky conversation.'

'Do you think they'll do it?'

Autumn shrugged. 'Depends. They might want to get rid of me quickly and pay up.'

Nadia hugged her. 'Good luck.'

'I'll see you tomorrow. Same time?'

'Thanks. You're an angel. I do appreciate this, you know.'

'I love having him. He really is no trouble.'

'Kiss Auntie Autumn goodbye,' Nadia instructed her son.

He wrapped his arms round her, kissed her warmly and stated, 'The *other* playground tomorrow.'

Autumn laughed and lowered her voice to say, 'He doesn't miss a trick, this one.'

Nadia sighed. 'Tell me about it. How will I cope when he's fourteen?'

It was a Tube ride across town to reach her parents' chambers and Autumn sat in the busy carriage with her eyes closed, letting the motion rock her. It was awful to say, but she had to brace herself for a meeting with her mother and father. To say that they had a hands-off style of parenting was something of an understatement.

As soon as she and Richard were old enough, they'd been

packed off to boarding school. Sometimes it even felt as if they were reluctant to have them at home in the holidays. Now she hadn't seen them for weeks. They'd not even called to see how she was coping without Rich. She'd tried phoning them, of course. Yet, every time she'd tried, their mobile phones had gone straight to voicemail. It was as if they were avoiding her.

Through their personal assistants, she'd finally arranged to meet them both at a restaurant – a high-end one, not surprisingly, so she'd dressed smartly today. Well, as smartly as charity shop finds allowed. Her mother, as usual, would be in her trademark sharp, black Armani or Versace suit. Autumn checked her watch and was relieved to see that she was on time. Her mother and father would be on a tight schedule and she couldn't afford to be late. It was something of a miracle that they'd both been able to make themselves available at short notice.

When she arrived at the restaurant, they were already seated and waiting. Her mother always sat as if she had a steel rod through her spine. Her father had the air of a man who'd rather be somewhere else and checked his watch every few minutes. Autumn felt her stomach clench as soon as she was in their vicinity.

'Hello, darling,' her mother said as she was shown to their table. She stood and air-kissed both of Autumn's cheeks.

Her father stood up and sort of rubbed her arm by way of greeting.

'Hi, Daddy.' She sat awkwardly between them like a floppy volume of poems between two rigid bookends.

'We've already ordered,' her father said. Watch check. 'They do an excellent carpaccio of beef here.'

'I'm vegetarian.'

'Ah, yes.' Another quick look.

'How are you feeling?' her mother asked.

'Lost,' she admitted. 'I miss Rich terribly.'

'So do we, darling,' her mother said, not a hair on her head out of place.

Autumn thought that she didn't really look as if she was suffering any kind of anguish.

'It's a terrible business,' her mother said, scanning the room.

Business? Is this how a person should describe their child dying? Autumn took a deep breath and let the word go.

'Your mother isn't sleeping,' her father said with an irritated shake of his head as if his son's death was an inconvenience.

'That must be dreadful.' If they heard the slight sarcasm in her voice, they didn't acknowledge it.

The waiter came and delivered her parents' meals.

'You don't mind if we start, do you?' Her father checked his watch again.

'Of course not,' Autumn answered tightly.

'I have a big case to prepare for,' her mother said. 'I can't stay long.'

The waiter came. 'Nothing for me, thank you.'

'You *must* have something,' her father said.

It was easier not to argue. So, Autumn ordered some food, the first veggie thing she saw on the menu, though the last thing she felt like doing was eating. The restaurant was noisy, the sound reverberating off the wooden floor. Plus it was filled with corporate types and lawyers talking loudly, which didn't help. It was the sort of place that her parents loved. They both tucked into their meals – raw meat on her father's part – while she sat and watched.

It was obvious that there was no further conversation forthcoming and there was no point beating about the bush, as she knew the clock was ticking. 'I wanted to talk to you about the Stolford Centre.' Both of their faces were blank. 'The place where I work,' she reminded them.

Her mother lowered her voice. 'The drugs place?'

'Yes. I have a pressing issue. The funding for the future is uncertain,' she pushed on, even though her nerve was beginning to falter. 'Addison wants to set it up as a charitable trust. I thought, perhaps, we could do it in Rich's name.'

They both look horrified at the thought.

'I don't think that's necessary,' her mother said. 'We should remember Richard in our own personal ways.'

Which in their case, Autumn thought, was to pretty much ignore that he'd ever existed. She knew that this was a waste of time. 'You have more money than you know what to do with. I thought you might like to do something noble with it.'

Her father sighed. 'How much do you want?' He took a surreptitious glance at his watch and glanced longingly at the door. It was clear he was keen to get away. Autumn's food hadn't even arrived yet.

'I was thinking a hundred grand,' she said more calmly than she felt. In for a penny, in for a pound. Literally. 'That should start us off.'

Even her father flinched at that. Though his usual inscrutable expression quickly returned. 'I'll transfer the money into your bank account. You can do with it what you will.'

'Thanks, Daddy. I appreciate it.'

He dabbed at his mouth with his napkin. 'I have to fly. Client meeting in five.' He patted her shoulder. 'We should do this more often.'

'I'll see you at home, darling,' her mother said to him. 'I'll be late tonight.'

He nodded and strode from the restaurant.

'How is Addison?' her mother asked when she turned back to Autumn.

'He's well, thank you.'

'Any plans for the wedding yet?'

293

'No.' She shook her head. How could she tell her mother that it was the last thing on earth that was on her mind, that she and Addison seemed further apart than ever? 'Not yet.'

'I won't look at hats for the moment, then.'

'Probably best not to.' She wanted to talk to her mother about Willow. She wanted to tell her that, after all these long, lonely years, she'd decided to look for her daughter. Perhaps she could ask why she'd thought it was the best thing to do for anyone to put the baby up for adoption. She wanted to understand their motivation. Yet, if she was honest with herself, she already knew what it was. Her parents didn't want any ripples marring their perfectly smooth pond. How would they have coped with a new baby in their busy, structured lives when they didn't really want much to do with the two children they had? It was pointless even raising it. She would be the only one who would end up hurting.

Instead, she bit down her questions and diverted her mother onto her favourite subject. 'How are things at work, Mummy?'

For the next fifteen minutes, her mother proceeded to tell her.

'Well,' her mother said when she'd finished her data download. 'I'm sorry to dash too.' She was already half out of her seat. 'I would rather you kept our family name out of anything to do with drugs. Daddy and I can't really be associated with that place. We do have our reputations to think of.'

'I realise that.' It was perfectly clear that mattered much more to them than creating a memorial to their son.

Her mother air-kissed Autumn's cheek. 'Lovely to see you.' Then she too was striding out of the restaurant as her father had done.

Autumn put down her knife and fork, appetite gone. She'd got the money as Addison had wanted, but there was no joy to be had in it. Everything felt wrong. Very wrong.

Chapter Fifty-Seven

'We need to go in a minute, Lewis.' Nadia was finishing the washing up from last night that she'd been too tired to do. She was still too tired to do it now, but couldn't face coming home to it later.

'OK.' Her son pushed his plate away and jumped down from his chair. 'Have I got two mummies?'

'No,' she laughed as she dried her hands. 'There's just me.'

'What's Auntie Autumn, then?'

'She's an auntie, silly billy.'

Lewis didn't look convinced. 'She acts like a mummy.'

Nadia came and knelt before him. 'That's because she loves you very much and she helps me out with looking after you.'

'Can she be my mummy too? Christian at nursery has got no daddy and two mummies. He says it's cool.'

'Ah.' The penny dropped. 'Well, I'm sorry to disappoint you but you have just one mummy and always will. You have a very special auntie, though. Tell Christian that.'

'OK. Can I have a chocolate off the Christmas tree please, Mummy?'

'Did you finish all your lunch?

'Yes.'

She checked his plate which was, indeed, empty. 'You can have *one*.'

'Yay!' Her son scurried into the living room.

'Just one!' she shouted after him as she took his plate to the sink.

She was working this afternoon at the shop and was due to start soon, so she'd need to hurry to get Lewis to nursery on time. One day it would be lovely to think that all this rushing about could stop. She'd enjoyed being a full-time mum when Toby was the breadwinner and now every moment she spent away from Lewis was hard. It was time that she would never get back with him. It was lovely that Autumn cared so much for him, but it was also difficult for her to see another woman – albeit a good friend – doing the fun things with him. Nadia wanted to be the one taking him to the playground, to the Winter Wonderland. It should be his mother who was the one playing Lego with him on the living-room floor when it was raining. Now they never seemed to have enough hours together. Nadia felt she was always hurrying him to eat his food, or into bed or out of the door. Today was no exception. She needed a partner to help her with all this and Lewis needed a good father figure in his life. Perhaps that person could be Jacob.

Lewis came back a moment or two later with chocolate round his mouth.

'Teeth. Quickly. Don't make me ask you twice.'

So, without argument, he rushed upstairs to brush his teeth.

When he bounded down the stairs again, she grabbed him into her arms and held on tightly.

'I love you,' she said. 'To the moon and back.'

'I love you too,' he said. 'Can I have another chocolate from the tree to take with me?'

'Don't push it,' Nadia said with a smile. 'Come on, or you'll be late for nursery.'

She got her son's coat and, while he wriggled and fidgeted, somehow managed to get it on him. Then they were out of the door and, his tiny hand nestled in hers, were rushing down the street.

When they reached the nursery, breathless and harried, one of the assistants, Hollie, came out to meet them. 'Hello, Lewis. Hello, Mrs Stone.'

'Hi,' Lewis said.

'We're going to do some painting this afternoon, Lewis. You'll like that.'

Lewis looked as if he could take or leave painting. Nadia wished that she could stay with him, both of them getting covered with paint.

'I'll take Lewis's coat off for you,' she said to Nadia. 'You look as if you're in a rush.'

'Thank you. I am. Story of my life.'

'No worries.' Lewis happily submitted himself to Hollie's ministrations.

'Mummy will be back soon,' Nadia said, glad to be collecting him this evening. The hours at work would fly by with that in mind. 'Be good.'

She hugged and kissed Lewis again as she left him in the corridor of the nursery. Some days it was more of a wrench than others and this was one of the tough days. Reluctantly, she left her son and headed towards the Tube.

Nadia was trying to distract herself from thinking about Lewis and, if she was honest, about Jacob too. So much was crowding her thoughts today. She was sorting through a rack of new dresses that Tarak had brought in. As if she didn't have enough to worry about, when she'd arrived he'd winked at her and given her a lascivious smile when her sister's back had been turned. Creep. Now he'd gone to visit the other stores, but he'd be back to lock up later. She shuddered at the thought.

Anita brought her a cup of tea and asked, 'Is everything OK with you?'

Nadia turned, distracted. 'Yes, fine. Just got a lot on my plate at the moment.'

'You've been quiet since you got here. You're not coming down with something?'

'No,' she said. 'I don't think so.'

'What are you and Lewis doing for Christmas? We'd love you to come over to us. It would be our first Christmas as a family again.'

'What about Mum and Dad? They still haven't spoken to me.'

'Give them time. Christmas might be the perfect opportunity to build bridges. Families should be together.'

'I think I'm going away with the girls from the Chocolate Lovers' Club.' She didn't like to add that they'd been more like family to her for the past few years. Plus there was the matter of her sleazy brother-in-law. That was enough to knock any Christmas spirit out of her. 'Chantal is organising something. I'm not sure what yet.'

Anita looked a little put out.

'But perhaps next year.' Nadia wrapped her arm round her sister. 'We're together again and that's all that matters.'

'I have to go to the bank. Tarak asked me to. Do you mind if I go straight home? It's parents' evening for Daman and I want to make sure that the boys have dinner before we have to go out.'

'Of course not. I'll finish up here.' She wondered if Tarak was simply trying to get her on her own again. This had to stop.

Sure enough, as soon as Anita had left for the bank, her brother-in-law appeared, grinning like the Cheshire cat.

'Just you and me, Nadia,' he said as he closed the door behind him. 'Cosy.'

'If you say so.' She busied herself folding the T-shirts and jumpers stacked on the shelves. 'I'll just finish up here and then I'd better go to collect Lewis. I can't be late.'

He caught her wrist as she passed him. 'Did you think about what I asked?'

'No,' Nadia said when, in fact, it had hardly been off her mind.

'Meet me,' he said. 'It will be fun. I'll book a room at a good hotel.'

'You think that's an attractive proposition for me?'

Tarak shrugged. 'We can have dinner, whatever you like.'

'Why don't you take your wife, my sister, to a nice hotel?'

'Sometimes a little spice on the side can help a marriage.'

'Shall I tell Anita that? Do you think she'd be interested to know what you've suggested?'

His face was impassive. 'She wouldn't believe you. Anita trusts me implicitly. Besides, what the eyes don't see, the heart doesn't grieve over.'

'It's never going to happen, Tarak. Never. I don't know how to spell it out any more clearly. I don't want to resign from my job. Despite your suggestions, I like it here. I enjoy working with Anita. You and I should maintain a professional relationship, nothing more.'

'You'll come round,' he said, cocksure. 'I know you like me. You always did. We could have some good times, you and I.'

'You're wrong. So very wrong.'

Her brother-in-law laughed and headed to the back of the shop.

This couldn't go on, Nadia thought, it was wearing. She'd have to do something – and soon – to put Tarak in his place.

Chapter Fifty-Eight

Chantal and Stacey, with babies in their buggies, were waiting patiently. Ted, less so.

A family trip to have a photograph taken with Santa had seemed like a good idea and Harrods' grotto had been deemed the best place.

'Is this really necessary?' Ted said, crossly. 'Neither of them has a clue what's going on. Can't we come back when they're three? Or five? Or maybe never?'

Chantal had bought both of the babies cute little red outfits, white woolly tights and sparkly red shoes. They were both wearing furry reindeer ears. Lana and Elsie couldn't register any higher on the adorable scale if they tried. She fussed with Lana's skirt. 'It will be something lovely to have for their memory boxes.'

Ted didn't look appeased.

'I have a bar of gorgeous salted caramel chocolate to while away the time.' She passed him a couple of squares.

He swallowed them without tasting. Obviously something more was required.

'I'll buy you coffee and a cake afterwards,' she promised.

'Just enter into the spirit. It's Christmas! Resistance is futile.'

Ted sighed. 'You're telling me.'

Santa was seated at the end of a glittering grotto of white frosted trees, flanked by two pretty – and rather shapely – elves in green velvet suits. He was on an oversized gold throne and looked every inch the part. His red suit was lavishly trimmed with white fur and his snow-white beard curled down to his chest. He was ho-ho-ho-ing on an industrial scale.

They moved forward in the queue and Elsie started to cry. Stacey lifted her out of the buggy.

'I'll take her.' Ted held out his arms and Stacey handed over their daughter.

'It might be a little bit of wind.'

Ted rocked her gently and rubbed her back. Elsie's grizzling subsided. 'Hush, hush,' Ted cooed. 'Hush, hush.'

'I wanted to talk to you about our Christmas arrangements,' Chantal ventured. 'I was thinking about us all going away together.'

Ted raised an eyebrow.

'Not just the five of us, but the other girls too. And maybe Clive and Tristan.' Maybe Nadia would want to bring Jacob too, but she hadn't addressed that. Ted would only need to know when it was confirmed. 'A big house party.'

He looked slightly relieved that it wasn't to be just him, Chantal and Stacey and the babies. But he didn't look overly convinced either. It was strange that she'd managed to come to terms with their unusual arrangement and yet Ted seemed to be the one struggling with it most. Stacey was doing much better now but, at the end of the day, she was still so isolated with no family around her. Whereas Chantal felt strong and capable, Stacey seemed so vulnerable. She was the one who needed help and support.

They were at the front of the queue now and Santa was waiting, open-armed with a beaming smile.

'You go first,' Chantal said to Stacey. 'You too, Ted.'

'Must I?'

'Yes,' Chantal laughed. 'This is your children's first Christmas. Be proud.'

He relented and when Stacey was settled on the throne next to Santa, he handed over Elsie to her and then joined them.

The official photographer took a portrait for posterity and Chantal took her own snap with her phone. They all gave winning smiles and there was no doubt that Ted and Stacey made a great-looking couple. Chantal felt a momentary pang of jealousy. Stacey looked like she'd stepped out of a Boden catalogue while Chantal was still wearing post-baby clothes and a harried expression. Chantal's frown deepened. Perhaps it wasn't Stacey who needed the support after all.

Before she had time to dwell on it too much, it was her turn and she fussed with Lana as she settled her. Ted stayed in place on his throne and she held Lana on her lap. This time Stacey did the honours with the camera phone.

When his ordeal was over, Ted took Lana from her and gently placed her back in the buggy. It must be difficult for him, but it needn't be. She wanted to make it as easy as it could be, so that both of their girls would have their father around as much as possible.

'I'm glad we came,' Ted conceded. 'It was a good idea. Elsie and Lana will like to look back on that, I'm sure.'

'Coffee now?'

'Great idea,' Stacey said.

They headed through the store, the aisles brimming with tempting Christmas treats. She still hadn't finished her Christmas shopping and would need to get a move on. There was little point, after all, in doing it in January.

'Did you think any more about Christmas, Ted? Could we all go away, do you think? I'll need to hurry up and find a place that could accommodate us all.'

Ted looked uncomfortable. 'I think we should talk about it at home, Chantal.'

'It's no big deal,' she assured him. 'We could manage. I think it would be great fun. We can take all the food, muck in with the cooking, pack lots of champagne, heaps of chocolate.'

Ted pulled at his shirt collar. 'Don't you think it would be a little . . . awkward?' He couldn't help his glance towards Stacey, who had flushed.

'It will be fine, really,' she said. 'In fact, Stacey and I have been talking.'

'Oh,' he said. 'You have?'

'I'm trying to be helpful,' she insisted. 'Practical.'

'And you thought you'd just go ahead and sort out my life for me without any consultation with the person whose life it actually is?'

'I always organise Christmas.'

'And that's my point. You organise everything, Chantal. Why can't you leave me alone, for once? Everything has to be on your terms.' Ted held up his hands. 'Well, I'm sick of it. I'm out of here. I've done my bit. I've played nicely with Santa and now I'll leave you to your plotting.'

She stood there speechless. Where had this come from?

'Consider this,' Ted continued. 'What if I don't want to play happy families? What if I don't want to spend Christmas together? Or any time? What if I'd rather live alone? I've been offered a great job back in the States and I might well take it. How does that fit with your plan?'

'Ted . . .'

But, before she could utter another word, he'd turned on

his heel and was marching away through the racks of teddies wearing jolly red and white scarves.

Chantal looked at Stacey. Her face was ashen, her eyes were agog and she'd been stunned into silence.

Chantal blew out a disappointed breath. 'I thought that went well,' she said as flippantly as she could manage.

'Should I go after him?' Stacey gazed in the direction where Ted had made his exit. It was clear that she was on the verge of tears.

'No. He's best left alone when he's like this.'

'He didn't mean it though, did he?'

Chantal shook her head. 'Who knows?'

'You don't think he'd really take a job in America?'

'No.' Chantal shook her head with as much enthusiasm as she could muster. 'I doubt it. He might be fed up with me, but he loves Lana and Elsie. He'll come round.'

Yet, knowing Ted, she could equally get home to find that he'd packed a bag and gone.

Chapter Fifty-Nine

The afternoon rush is slowly subsiding and I take five minutes to have a cuppa and some restorative chocolate. A nice 70 per cent cocoa from a plantation in Venezuela seems to hit the spot. I wonder if there has ever been a busier Christmas. There are all kinds of talk on the news of recession doom and gloom, but you wouldn't know it to see the business in here. The till has hardly stopped ringing all day.

From beneath the counter, I pull out the sales details for Chocolate Heaven and gaze at them in a wistful manner. If Father Christmas really existed he would give me the means to buy this place.

As I look up a familiar red Ferrari pulls up outside. Marcus. My heart sinks. I've a good mind to rush and bolt the door.

I don't and a second later my dastardly ex-fiancé swings in.

'I'm not even speaking to you,' I tell him tartly.

'I've come to say that I'm sorry,' he begins.

I put my fingers in my ears. 'La, la, la. Not listening!'

Marcus has the gall to laugh. 'You can't blame me for trying.'

'It was a horrible thing to do,' I counter. 'Once a bastard always a bastard, Marcus. I know that now.'

'We had fun though, didn't we?'

'Yes,' I say. 'Right up until the point you tried to snog me and then I fell in the canal.'

Now his laugh becomes a guffaw. 'You didn't?'

'I did.'

'I wondered what all the commotion was.'

'It was me. And Aiden came to my rescue. He was on to you before me, Marcus Canning. That fake client routine didn't fool him.'

'It nearly did.' He isn't even remotely shamed.

'I'm done with you.' I give him my crossest face. 'You've had too many second chances.'

'I love you,' he says, starkly. 'That won't change.'

'No, Marcus, what won't change is *you*. You'll always be the same.'

'We're soul mates, Lucy Lombard. Whatever happens, we're meant to be together.'

'Have you had a blow to the head?' I couldn't be any more exasperated and yet Marcus is still standing here as cool as the proverbial cucumber. 'I love Aiden. I love him more than I ever loved you.'

'That's harsh.'

'And true.'

'I am a winner, Lucy. I *will* get you back.'

'You'd have to crawl over broken glass.'

He shrugs. 'Faint heart never won fair lady. Can I have a coffee while I'm here?'

'No. Clear off.'

'You never used to be this cruel.'

'I never used to be this stupid, either.'

'A cappuccino would be good.'

I fold my arms, unmoveable.

'What's that you've got there?' He picks up the sales details for Chocolate Heaven. 'Oh. They're really going to sell?'

I sag a little. 'It looks like it.'

'No wonder you're tetchy.'

It's pointless telling Marcus that I wasn't *actually* tetchy until he arrived. I was sad, that's what I was. Sad that I wasn't born into a banking dynasty in the style of the Rothschilds and could, therefore, afford to buy Chocolate Heaven with my spare change.

'You should go, Marcus,' I say. 'Aiden is due to come here soon and you wouldn't want him to find you here.'

His face registers a moment of panic. 'Right. I've got a meeting, anyway. I'll be on my way.'

'And don't come back.'

'I love you.' He grins at me. 'Don't forget that.'

'Forget what?'

'Hahaha.'

He breezes out of the door, jumps into the Ferrari and roars away. I'm disappointed to see that he didn't even get a parking ticket. There really is no justice in this world. Then I notice that he's taken the sales details for Chocolate Heaven, just when I wanted to torture myself with them a bit more, and I give an extra dark scowl to his disappearing tail lights.

Chapter Sixty

While I'm still grumbling to myself about Marcus, Nadia arrives and, thankfully, distracts me.

'I am in serious need of chocolate,' she says, throwing her handbag onto the nearest chair.

'Any preference?'

'No. Just give me more than is good for me.'

'Coming up.'

She sinks into the chair next to her handbag and lets out a tired and disgruntled huff.

So I make Nadia one of my Christmas specialities – a strong black forest latte flavoured with chocolate and topped with cream, cherry syrup and chocolate flakes – as she looks as if she needs it. I serve it with a slice of chocolate-chip banana bread, because bananas are nearly as good for you as chocolate. They're full of plutonium or something.

'Here you are,' I say to Nadia when I deliver it. 'All of your five a day in one hit.'

'Thanks, Lucy.'

'You look stretched. Everything all right?'

Nadia shakes her head, wearily. 'I've just had another run

in with Tarak.' A sigh escapes as she takes a welcome glug of her latte. 'This can't go on. I have to do something to stop it.' She looks up at me. 'Can you believe this? He's still banging on about me going to a hotel with him. Offered me dinner in return for an illicit shag. Bloody cheek. I even threatened to tell Anita, but he practically laughed in my face. He has a point, too. My sister adores him. She can see no wrong in him.' Her expression is bleak. 'What am I to do?'

'Let me give it some more thought. I've yet to come up with a cunning plan, but there *will* be a way to call a halt to this harassment.'

'Anita would probably have to catch him in the act to be convinced of his cheating ways and I certainly don't want it to be with me.'

There's a queue of customers forming at the counter. 'I have to go,' I tell Nadia, 'I think I'm on for the Guinness World Record for selling chocolate Santas. I'll keep thinking, though. You can count on me.'

She smiles at me in a jaded manner. 'Thanks, Lucy. You're a pal.'

When I've served a dozen people with Christmas treats, Autumn appears. She too has a long face.

'Everyone's glum today,' I say. 'What's the matter?'

'I have just had the most depressing lunch with my parents,' she reveals as she unwinds her scarf.

'Couldn't you get the money for the charity from them?'

'They've just agreed to give me a hundred grand.'

'Wow.' My eyes nearly pop out of my head. 'That's the kind of depressing I could do with now.'

'Sorry, Lucy,' she says. 'That sounds really selfish of me. I'm morose because they hardly talked about Rich at all. Their own son is dead and they don't seem to give a damn. They're such cold fish.'

'But they produced a lovely, warm and caring daughter,' I remind her. 'They must have done something right.'

'I've spent all of my life trying *not* to be like them,' she admits.

'Have you told Addison about the money yet?'

'No. I'm going to mull it over for a few days first.'

'Why? I thought he'd be thrilled.'

Autumn frowns. 'I don't know why. Maybe I don't want him to think it was as easy as it was.' She lowers her voice. 'I have an awful feeling that he's taking advantage of my situation, Lucy, and it's sitting a bit uncomfortably. I'm more than happy to help out with the charity, but I don't want to be nothing more than a cash cow for Addison. If I'm going to do something in Rich's memory, then I actually want to raise the money for it myself. The less it has to do with my parents the better. Does that make sense?'

'Of course. You must do what you need to do. Don't be rushed into making a snap decision. You could regret it. It's your money. Sit on it until you feel comfortable.'

'I think I will. Just for a short while.'

'What are you having?'

'A coffee and one of those reindeer cupcakes, please. I'm just in the mood to bite that shiny red nose off.'

'Wow. Things must be bad,' I tease. 'And you a vegetarian.'

That, at least, raises a smile. She goes over to Nadia and they exchange a kiss. 'Hey.'

Fortunately, there's a brief gap between customers and I make myself a quick and rather generous espresso as a pick-me-up and join them both.

'I've just been telling Autumn about Tarak,' Nadia says. 'Cheating scumbag.'

'That's horrible,' Autumn agrees when she knows the story. 'How could he ask you to go to a hotel with him? So sleazy.'

'Wait!' A light bulb pings on in my brain. My dormant criminal mastermind lobe is finally fully functioning! 'Accept,' I say. 'You must accept.'

'Have you lost your marbles, Lucy? Nothing on God's earth would get me there.'

'I have a plan. A brilliant one. We've done our best and most dastardly work in hotels. We must call a full meeting of the Chocolate Lovers' Club immediately.'

Nadia looks wary. 'Now you're worrying me.'

'All you need to do is say yes to Tarak. I'll organise the rest.'

Now her wariness turns to sheer disbelief. 'You're kidding me?'

'Trust me,' I say, barely able to contain myself. 'This is my best plan yet. You have to believe in me. After this, your horrible brother-in-law will never bother you again.'

Then the door opens and Crush comes in.

'Don't say anything about this,' I whisper. 'Crush mustn't know what we plan to do.'

'*We* don't know,' Nadia reminds me.

'Oh, yeah.' Mere details. 'It will be fine. Leave it all to me.'

'Are you sure?'

I nod. In for a penny, in for a pound. Somewhat too late, I've remembered that I'm supposed to be sensible and grown-up Lucy now. I'm not sure that Crush would be altogether keen on my plans, so it's probably best that I don't tell him everything. Or anything.

I leave the girls and dash over to see him.

'Hey.' He takes me in his arms and kisses me. 'I've finished my meeting early and thought I'd swing by instead of going back to the office.'

'I'll be finished soon.'

'What about we go out for a pizza and catch a movie?'

312

'Sounds great.'

He studies me. 'Are you sure that everything's OK?'

'Brilliant.' I kiss him to convince him of my sincerity. 'Never better.'

But I don't tell him I'm still utterly miserable about the impending sale of Chocolate Heaven. I don't tell him about Marcus's visit or what I'm planning to pull off to save Nadia from Tarak's unwanted attention. Sometimes I've been known to overshare and that gets you nowhere.

Chapter Sixty-One

Autumn stoked up the fire in her living room and then settled back under her blanket. She'd finally relented and had decorated her living room for Christmas. It was now looking very festive – a small tree stood in the corner, decorated with multi-coloured lights. It was artificial as she couldn't bear the thought of all those trees chopped down in the name of Christmas, but it looked quite realistic. There was the glow from the fire and she'd lit some candles too, scented with ylang ylang, frankincense and patchouli, to help her relax.

Yet, whatever she did, she couldn't get warm this evening. Deep inside her there was a cold, unidentifiable knot – was it anxiety, disappointment, loneliness? She wasn't sure but, whichever, she didn't like how it felt.

Even a bar of her favourite dark chocolate studded with delicious nips of ginger, eaten straight from the fridge, had failed to take the edge off her turmoil. There was no need to be alone; she could call Addison. Worryingly, the thought of that didn't comfort her either. He'd want to know about her lunch with her parents – in fact she was surprised that he hadn't called her already. Then they'd probably have a row about something and nothing. Once upon a time she could call on the girls and they'd all come running right away. There was no doubt that they were all still there for each other, but the practicalities of getting together were considerably more tricky now. Lewis would be in bed, so Nadia would need to find someone to look after him. The same went for Stacey and Chantal with their babies. Lucy would drop everything and come round, but that wasn't fair on her. She had hardly any time with Aiden as it was. It was moments like this that she missed Rich, missed having a family of her own.

There was nothing worth watching on the television, so she pulled her laptop towards her. Autumn had done a little bit of searching already, but now she was determined to put out the first feelers to make contact with her daughter again. It could be years before Willow might look for her. Perhaps she never would, and Autumn understood that. However, she felt she had to try. So far she'd learned that you could only search for your birth mother with the consent of your adoptive parents if you were under eighteen. That's if Willow even wanted to find out where she'd come from. It was a potential minefield, but Autumn felt she had to know. She could understand if her daughter didn't want a relationship with her and, if she had a happy and settled life, then Autumn wanted to do nothing to disrupt that. But, despite being able to rationalise all the reasons why Willow wouldn't want to make contact with her, Autumn knew that she would love to be able to see her daughter at least once and tell her that she hadn't wanted to give her away. Willow should know that she was very much a loved and cherished child. As always, she had flashbacks of her daughter being wrenched from her arms. It would also be lovely to hear from Willow's lips that she'd had a good and happy life with her adoptive family. She could hope for no more.

Autumn found the site that she'd looked at before – an agency that helped to put people who were searching for adopted children or birth mothers in touch with each other. This could change both of their lives – for the better, she hoped. Before she could have any second thoughts she entered her details, her hands shaking as she completed the online form. When it was done, she pressed 'send' and closed down the laptop.

It wasn't like her to drink alone, but she went to the kitchen and poured herself a large glass of wine. She'd downed half of it before she'd even moved away from the counter. Then the doorbell buzzed and she went to answer, frowning as she wasn't expecting anyone so late. The awful thought went through her mind that she hoped it wasn't Addison. She couldn't face him right now.

But, when she pressed the intercom button it wasn't Addison's voice that came through.

'It's me,' Miles said. 'I need to talk to you.'

Autumn was flooded with both relief and anxiety. So easily she could picture him outside her flat in the cold and dark, leaning up against the door, coat buttoned up, beanie hat jammed on his head. She felt a surge of affection for him. What was he doing here so late? Especially as she'd been trying to avoid him.

There was only a slight hesitation before she said, 'Come up.'

She buzzed him in. Then stood fretting, while she waited impatiently for him to make the climb up the stairs to her second-floor apartment. It was unfair of her to be cutting him dead. Of course it was. Far better to explain to him why she needed to keep her distance. But how on earth could she tell him that she'd had to stop their friendship because she was worried that she liked being with him a little bit too much?

She wished she'd thought to rehearse this speech as, before she'd worked out exactly what she wanted to say, he knocked at her door. When she opened it, he stood there in a black jacket, collar up, and beanie hat just as she'd imagined. He was soaked through and his face was damp from the sleet. Her heart was beating in a way that it really shouldn't.

'I don't want to drip on your carpet,' he said.

She smiled. 'That's fine. It can take it. Come on in. You look freezing.'

'This isn't a bad time?'

'No.'

'You're alone?'

'Yes. Quite alone.' Their eyes met as she said that and she turned away from the intensity of his gaze. 'I just poured myself a glass of wine. Would you like one?'

He nodded and pulled off his hat. His hair was a terrible mess, more so than usual, but it still made her want to run her fingers through it. He left his sodden coat on the rack.

She went through to the living room and Miles followed. When she poured his glass of wine, she was shaking. They hadn't ever been alone together until this point. They'd always had Florence and Lewis with them. Without them as a distraction the atmosphere was charged. He was close to her and she was aware how tall, how solid he was in her small room. His presence was comforting, reliable. She knew, instinctively, that Miles was a man that you could depend on.

'I'm sorry to have turned up like this, out of the blue. I didn't know what else to do.' He looked at her bleakly.

'I'm pleased to see you,' she admitted. 'Very pleased.'

'Then why have you cut us off, Autumn? I've been going out of my mind. You've not answered my texts or my calls.'

'I'm sorry.'

'Have I done something wrong?'

'No. Not at all.' She glugged her wine and poured some more.

'I thought we were all getting on great.'

'We were. We *are*.'

'Florence has missed you both.' Colour flushed into his cheeks. 'I've missed you, too.'

'The difficult thing is, Miles . . .' Her throat felt constricted. 'I feel the same.'

'Then why in heaven's name are we not seeing each other?'

Looking into his anguished face, Autumn felt that she had to be straight with him. She took a deep breath. 'You see, even though I'm with someone else and I'm engaged to be married, I have a problem.'

He waited patiently.

'The problem is that I actually want to see you that little bit too much. When I'm with you, I completely forget that I have a future with someone else. And when I'm not with you, I think about you all the time.'

They stood looking at each other. She could hear Miles's breathing, as ragged and as uneven as her own.

'Right,' he said, risking a smile. 'That clears that up.'

She nodded. 'Yes. Good. It does.'

'So? What do we do now?'

Autumn smiled too. 'I'm not really sure.'

He put down his glass, then took hers and placed it on the coffee table beside his.

'What about this?' Slowly, he moved towards her and took her face tenderly in his hands. His mouth found hers and he kissed her deeply, warmly. She reached up to meet him and her fingers twined in the mop of hair that she'd so been longing to touch. They kissed until her lips were bruised and then held each other tightly, silently.

Autumn wasn't entirely sure what happened next or who

made the first move, but she was unbuttoning his shirt, tugging at his belt. Miles pulled off her jumper, covering her face, her neck with kisses, as he did. She tried to wriggle out of her skirt as she stripped him of his shirt. His bare chest was toned, covered with a fine down of hair the same colour as his head. It only made her want to see more of him. Half-dressed, half-crazy they stumbled, unspeaking, still kissing, still touching, towards her bedroom.

They made love with a passion that Autumn never knew she had inside her. She felt abandoned, reckless, loved. Miles held her tightly, and showing considerably more restraint than she was, moved slowly above her as she urged him deeper into her. It was beyond bliss and she had no thought as to whether it was right or wrong. She only wanted his body covering the length of hers and nothing else seemed to matter.

Afterwards, they curled into each other's arms and snuggled beneath the covers. His touch was strange, yet somehow familiar. She knew it would be like this with him. Miles stroked her hair.

'Did we really just do that?' Autumn asked.

He looked into her eyes. 'I think we did.'

They giggled together like naughty kids.

'I feel giddy and guilty at the same time,' Autumn admitted.

'You don't regret it?'

'Not at all. It was wonderful, Miles.' She blushed. 'More than that.'

'I know that you're with someone else, but I've grown very fond of you.' He laughed. 'What am I saying? *More* than fond. You know what I'm trying – very badly – to say.'

'One of the reasons I haven't been able to see you is that I felt our closeness was pulling me away from my relationship. I'm engaged to be married and yet, if I'm honest, the thought of it fills me with dread. Recently, I've looked forward to spending time with you more than I did with my fiancé.'

'I don't want to create any difficulty for you.' Miles twined her curls round his fingers. 'This honestly wasn't what I intended.'

'I have no regrets,' she said. 'This has happened for a reason. I'm a strong believer in fate.'

'Where does that leave us?' His thumb grazed her cheek. 'I've missed you so much. I know this is a big decision for you, Autumn, but I don't want this to be a one-off.'

'Me neither.' She let out an unhappy exhalation. 'I have to speak to Addison. Being here with you, like this, only confirms to me that he and I have come to the end of the road. There's no future for us.'

'I hope that there might be one for us.' Miles toyed with her fingers. 'I think we could have something really special, Autumn, but it depends whether you'd like to take on a slightly battle-scarred single dad with a bossy three-year-old in tow.'

'I love her,' Autumn said. She cupped his face with her hand and looked into his eyes. 'I think I might love you, too.'

'You don't know how happy that makes me,' Miles said and he kissed her again.

Autumn held onto him tightly. There was no way that she wanted to let this man go. Now all she had to do was face the fallout.

Chapter Sixty-Two

Nadia and Anita were tidying up the shop. They'd decided to reorganise it and move some of the racks, to make it look more streamlined and easier for the customers to walk around.

Perhaps it was due to the festive season and the cheery songs blaring out, but they were both in high spirits this morning. They'd done nothing but laugh together over the rails of clothes as they shuffled them around, reminiscing about happy times from their childhood.

'Nadia, remember the hamster you got one Christmas?'

'Ah, yes. Poor Chocolate Button.'

'You said it was the best day of your life.'

'Until he went missing a few hours later.'

'There were scrabbling noises under the bath for days.'

'Oh, don't. I was completely traumatised. My Christmas present had done a runner!'

'We never did believe it when Mummy and Daddy said they'd managed to get him out.'

'No. The replacement that suddenly appeared in his cage as soon as the shops opened again. Perhaps they thought I wouldn't notice that Chocolate Button Mark Two was a completely different size and colour.'

'He was still very sweet, though.'

'And he fared much better. We had him for over a year, maybe two.'

'Perhaps one day we'll confess to Mummy and Daddy that we didn't buy their story.'

'I'd like that,' Nadia said.

Anita touched her arm. 'Come to the house, over the Christmas holiday. Perhaps when you're back from your trip with the girls. They would like to see you, I'm sure.'

'I will,' Nadia said. If there was any chance of reconciliation with her parents she should take it. They had given her and Nadia a good and happy childhood and still part of her didn't understand how they'd come to this. She'd been pig-headed in her determination to marry Toby, but she'd been young, foolish. That was all behind them now. Nadia had always thought that, eventually, they would come round to her way of thinking, but it seemed as if she'd pushed them too far. She had underestimated her parents' ability to harbour a grudge. But surely they couldn't still hold her mistakes against her? Hadn't she been punished enough by now? Perhaps if she held out an olive branch, then they'd be willing to respond. Nadia felt as if she'd been out of the fold for too long and nothing that her sleazy brother-in-law could do would ever drive her away from her family again.

When Tarak arrived an hour later, she and Nadia were still giggling away over some silly shared story. 'You ladies seem to be having a lovely time.'

'Just reminiscing, Husband,' Anita said. 'My sister and I did have some fun times when we were girls.'

'Too much, our parents would have said,' Nadia added.

They chuckled again.

'Anita,' Tarak said. 'I have some letters to post, recorded delivery. They must be handed over at the counter. Can you go to the Post Office for me?'

'Yes, of course. Shall I do it on my way home?'

'Now is a good time,' he said.

She shrugged. 'I'll get my coat. I could be a while. The queues are terrible at this time of year with everyone posting parcels and what-not.'

'I'm sure Nadia will hold the fort for you,' he said and glanced over at her. His eyes held the promise of trouble.

'I could go to the Post Office for you,' Nadia shouted after her sister. There was no way she wanted to be left by herself with him.

'Anita doesn't mind,' Tarak countered.

Even a sleazy look from him made her blood run cold. Her brother-in-law seemed to be contriving more and more reasons for Anita to be dispatched on errands while he spent time alone in the shop with her.

A few minutes later Anita appeared from the back of the shop, all swaddled in her coat against the winter cold. She gave a mock shudder. 'It looks freezing out there.'

Her sister had always preferred the warmer weather.

'I could go,' Nadia reiterated. 'I don't mind.'

'I'm booted and suited now. You wanted to rearrange the Christmas jumpers. If you make a start on that, then I can help you when I get back. I hope I won't be long,' she said as she took the bundle of letters from Tarak.

Nadia hoped so too. She watched her sister as she swung out of the door and walked briskly along Brick Lane, joining the throng of other pedestrians who all scuttled along, heads down, huddled into their coats.

Sure enough, the minute that Anita was out of sight, Tarak sidled up to her again, as she knew he would. This was going beyond annoying and was becoming decidedly disturbing.

'Did you think any more about meeting me at a hotel?' he asked, as he fiddled with the till, avoiding her eyes. 'I'm discreet, Nadia. No one would need to know.'

She had to admire him for his persistence, if nothing else. 'Not even Anita?'

'Especially not Anita,' he confirmed, failing to recognise her barbed tone.

Nadia sighed. She didn't know what sort of plan Lucy had in mind, but anything was better than this. If she simply resigned, Anita would wonder why she was leaving when they were enjoying being together so much. Unless she had another job to go to, she wouldn't believe her excuses. Plus, Nadia wanted to give Tarak a jolt. Something that would make him change his ways. One he wouldn't forget in a hurry. She didn't want to see her sister tied to a cheating scumbag.

'OK,' she said. 'Let's organise it.'

He looked as if he couldn't quite believe his luck.

Tarak went to snake an arm round her waist, but she sidestepped him. Creep. 'Not here,' she said. 'Someone might come in.'

Her brother-in-law moved away from her. Good job, otherwise she might have been tempted to slap him.

'Where were you thinking of?' Nadia asked, trying to keep her voice under control. She wanted to rant and rage at him, tell him exactly what she thought of him.

'I like the Soho Strand Hotel.'

It came from his lips too easily, too slickly and Nadia wondered whether this was his regular haunt for illicit assignations.

'I don't know it.'

'It's secluded,' Tarak said. 'High class. We could have dinner sent to the room.'

'No need for that,' Nadia said. There was no way she wanted a reason to linger. Whatever this meeting threw up, she wanted it to be a short, sharp shock. 'I'll meet you there.'

'When?'

'The sooner the better.'

Tarak brightened considerably. 'This weekend? Saturday night. Meet me at seven thirty.'

'Fine. I'll organise a babysitter and book the room.' Or Lucy will, Nadia thought.

'I can't stay the whole night, obviously,' he said.

'Obviously.' She had no idea how she was managing to stay so cool when she felt like committing bloody murder. How could he behave like this towards Anita when she'd done nothing but be a good wife to him?

He caught her eye and did his very best to look sincere. 'You won't regret this,' he said.

Possibly not. But, depending on how good Lucy's plan was, she very much hoped that he would.

Chapter Sixty-Three

It was a bright and beautiful winter morning. If you were wrapped up against the cold, of course. The sky was ice blue, the sun a milky disc, the wind sharp. Chantal had brought Lana for a trip to Kensington Gardens as she was in the mood to get out and enjoy the morning while promenading up and down the wide pathways with her baby snuggled down in her buggy.

Ted was spending the day with Stacey and Elsie. She'd nearly suggested that they all have a day out together. Now that Stacey was her friend, it felt odd for them to be having time alone without her. It was fair to say that her nose felt a little pushed out of joint. Yet neither Stacey nor Ted had suggested she join them.

Plus Ted had been rather cool with her since her last attempted conversation about their Christmas arrangements, when he'd stormed out of the department store. He'd mentioned nothing more and she hadn't felt able to broach the subject either – though it was a discussion that they needed to have as time was running out. He'd made no further mention of his job offer in the States and she wondered if it was just posturing on his part. She'd thought about going through his emails, but felt that would be a step too far. Ted would have to tell her in his own good time.

At one point, she'd felt that they were becoming closer again, but the gulf between them seemed to have opened up once more. Were all relationships this exhausting? At best, it was two steps forward, three steps back. She wanted to spend all her time on Lana, not treading on eggshells with the person who was supposed to be supporting her through this.

Chantal had a fur-lined hat pulled down over her ears and her warm UGG boots on. Lana was cocooned in her buggy with an extra blanket over her, only her long eyelashes and tiny pink nose visible. They'd had a good, long walk in the bracing air – also part of her resolution to finally start shifting some of her baby weight. Coming up to Christmas probably wasn't the best time to start on a fitness plan, but it might as well be now as never.

The statue of Peter Pan had still been tinged with frost when they'd arrived, but now the weak but willing sun was doing its level best to bring some warmth to the day. She'd skirted past the Italian gardens, had headed up Budges Walk to Round Pond and was now turning into the Broad Walk.

There were relatively few people out in the park today. Most were probably finishing off their Christmas shopping in Oxford or Regent Street – a reminder that she still had much to do herself. She had been surfing the internet for places to stay at Christmas and – a miracle at such short notice – had found somewhere that looked wonderful. They'd had a last-minute cancellation and the cottage seemed plenty big enough to accommodate all comers. Chantal hadn't even discussed it with Ted before she'd booked it – something she'd have to address before too long and certainly before the credit card bill came in. A place so big over the Christmas period certainly hadn't come cheap. But she felt that they needed this, to get away, have a change of scenery. She wanted to make Lana's first Christmas memorable – not that her darling daughter would appreciate her efforts. The place looked amazing and she couldn't wait to tell the girls.

Lost in thought, she didn't see the man jogging towards her until the last minute. He had his head down, earphones in, and was speeding along. Clearly he hadn't seen her either as it was only as they were about to collide that they both pulled up short.

Instantly, they grinned at each other.

'Jacob,' she said. 'This is a nice surprise.'

He stopped, hands on hips, breathing heavily. When he kissed her cheek his skin was dry with the cold. His eyes were a little bleary and he was unshaven. Stubble grazed her skin. Even with a tracksuit and a beanie hat on, he still looked attractive.

'What are you doing here?'

'I needed some fresh air.' His voice was raspy, though his breath was more even now. 'I had a heavy session at an event last night.'

'Hence the bloodshot eyes and the Bonnie Tyler impersonation.'

Jacob nodded. 'I couldn't speak at all an hour ago. Vodka is evil. Especially when drunk in an enormous quantity.'

Chantal laughed at him. 'Not the party animal you once were?'

'No. That man is long gone. I'm getting *way* too old for this,' he conceded. 'I thought a run would either kill or cure me.'

'Is this a regular haunt?'

'Quite often,' he said. 'But it's well away from your patch.'

'I'm home alone today,' Chantal said. 'It's Ted and Stacey's turn to play happy families.'

'How's that working out?'

'I don't know,' she admitted. 'Catch me on a good day and I'd say that we're making a great job of it.'

'But this isn't a good day?'

'Not especially.' She shook her head. Today she was struggling to see a way forward. 'I had to get out of the house. A change is as good as a rest – so they say. We were just headed to the Diana Memorial Playground. I'm going to show Lana where I'm going to bring her to do fun stuff when she's big enough.'

Jacob peered into the buggy. 'How's my favourite girl?'

'She's good. Getting bigger by the minute.'

'I'm just about done with my run,' Jacob said. 'I think my lungs might burst if I push it any further. Mind if I come with you?'

'There's a nice café there,' Chantal said. 'I'll treat you to a coffee and something with lots of chocolate and calories.'

He grinned at her and her stomach did a funny little flip. 'Sounds good to me.'

'You can go on buggy-pushing duty,' Chantal said and she moved aside to let Jacob push the pram.

She linked her arm through his as they walked, always so comfortable in his presence.

They passed the clock tower and the Elfin Oak, an ancient trunk elaborately carved with figures of elves and fairies, and reached the playground. In the height of summer there was always a lengthy queue to go inside and she always wondered how parents had the patience to do so. Now she knew that she'd stand in line for hours to give Lana a taste of this magical place.

Today there were only a few hardy souls in evidence. Small children in big coats and wellington boots clambered over the massive pirate ship which formed the centrepiece to the play area. There was a fort, too, and an area of wigwams, all inspired by the story of Peter Pan.

'This is a great place,' Jacob said. 'Much better than we had when we were kids. When I'm a dad, you won't be able to keep me out of here.'

'I can't wait to bring Lana to play here either.'

'Can I get her out of the buggy? She needs a cuddle with her favourite uncle.'

'You do that while I get us a hot drink. What do you want?'

She took his order and went over to the café. Jacob found them seats outside, sheltered from the breeze.

When she came back, he was jiggling a very contented Lana on his knee. Her daughter was beaming widely and gurgling as Jacob pulled funny faces for her.

'You're great with kids.' She put down the cardboard cartons of coffee.

'I can't wait to have my own.' Then he glanced up at Chantal. He fixed her with his eyes. 'You know, there are times when I wish she was mine.'

Chantal felt herself flush.

'I never thought that I'd want to find a wife and settle down, but this little one is making me feel very broody,' he admitted, laughing at himself. 'She's great.'

'It is life-changing.'

'Do you think you'll have more?'

'I'd love another child, but I'm not sure that it will be with Ted.'

Jacob raised an eyebrow at that.

'I've tried really hard,' she said. 'But I'm beginning to think whatever we had has long gone. We get on much better as friends than we do as husband and wife.'

'I'm sorry to hear that.'

'We've got Lana to consider. Perhaps it's just a rough patch.

Having children isn't easy.' She looked at Lana lovingly. 'I'm sure we'll manage to work something out.'

Jacob frowned. 'It will be hard to raise a child on your own. Look at Nadia. I know how she struggles.'

They exchanged a glance at the mention of her name and Chantal wondered how it was going with Nadia and Jacob. She'd said very little recently.

'Ted would be mad to let you go. You're a great woman, Chantal. Beautiful and feisty and . . . well . . . I've said too much.'

She laughed. 'Really? I hoped you were just getting warmed up.'

Oh, it was far too easy to flirt with Jacob. They'd always been the same with each other. They were like old friends, comfortable in each other's company, all underpinned by more than a hint of attraction. Suddenly, it seemed so very hard to think of him in a relationship with Nadia. She felt as if she was losing Ted to Stacey and now she faced losing Jacob to Nadia. How would she cope when she was the one who was all alone?

Chapter Sixty-Four

Miles had stayed overnight. Autumn hadn't wanted him to leave and they slept snuggled together as if they'd been sharing a bed for years. Florence had been staying with her mother who, thankfully, was also charged with today's nursery run.

Which meant that Miles had been able to stay for breakfast, too. They were shy, but held hands over the table and lingered for as long as they could, chatting and looking dreamily at each other. It had been hard for her to leave to come to work.

They'd kissed warmly as they parted and had arranged to meet later in the park. Miles would be collecting Florence this afternoon and she would be looking after Lewis until Nadia came home from the shop.

Now it was mid-morning and Autumn had just arrived at the Stolford Centre. She had no classes arranged for today, but she needed to see Addison sooner rather than later.

She swung through the main door, kicking the slushy snow from her boots on the mat. Autumn walked along the corridor to his office, spirits low. She hoped that he would understand. It was no reflection on him, but she realised now that they simply weren't suited. As people they were too different. After the first flush of love, there was very little underpinning their relationship and it was better that they'd found out now rather than a few years down the line when they might have had children together.

Addison was sitting over some paperwork at his desk, the winter sunshine throwing him into silhouette. Next to him, so close that she couldn't see the daylight between them, stood Monica Desmond.

'Hi.' Addison glanced up at her. Monica took a subtle but noticeable step away from him. 'Didn't expect you today.'

Autumn stood there, heart hammering in her chest. She looked at him and suddenly felt as if she didn't really know this man at all. And he didn't know her. She'd talked more, shared more secrets with Miles in the short time that she'd known him than she ever had with Addison. It would have been a truly terrible mistake to have married him.

'I need to have a word with you,' she said. 'It can't really wait.'

Monica gathered up her papers. 'We can catch up later.'

'Fine.'

The look that passed between them, if only for the merest second, made Autumn think that she wasn't the only one who was having doubts. It was too soft, too raw. Was there something going on between Addison and Monica? If there was, then it was really too late for her to worry about it.

When Monica left, Autumn sat in the chair opposite him.

'Did you have lunch with your parents yesterday?' he asked.

'I did.'

'Were you able to get any money from them?'

She thought about the hundred grand sitting in her bank account. If she gave it to the centre, then that would tie her and Addison together for the foreseeable future and she didn't

333

really want that. Suddenly, she wanted a clean break from him, from this place. Part of her wondered if they'd only stayed together for so long because he thought that she could bring some money to the table. It was sad, but she also thought it might be the truth.

'No,' she lied. 'Their investments are all tied up at the moment.'

'Ah.' He looked disappointed but not entirely surprised. 'It's probably just as well.' Addison stood up and came round to perch on the desk next to her. 'This is difficult, Autumn.'

Addison took off his glasses, deliberately, slowly, acting regret to the gallery. 'Monica and I have been talking. We feel that the creative classes have to come to an end. We have to make savings.'

'And they're the easy target.'

'We feel that the money needs to be channelled elsewhere.'

'I see.' She wondered whether Addison would have taken her parents' money and still have got rid of her.

'I know you'll be disappointed.'

'Yes.' She'd put a lot into this place, sat for hours talking to the troubled kids, turning fingers that were as clumsy as sausages into something remotely skilful, giving them a sense of pride in themselves. It wasn't a lot, but she liked to think that she'd helped to give some of them a little respite from the tragic worlds that they normally lived in. She'd seen this coming – admittedly, not quite so quickly and not quite in this way. She couldn't deny that it hurt. It seemed that Addison wasn't keen to fight her corner for her. A telling sign of what she really meant to him.

'I've put your personal belongings together.' He nodded towards a small cardboard box on top of his filing cabinet. 'I collected them for you.'

'There's nothing in there that I want.'

'You've realised, I suppose, that it's not working for us either.'

'Yes. So it seems.' Yet the relationship had once been so full of promise.

'We're too different. We don't want the same thing.'

Autumn wasn't sure what it was that Addison wanted but, obviously, it no longer included her.

'Your brother, he was always at the top of your list. It was never me.' He stood up then and paced the room. 'I want to be straight with you, Autumn. Monica and I have grown close. Very close.'

Autumn managed to keep her face impassive. She had guessed as much a few moments earlier and wondered why she hadn't realised before.

'I think we're more suited to each other,' he continued solemnly.

'I see.'

'I didn't want you to hear it from someone else. I wanted to be upfront with you.'

'Well. Thanks for that.'

'You're a lovely woman,' Addison said, though his tone sounded patronising. 'I'm sure, in time, that you'll meet someone else.'

'You're right.' She smiled at her ex-boyfriend kindly. Addison had been a mistake, an error of judgement. She could see that now. He wasn't the one for her at all. Then Autumn thought about Miles. She thought about his kind eyes, his lovely sensual mouth, his mad hair. His solid, kind, caring presence. She thought about being in his arms, being in his life. She was free to love him now and that, suddenly, seemed quite appealing. 'In fact,' she told Addison, 'I already have.'

And she left Addison gaping at her as she headed out of the door and to Chocolate Heaven to tell the girls her news.

Chapter Sixty-Five

We, the good ladies of the Chocolate Lovers' Club, are masters of the art of subterfuge. A room at the Soho Strand Hotel has been booked in Tarak's name and, at the allotted time, we convene in the lobby to put into action our dastardly plan. Well, *my* dastardly plan, if I'm honest. The girls still have very scant details and probably just as well.

The rather salubrious hotel is looking particularly lovely in its festive garb. A huge Christmas tree dressed in red and gold bows dominates the entrance. The reception desk is festooned with garlands in the same theme and the area is busy with guests here, it would seem, for seasonal celebrations. It's a lovely choice – even though it is Nadia's sleazebag brother-in-law's favoured shag palace and we are here for *dark* reasons.

'You didn't tell Stacey, did you?' Chantal asks anxiously.

'No. I'm not sure why, though. I thought everything was OK between you two.'

'It is.'

'Don't you trust her?'

'Yes, of course.' She gnaws on her fingernail. 'I don't know. Maybe not.'

'There seems to be a bit of tension creeping into your relationship.'

'We're fine. Everything's fine.' Said with the air of a woman who believes that everything is definitely *not* fine. 'I just don't want Ted to know about this.'

'And you think she'll tell him?'

'Yes. No. Maybe.'

I'm glad we cleared that up.

'I'm not sure how we'll keep this from her, now that she's part of our gang,' I confess. 'She might be hurt that she wasn't invited.' Still, at the moment, that's the least of my problems.

'It's too late now,' Chantal says. 'She's babysitting Lana. I can hardly ring her up and tell her to get her ass down here.'

Nadia, too, is biting her nails. I'm going to have to book them all in for recuperative manicures at this rate. With Chantal placated – sort of – I turn my attention to soothing Nadia.

'It will be fine,' I assure her. 'Some of my best work has been in hotels. You know that. Don't be nervous.'

'I'm *beyond* nervous, Lucy.' She does look anxious. 'I'm terrified. What if he doesn't turn up?'

'He will.'

'Even worse, what if he *does* turn up and my sister finds out that he's meeting me? My renewed relationship with her is still in its early stages. If this gets out, it could kill it stone dead.'

'Then we'll have to make damn sure that it doesn't.'

'We don't even know what the plan is yet,' Autumn notes. She has a fair point. 'Let's get the room key and then I'll fill you in. We might need a drink. Or two.'

'What's in there?' Chantal points at the little wheelie case I've brought along.

'All in good time,' I tell her.

Chantal shakes her head. 'Why did we let you organise this, Lucy?'

'Because I am a past master,' I remind her a touch haughtily. 'I got your jewellery back for you from the gentleman thief, didn't I?' Something else Ted still doesn't know about.

'Yes,' she admits. 'That was nice work.'

It's good to blow your own trumpet sometimes.

'Does this plan involving drugging someone with spiked chocolates, as you did last time we let you sort something like this out?'

'No,' I say. 'It is more cunning than that.'

'Time's marching on.' Autumn glances at her watch. 'Isn't Tarak due soon?'

I note the lateness of the hour. 'Yes. Better get a move on. I'll check us in. You lot loiter here, while I do the business.'

So I go to the desk and complete the formalities.

'Can we take a credit card, please?'

'I'll give you mine, but Mr Patel will be paying the bill when he arrives,' I inform her. 'He's one of your regular guests.'

In return, I get the swipe card to the room I've reserved in Tarak's name.

We head to the lift. When it comes we squeeze in, all silent. Christmas carols fill the space.

'*Glad tidings of great joy we bring,*' a tinny voice trills from the speaker, '*to you and all mankind.*'

Hmm. We're definitely not bringing glad tidings of great joy and one particular member of mankind is going to be distinctly unhappy at the end of the day.

We tiptoe along the plushly carpeted corridor, aware of every noise and I let us into the room at the end.

Chantal throws the light switch and illuminates a chic room that's decorated in the routinely anonymous style in varying shades of beige employed by most hotels. It's fine, though. Suits our purposes perfectly.

The television is already on and the screen displays the

legend 'The Soho Strand Hotel welcomes Mr Tarak Patel'.

But, unfortunately for Mr Tarak Patel, he will get more of a welcome than he imagined.

'Right. Chantal, you need to break out the mini-bar.'

'Will do.'

'I'm going to get Tarak to pay for all of this, so tuck in.'

'I have no idea how you're going to manage that,' Nadia says. 'He's as tight as two coats of paint.'

'You'll see,' I tell her mysteriously.

'I have emergency supplies in here.' I lift the wheelie case onto the bed and flip it open. Then I lift out the box of chocolates I've brought from Chocolate Heaven and hand them around. I smile as each of the girls zooms in on their own favourites. The tension in the room lessens considerably.

'Champagne, I think.' Chantal brandishes a bottle from the bar and then pours out a glass for us all.

'To the Chocolate Lovers' Club,' I propose. 'Long may we reign.'

'To the Chocolate Lovers' Club,' the girls echo and we toast each other.

Nadia swigs her fizz and says, 'Come on, Lucy, spill the beans. There isn't much time.'

I hastily take another fortifying sip and put my glass down. Out of the wheelie case, I produce a carrier bag. 'Ta-dah!'

Chantal frowns. 'You've been to a sex shop?'

'A nice one,' I counter. 'They don't have any itchy lace tat in Sirens. It's all proper silk and stuff. A lot of celebs shop there.'

My friend rolls her eyes. If I'm not mistaken Chantal would once have been their target customer.

Autumn takes the bag from me and peers inside. 'What's this got to do with us?'

'Weeeell,' I say. 'This is what we're going to do. We're all

339

going to dress up in sexy underwear and, except Nadia, we'll hide. When Tarak arrives, just expecting a cosy evening, we all jump out and take photographs of him in compromising positions. Then we'll threaten to show them to Anita if he doesn't leave Nadia alone and keep on the straight and narrow.'

They all stare at me, aghast.

'What?' I feel my courage waver.

As everyone else seems to have been struck dumb, it's Chantal who finally manages to speak first. 'You're kidding me?'

'It could work,' I offer. 'We've pulled off more audacious things.'

Chantal dips into the carrier bag and pulls out a lacy basque and thong set. She holds it high. 'There is no way on God's earth that I'm letting myself be seen in public in these.'

'It's hardly in public,' I counter. 'It's only us. And we're all friends together.'

'I'm packing nearly two stone of baby weight.' Chantal pats her rounded tummy. 'I have stretch marks that are like a map of the Andes. This is *not* going to happen.'

Despite feeling deflated at her lack of solidarity, I refuse to be thwarted. 'You could take the photographs,' I suggest.

'Done,' she agrees quickly.

Out of my trusty case, I produce Crush's very fancy camera which I've secretly purloined for the specific purpose of taking a decent shot. This is too important to be left to the variable quality of a camera phone. I hand it to Chantal and she grabs it gratefully.

'What else have you got in there?' she wants to know.

'A pair of fluffy handcuffs, a gimp mask and a whip.'

Everyone falls about laughing.

'What?' I fear that they're not taking this seriously.

'I don't want Tarak to see me in underwear,' Nadia says when she's stopped laughing. 'It's bad enough that he looks at me in the way he does now. I don't want to give him any more reason.'

'Fair enough.' Hadn't thought of that one. Now my confidence really is failing. If that's Chantal and Nadia out of the picture – literally – what am I going to do?

Chantal continues to pull the skimpy garments out of the carrier bag with a disdainful face. 'This is a dreadful plan, Lucy. Even for you.'

'Can you do better, Chantal?' I sound very peevish. 'Be my guest.'

She puts down a wisp of black lace with a sheepish expression.

'I think it's a great plan,' Autumn says, enthusiastically.

Hurrah! Finally someone realises that I am not a complete airhead, but a borderline criminal genius.

'But I can't wear these either, Lucy. I've never had anything like this before. I haven't the nerve.' She pulls an apologetic face.

'So you don't actually think it's a good plan?' Chantal notes.

'No,' Autumn confesses. 'Not really. I'm happy to stay in the background and be supportive, though.'

I realise that this is, indeed, out of her comfort zone. I should have bought Autumn something in cheesecloth or tie-dyed at the very least.

'That leaves me then,' I say.

'That could still work.' Nadia does a face palm. 'I can't believe I just said that. This is how desperate I am.'

'He might be a total sleazebag,' Autumn says, 'but does he really deserve this?'

We all turn on her and say as one, 'Yes!'

'Couldn't we all just sit down and talk it through with him like rational people?'

'No!'

'Fine.' She holds up a hand in submission. 'Just checking.'

Nadia rallies herself. 'I've tried talking to him and he hasn't listened. Lucy's right. It needs something drastic.'

'This is drastic, all right,' Chantal agrees.

Nadia paces the floor. 'What if I'm here to welcome Tarak? Fully dressed. I give him a drink, play nicely. Get him to take his clothes off.' She shudders just a little bit. 'I could tell him I've brought a friend along to make a threesome. He'd like that. Bastard. Then Lucy – dressed in the hooker underwear – can spring out of the bathroom, and Chantal, you can take some compromising photographs. Just of Tarak and Lucy.'

'That's sort of what I'd planned,' I chip in. 'Except I wouldn't be the only one in my skimpies. And the look I'm aiming for is classily sexy rather than hooker.'

'I don't want to be in any photographs,' Nadia stresses. 'How could I ever explain it to Anita if she saw them?'

'They're just for insurance. Anita never needs to see them. I hope that if we have evidence of his infidelity to use against him, he'll leave you alone and also think twice before he does the same with another woman.'

Nadia chews her lip. 'I don't know,' she says. 'I'm frightened. I don't know if I can go through with this.'

'He'll be here soon,' Autumn notes. 'We'd better decide quickly.'

'While we're here, let's give it a go,' Chantal puts forward. 'We've come this far, we might as well.'

I feel as if this is being taken out of my hands.

'Lucy, you nip into the bathroom and get yourself kitted up,' Chantal orders. 'Make sure that you put the most revealing outfit on. Lots of slutty make-up too.'

I pick up the carrier bag and, a little sulkily, ask, 'What am I going to do with this lot?'

'Take it back,' Chantal says. 'Just don't take the labels off. This must have cost you a small fortune.'

'It will be worth it if it keeps Tarak off Nadia's back.'

Nadia comes to hug me. 'I don't know if this will work, Lucy, but thank you for trying.' She gives me a hug and kisses my cheek, which puts a smile back on my face.

'I'd better go and get undressed then.'

'Yeah,' Chantal agrees. 'Great plan. We'll just stay here and open another bottle of champagne.'

So, with a heavy heart, wondering why I don't just keep my meddling under control, I take the carrier bag of sexy Siren lingerie and my wheelie case, and then head alone to the bathroom.

Chapter Sixty-Six

I apply another layer of make-up and slick on a bright red lipstick from my bag that I must have bought once for a fancy dress party. Probably something to do with zombies. I'd never wear lipstick this vibrant shade of crimson.

Then I dip into the Sirens carrier bag and pull out the basque, thong and stockings that I've chosen for myself. I regard them with an emotion that comes close to horror. What was I thinking? I divest myself of my sensible black trousers and floral blouse and, with much huffing and puffing, squeeze myself into them. Now I know what a sausage must feel like. I slip on my black patent stilettos with the heels that aren't meant for walking in.

When I risk a tentative look in the full-length mirror, I'm startled at what looks back at me. I think I might even gasp out loud. This underwear is positively obscene. Bits of me pop out everywhere. In my defence, it came across a lot bigger on the hanger.

I emerge from the bathroom more self-conscious than I'd imagined. I'm among friends here. This shouldn't be intimidating. I try to keep my hands over my boobs and my lady bits.

'You look fabulous,' Chantal says.

Then they all burst out laughing.

'Thank you,' I say, crossly. 'Thank you very much.'

'You look as if you're on your way for a night on the streets at King's Cross.'

'I was aiming slightly higher than that.' Now I feel dreadful and so exposed. I wish I'd waxed my bikini line.

Nadia comes to comfort me. 'You're the only one who has the nerve to do this, Lucy.'

That fact hasn't escaped me. So much for the solidarity of the sisterhood.

'Tarak's just texted me,' she adds. 'He'll be here any minute.'

'Give me champagne,' I say. 'Quickly.'

Chantal replenishes my glass and hands it to me. I gulp it down.

'We all need to go and hide in the bathroom,' Autumn says.

'I don't want you to leave me.' Nadia clings to my arm.

I give her a chocolate and Chantal gives her champagne.

'You'll be fine,' I assure her. 'You just have to put him at ease.'

'That's the bit I'm worried about.'

'We'll do the rest.' By 'we', I obviously mean 'I'.

'Call me when you want me to come out of the bathroom,' I say to Nadia, who only stops clinging to me to hug herself protectively.

'You'll have to give us a signal for when we're to spring our little surprise on him,' Chantal says. 'You'll have to say a particular phrase or something.'

'What about "Are you sitting comfortably?"' Nadia proposes.

345

Chantal nods her agreement. 'Sounds good to me. Don't forget to say it loudly.' She glances nervously round the room. 'We'd better make ourselves scarce.' She gives Nadia the bottle of champagne. 'Liquid courage.'

As one, all three of us troop into the bathroom, squeezing tightly together. We close the door behind us.

Chantal is clutching Crush's camera. 'Does he know where you are tonight?'

'No,' I admit. 'I think a couple should have some secrets.'

'Oh, Lucy,' she smiles. 'Only you. Only you.'

'What?'

But before she has a chance to explain, there's a gentle knock at the hotel room door and, seconds later, it opens.

Chantal looks at me and our eyes meet. There is apprehension in hers and I think there is more than a little fear in mine. To think I could be safely at home stretched out on the sofa in Crush's arms watching the *X-Factor*.

'Game on,' Chantal whispers and, filled with trepidation, we all fall silent.

Chapter Sixty-Seven

Nadia quickly switched on the voice recorder of her mobile phone. Her knees were shaking as she heard Tarak swipe his key card and open the door. She thought Lucy's plan was, at best, risky. At worse, foolhardy. There was no way that she could see Tarak falling for this. He was a seasoned and serial adulterer, surely he'd be wise to the fact that he'd been conned?

'I hope you haven't been waiting for long,' he said as he came into the room, his usual swagger and smarmy smile firmly in place.

'Not too long.' She tried not to glance nervously at the bathroom door behind her and give her friends away. All she had to do was hold her nerve. Easier said than done.

Tarak held out a bottle of champagne. 'I brought this.'

She held out one too. 'I've already started. I helped myself to the mini-bar.'

Her brother-in-law looked slightly shocked at that, probably considering the price. She splashed champagne into a glass for him.

'Cheers,' he said. 'To us.'

Nadia sucked in a deep breath. This was torture. She knocked back her champagne and, steeling herself, let her fingers go to the buttons of his shirt.

'Keen,' Tarak said.

Nadia bit down a wave of revulsion. If only Anita could hear him now. She might think differently about what a good and loving husband he was. 'We don't have long.'

'I knew that you'd be more enthusiastic than you are in the shop.'

'I want this to be a night that you'll never forget,' she said as huskily as she could manage.

He laughed, but there was a frown on his forehead. 'You make it sound as if this will be the only time.'

'Let's see what happens. I might be more than you can handle.'

He grinned at her. 'It's that spirit in you that's always attracted me. You're so much more woman than your sister.'

Nadia wanted to slap his stupid face. She held a finger to his lips. 'Let's not talk about Anita.'

Tarak shrugged and she put down her glass. She hoped that Lucy was ready and waiting in the bathroom. The sooner they got this over with the better.

'Do you do this often?' she asked.

'When I can,' he admitted without shame. 'A man has needs.'

The neck of his shirt was already undone, so Nadia moved her hand down to the next button and opened it.

'I'm discreet,' he said. 'You can trust me.'

Trust. It was clear that Tarak didn't even know the meaning of the word. However, he was about to find out that he couldn't trust her. Nadia seethed inside. Then Tarak moved forward to kiss her and a gulp of terror travelled down her throat. Oh, this was a bad idea. A very bad idea. She would kill Lucy for getting her into this situation.

Nadia fumbled with another button.

Tarak smiled. 'I didn't know you'd be in such a hurry.'

'Why waste time?'

'We're of the same mind.' He put his glass down and rapidly undid his own buttons.

His body beneath was soft and mildly overweight. His pot belly sat on the belt of his trousers. It was repulsive. What did her sister see in him?

Nadia tugged at his belt and Tarak ran his hand over her breast. She shuddered and Tarak took it as desire rather than disgust.

He kicked off his shoes and it took seconds to divest him of his trousers. He stood there looking pathetic in his boxer shorts and socks.

'I have a surprise for you,' she purred. 'I thought I'd have someone join us.'

'Join us?' Tarak raised an eyebrow. 'Who?'

'A friend of mine. I think you'll like her.'

'A threesome?'

'Would you like that?'

'It wouldn't be the first time,' he boasted. 'For you?'

'I'm very *close* to my friends,' she said as she pushed Tarak down onto the bed. If she was in her right mind, she'd stop this now and run for the hills.

But she wasn't and there was no other plan in place to stop Tarak's harassment of her. Well, what you reaped was generally what you had sown by your own selfishness. Tarak most definitely was due a dose of humiliation and it might as well be her that administered it. Having got this far, there was no going back now.

'Lucy!' she shouted. 'Come and join us.'

Chapter Sixty-Eight

I stand there in the bathroom in nothing but my underwear – and not much of it at that – frozen with fright.

'Get out there, Lombard,' Chantal hisses. 'Take one for the team. Deep breaths, deep breaths.'

I look to Autumn for succour.

'Rather you than me,' she whispers, with a pitying expression on her face.

This all seemed like such a good idea when I thought we'd all burst out of the bathroom *en masse* in our skimpies and execute my plan. Doesn't seem such a good scheme now that it's me on my tod.

Chantal gives me an encouraging shove. At least that's what I think it is. 'Let's get this over with.'

'Nadia will be desperate for you to get out there,' Autumn says.

She will. And I must do this for her. Particularly as it was my stupid idea. I take the deep breaths that Chantal advised, but it makes no difference at all. None. I'm still borderline hyperventilating and my heart is pounding in my chest.

'Be sexy,' Chantal says. 'Otherwise he'll smell a rat.'

'You're so much better at this sort of thing than me,' I tell her. 'I'm not a natural *femme fatale*.'

'Yes, and I look like a blimp, so get out there and be fabulous.' Then she hugs me fiercely. 'Come on. You can do this.'

At that moment my phone pings and they all go, 'Sssshhh!'

'It's Crush,' I whisper. Oh, God bless him. The love of my life is going to make me a romantic dinner for when I get home. I'd envisaged collecting a takeaway in Camden High Street. How lovely is he?

I start to text back.

'You haven't got time for that,' Chantal says and grabs my phone from my hand.

Autumn yanks open the door and Chantal hands me the whip and the fluffy handcuffs, and suddenly I'm in the bedroom with Nadia. There is terror in her eyes too and we give each other a comforting glance. Then a smile breaks out on her face and that makes me relax as well. She puts her hand over her mouth to hide the laughter that threatens to erupt. The stupidity of what we're doing hits us both, I think.

Sitting on the bed is a rather podgy middle-aged man. He's wearing just his boxer shorts, socks and a creepy grin. This must be the troublesome Tarak. He doesn't look that troublesome. He looks a little bit pathetic and desperate. But he also looks as if he thinks his birthday and Christmas have come together. That makes me more determined to see this through.

'Hello, Gorgeous,' he says in an oily manner.

I hate that he uses the same pet name that Crush has for me. Then I get a pang of guilt. If Crush could see me now he'd be flipping furious. And maybe a bit beyond. That's why I haven't told him, of course.

Whip over my shoulder, I saunter towards the bed, trying to look alluring. 'Are you sitting comfortably?'

Then Chantal bursts out of the bathroom door, camera raised. Tarak looks as if he's about to have a heart attack – which wasn't quite in the plan. She makes me and Nadia jump like scalded cats too.

'You're not doing anything!' Chantal complains. 'Why did you say that?'

Omigod, I'd forgotten 'Are you sitting comfortably?' was to be our key phrase for action. Stupid, stupid, stupid.

'Do something,' she shouts.

Quickly, while Tarak still looks like a rabbit caught in the headlights, I dash to his side and, before he realises what I'm doing, I pose against him. He's too startled to complain or move. I hitch my breasts and point them towards the camera, giving my best duck pout. I put my high-heeled foot on Tarak's naked thigh.

Chantal snaps away with the camera while I drape myself this way and that over the hapless brother-in-law.

Finally, he finds his voice. 'Wha . . . wha . . . what are you doing?' he splutters. 'Is this a joke?'

Nadia, who had dissolved into the background, steps forward. 'It's not a joke, Tarak. This is my insurance policy.'

He stares at her and blinks a lot.

'If you ever come near me again or even make a sleazy comment, then I'll show these pictures to Anita,' she tells him.

'You wouldn't,' he says, eyes wide.

'Try me.'

I climb onto the bed behind Tarak and put my boobs on his head, dangling my whip over his shoulder. Chantal takes another snap.

'Will you stop that!' he yells.

Actually, I'm quite getting into this now.

'You're going to get dressed and get out of here,' Nadia

says, taking charge. 'And we're never going to mention this again. From now on you'll treat me with the respect that you should give to all of your employees. Especially one who is your sister-in-law, your own family.'

I expect Tarak to kick off but, instead, he keeps his mouth shut and looks slightly shamefaced. I thought he'd be difficult, aggressive even. Instead, his shoulders slump. He looks like a man who is defeated. Someone whose bubble has been most categorically burst. I slide down and sit next to him.

'Sorry we did this,' I say. 'But we didn't know what else to do.'

He looks up at Nadia, his piggy eyes bleak. 'You could have just said no.'

'I did,' she counters. 'Many times. You weren't listening.'

Tarak scratches his stubble. He looks a bit pitiful sitting there in his pants. 'I won't do it again,' he promises. 'I've learned my lesson. Can you delete those photographs? Anita would kill me if she saw them.'

'No,' Nadia says. 'I'm going to keep them in a safe place. Whenever you think you might like to cheat on my sister, just remember that I have them tucked away.'

He hangs his head.

'My sister is a devoted wife, Tarak. I want you to love her as she deserves.'

'I will,' he says. 'I definitely will.'

'She adores you. She's the mother of your boys. I don't want you to take that for granted.'

'Can I get dressed now?' he asks.

'Yes.'

'Can I go into the bathroom?'

'No,' Nadia says. Then she looks a bit embarrassed. 'There's another woman in there.'

That makes him looked shocked again.

'We'll get out of the way,' I tell him nicely. 'Leave you to it.'

'Thank you.' He crosses his arms over his body, clearly feeling very self-conscious now. I can empathise with that.

'We could all get dressed and have a drink together,' I suggest. 'We might laugh about this.'

'I'd rather not,' Tarak says in the manner of a man who'd rather stick pins in his own eyes than share a glass of fizz with us. 'If you don't mind.'

I stand up and shake his hand. 'It's been very nice meeting you.'

The glare he gives me says that he doesn't feel quite the same.

'I have one more piece of bad news for you,' I confess. Tarak braces himself. 'This room is on your account. And the champagne.'

'OK.' Clearly a broken man.

'Now we'll go.' I signal to Nadia and Chantal and we all back up towards the bathroom. 'We won't come out until we hear the door close. Give it a good slam.'

'I don't think that will be a problem,' Tarak says.

The door opens behind us and we tiptoe away. I give Tarak a last hesitant wave before we disappear inside. I'm sure I see him roll his eyes.

We turn to Autumn and all do a silent air punch.

'We did it,' I whisper. 'I *actually* think that we did it.'

'Thank you, Lucy,' Nadia whispers back.

The Chocolate Lovers' Club have pulled it off again. Mission accomplished. We have a group hug and do a little dance, trying not to make any noise.

Then we wait, listening while Tarak gets dressed. Only when the door slams – and it does, very loudly – do we let out a celebratory cheer.

Chapter Sixty-Nine

When I'm dressed again, we all go downstairs to the bar. If things had gone badly with Tarak I'd have put this on his bill too but, in the end, he was suitably penitent.

Around us are a few parties getting into the Christmas spirit – a boisterous group of estate agents, a cackling bunch of ladies who are heckling them. I can see late-night drinking ahead and red faces in the morning.

Having used up all our emotional energy, we are having a much more sedate evening. That doesn't stop us ordering some amazing cocktails, though. We've already polished off a vodka martini or two and are now onto mojitos laced with rum. Yum. I feel my equilibrium is starting to return. I think I was unsettled by how much, once I got going, I enjoyed prancing round in my underwear being photographed, tormenting a man. Somewhere deep inside I have a latent dominatrix. Yikes. I have another swig of mojito.

Chantal raises her glass. 'To the ladies of the Chocolate Lovers' Club.'

We all echo the toast and clink glasses together around the table.

'I thought it was a completely hare-brained scheme, Lucy,' she admits. 'But, somehow, you've done it again.'

'It's my forte,' I tell her.

Then we all splutter with laughter.

'I hope it works,' says Nadia, who remains anxious despite the amount of cocktails she's consumed. 'I've still got to face Tarak again. I'm definitely not looking forward to seeing him at work next week.'

'At least you've given him a fright,' Chantal says. 'He'd be a fool to come on to you now we have photographic evidence of his philandering. We've done the best we can.'

'I appreciate it,' Nadia says. 'It's down to me now.'

'No one must ever see those photographs,' I say. 'I'll put them on a plug-in as soon as I get home and then hide them somewhere very, very safe. I don't want them falling into the wrong hands.'

You know what it's like these days. One slip up and they're on the internet for everyone to see. Imagine that! I shudder at the thought. No one is getting an eyeful of these babies.

'I've been dying to tell you all. I managed to book a cottage in the Lakes for Christmas,' Chantal says. 'Well, that's what the blurb said. I'd call it a farmhouse. It's massive. There'll be room for all of us and a few more. Is everyone coming?'

'I can't wait,' Autumn says. 'Miles has Florence this Christmas and I'd love to bring them. Is there enough room?'

'We can accommodate all comers,' Chantal agrees. 'We should all bring our other halves. Though Ted isn't all that keen.'

'Is Stacey coming?'

'I think that's part of the problem. He's being very cagey. I don't think he wants both of his women under one roof.'

'I can't say that I blame him.'

Chantal grimaces. 'I know. Tricky. I'm sure I can talk him

round. What else can I do? We can't leave Stacey behind.'

I don't point out that she's not here with us now. And the question that remains unasked is how *will* they all cope under one roof for the first time?

'I'll call Clive and Tristan too,' I say. To be honest, I need an excuse to speak to them to see if they've had any interest in Chocolate Heaven. I can only hope the answer to that is a resounding no. 'I'll ask if they want to join us.'

'That would be great.' Chantal turns to Nadia. She sounds overly bright when she asks, 'Are you going to bring Jacob?'

'I'd love to. Do you think he'd come?'

'He'd love it, surely. Jacob knows how to get a party started,' I offer. I just hope that Nadia and Chantal don't come to blows over him. I know that Chantal is trying to work on her marriage, but there's no doubt she can be a little bit possessive when it comes to Jacob. She hasn't said anything, but I do wonder how she feels about Jacob and Nadia getting closer.

'He's a great cook,' Autumn adds. 'Perhaps he can help with the food?'

'It is going to be a full house,' Chantal concedes. 'I did think about getting caterers in to feed us all, but I'll just fill up the Range Rover with supplies. I might not be a domestic goddess for the rest of the year, but I do love cooking Christmas dinner.'

'We should help,' I offer. 'This sounds very expensive. Why don't we all chip in what we can?'

Chantal won't hear of it. 'I've got it covered. You've all been so fabulous this year; I'd like this to be my Christmas present to you. End of discussion.'

'I hope it snows.' Even to my own ears I sound wistful. A snowy Christmas in the countryside curled up with Crush. I can't wait. I feel like hugging myself. Then I glance at my watch and think that I'd better be getting home. I don't want him to feel as if I've abandoned him. Call it baggage from the Marcus era, but it's always at the back of my mind that a boyfriend shouldn't be left unattended for too long. I couldn't leave Marcus alone for five minutes before his eyes – and hands – started wandering. Chantal had kindly texted Crush on my behalf – unbeknown to him – to say that I wouldn't be too late.

'I hope it snows *after* we get there,' Chantal says. 'I don't want to be spending Christmas on the motorway. I'm planning that we'll go up there on Christmas Eve. Everyone else can arrive whenever you can. We'll set off as early in the day as possible to get everything ready.'

'I should be able to come up at the same time as you,' Autumn says.

'You're an angel.'

'I think Crush finishes work at lunchtime, but I've got to stay and man Chocolate Heaven until five o'clock.' No one will want to go into the frenzy of Christmas lacking in chocolate supplies, so no doubt I'll have customers coming in right down to the wire. Plus I still have several dozen chocolate Santas to shift before then. 'We can drive up together straight after that.'

'Great. I'll do a one-pot supper and you can eat whenever you arrive.' Chantal rubs her hands excitedly. 'I can't wait. This will be the best Christmas ever.'

Christmas. It's just around the corner now and, for the first time in years, I'll be spending it as a loved-up person, not a sad spinster. It will be so magical. I simply can't wait.

Chapter Seventy

I'm exhausted when I get home. Emotionally and physically. Being mean is draining and quite depressing. I'd much rather be nice all the time. But, hopefully, tonight's activities will have served their purpose.

When I open the door to the flat, the scent of something wonderful cooking wafts its way towards me. In the living room, the table is set. There's an arrangement of red roses in the middle, flanked by two candles, already lit, which are giving the flat a mellow glow. Soft music fills the room. Normally, we eat on a tray on our laps in a slightly comatose manner. But not tonight. This is the full-on romantic works and I am beyond happy. Any thoughts of that horrible hotel room are behind me. I am home and I am loved. It makes me want to lie on the floor and weep with joy.

'Hey, Gorgeous,' Crush shouts from the kitchen. 'Dinner won't be long.'

I dump my coat and try to hide my wheelie case at the bottom of the coat rack. Most of the stuff will have to go back to Sirens unworn, but I might manage to get another wear of my revealing outfit because, tonight, lurrrrrve is clearly on the menu.

In the kitchen, Crush wraps his arms round me. 'Did you enjoy your cocktails with the girls?'

'Yes. It was lovely to go out with them. We don't do it enough.' You cannot believe how guilty I feel about what I've really been up to. Mega guilty. More guilty than anyone has ever been about anything. I'm surprised that it's not written all over my face. I try to deflect his attention from me. 'What have you been doing today?'

'Oh, not much.'

But I can tell that Crush is also being slightly shifty. That always makes me think the worst. 'What, though?'

He must see the anxiety in my eyes as he sighs and says, 'I did a bit of shopping.'

That makes me brighten up. 'Christmas shopping?'

'Sort of.'

'Ooo. Have you got me something nice?'

Crush grins. 'I think you'll like it.'

'I hope it's something completely impractical. If it's a food processor we could have an issue.'

'It's fair to say that it's nothing useful.'

'Good. I like the sound of it already.'

'If you can just untwine yourself from me for a moment, then I'll make sure that dinner isn't burning.'

'What are we having?'

'Beef bourguignon, followed by chocolate mousse.'

'Sounds fabulous.'

'Are you ready to eat?'

'Starving.'

'You've got five minutes for a quick run round the shower, if you like.'

'That would be great.' I think in honour of all this effort, I should slip into something distinctly more slinky.

He smacks my bottom. 'Hurry up, then.'

I salute him. 'Yes, sir.'

A bit furtively, I retrieve my wheelie case from its frankly inadequate hiding place, take it through to the bedroom and flick it open. As soon as I possibly can I must get Crush's camera out and download or upload those pictures or whatever. If I had another five minutes, I'd do it now, but I don't want to keep Crush waiting. Though that hard-gained photographic evidence needs to be hidden in a secret file that no one can ever find. I never want to be in a situation where I accidentally text one of those saucy snaps to my dad.

Jumping in the shower, I stand and let the soothing water flow over me. My eyes are as heavy as lead. I'm so tired that I hope I don't fall asleep during dinner. Crush has gone to such lovely trouble that I want to be the ideal companion.

'Lucy!' I hear him call.

'Coming.'

Before I can think better of it, I slip on my cheeky outfit again. He wanted to give me a surprise. Well, two can play at that game and this will give him a bit of a treat.

Crush is putting dinner on the table when I emerge from the bedroom. It gives me a slightly unwanted flashback to me doing this not too many hours ago. I also check that, this time, we don't have any unexpected guests that I wasn't aware of before I bare my all. That would be a surprise too far. When I see that it is, indeed, only Crush in the room, I emerge to lean on the door frame in my stilettos and a filmy bit of naughty nothingness, rocking my best seductive pose.

Crush glances up from the beef bourguignon and his eyes go out on stalks when he sees me. 'Wow.'

'I thought I'd slip into something more comfortable.'

'It actually looks as if you've pretty much slipped out of everything.'

I give him a twirl. 'You like?'

'I love.' He comes and holds me, running his fingers over my ridiculous wisps of lace. 'I'm actually going to struggle to concentrate on my food.'

'Me too. But that will make it all the more fun.'

'If you say so. Are you sure you're going to be warm enough?'

I look down at myself. I'm really not wearing very much at all and my nipples are certainly standing to attention. It would spoil the effect to go and get a cardigan, wouldn't it? 'Better turn the fire up a bit.'

Crush laughs and I sit at the table.

'Are you sure that you want to eat dressed like that?' he asks. 'I could put this back in the oven to keep warm and we can make love now.'

'I'm ravenous. Both for your body and your beef bourguignon. Besides, this is a bit thrilling. You'll be mad for me by the time we've eaten.'

'I'm mad for you now, Gorgeous.' But, nevertheless, he dishes out the dinner.

With the beef he's made horseradish mash and green beans and it's all very delicious. I don't think I've ever had such a very clever and wonderful boyfriend. I eat up every morsel and soon I'm bursting out of my flimsies even more.

'My,' Crush says, as he clears the plates, 'you were hungry.'

'I'll clear up.'

'Stay out of the kitchen, Lucy. I'm not sure that's fire-resistant material. You might go up in flames.'

'As if.'

A second later he brings back a plate of chocolates and sets them in the middle of the table.

'Yum. You've been buying chocolates from one of my competitors?'

'With very good reason.'

'They look amazing. Can't wait to taste one.' I reach out and Crush slaps my hand.

'They're for *after* dessert.' He wags a finger at me. 'Leave them alone. I just have one more thing to do to the mousse and I'll be back.'

I give them a longing look.

'*Leave*,' Crush reiterates. 'Those are *very* special chocolates.'

I laugh. 'You can trust me.'

'I'm warning you,' he says sternly as he heads back towards the kitchen. 'Leave them alone.'

I pout after him, giving him my butter-wouldn't-melt-in-my-mouth look.

He shakes his head, laughing.

Butter might not melt in my mouth, but chocolate would. And I'm feeling very naughty and a little bit reckless. So, despite my fervent promises, I need one of these *now* and am willing to take the consequences. I eye all the chocolates greedily and then take one from the plate – the biggest there is – and pop it into my mouth.

Chapter Seventy-One

'Stop!' Crush shouts and that makes me spin round in my seat. As I do, I bite down on the chocolate in my mouth and my teeth connect with something metallic. He's across the room in two strides. 'Don't swallow it!'

In my shock I swallow it whole. Of course I do.

'Oh, hell!' Crush says.

I want to tell him that it will be OK, but I can't as I'm starting to choke. Something is lodged in my throat. I cough and cough and cough, but nothing is happening. Whatever I've swallowed is very firmly stuck.

Crush bangs me on the back and I cough some more. But I still don't cough up the offending and potentially lethal chocolate. Now Crush tries standing behind me and performs his very own version of the Heimlich manoeuvre. My boobs burst out of my bra, but I'm still choking.

'Think of it as a fur ball,' he advises. 'Make a gravelly noise. Gurgh. Gurgh.' He does a passable impression of a cat sicking up a fur ball.

I make a similar gravelly noise, but nothing happens. No fur ball. No chocolate.

'This could be serious,' Crush says, alarmed. 'I'm taking you straight to hospital.'

I manage to indicate my clothing. Or lack of it.

'I'll get you a coat.'

I'd rather die than rock up in A&E looking like this. Then I realise that death might be a very real option, so I nod vigorously.

So he throws my coat over me and hustles me towards the door. There is blind panic in his eyes now and I'm starting to be more than a little concerned, too. Is this how it ends? With me choking on a chocolate while wearing skimpy under-wear?

Crush bundles me into his car. Thankfully, the hospital with an A&E department is a minute or two down the road. I'm still making cat fur ball hawking noises to try to dislodge it.

'Hold on, Gorgeous,' he says. 'We'll be there before you know it.'

So Crush drives like Lewis Hamilton in a bad mood, cutting up taxis and buses, until we reach the hospital. As there's nowhere else to park, he throws the car onto a double yellow line and rushes me inside.

'She's choking,' he shouts at the nearest nurse while I point helpfully at my throat and gasp.

'Straight through,' the man says and leads us into a curtained area. The burly nurse with a five o'clock shadow zips the curtain around us. 'Take your coat off.'

I shake my head vigorously. If it was a woman, I might think differently.

Crush snatches it from me.

Yet, if the nurse is surprised by my attire then he says nothing. The ultimate professional.

'She's swallowed a chocolate with a diamond ring hidden in it,' Crush says.

Have I? That makes me jolt upright and cough with surprise. The chocolate and diamond ring combo slides happily down my throat unaided.

'I've swallowed it,' I say hoarsely.

For some reason, Crush looks relieved. 'Are you all right?'

I nod weakly.

'Thanks,' Crush says to the nurse. Who frankly has done nothing, but now stands here looking bemused. 'I thought she was a goner.'

'Maybe getting down on one knee would have been the way to go, mate,' he suggests. 'But congratulations.'

'She hasn't said yes yet,' Crush notes.

'Yes,' I say.

Crush laughs and takes me in his arms. 'Really?'

'Yes.' Tears fill my eyes. 'Yes, please.'

The nurse looks embarrassed now. 'I'll give you a moment to get dressed, Miss.' He leaves, pulling the curtain behind him.

'So are we actually engaged?' I ask.

'Well,' Crush says. 'I had planned for the ring to be on your finger rather than in your digestive tract, but yes we are.'

I throw my arms round his neck. 'I love you. Even though you nearly choked me to death.'

'I might have known that it wouldn't be straightforward with you, Lucy Lombard. Nothing ever is. But, despite that – and possibly because of it – I would very much like to spend the rest of my life with you.'

We kiss in a manner that's probably not quite appropriate in a hospital.

When we break apart, I say, 'What about the ring? How am I going to get that back?'

Crush grins at me. 'There's only going to be one way, I'm afraid, Gorgeous.'

When I realise what that way might be, all I can say is, 'Oh.'

Chapter Seventy-Two

So the nice nurse advised me to take some laxatives and wait for nature to take its course. I have done just that. I'm lying in bed, unable to speak as my throat is swollen due to all the coughing, waiting for *things* to happen.

Crush phoned Autumn as soon as it was light and asked her to take over at Chocolate Heaven today. Bless her, she was not only concerned for my welfare but selflessly agreed to help out. Honestly, where would I be without my girls?

'Anything yet?' Crush comes back into the bedroom.

I shake my head and whisper, 'No. I'll take a couple more.'

'You've probably had enough.' He gives me a worried look.

But I swallow two more laxatives. I want that diamond ring out of me and I want it out now.

'Be patient. It might take a while,' he advises as if he knows about these things.

I wish it would hurry up as I want to be wearing it on my finger. After scrubbing it thoroughly in bleach, of course. Bleach doesn't dissolve diamonds, does it?

'I'm going to pop out to the chemist and see if they can give me something to help soothe your throat.'

'Thank you,' I manage to croak.

'We don't want both ends suffering at once.'

'No.'

'I'll be half an hour at most. Anything else you want?'

I shake my head.

Crush comes to kiss me. 'Text me if you think of anything. Love you.'

I lie still until I hear the sound of the front door slamming then, as soon as I'm sure that Crush has left, I jump up and grab the camera out of my wheelie bag. I need to upload the compromising photographs of me with Tarak and file them for safekeeping. Sometimes Crush takes his camera to work and there's no way that I want these doing the rounds of Targa's offices. They need to be deleted from the memory card as soon as humanly possible.

Crush's desk is set up in the corner of the living room and, as we're currently sharing the computer, I need to make sure that I bury this deep. As I sit down my stomach starts to gurgle. Ah, finally, something seems to be moving. I can't wait to see this diamond ring as I didn't get a glimpse of it before I ate it. What a nice surprise it will be. Once cleaned.

I hook up the camera and upload the images. Wow. They look pretty good. Pretty good in the sense that they're quite candid shots, perfect for blackmail purposes should they ever be needed. I do look quite startlingly slutty in my underwear, though. No wonder that poor male nurse couldn't look me in the eye last night. The one of me jutting my breasts towards the camera over Tarak's head is particularly lewd. Blimey. I can hardly bear to look at it myself. Still, I did what I had to do, all in a good cause. I hope that Tarak now stops coming on to Nadia and lets her get on with her work and her life.

Then I'm gripped by the most alarming sensation. It feels

as if a whirlwind is whipping through my guts. 'Oh, no. No, no, no. Not now!'

I don't even have time to unhook the camera from the computer before I have to make a frantic dash for the bathroom. Really, Mo Farah could not have covered my living room any quicker. I make the loo just in time. Thank goodness. Who knows what damage an internally lodged diamond could have done? Explosive is the only word I can think of to describe my current situation. My head is in my hands, ready to weep with relief, when I hear the front door open.

'I'm back,' Crush shouts. 'Are you OK?'

Oh, no. I've left the photographs open on the computer screen. No, no, no! How can Aiden fail to see them?

'Yes,' I call back, heart pounding. 'In the loo!'

Then I hear him say, 'What the hell . . .' and I know that he's seen the very thing that I didn't want him to see.

The bottom might be about to drop out of my world but, thankfully, the world has stopped dropping out of my bottom for a moment. I jump from the loo and rush into the living room.

Crush is stood frozen in front of the desktop, mouth open, eyes agog. In front of him is the worst photograph – the particularly lurid image of me pushing my boobs towards the camera above Tarak's shiny, bald head.

'I can explain,' I say.

He turns to me, ashen. 'This, I can't wait to hear.'

'It was for Nadia,' I tell him. 'Her brother-in-law has been coming on to her at work and she didn't know how to stop him, so I thought—'

'*You* thought?'

'Well, it was sort of my plan.' It sounds like a bad one now. 'We lured him to a hotel and then, when he thought he was about to get down to it with Nadia and me, Chantal took some photographs.'

His jaw tight, he asks through clenched teeth, 'So why isn't Nadia in the photo?'

'Because I was the only one wearing . . . um . . . lingerie.' His face darkens now and I realise that might not be what he wanted to hear. 'The other girls were supposed to be in their skimpies too, but they all bottled it.'

'And you didn't?'

'No.'

His jaw tightens. 'At some point they probably realised that it was a really stupid, stupid idea.'

He looks as if he might explode. I don't think I've ever really seen Crush angry before – not *really* angry – but he looks as if he might be now.

'I'm not saying it was a *great* plan,' I offer.

'I don't know quite what to say.' Crush rubs his hands over his face. 'I thought I could cope with you, Lucy. I thought all this ditzy shit would be fun. You might be infuriating, but you're also kind of endearing.'

That's good, isn't it?

'I also think I've handled the fact that your ex-boyfriend is always somewhere lurking in the background remarkably well.'

'Marcus is out of my life,' I plead.

Crush holds up a hand. 'But this,' he says, pointing at the screen. 'I never know what you're going to do next. Why did you think that getting naked with another man in a hotel bedroom was ever going to be anything but a seriously bad idea?'

'I'm not quite naked,' I counter.

'You're probably *worse* than naked. Look at yourself.'

To be honest, I don't really need to.

'You liked it well enough last night,' I point out a little petulantly.

'But I thought it was for my eyes only.'

'I did it for Nadia,' I say apologetically.

'And what do you do for me?' he asks, bleakly. 'When do *I* ever come in the equation? At what point do you ever consider what *I* would think? Why didn't you tell me you were doing this? Did you think you were going to hide it from me for ever?'

'Yes,' I confess.

'What the eye doesn't see the heart doesn't grieve over?' He paces up and down while blowing out ragged, unhappy breaths. 'Well, I have seen it and I am grieving.'

I don't know how we've come to this. Last night I was an engaged person, albeit with a slightly indisposed diamond ring. Now Crush seems to be questioning whether he wants to be with me at all.

Panic starts to rise in me. 'How can I make this right?'

He shakes his head, seemingly robbed of speech.

I'm on the verge of tears. 'I'm sorry. Really sorry.'

'You're not, Lucy. You're only sorry that I found out. You would have been quite happy to keep this secret from me.' His expression is agonised and I realise that this is more than just a hissy fit. This is deadly serious. 'I thought I wanted you to be my wife . . .' His words tail away.

My voice is so quiet that even I can hardly hear it when I ask, 'But now?'

He stares at me levelly and the love that I normally see in his eyes simply isn't there. It's gone. Perhaps for good. And it's all my fault.

'I need to leave,' Crush says.

'No.' I grab his arm. 'Don't do this. We can talk about it.'

'I need to be alone, Lucy. I need to think about this.'

He goes into the bedroom and I follow him. Crush gets a bag out of the wardrobe and throws in some clothes.

I can't believe that he's really leaving.

'Is this because I swallowed my engagement ring? Are you cross about that?'

'Oh, Lucy.' He looks at me again. This time with something approaching pity. 'Grow up.'

'I'll try,' I promise. 'I'll try very hard. I'll never do anything stupid ever again. Never. Cross my heart and hope to die.'

His shoulders sag and, for a brief moment, I think he might change his mind. Then there is an almighty rumbling and groaning from my stomach.

'Oh, no.' From my experience of a few minutes ago, I know exactly what's going to happen and I know that I have only a couple of seconds to make it to the loo. 'Don't go,' I beg. 'Please don't go. Wait for me and we can talk it through. But I have to dash. This might be my ring.'

Before he can speak, I bolt for the bathroom. As I sit on the loo waiting for my diamond ring to make an appearance, I hear the wardrobe door close, then the bedroom door.

'Aiden,' I shout. 'I love you!'

But I hear the front door close and even though I sit on the loo and wait patiently for nearly an hour, until both my bottom and my heart are numb, he doesn't come back.

Chapter Seventy-Three

Nadia was dreading seeing Tarak after the weekend. She had half-expected him to text or call her to say that she needn't come back into work, but she'd heard nothing. Perhaps that was a good sign.

'Come on, Lewis,' she said. 'Auntie Autumn will be here to collect you in a minute. Have you brushed your teeth?'

'Yes, Mummy.'

'Coat on then.'

She followed Lewis through to the hall and handed his coat down to him from the rack. As she did there was a knock at the door. Lewis jumped into Autumn's arms the minute she was through the door.

'Whoa,' Autumn said. 'You are *so* getting too big for this.' She lowered him to the ground. 'Or I'm getting too old.'

'Hey.' Nadia hugged her friend in a more sedate manner.

'Are you all right?' Autumn asked.

'I'm fine,' Nadia said. 'Just a bit tired.'

'You and me both. I'm dead on my feet. I had to step in at the last minute to work at Chocolate Heaven yesterday.'

'Oh?'

'Crush proposed to Lucy on Saturday night . . .'

'Really?' Nadia brightened instantly. 'That's fabulous. I'm so pleased for Lucy.'

'. . . but there's more. He put the ring inside a chocolate and Lucy nearly choked on it.'

'Nooo!' Nadia laughed. 'I shouldn't find that funny, but it's *so* like Lucy. Is she OK?'

'She's fine now. I believe she was permanently attached to the loo hoping for it to reappear, but other than that unharmed. I'll catch up with her later and see how she's faring.' Autumn lowered her voice so that Lewis couldn't hear. 'Make sure that you take it easy today. There was *far* too much excitement on Saturday.'

'Yeah.' Nadia rolled her eyes. 'I still can't believe we actually did that.'

'No regrets?'

'Lots,' she admitted. 'It was complete madness. I can't believe that we let Lucy talk us into it.'

Autumn laughed. 'There is no one quite like her. It was a rush at the time, but it's probably catching up with you. Will you be OK going into work?'

'I confess that I'm more than a bit nervous.'

'I'm sure that Tarak will be fine. He seemed very contrite. But you know where we are. Any trouble, just call one of us.'

'You're a lifesaver, Autumn.' She kissed her friend's cheek.

'Come on, Lewis,' Autumn said. 'We've got a date with the park.'

'The *proper* park,' Lewis observed.

'Yes.' Autumn smiled. 'Normal service resumed.'

Tarak was in the shop when she arrived and Nadia felt the urge to turn and run. It was only that there were a couple of customers that stopped her from bolting down Brick Lane.

'Nadia,' Tarak said, tightly. 'These ladies could do with your help.'

'I'll be right there.' She smiled at the customers, who were leafing through the racks. 'Give me a second to take my coat off.'

In the grubby staff room, she hung up her coat and shook out her hair. When she turned Tarak was standing right behind her and she jumped.

'You didn't have to do that, you know.' He avoided looking directly at her. 'You could have said no.'

'I felt that I had. You weren't listening.'

He sucked in a breath and she was worried that he was blocking the way back out to the shop. There was just the two of them in here. What could she do if he decided to make things difficult for her?

She summoned up her courage and said, 'Is it going to be hard to work together, Tarak? If it is then I'll leave now and you can explain it to Anita.'

'It'll be fine,' he said. Though he didn't sound convinced. 'It was a misunderstanding. Nothing more. Just make sure that those photos never see the light of day.'

'They won't,' she promised.

Tarak flicked a thumb back towards the shop. 'The ladies are looking for outfits for a Christmas party.'

'I'll go and help them. Straight away. Is Anita coming in today?'

'Later,' he said. 'I'll be out of your hair soon. I'm going to the warehouse to get some stock.'

'We're family, Tarak,' she said as he went to walk away. 'For Anita's sake, we should be able to get along. In time we could even be friends. I'm prepared to give it a go, if you are. Let's forgive and forget?'

He nodded and said, non-committally, 'Let's see how it goes.' However, she was relieved to see that he didn't look quite so cross as he had a moment ago.

Chapter Seventy-Four

I'm sick with worry. So sick that I have eaten no chocolate this morning. None. I fear I might fade away to dust if Crush doesn't return my calls. I know the fashion is to play it cool, but I have left him a hundred begging messages on his voice-mail and I've texted him a million times, too.

But nothing. No reply.

Sod it. I am going to have some chocolate. Calories are the best way to mend a broken heart. And heartbroken I very much am.

I was engaged for such a ridiculously short time and now I'm not. To make matters worse, I spent nearly all day yesterday on the loo and still didn't find my diamond ring. It has gone, whizzing down the deepest, darkest, smelliest sewers of north London, never to be seen again.

That has to be worth a chocolate brownie or two. Then I think of how I spent yesterday and my appetite for anything brown and squidgy suddenly goes. I have a Santa cupcake instead.

I texted the girls 'CHOCOLATE EMERGENCY!' and, in adherence to our sacred code, they're all coming in as soon as they can. Quite frankly, they can't get here soon enough. I need their collective shoulders to cry on before I fall apart completely. If I wasn't the only operative here, then I might have stayed in bed with the duvet over my head wallowing in my pain. As it is, I've had to come and face my public. The chocolate show must go on.

Chocolate Heaven is full and I've had a morning filling a mammoth number of orders for Christmas cakes and novelties. Alexandra is run off her feet.

They say that bad things come in threes and, of course, as well as losing short-term fiancé and diamond ring, there is also the small matter of the sale of Chocolate Heaven hanging over my head. I can hardly bear to think about it, but I'm aware that time is marching on. If I'm going to do anything, then I have to do it soon. But what?

While I'm considering this dilemma, I hear the roar of a throaty engine as a red Ferrari pulls up outside the front door. Marcus. Make that four bad things.

Seconds later, he strides in, shaking snow from his hair in the manner of a screen idol rather than a sneaky, low-life, ex-boyfriend.

'Get out,' I say. 'You're barred.'

'I've only come to wish you merry Christmas, Lucy,' he says earnestly. 'Then I'll be on my way. I'll be out of your life for ever.'

At that I burst into tears.

All my customers look up from their cake and coffee.

'I'm sorry,' I say, loudly and snottily. 'I'm having a bad time. A *very* bad time. Go back to your beverages.'

Marcus is round the counter in a flash. Sometimes I'll swear that he moves like a vampire as I'm in his arms before I know what's happening.

'Shush, shush,' he soothes. 'Everything will be all right. I'm here now.'

And, for a moment, just a moment, it feels so good to be held. He passes me a tissue before I get snot on his suit.

'What's all this about?'

'Aiden has left me,' I sob.

'Really?' Marcus doesn't look as if he's sharing my disappointment.

'He found some photos on his computer with me in my underwear with another man,' I confess.

Marcus laughs out loud now and I whack him. 'It's not funny.'

'It is,' he insists. 'What were you up to? It doesn't sound like you at all.'

'You don't need to know,' I say. 'But it's not what you think. It was your fault, too. Aiden says that you're always there in our relationship.'

'I like to think so,' Marcus chips in.

'But you're not. I don't think of you at all. Ever. It was the Bruges episode, the ball and the attempted snog and the canal swim. Aiden's had enough of me being silly.'

Marcus looks into my eyes, his smile gone. 'Then he can't love you as much as I do.'

'Oh, bog off, Marcus.' I weep noisily again.

Some of the customers hurriedly finish their drinks and leave. 'Come back,' I call after them. 'Don't leave me.' Even my customers are fickle.

'They'll be back.' Marcus strokes my cheek. 'Don't you worry.'

'Perhaps this is the way to keep Chocolate Heaven – lose all of Clive and Tristan's customers and then they won't be able to sell it after all.' There is a glimmer of hope in my despair.

'How's that going?'

'I don't know,' I admit. 'I'm taking the head-in-the-sand approach.'

'Something will work out.'

Everyone keeps saying that, but what?

'I brought you a Christmas present,' Marcus says and he produces a beautifully gift-wrapped box from his pocket.

'I don't want a Christmas present from you.'

'That's not really in keeping with the spirit of the season,' he chides.

Reluctantly, I take it.

'Open it now,' he urges.

Accepting that resistance is futile, I tear off the pretty paper. It's jewellery. That much is obvious from the shape of the box. Sure enough, when I open it, inside there's a stunning bracelet. 'Tell me that's not real diamonds.'

'It is,' Marcus says. 'Nothing but the best for my Lucy.'

'I'm not *your* Lucy,' I remind him.

'Technicalities,' he says.

'It's very lovely, Marcus.' Though it does make me pine more for my diamond ring that's down the toilet. 'However, I can't accept this. It's too much.'

This is worth hundreds, if not thousands of pounds. If it was a box of chocolates or some smellies – even posh ones – then I might feel differently. But with this bracelet comes great responsibility and great indebtedness. And I don't want to be indebted to Marcus.

Again, using his vampire moves, he takes the bracelet and clips it around my wrist before I know what he's doing.

'There.' He pats it in a very proprietorial way.

It does look extraordinarily beautiful.

'I want you to have it.'

'Thank you, Marcus. But I want you to take it back.' I unclip it from my wrist. I am a woman who is not destined to be adorned in diamonds. Gently, I lay it back in the box.

'Don't be alone at Christmas,' he says. 'Let me take you

380

away. We could go somewhere fabulous, the Bahamas or the Seychelles. Or we could get a cosy place here, the New Forest or somewhere.'

'I'm spending Christmas with all the girls. Chantal has fixed us up with a cottage in the Lake District.'

'Oh.' He looks crestfallen.

Ha! Take that, you and your plans to whisk me away somewhere wonderful.

'There wouldn't be a little space for me?' Marcus asks meekly.

'No,' I say. 'There's definitely no room at the inn for you, Marcus Canning. They'd kill me if I even suggested it.'

'Does that mean it crossed your mind?'

I sigh tiredly. It's exhausting trying to keep one step ahead of Marcus. 'You should go now,' I say. 'I have customers to alienate and a broken heart to nurse.'

'I love you.' Marcus's eyes are bleak. 'I love you more than you can ever know. One day, Lucy Lombard, I'll make you realise just how much.'

Marcus kisses me tenderly and then turns to leave. At the door, he looks back at me and blows another kiss. A second later, he's in his Ferrari and roaring away.

It's then that I notice he's left the beautiful diamond bracelet behind.

Chapter Seventy-Five

I'm still in a state of shock when the rest of the Chocolate Lovers' Club arrive just as I'm closing up for the day. When the last of the customers have left, I get us all drinks and a plateful of treats – some leftover mincemeat cupcakes with brandy icing, a few with candy canes on top and there are brownies that I can't put out again tomorrow as they'll be a bit past their best by then. Much like me. We sit in our favourite spot by the window.

It's only a short time before Christmas now and the weather is determined to be as seasonal as possible. We very rarely have snow in London, but again today, there are a few flakes in the air.

'Those brownies need eating today,' I say and the girls oblige me by taking one each. 'Where's Stacey?'

'She said she was busy,' Chantal says. 'Couldn't make it.'

'Oh. Is everything all right?'

'I think so.' Chantal shrugs. 'Perhaps I'll pop in on the way home to see her.'

'We should toast you, Lucy,' Nadia says, lifting her coffee cup. 'Autumn tells us that you and Crush are engaged.'

'That was yesterday,' I sigh. 'A lot can happen in a day.'

'It can in your life,' Chantal agrees.

'He proposed during dinner on Saturday night,' I tell them, filling them in on the whole story. 'Well, not quite. We didn't get that far. He'd hidden the ring in a chocolate and I ate it.'

They all fall about laughing.

'I could have died,' I point out, tearfully. 'The ring got stuck in my throat. He had to take me to hospital and everything.' I flush as I admit, 'I was wearing the same skimpies as I had on in the hotel.'

'Oh, no!' Autumn says.

More laughter. Guffawing, even. I don't think that my friends are taking this as seriously as they might.

'I was mortified. Then I had to take loads of laxatives to try to . . . um . . . *retrieve* . . . the diamond ring.' My eyes fill with tears again. 'I spent most of Sunday peering down the loo at my own poo looking for something sparkly in it.'

The girls exchange a look and, as one, put down their brownies.

'Sorry.'

'You can get another ring,' Autumn says, soothingly. 'It's not the end of the world.'

'It is,' I sniffle. 'I don't even have a fiancé now. Crush left me.'

'Have I missed something?' Chantal asks, frowning.

'He saw the photos of me in the hotel with Tarak and was so angry. I'd put them up on the computer, then had to dash to the loo. I didn't have time to hide them.' I sniff back my tears. 'I've never seen him as cross. He said he'd had enough of my stupidity. He thinks I'm a liability.'

Chantal frowns. 'Crush said that?'

'Not in so many words. I'm paraphrasing. But it all adds up to the same thing. He packed a bag and walked out. I don't even know where he's gone.'

'He'll be back,' Nadia assures me. 'He loves you.'

'I'm not so sure. It sounded pretty final.' My lower lip wobbles. 'I have no fiancé and soon I'll have no job.'

'Call him,' Chantal suggests, as if I haven't tried a million times.

'He's not answering my calls. This really is it.'

'Lucy, my love, don't worry,' Autumn says. 'When he's had time to cool down and think about it, he'll come home.'

'I hope so.'

'He won't be able to stay away,' she adds.

But it's Marcus who can't stay away. Aiden is so much more resilient, more determined. I'm the one who needs him more than he needs me. The thought nearly has me in tears again.

'You'll both laugh about it in time,' Nadia assures me. 'Just as you have with all the other crazy things you've done.'

The girls fall silent and exchange nervous glances. We all realise that there have been quite a lot of very silly incidents that I've subjected Crush to over the time we've been together. And this one could be the straw that breaks the camel's back.

'Have Clive and Tristan been in touch?' Chantal asks, clearly in an attempt to distract me from my woes. But there are more woes lining up and we just go straight into another one.

'Not yet. But it's only a matter of time.' I put my head in my hands. I feel like a sitting duck, here for everyone to take pot shots at. How depressing. I have no idea what to do for the best. Then, of course, I realise there's only one thing for it. 'Pass me a cake. Not a brownie.' Thankfully, my appetite has come back with a vengeance and is fully embracing the concept of comfort eating. That's one thing going my way then. Excellent.

'I could lend you the money, Lucy,' Autumn blurts out. 'Or I could buy Chocolate Heaven and we could go into business together. I don't know why I didn't think of it until now. I have a hundred grand sitting in my bank account from my parents. Now that Addison and I have split up, I'm not going to give it to him to squander. My parents would be just as happy if I used it to buy this place. In fact, they'd probably prefer it. No taint of scandal with a chocolate café.'

For a moment there is a spark of hope. 'Could we really do that?'

Autumn shrugs. 'I don't know, but we should give it a go. Surely? You and I could work well together. How much is it?'

I tell her.

Everyone round the table takes a deep gulp. It's a lot of money by any reckoning.

'Wow,' Autumn says when she's regained her power of speech. 'It might not even be enough as a deposit. The mortgage would be colossal.' She looks slightly deflated. 'Who knew that commercial property cost so much?'

'This place has such potential, though,' I tell her. 'The flat upstairs is huge and that's currently standing empty. You could move into it, rent it out or even use it to expand the business. There are days when some extra tables would be most welcome.' Listen to me talking as if it might actually happen.

'Let me see what I can do,' Autumn says. 'I'll see if I can borrow enough to be in with a chance. I'm reluctant to ask my parents for any more but, if push came to shove, then I could.'

That sets me off crying again. 'You'd do that for me?'

'Yes. And for me too. I'm also out of a job now. Addison has cut my sessions at the Stolford Centre and I've nothing else on the horizon.' She looks quite animated now. 'This could be a really great move.'

Suddenly, it seems like a wonderful suggestion.

'It's a brilliant plan,' Chantal confirms. 'Surely Clive and Tristan would rather sell to Autumn than anyone else? Lucy has already proved herself to be a brilliant manager. It keeps it in the family then.'

'I'll call them,' Autumn says. 'Then tomorrow I'll get onto the estate agents, see what I'd have to do. Don't give up hope just yet, Lucy.'

That gives a lift to my tired heart. One day, I'd like everything in my life to run smoothly and to stay that way for more than twenty-four hours.

Chapter Seventy-Six

Autumn dished out the Chinese takeaway. It was her first proper date night with Miles. Florence was with her mother this evening and she had no babysitting duties for Lewis. They'd been planning to go to a restaurant, but Autumn was just so tired that she couldn't really face it. All she wanted to do was curl up on the couch with Miles, so she'd called him and asked if he'd mind if they stayed in instead. It was Miles who'd volunteered to pick up some food on the way over.

Nadia had collected Lewis an hour ago, but she'd seemed very distracted. Autumn hoped that everything was all right in the shop with Tarak and she wasn't hiding anything from them. She'd find time to sit down and have a proper chat with her tomorrow.

'Can I do anything to help?' Miles asked.

'You could open some wine. Or there are a couple of beers in the fridge if you prefer.'

He came and slipped strong arms round her waist. Autumn turned to kiss him. 'I hoped that we'd be just like this together,' she said.

'Me too.'

She rested her head against his. 'I feel like I've known you for years.'

Miles laughed. 'Then I'll have to come up with a couple of surprises. I don't want to be like old slippers just yet.'

'That's not what I mean. You're easy company to be with, that's all.'

She'd heard nothing from Addison and hadn't really expected to as they had nothing to tie them together now. Autumn was sad not to be working for the charity anymore, but she'd find something else to do in that area when she'd decided where her future lay. For now she wanted to pour her attentions into the possibility of acquiring Chocolate Heaven for her and Lucy to run. Then there was the matter of her new relationship to concentrate on. This one felt right. Very right. It was only really when you met the person that you were meant to be with that you realised how wrong the others had been.

They pulled apart and Miles fixed them some drinks. She put the Chinese food on a tray and took it through to the living room, spreading it out on the coffee table. She'd switched off the main light earlier and the room was lit only by the fairy lights from the tree. It looked sparkly and warm. On the mantelpiece, she had a few festive candles and lit those too. She didn't think the place had ever looked more romantic.

'These are all the DVDs I have,' Autumn said, indicating her bookcase. 'Not the most extensive selection and many of them are Disney or Pixar films for Lewis.'

'Florence would be in heaven.'

'Next time I'm babysitting for Lewis, we'll do a film night for them both. Get some popcorn in.'

'That would be great.' Miles rifled through the shelves. 'What about this one?' He held up *Love, Actually*. 'This looks suitably festive.'

'You don't mind a chick flick?'

'Love them. You'll have to cope with seeing a grown man cry.'

'I have tissues,' Autumn said. 'But let's eat first before it gets cold.'

They tucked into the food. She'd let Miles choose and he'd remembered that she was a vegetarian and had chosen some lovely dishes. The mushroom chow mein and the vegetable pancake rolls were a big hit.

'You've heard nothing from the adoption sites?' he asked.

'Not yet. I can only keep hoping.'

'I'll keep my fingers crossed for you.'

'You'd be OK with it?' she ventured. 'If my daughter does come back into my life? It's so important to me.'

'Of course. She's a part of you,' he said. 'Eventually, I hope she'll be a part of *us*.'

That would be nice. She'd always wanted a family of her own and Autumn could finally see it happening with this man. It was clear that he adored his own daughter and there was no doubt that he'd want more children in the future.

'I have one other problem,' she said. 'My parents.'

He waited for her to explain.

'They're very rich,' she continued.

He laughed. 'How is that a problem?'

'They have very little to do with me unless it's to give me money,' she said. 'They have taken hands-off parenting to the extreme. They always have.'

'That's a shame.'

'I rely on them too heavily,' Autumn admitted. 'Even at my age, I'm not independent.' She hadn't yet shared with Miles the prospect of her buying a business. 'They still have a hold over me.'

'None of us is perfect,' Miles said. 'My parents are suffocatingly nice. They're well-meaning and don't have a nasty bone in their bodies, but they'll try to kill you with kindness.'

'There are worse ways to go.'

'They live for Florence and they're used to me leaning on them heavily too. But I'm sure we'll negotiate the inadequacies of our families together.'

'I hope so.' She sighed with contentment. 'I can't wait for Christmas now. I'm so glad that you and Florence can join us in the Lake District.'

'That's something I haven't broken to my parents yet,' he confessed. 'I'm putting it off for as long as I can.'

'If it's a problem, we can work round it. Don't feel obliged to come.'

He hugged her tightly. 'I wouldn't miss it for the world. We're in this together now, Autumn.'

Next year was looking as if it could be amazing. She was finally beginning to let go of Rich, she'd started her search for Willow, Miles and Florence were in her life and there was even a chance that she could be the owner of Chocolate Heaven. The future was definitely looking up.

Chapter Seventy-Seven

I feel like I'm going out of my mind. If I didn't work in a chocolate shop and café, I really don't know how I'd be coping. I would have to stockpile Mars bars or Double Deckers or something.

I've been calling Crush like a mad thing, but he hasn't replied at all. All my texts just vanish into the ether.

It's over between us. There's no doubt about it.

I have a dark chocolate truffle to soothe my pain. Then another.

Even though it's very, very nearly Christmas, Aiden Holby has hardened his heart against me. Bugger.

A giggling couple, arms entwined, come to the counter to pay their bill. They've been slobbering all over each other while they drank their coffee and ate their chocolate-chip muffins. They were practically having sex on the coffee table. I hate them. I hate them both. Probably her more than him, actually, because she has a lovely, lovely boyfriend who's just bought her a Christmas reindeer and I have not.

'That will be twenty-two pounds please.'

They pay up and go out into the snow still giggling and clinging to each other tightly.

Nothing in this world is fair. Nothing.

You take one set of risqué photographs in a hotel room with a total stranger and your relationship goes up in smoke. Pfft.

Most of Crush's clothes are still at the flat and he hasn't come back for any of his belongings. So all he has is what he left with. I wonder where he's staying. Perhaps he's gone back to an ex-girlfriend and thrown himself onto her mercy and her sofa. That would be Marcus's first port of call. Then I think that I will not tarnish Crush's image by thinking of him in the same sentence as Marcus. I'm the one who has let Aiden down, not the other way round.

Autumn comes in and I pin a smile on my face. She looks nearly as happy as the couple who just left, but this time I'm not jealous. My friend is as loved up as loved up can be and I'm pleased for her. It's about time.

She's wearing a smart black coat over a well-cut black suit and has her mad mass of auburn curls tamed and pinned in a sophisticated up-do. Autumn – *our* Autumn – is sporting a briefcase and is wearing stilettos. The boho hippy chick has turned into Anna Wintour. I have clearly slipped into an alternative reality.

'Blimey,' I say, mouth gaping. 'You look like a supermodel who works in the city. I didn't know you even possessed clothes like that.'

'I don't. But my mother does,' she admits. 'I raided her wardrobe while she was at work.' Autumn admires herself in the glass of the counter. 'Mummy has two dozen suits in there that all look exactly like this. She'll never miss one.'

'And the coat?'

'Same.' She slips it off and gives me a twirl, so I can get a proper eyeful of the suit.

'Wow. Well, I'm impressed.'

'I hope the bank manager will be, too.'

'No!'

'Yes! I've got an appointment with the bank this morning,' she adds joyfully. 'I'm only stopping by for a quick coffee and a pep talk.'

'I can give you accounts, spreadsheets, stuff like that to take with you,' I tell her as I make her coffee.

'Perfect. I'm sorry I've not given you more warning, but I thought I should strike while the iron's hot. He only had one appointment open today, so I grabbed it with both hands.'

'Good girl.'

'Now I'm terrified.'

'I'm sure they'll be able to tell instantly that it's a great business.'

'It is. But it's a lot of money, Lucy. A frightening amount. I'm sure I can get more backing from my parents, but I'd rather not if I don't have to.'

'I can understand that.' I hand her drink over the counter. 'I have to admit that I'm terrified at the amount of debt you'd be taking on.'

'I know,' she says. 'It is quite daunting.'

But, if Autumn doesn't do this, then what do I do? I can see me ending up working as a temporary secretary again. God forbid. I might even end up back at Targa! Aaargh. Except, of course, that I've been banned from working there ever again and I'd have to torture myself by seeing Crush every day. And I've been there, done that.

So pretty much everything is resting on Autumn now.

'Thanks for trying to do this,' I say. 'I really mean it. I wish I could come with you.'

'I'd love you there, too. As the manager, you'd be the best one to put our case to him. It's just the timing that's off. You can't leave this place and we need to strike while the iron's hot. I'm sure Chocolate Heaven won't stay on the market for long. As soon as we have approval from the bank, we can put an offer in to Clive and Tristan.'

'Do you think they'd give us mates' rates?'

'It's their future, Lucy. They'll need all the money they can get for it. I think I'll have to be prepared to pay top whack if there are other people in the picture. My hands are tied until I get a yes from the bank.'

'Just thinking about it makes me feel giddy.'

'Apart from the money side, I'm excited about it,' she admits. 'I really believe that we could do great things together.'

We both have a little jump up and down and a restrained 'squeeee'.

'We should call Clive and Tristan.'

'Already done. I've left a dozen messages for them but, as yet, they haven't called back. I put one on Clive's phone just a few minutes ago to say that I was hoping to put in an offer.'

I clap my hands, unable to contain my glee.

'Hold the fort here for me while I run into the office and get some printouts for you.' So while Autumn takes my side of the counter, I sprint up the stairs and get busy with the computer – dashing off bank statements and sales figures like a thing possessed.

Minutes later, I have a sheaf of paper in my arms for her.

'Wow,' she says. 'Instead of cuddling up on the sofa with Miles last night, I could have done with studying this lot.'

'How's it going there?'

'Great,' she says. 'I really like him. A lot.'

We grin goofily at each other.

'Wedding bells?'

'Lucy!' She looks outraged. 'We've barely started dating.'

I stare her down.

'But yes, maybe.'

'Hurrah!' I say. 'At least someone's love life is going well. You're our only hope at the moment.'

'Still nothing from Crush?' She looks at me with pity. Stupid Lucy who can't keep a boyfriend.

'No.' I shake my head. 'I'm dead to him.'

'He'll come round,' Autumn assures me. 'He loves you too much to stay away. It must have been quite a shock for him. Give him a bit of time.'

'I hope it was worth it.' I get a flashback of those terrible, revealing photographs and shudder. 'Do you know if your dastardly plan worked? Has Tarak still been bothering Nadia?'

'I don't know. She looked a bit distracted when she picked up Lewis last night but she clearly wasn't in the mood to talk. Obviously, there's something on her mind. I'll try to catch her later for a chat.'

'I'll put a box of chocolates together for you to take to the bank manager.' My future depends on this meeting so I hope he's not someone who's allergic to chocolate or on a diet or something ridiculous like that. It would be just my flipping luck. As Autumn already looks terrified enough for the both of us, I decide not to share these fears with her. Instead, I offer, 'He'll be putty in your hands.'

'I do hope so.'

I get a gift box and fill it with a dozen of our very best chocolates. If that doesn't work, then nothing will.

Autumn knocks back the last of her coffee. 'I'd better get a move on. Wish me luck.'

I give her the biggest hug I can manage. 'Here. Take emergency chocolate for yourself, too.' I press a bar of single plantation Madagascar into her hand along with her gift box for the bank manager. These are the best chocolates we have, the most expensive. This is what the occasion warrants. She puts them into her briefcase along with the papers.

Hugging her again for good measure, I say, 'Autumn Fielding, businesswoman extraordinaire, go and knock them dead.'

I brush down her suit which, for once, isn't only *not* made of cheesecloth, but looks suspiciously like Armani. *Proper* Armani! I help her on with her coat.

'I'll do my best.' Then, in her finest Terminator voice, she says, 'I'll be back.'

Watching her go out into the cold and snow with only a posh coat and a designer suit for protection, my heart is in my mouth.

Chapter Seventy-Eight

Nadia stood in the kitchen, her fingers shaking. She held a cheque in her hands and it was for an astonishing amount of money. Finally, the insurance had paid out for her claim after Toby's death. Thank God that they had eventually deemed it to be an accident and not suicide.

With this amount of money, she could pay off the mortgage, move to somewhere smarter, somewhere that didn't hold such terribly painful memories. If they lived in a nicer area, then she could get Lewis into a better school. They could go to a place where they could breathe clean, fresh air rather than the London fog of fumes and pollution. It opened a whole world of possibilities to her that had previously been closed. It was making her dizzy to think about it.

At the table, Lewis was eating his supper, unaware that something life-changing had happened. He ate his spaghetti bolognese, humming happily and chattering half to himself. She loved him more than life itself and she wanted him to have the most wonderful childhood. This money made sure that she would be able to provide it. What she did now would shape his future.

Autumn would be devastated if they moved away from London, though. Lewis was like a nephew to her – more than that – and she saw him virtually every day. Could Nadia do that to her dearest friend? Would she want Lewis separated from Autumn? She was a very big part of her son's life. Nadia thought that she'd have to consider all this very carefully. It was the first time in her life that she was free, and financially able, to do exactly as she wanted.

She could look for another job, too. Nadia enjoyed her job at TD Fashions and working with her sister, but she'd been foolish to think that she could carry on working there after what had happened. There was simply too much unspoken tension between her and Tarak and, instead of looking forward to going to work, she now dreaded it. Her day was spent feeling as if she was walking on a tightrope. The new year would bring change on many fronts.

The doorbell rang and she went to answer it. These days she always looked through the security spy hole in case it was another unexpected visit from her brother-in-law. This time it was Jacob standing at the other side of the door, which filled her both with relief and trepidation.

'Hey,' he said when she opened the door. 'Is this a good time?'

'Of course. Come on in.'

'I've only popped by to say hello.'

He followed her through to the kitchen and Lewis had, thankfully, just finished his supper as he immediately jumped down from the table to clamber up Jacob for a hug.

'Hiya, champ,' Jacob said. 'What have you been up to today?'

Nadia smiled as her son launched into an elaborate description of his day's activities, giving Jacob more than he bargained for.

'Leave Jacob alone,' she said eventually. 'You can go and play for an hour before bedtime.'

'Can Jacob play too?'

'In a minute. If he wants to. Mummy needs to talk to him.'

Jacob lowered Lewis to the floor and he scampered upstairs. She fought the urge to shout 'Don't run!' after him.

'Sounds serious,' Jacob said.

'I've been meaning to talk to you.' This seemed as good a time as any. She sat down at the kitchen table and, without her needing to ask him, he pulled out a chair and sat down opposite her. 'Chantal has hired a cottage in the Lake District for Christmas.'

'Sounds great.'

'I'd really like it if you'd come with us. Lewis adores you and he'd love to have you there.' She paused and took a deep breath before she said, 'I'd like it, too.'

'I can hear a hesitation there.'

Nadia sighed. 'I'm not sure what we are to each other. I've been thinking long and hard about what I want from my future . . .'

'Does it include me?'

'I suppose . . . I need to know what I mean to you.'

Jacob frowned. 'What's brought this on? Have I done something wrong?' he asked. 'Have I upset you?'

'No.' This was so much more awkward than she'd imagined. Yet she was the one who'd shaken up this particular can of worms and had prised it open. 'You've always been kind, sweet, supportive. In short, you've been wonderful.'

'I like you, Nadia,' he said. 'And Lewis is a great kid. I thought you needed a friend.'

'I did. I still do.' Nadia cleared her throat. 'This is very hard for me to say. If we went to the Lake District for Christmas, would we go as friends or would it be more than that?'

Jacob hung his head. 'To tell you the truth, Nadia, I don't know.'

Looking across the table at him, she dearly wished that she could take the troubled look out of his eyes. At that moment, she fully realised that she cared for him more than she liked to admit. She could so easily love Jacob and life would be much simpler if he felt he could love her in return. He would be a great father figure for Lewis, but it was no good letting herself fall deeply for someone who didn't reciprocate her feelings.

Jacob put his finger on the toy car that Lewis had left on the table. He moved it slowly, thoughtfully, avoiding her eyes. 'There's someone else. You know that. You must do.'

They both knew that they were talking about Chantal and they both refused to say it out loud.

He looked so sad; she hated to hurt him, and she was hurting herself. But surely it was better to nip this in the bud now rather than give herself false hope. She was in no doubt about that. Of course, he'd always loved Chantal. They had something very special between them and Nadia couldn't hope to compete with that.

'I've never promised you anything, Nadia. I've just tried to be here for you.'

'I know.'

'I thought this . . . situation . . . suited us both.'

'It does. Absolutely. And I hope we can carry on exactly as we have been. I'd still like you to be in our lives. Nothing needs to change.'

'You're a great woman, Nadia. The best. In different circumstances . . .'

They were strained, stilted with each other now. He was slipping away from her. She felt her cheeks burn.

'I can't help it,' he said. 'God knows, if I could move on I would. She's with another man while I'm on the outside. But there it is. We can't choose who we love.' He stood up. 'I should leave.'

'Don't walk out,' she implored. 'We'll pretend that this conversation never happened. Stay. Go upstairs and play with Lewis for a short while. He'd love it. You know that. We can carry on exactly as we were. Except that we both know where we stand now.'

She stood up and hugged him. For the first time, there was tension, a resistance in his body. This could be the last time she could hold him. Her eyes filled with tears. If she could take back what she'd said at this minute, she would. Then she could still have pretended, hoped, that she and Jacob could be together one day.

Instead, she forced herself to drop her arms and move away from him. She steered the charged conversation back to the banal. 'Have you had dinner?'

He shook his head.

'I can heat up some chicken curry?'

'You know, Nadia, I'm not that hungry.' He flicked a thumb towards the door. 'I'll go up and spend a few minutes with Lewis and then I'll be on my way. There are things I should be doing.'

'Of course.'

With a sad smile, he left the room. Nadia wrapped her arms around herself and stared at the ceiling. It felt like a break-up, even though they'd never truly been together. She could have loved Jacob. Perhaps she already did. But he loved someone else. Life could really be rubbish sometimes. Only when she heard Jacob slowly climbing the stairs to Lewis's room did she allow herself to cry.

Chapter Seventy-Nine

It's late afternoon, near closing time, when Autumn comes back into Chocolate Heaven. If I hadn't been so busy, I'd have been going mad with worry, as she didn't ring me after her bank appointment to let me know how she'd fared.

'I thought you'd run away with the circus,' I say as she comes in. 'Why didn't you phone me? Where have you been?'

Autumn looks shell-shocked. Her hair is escaping from her up-do and she's a lot more dishevelled than when she left here this morning. The Armani suit is slightly crumpled.

'How did it go?'

'Chocolate,' she says. 'I need chocolate. And coffee. A strong one. Maybe a double brandy, too.'

'I can do all of those,' I say and hurry to fulfil my friend's needs.

'I have good news and bad news,' she informs me.

'I can't bear the suspense.' I hand over her drink and quickly nip into the back to give her a sly tot of brandy in an espresso cup. I have a quick one myself.

When I take the brandy to her, there's a queue forming at the counter with people stacked up with chocolate reindeers,

Santas and God knows what else. I know this is Christmas but, bloody hell, can't they see that I've got important business to attend to? If I don't sort this out, then next year there won't be anywhere for them to buy their festive chocolate fancies.

I serve them as fast as I can and, the minute they're gone, nip round to join Autumn.

She's collapsed into our favourite sofa, pale and tired-looking.

I flop down next to her. 'Was it hell?'

'The meeting with the bank manager was tough,' she admits. 'He trawled through the paperwork you'd given me with a fine-tooth comb and I answered his queries as best I could, but I realised that I was hideously under-prepared. We should have gone together. You're the one in the know when it comes to Chocolate Heaven.' She lets out a shuddering sigh. 'Despite that, he was quite impressed. There were a few questions outstanding and we agreed to schedule another meeting so that you could be there. I'd have needed to get some more money from my parents, too, but in principle he agreed to give me a loan.'

'He did?' Euphoria bursts forth from my heart. 'I can't believe it!'

'Don't get too excited, Lucy,' Autumn warns. 'I then went straight round to the estate agents to talk about making an offer.'

'Yes?'

'I thought it would be a lovely surprise for you if I could come back with a deal that was pretty much sewn up.'

'Tell me you did,' I beg. 'Tell me you did.'

Her shoulders sag. 'We're too late.'

'What? We can't be.'

'Someone else put in an offer as soon as their office opened this morning – before I'd even got anywhere near the bank. I finally managed to speak to Clive and Tristan as soon as I could, but they've accepted it.'

'It's only just gone on the market. As far as I know, no one has even come to view it.'

'I guess it's a good business. They don't come up around here that often. Someone must have spotted a golden opportunity. As we did.'

'Who?'

'The agent wouldn't say. Client confidentiality and all that, but they did tell me that a company had bought it. Clive confirmed it.'

'Noooo.' I can't quite get my brain round this. We're too late! My heart is in despair.

If a company has bought it they might not care about this place at all. They might just want to get their hands on some prime-location property.

'I'm so sorry.' Autumn looks as shattered as I feel.

'How could they? Chocolate Heaven should be ours.' It has my name all over it. Autumn and I would be the perfect pairing. I thought the bank would be the stumbling block. I didn't reckon on anyone else putting in an offer before her and snatching it from under our noses.

'I tried, Lucy. Clive understood our situation, but he's decided to go with them. He went back to the agents and told them that someone else was interested, and the company who's buying it simply upped their offer. Looks as if they have unlimited funds to play with and they're determined to have it. I couldn't compete with that. All I could do was leave my details with the agents in case anything goes wrong with this sale and it doesn't go through. But, by all accounts, it's full steam ahead. The agent said it's a cash purchase and there was nothing to make them believe that contracts couldn't be exchanged quickly. It could all be done and dusted at the start of the new year.'

I can hardly believe what I'm hearing. A few short weeks and I could be out on my ear.

Autumn looks wretched but, already, she's resigned to our fate. 'Clive was really apologetic.'

That doesn't make me feel much better.

'I don't know what else to do,' she says. 'I don't think there's anything else we *can* do.'

'Wow.' I feel as if I'm about to have a panic attack. 'It looks like Chocolate Heaven will have a new owner at the beginning of next year.'

'I'm sorry.' Autumn looks totally miserable.

'You did your best.' I give her a hug and she holds on to me tightly.

'I thought it would be great for us,' she says. 'We'd have made a super team. Now we'll probably both have to find something else to do.'

The thought fills me with dread. I wish Crush was here now. He'd know what to do, what to say. Instead, I'm facing going home to an empty flat and having a good cry by myself. I've never felt so lonely or so all at sea.

Autumn wipes a tear from her eye. 'What else can we do? Any bright ideas?'

'Yes. There's only one thing for it,' I say, standing. 'I'd better get us more chocolate.'

Chapter Eighty

Chantal stoked the fire in the grate. It was roaring away and she didn't really need to fiddle with it, but she was anxious now.

This morning, all the Christmas decorations had arrived from Harvey Nicks and it had taken her four hours to dress the tree and make the rest of the room pretty. It had been hard work and she could definitely have done with Jacob's help, but he was busy with his own events this week and she had managed. Just about. The tree was eight feet tall and she'd had a good wrestle with that. If there had been more time, she would have got someone in to do it. Her forte definitely leaned more towards titivating than ground work. Still, that was the price you had to pay for coming late to the party and she'd put her shoulder into it.

Now the lights twinkled and the tree looked glorious. Very festive. Chantal had decorated the mantelpiece with a garland of holly – artificial, but it was amazing. In some ways it was a shame that they weren't staying here to enjoy it, but they could make the most of it for the next few days and it would still be here when they returned for New Year. Perhaps, if they weren't all ready to kill each other after a week in the cottage, she'd throw a party. Suddenly, she felt as if there was much to celebrate in her life.

She'd bought a few canapés from the deli and had opened a good bottle of wine. Ted's favourite. Though she was already well into her second glass to calm her nerves and, if he didn't come home soon, there was a very real danger that she'd have drunk the lot. There were also some of the Christmassy cakes from Chocolate Heaven for afterwards.

She'd been watching the weather reports with trepidation and hoping that they would actually be able to get up to the cottage in the Lakes. It was quite bad up there compared to the few measly flakes that they classed as snow in London.

The Discovery was sure-footed enough to tackle it, she was certain. However, Chantal was also slightly worried about the amount of luggage and boxes that had to be loaded into it. Not only was there all of the food and booze for the duration of their stay, but there was also Lana's extensive paraphernalia to consider. If there was one thing she'd learned about having a baby it was that you could never leave the house again without being equipped as if you were going on an expedition.

They were also taking the lavish amount of decorations that she'd ordered. The plan was that Stacey and Elsie were coming up with her in the car and, no doubt, they wouldn't be travelling light either. At this rate, they were definitely going to have to take both cars. If she was honest, Ted might prefer to follow them at his leisure with only some suitcases for company. It would be a very long journey if the weather was bad and there were two fractious babies in the car. She'd yet to broach it with him, but there was no putting it off now. Hence the good wine.

Chantal glanced at the clock, nervously. It was late and Lana had already been in bed for a good while. He should be home any moment as he hadn't texted to say that he'd be delayed at the office. It seemed to be back to their old pattern of Ted working well into the evening, avoiding her. This Christmas break would do them good, she was sure.

She resisted the urge to pour another glass of wine and, to her relief, a few moments later she heard Ted's key in the lock and waited patiently as he stripped off his coat and took his briefcase through to the study.

'Hey,' he said when he came into the room a few minutes later.

'Long day?'

He nodded. 'Long enough.'

'I've opened a bottle of the Rothschild you like.'

He took the glass and gratefully gulped it down, then flopped into the sofa. 'What's this in aid of?'

Today Ted looked his age and very tired. It couldn't be easy trying to juggle the demands of two families.

'Nothing. I thought you could put your feet up, relax.'

He looked at her suspiciously, as well he might.

She should wait a little longer until he'd had time to chill out, but she simply couldn't. Instead, she rushed on. 'We need to talk about our Christmas arrangements.'

Ted closed his eyes. 'I can't do this, Chantal.'

'I've organised everything. All you have to do is turn up. It'll be great. I'll show you the brochure for the place I've rented. It's fabulous. So festive. If it snows it will be like a winter wonderland.'

'I don't mean Christmas.' Ted opened his eyes and stared at her hard. 'I can't do this "happy families" thing. We've messed up, Chantal. You, me, Stacey. I can't live in the middle of it all.'

'It's not easy. Of course not. But we're picking our way through it, aren't we?'

'I can't dress this up nicely, Chantal, and I'm sure you wouldn't want me to. You might as well hear it straight.'

Instinctively, she braced herself for what was coming.

'I don't love you anymore,' he said flatly. 'I love Stacey. It's her I want to be with. I've taken a job in New York and they want me to start straight away. We're going to be moving there as soon as Christmas is over.'

The words hit her low.

'You and Stacey?'

He nodded. 'And Elsie, of course.'

'What about Lana?'

'She'll stay here with you. It will be better for her.'

'She's your daughter too. You can't just leave her behind, Ted.'

'Of course, I won't. We'll come back as often as we can. I'll be here on business regularly. I'll see as much of her as I possibly can.'

'But you won't be just around the corner.' And that was heart-breaking. 'Lana and Elsie are like sisters. They should grow up together.'

'That's what happens in fairy tales, Chantal. This is real life. The harsh reality is that this is an unworkable situation. We need some space.'

'I've befriended Stacey. Taken her and Elsie under my wing. So have the girls at the Chocolate Lovers' Club. I thought she was our friend.'

'Well, that's as may be. But I've asked her to come with me and she's said yes.' Ted faced her, his expression unreadable. 'It's never really ended between us,' he admitted. 'I know that's probably not what you wanted to hear, but that's how it is.'

'All the time that she and I have been friends? When you asked me to help her as she had no one else?'

Ted had the grace to look slightly discomfited. 'Yes.'

'What a fool I've been,' Chantal said. She wanted to rail and shout, but felt as if all the fight had flooded out of her. She'd battled against the odds to keep this marriage going for too long and, if she was honest, she wasn't entirely surprised that it was over. It was just that she hadn't seen it coming in this way.

She'd anticipated a slow fizzling out, an amicable split, a forging of a new but lasting friendship. Perhaps Ted was right. That only happened in fairy tales. He was going. Abandoning his daughter, her too.

'I'll pack a bag now and go. No point in prolonging these things.'

'We should have Christmas together,' she said forlornly. 'At least give me that. For Lana.'

'There's very little point.' He stood up, decisively. 'Lana's so young that she won't miss me this year. You're the only one she needs.'

It broke her heart to hear him speak like this. 'Does she mean nothing to you?'

'Of course she does. I adore her. But I also have to think what *I* need in all of this,' he said, as if it was the most reasonable thing in the world. 'We can sort out what we have to in the new year – the house, the finances. You won't want for anything. This is the right thing to do. It will be a fresh start for both of us.'

She looked at him, speechless. For a moment she thought she saw a glimmer of regret in his eyes, but it was fleeting.

With that he walked out of the door and she stood staring after him, rooted to the spot. Was this it? Was this *really* it? Her marriage ended, just like that? It certainly looked like it.

Chantal's shoulders sagged and she said into the empty room, 'Merry fucking Christmas, Ted.'

Chapter Eighty-One

Closing up Chocolate Heaven, I stand in the street beneath the falling snowflakes. I love snow and this should lift my spirits but it resolutely fails to do so.

I've stayed late, cashing up, restocking the shelves, tidying up the counter display. All necessary, but also an avoidance technique so that I don't have to go home to my cold and lonely flat. Actually, it's not that cold if I'm truthful, but you know what I mean. It feels cold without Crush there. Even my ridiculous singing and dancing reindeer can no longer raise a smile.

I stand back and look at the front of Chocolate Heaven. Christmas is now only a few days away and soon I could be locking up as manager for the very last time. My heart is as heavy as lead.

Before I even know what I'm doing, I'm on the Tube and heading, not home, but towards Targa. I have to speak to Crush. I miss him so much that it's a physical hurt. He has always been my rock, my support and I'm lost without him. It's like Shaggy without Scooby. Ant without Dec. Unthinkable. I must find him. He will know what to say, what to do.

Getting off half a dozen stops later, I'm being carried forth from the Underground on a wave of commuters. Targa's offices are just behind the Tube station here and I walk up the road, hands in pockets, shivering against the cold.

I don't even know if Crush is working there today. He could be anywhere and, as he doesn't reply to my texts, I have no way of finding out. I'm hoping that he is here and that the element of surprise will work in my favour. If he sees me – sodden and shivering – perhaps that will soften his heart towards me.

There's a newly opened coffee shop directly opposite the entrance to Targa's offices and I prepare to take up station on one of the stools set at a counter in the window. I can't fail to see him now. Unless he's somewhere else entirely and, knowing my luck, he is.

I order a cappuccino and scan the competition's meagre choice of chocolate-based goodies. Chocolate Heaven would beat them hands down. And that brings another wave of sadness. It's a great café, a great business and now someone else will benefit from all my hard work.

Sitting in the window, I prepare for a lengthy stake-out of my former employer's premises. I have hope in my heart. When Crush emerges from his daily toil, I'll dash out and stand in front of him doing the I'm-just-a-girl-standing-in-front-of-a-boy thing and it will hit him like a hammer how much he's missed me and he'll be overwhelmed with love for me once more and we'll fall into each other's arms. Hurrah! Happy ending. Love, love, love!

We could be back at my flat and having sex under the Christmas tree while the night is still young. Hope is a truly wonderful thing.

But I'm only halfway down my coffee when a raucous party bursts out of the main doors of Targa and spills out into the street. I recognise most of the faces instantly and one more than all. In the middle of the fray, wearing a pink paper hat and puffing into a rainbow-coloured party blower with a pink feather on the end is my beloved Crush. He's also wearing a pink feather boa. Normally, I like a man in touch with his feminine side but he's enjoying himself cavorting down the road in his feathers so much that I die inside a little bit. He's having such fun, a great time without me. He's not sitting moping in an overly lit café in a stalkery way, with a luke-warm cappuccino and an inadequate selection of chocolate products.

It must have been the office Christmas lunch today. Always an excuse for high-jinks. As if one was ever needed at Targa. There was always too much wine drunk, too many colleagues taking risks with their employment status or their future promotion chances. There was always lots of snogging in the stationery cupboard afterwards and, inevitably, a call needed for the photocopier engineer the next day.

And now Crush – *my* Crush – is right in the middle of it.

A woman – who I don't recognise – dances in front of him and then grabs the end of his feather boa. Crush puts up no resistance at all as she leads him further along the pavement and towards the bar that is just a few doors down from Targa. It seems as if the party isn't yet over.

I know only too well what could go on tonight. Crush obviously sees himself as a single man now and who can blame him? This woman probably isn't a complete fuck-up. She probably has a successful career at Targa, her own place which isn't subsidised by her mother and can send sex texts without them going to her dad by mistake. She'll make a much more suitable girlfriend for Aiden Holby than I ever have.

With much pushing, shoving and laughter, they elbow their

way into the crowded pub. I down my coffee, pay my bill and brace myself to go out into the cold once more.

The wind is cutting cruelly down the street and I pull my coat around me. Then I head across the street to the pub. I want to get one last glimpse of Crush that I can fix in my mind. With the way he's behaving, he looks more like Marcus than I can bear and I never in a million years thought that I'd be making a comparison between the two of them.

He's not *my* Crush. He's someone else's. That couldn't be clearer. He's gone from me. Gone from me for ever. I know that in this moment.

I stand in the doorway of the pub and watch the group as they carry on their party oblivious to my pain. Hope really is a fucking bastard. Because once it has left the building there is nothing remaining but a big, fat frigging hole in your heart.

Crush has his arm round the woman and is singing now at the top of his voice. It's so bad that I can't actually tell what he's singing.

Then, as I stand there, he looks up. 'Lucy,' he says.

But I shake my head sadly at him. I've lost him. I have to learn to accept that.

Then I'm gone, out of there and I run down the road, snowflakes stinging my face as the tears burn my eyes. Without looking back, I head straight into the Tube where no one even notices or cares that I'm crying my heart out.

Chapter Eighty-Two

Nadia had spent a sleepless night mulling over her decision. At four o'clock in the morning she knew that it was the right one.

As soon as she got into the shop in the morning, she would hand in her notice. In the new year she wanted a completely fresh start. She didn't want to start dipping into the money from the insurance pay-out but it would tide her over until she could find something else. She'd enjoyed working in the shop – apart from the issues with Tarak – but she also knew that she had so much else to offer. In January she would look for a new place to live, a new job.

She was tired when she dropped off Lewis at nursery and took the Tube to Brick Lane. Tarak and Anita were both standing behind the counter chatting and there were no customers, as yet, in the shop. It was as good a time as any.

'Morning.' Nadia slipped off her coat and dropped her handbag into the backroom.

'The kettle has just boiled,' her sister said, so she made herself a drink.

'I need to talk to you both,' Nadia said when she went

back into the shop. 'I'm really grateful for this job, but I'm going to look for something else in the new year.'

She saw Tarak's shoulders sag with relief.

'I've loved working with you, Anita, but I need to do this for me.'

'Why? I don't want you to leave.' Her sister's eyes filled with tears. 'Who will I gossip with?'

Nadia laughed. 'I'm sure you'll find someone.'

'But it won't be the same. We've just found each other again.'

And, Nadia thought, they'd nearly lost each other again due to her husband's cheating. She hoped that Tarak had learned his lesson. Lucy's plan had been a bit extreme, but if it helped then it wouldn't be time wasted.

'You must do what you have to,' Tarak said solemnly. However, she could tell in his voice that he was glad she was leaving. She wasn't going to let him push her away from Anita; he knew now that he had to watch his step with her.

Then the shop started to fill with customers and the moment passed. The rest of the morning was so busy that they didn't have time to chat at all. It seemed as if everyone was coming in for last-minute fashion purchases for their Christmas parties. If Tarak didn't go to the warehouse today, then they'd be cleared out of itsy-bitsy sparkly numbers.

Shortly before lunchtime, he picked up the keys to the van and went to leave. Anita was in the backroom. Tarak stood before Nadia and lowered his voice. 'We are OK, aren't we?'

'Yes,' she said. 'This really is something that I need to do for myself.'

'Good.' He glanced anxiously towards the back of the shop where his wife was. 'I didn't like what you did,' he said in hushed tones. 'But it did teach me a lesson. I thought I was the one in control.' He raised an eyebrow. 'I never bargained for a bunch of vindictive women.'

'I'd like to think of us as educational rather than vindictive. It wasn't done out of malice, Tarak. The very last thing on earth that I want is to jeopardise your marriage. I want you to appreciate it. Next time you might not be so lucky. It would only take one phone call to Anita from a bunny boiler and all this could come crashing down.'

'There won't be a next time,' he whispered. 'I promise you that. I'm really trying to be a good husband. I don't want to lose Anita or my boys.'

'It's not easy to start over again, Tarak. I know that. Treasure your family. They all love you.'

He nodded. 'I want to make this a good Christmas.'

'Just be there for them. That will be enough.'

'Does anyone want a cup of tea?' Anita called from the back.

'Let's leave it there,' Tarak said.

She nodded her agreement. 'Merry Christmas, Tarak.'

'To you too, Nadia.' He walked briskly out of the door and jumped into his van.

Anita popped her head out of the curtain, holding two cups of tea. 'Has Tarak gone?'

'Yes. To the warehouse. Those new dresses are flying off the racks.'

She laughed as she handed Nadia a mug. 'That will keep him happy. Until I give him the bill for the boy's Christmas toys. All they want now is iPads, iPhones, iEverything else. It costs a small fortune.'

'Are you happy with him?' Nadia asked as she sipped her tea.

Anita nodded. 'I know that he's not perfect.' She avoided looking at Nadia. 'What man is?'

Her sister sighed and, for the first time, Nadia detected a hint of weariness in her tone. 'He always comes back to me. Eventually. I've learned to cope by turning a blind eye. Don't pity me, Nadia,' she said. 'I'm not weak like you think.'

'I didn't say that.'

Anita held up a hand. 'I'm the strong one. I'm the one who keeps the family together. That's my job. That's what we women do.'

Nadia took her sister in her arms and hugged her. 'It will be fine,' she said. 'You see, it will all be fine from now. Tarak loves you.'

'I know,' she said. 'Underneath it all. He's my husband. If I thought that he didn't love me, then I *would* leave.'

'I'm going to miss you at Christmas. It's a time for families.'

'You'll have a lovely break in the Lake District. I'm very jealous. I've never been there.'

'Me neither. I feel quite excited about it.' She'd been on Google and had clicked through some of the images. It looked amazing. That was another thing that she and Lewis would do next year. They'd go on holiday together. She'd seen very little of Britain and even less of the rest of the world. She hoped that would change. There was part of her that wished she'd be doing this with Jacob, but that wasn't to be. She was sad, but there was also a feeling of relief accompanying it. It meant that she was free for new experiences in that part of her life. Eventually, she would find someone who was free to love her.

'I will be thinking of you every day,' Anita said. 'We're together now and we won't be parted again.'

'I hope we both have a wonderful Christmas time.'

'I want to hear all about it,' Anita begged. 'You and Lewis must visit us as soon as you come back.'

'I promise.'

'You are very lucky to have such friends, Nadia,' her sister said.

'I know.' Now she couldn't wait for Christmas. Bring on the snow, the fun, the chocolate.

Chapter Eighty-Three

Chantal went to knock on Stacey's door. She hadn't heard from Ted at all. The calls she'd made and texts she'd sent to Stacey had gone unanswered. She took a deep and steadying breath and, seconds later, the door opened.

Stacey stood there, Elsie in her arms. She looked taken aback and, at first, she bristled. Then her whole body sagged and she said, 'You'd better come in.'

It was as awkward as the first time she'd come here. The time she'd offered Stacey the hand of friendship. Chantal manoeuvred the buggy into the small space. Lana was, thankfully, fast asleep. The hall was filled with packing boxes, some of them still half full. One was crammed with books, another with Elsie's toys.

Chantal took them all in. 'You're really leaving?'

Stacey nodded. 'I'm sorry it turned out like this. I never planned it this way.'

'Is Ted here?'

She shook her head. 'He's staying at the apartment in Islington. I thought it was better if he was out of the way while I packed.'

'Ted would appreciate that. He never did like getting his hands dirty.'

'Come through to the kitchen,' Stacey said. 'The kettle hasn't been dispensed with yet. I could make us a cup of tea.'

'I'm not really planning on staying. I've got a lot to do. I just wanted to wish you well, I suppose.' Chantal also wanted to ask her why she'd done this, probably have a rant and rave, but now that she was here all the fight had gone out of her.

'I'm sorry,' Stacey said. 'You and the other girls have been so kind to me. I've never had such good friends.'

Chantal couldn't help herself and before she could think better of it said, 'It's an interesting way to repay that.'

Stacey looked stung. 'I know. Can you ever forgive me?'

'You love him?'

'I do.'

Of course she did. It had been obvious from the start, but Chantal had hoped for the sake of the babies they would have come to some sort of working arrangement. Perhaps it had been pie in the sky.

'Make sure that he comes back to see Lana,' Chantal said. 'I don't want her to lose her father.'

'Of course not. I promise I'll do all I can. I love Lana and so does Ted. He said that we'd be back regularly.'

'I hope so.'

Stacey's expression was bleak. For someone who was about to start a new life with her lover, she didn't seem overjoyed.

As if she'd read her mind, Stacey lowered her voice and said, 'I know what I'm losing, Chantal. I wish there had been a way to make this work, too. But Ted is adamant. This is a great opportunity for him.'

'It's you and I who are left to pick up the pieces.'

'I know. But I'd like it if we could stay in touch,' Stacey

suggested tentatively. 'I could fully understand if you didn't want to.'

'We have to make a relationship, Stacey. Our girls are bound together by blood. Whatever happens we should try our best for Lana and Elsie.'

'Thank you.'

'I'd better go. I've got an early start tomorrow and I want to load up the car as much as I can tonight.'

'You're still going to the cottage in the Lake District?'

'Yes. Everyone's coming.' Well, nearly everyone.

'The place seemed amazing. I was so looking forward to it . . .' Her words trailed away.

'What are you doing instead?'

'Ted's booked us in at a local restaurant. Everything will be packed up by then. Our flights are on Boxing Day.'

'So soon?'

'Yes.'

'He's not answering my calls,' Chantal said. 'And I don't have the inclination or the energy to go to the Islington apartment. Give him my best. I hope it works out for you both. Really I do.'

'Thank you, Chantal.' Stacey hung her head. 'It's more than I deserve.'

'We can salvage something from it,' Chantal offered. She'd been angry with Stacey, but she could see now that she was between a rock and a hard place. She had to choose between the man she loved and her friends. It was an awful position for Ted to put her in and, if anything, Chantal felt sorry for her. 'I'm sure we can.'

'I'd like that.'

'Give me a hug.' She stepped forward and Stacey stepped into her arms where she sobbed and sobbed.

'I'll miss you,' Stacey sniffed. 'I'll miss you all.'

Chantal stroked her hair, her back and soothed her. 'Don't cry,' she said. 'It's Christmas. You have a new life to start. It will all work out fine.'

Chapter Eighty-Four

'I'm not sure we'll get another box in there,' Miles said, scratching his head. 'How long are we going for? I thought it was only for four days. We could stay there for about six months at least.'

'Some of it is food,' Autumn said. 'Vital supplies.'

'That probably means there's a whole box just for chocolate, if what I've heard about the Chocolate Lovers' Club is true.'

Autumn laughed. There was. Lucy had made sure of that. Each of the children had a chocolate Santa and reindeer wrapped and labelled for under the tree. 'You could be right.'

They were loading up ready for their trip to the Lake District in the parking bays outside Miles's terraced house. There still seemed to be a lot of luggage on the pavement but Miles was coping admirably with the task of trying to fit a quart into a pint pot.

'Nadia, will you and Lewis be all right in the back with Florence?' he asked.

'Of course. I'll sit on the roof rack if you need me to,' Nadia answered. 'I'm just very grateful that we're travelling up together in this snow.'

'We'll take it in turns to be with the children, if you want to,' Autumn said. Both of the kids were over-excited and would probably be more easily managed in short shifts. She'd made up a little goodie bag for each of them with crayons and colouring books to keep them amused and the internet had thrown up some useful I-Spy games for the motorway.

The snow was coming down quite heavily now, even in London. The bookies had stopped taking bets on a white Christmas as most of the UK was under a blanket of white.

'I'm very glad that you've got a beefy car, Miles,' Autumn noted.

'We'll be fine,' Miles reassured them. 'This thing can cope with anything.' He patted the car fondly. 'Plus, as it's been snowing for a while, they've cleared a lot of the main roads. The lanes in the Lake District could be fun, though. It's a long time since I've been up there in the winter.'

'I never have,' Autumn admitted. 'Mummy and Daddy were much more into Kenya than Keswick.'

'When I was young and foolish, I camped up there in November.' He shivered at the memory. 'Mind you, we did abandon the tent and get back in the car halfway through the night.' Then he clapped his hands together. 'Are we nearly ready?'

'Last trip to the bathroom for everyone?' Autumn suggested.

'Yes,' Miles said. 'I don't want to hear "I need a wee" until we're past Birmingham.'

'What time was Chantal leaving?' Nadia asked.

Autumn checked her watch. 'She should be on the road by now. I texted her first thing this morning and she and Lana were pretty much set to go then.'

'Perhaps I should have travelled up with her. I don't like to think of her going all that way on her own.'

'I did offer,' Autumn said. 'But she insisted she'd be fine. If they've made good time, they might not be too far away now. I know that she wanted to have the house decorated for when we arrived.'

'Is she doing all right without Ted?'

'I'm not sure that it's entirely sunk in yet, but she seems to be managing OK so far.'

'It's really very kind of her to have us all,' Miles said. 'She might not feel like it with the way things have turned out.'

'She'll definitely want us all there. I'm just glad you could come too.' Autumn smiled, delighted to be spending her first Christmas with Miles and Florence. 'We'll do our best to make sure that it's a lovely Christmas for her.'

'I've organised a little surprise that I think might put a smile on her face again.' Nadia looked smug and secretive.

'Care to share?'

'Not yet,' she said, mysteriously. 'Wait and see.'

'What's happening with Ted and Stacey?' Autumn asked.

'I don't know.' Nadia checked to see if the children were listening, but Miles was ushering them back towards the house for a last-minute bathroom visit. 'Chantal hasn't spoken to him since the revelation, but she went round to speak to Stacey yesterday and, from what she said, they've come to some kind of truce.'

'Stacey seemed so nice. I thought she'd fitted in so well with us all. A fellow chocoholic and all-round nice person. I'll miss her.'

'Me too,' Nadia agreed. 'I hope they can resolve their differences for the sake of those beautiful little girls. Chantal seemed hopeful.'

Miles returned. 'Let's see if we can squeeze this final bit of luggage in and then we can get going before the roads are too busy.'

426

Nadia laughed. 'Have we really brought so much stuff? I don't think any of us can travel light.'

'This cottage looks amazing already. I can't wait to see it when Chantal has finished with it. I think she bought up the whole of Harvey Nicks' Christmas display.' Autumn's phone rang. 'That might be her now with an update on their progress. I asked her to check in with me en route.'

When she got her phone out of her pocket, it wasn't a number she recognised. Who could be calling her on Christmas Eve? 'Hello?'

'Is that Autumn Fielding?' an unfamiliar voice asked.

'Yes.'

'Hello, Ms Fielding. This is Eleanor from the Find Families adoption agency. You registered on our site a little while ago.'

'I did.' Her heart was thumping in her chest.

'Well, I have some lovely news for you.'

Autumn clutched her phone.

'I'm very pleased to be able to tell you that we have someone who wants to make contact with you.'

Autumn sat down heavily on the wall outside Miles's home as her legs seemed unable to support her. Her chest was tight, her throat closed.

'Are you still there?'

She could hardly speak. 'Willow?'

'Her adoptive mother.' There was the rummaging of papers at the other end of the phone. 'Mrs Mary Randall. She's made contact with us. Willow would like to meet you. Are you happy for me to organise that?'

'Yes,' Autumn gasped. 'Yes, of course.' She could hardly process this. Willow was trying to find her. There was a longing ache in her heart. It was more than she could possibly have hoped for to hear something so quickly. And her darling daughter still had the name she'd given her at birth.

'I think they'd like to try to organise a meeting in the new year. If that's acceptable to you.'

'Oh, yes,' Autumn breathed. 'That's very acceptable indeed.' How would she wait until then? She wanted to see her now, this minute, make up for all the years that they had lost.

'Good. I'll be in touch again soon. We can co-ordinate diaries and sort out the details. I'd like to fix this up for you as soon as possible,' Eleanor said. 'You must be dying to meet her.'

'I am,' Autumn said. 'Please tell her that I am.'

'I most certainly will. Merry Christmas to you, Ms Fielding.'

'Merry Christmas,' Autumn said. 'Thank you. Thank you very much.'

The tears were streaming down her face as she hung up.

Nadia came over and touched her arm. 'Everything all right?'

She nodded – dazed, stunned, amazed. 'More than I could possibly have hoped for.' She looked up at Nadia. 'Willow's adoptive mother has made contact.' Standing up from the wall where she was perched, she felt as if her legs might give away beneath her and she held on tightly to her friend. 'Oh, Nadia. I'm going to see my daughter again.'

'That's fantastic news, Autumn. Brilliant.'

'I can hardly believe it.' She put a hand to her forehead. 'I've dreamed so many times of this day and now it's here.'

Her heart was beating like a drum, her breath high in her chest. She thought she might burst with joy. She would see Willow once more. It would be the best Christmas present that she could ever have. Her very own Christmas miracle.

Chapter Eighty-Five

The journey was slow, the motorway congested. But it was Christmas Eve and it was snowing, so it was only to be expected. Chantal had factored in plenty of time to arrive ahead of the others and, due to a crack-of-dawn start, they'd arrived in the Lake District shortly after lunch – even with a few cuddle stops for Lana scheduled in. The baby had coped well with the lengthy journey, dozing on and off in her car seat or happily talking in her own scribble language to herself, essential supplies stacked up around her.

Cumbria Cottage was a grade II listed building in traditional local stone and nestled comfortably into the landscape. To call it a cottage was a bit of a misnomer as it was a low, sprawling building with enough bedrooms to sleep sixteen people comfortably. They might even have a few rooms to spare. Perhaps it had always been foolish to think that Ted and Stacey might come here too. As it was, she'd probably have a more relaxed Christmas without them.

Last night she'd finally spoken to Ted and he'd come round to see Lana. He'd cried when he'd held her in his arms and Chantal wondered if he was beginning to regret his haste in taking this job in New York. The only good thing in all of this was that, thankfully, Lana was too young to realise any of the drama unfolding around her and was her usual contented self. He'd brought a Christmas card and a carrier bag full of presents that had Stacey's stamp all over them. Ted had never done his own Christmas shopping and he wasn't likely to start now. First thing this morning Stacey had phoned her to wish her and Lana a safe journey. The conversation had been OK, not too difficult. Perhaps they could be friends once again. The sad thing was that Chantal actually missed Stacey as a chum, despite what she'd done. She guessed it was all about the survival of the fittest in this world and Stacey probably reckoned she was better off with Ted than four female friends with a fixation on chocolate. Well, Stacey would have to see how things panned out. If Chantal knew Ted he'd immerse himself in his new job in New York and Stacey would be left dangling. She'd be even further away from friends and family than she was here. Yet, that was her problem now. What was done was done; they had to move forward from this point and all Chantal could hope for was a fair settlement from Ted and a quickie divorce.

Still, she'd put all that behind her for a few days and enjoy Christmas. This setting couldn't be more perfect for forgetting your troubles. The cottage sat in an enviable position above Derwentwater, a slice of pewter in the white landscape and, behind the cottage, the mountains towered over them. It looked as if they'd all been sprinkled with icing sugar. Perhaps it would be nice to come back here next year and see it in its summer glory. But maybe it would be wise to see how they all survived Christmas first.

She conducted a whistle-stop tour of the cottage and mentally allocated bedrooms for everyone. This was a wonderful place, Chantal thought as she looked out of the window and took in the spectacular view. The trip might have been a bit of a marathon, but she was so glad that she'd come. Now she'd started to unpack and Chantal was itching to get going on making the cottage feel as festive as she could. She wanted the other girls to be completely blown away when they got here.

To get her into the festive mood, she opened a bottle of champagne. It was already cold from being in the boot of the car on her journey up here. The first of many over the next few days, she suspected. Chantal trawled the vast farmhouse kitchen to find the glasses. Just a few sips and then she should get going on preparing the supper.

She'd brought the ingredients for a chicken casserole which she planned to do in one big pot on the range, so that people could help themselves when they arrived. There were a couple of wholemeal loaves that she'd got out of the freezer this morning, which they could cut into chunks to go with it. Lana watched all her mother's industry contentedly from her car chair by the warmth of the range.

For a moment, panic gripped her. She'd be a single mum next year, facing the world alone. How would she fare? She held on to the edge of the butler's sink to steady herself, trying to calm her thoughts by looking out at the solid, timeless mountains around her. As she stood there, a car came meandering up the drive towards the cottage, its tyres crunching on the gravel. She hadn't expected anyone just yet. Miles, Autumn and Nadia were the next ones she thought would arrive, but they would be a few hours at least yet. It certainly wasn't Lucy as the driving was far too sedate.

Perhaps it was a delivery or something. She wiped her hands and headed to the door. The car came to a stop as she opened it and her heart did a somersault as she saw Jacob climbing out of the driver's seat and stretching.

He grinned when he saw her and, in return, her heart thumped in her chest. 'I hadn't expected you.'

'Nadia invited me a couple of days ago,' he confessed. 'She thought you might like it if I joined the party.'

Chantal threw her arms round him. 'Of course I would. Oh, Jacob, this is a lovely surprise. Have you had a good journey?'

'Yes.' He held tightly to her waist and they swayed slightly together. 'I had Christmas songs on all the way to get me in the festive mood and I brought some more decorations.'

'This is perfect timing. I was about to make a start.'

'I'll get my bag then.' He lifted a holdall from the boot and Chantal linked her arm through his and steered him back to the cottage.

'I've just opened a bottle. We can start toasting Christmas early.'

He stopped and turned to her. 'It's good to see you looking so well.'

'Thanks,' she said.

'I'm sorry about you and Ted.'

'It was really horrible how it ended, but it had been on the cards. And I'll be fine. I've got Lana to think of. She's all that matters.'

He stroked his thumb over her cheek, tenderly. 'We'll make this a great Christmas.'

'We will. Now let's go and titivate that tinsel.'

When she'd made him a sandwich and furnished him with a glass of bubbly, she and Jacob went through to the living room. He carried the car seat for her, while Lana was nestled in her arms.

'Wow,' Jacob said. 'Where did you find this place? It's stunning. I could see myself living somewhere like this.'

The photographs on the website really hadn't done this beautiful room justice. In reality, it was warmer, cosier and more impressive than she could have hoped for. It had stone walls and low, original beams. There were comfy sofas huddled around the fire, enough so that they could all gather together, and she was looking forward to snuggling down in them later. But, for now, there was plenty to do. As she'd requested, the owners had put the tallest Christmas tree possible in the corner of the room and it was a splendid specimen, broad, bushy and so high that it was touching the ceiling.

'That's one hell of a tree,' Jacob noted. He started to open the boxes of decorations, pulling out strings of lights and baubles. 'This is going to take us a little while to dress. I'm glad I brought some more supplies.'

'We are Team Christmas. We can do it.'

'How long have we got?'

'The others won't arrive for a few hours yet,' Chantal said. 'We should take our time and enjoy it. Clive and Tristan won't be here until this evening and Lucy's got to spend all day at Chocolate Heaven, so it will be really late by the time she arrives. Miles and company set off just after nine, so they should be the next to arrive. But I guess it depends on how many stops they have to make with the children.'

They clinked their glasses together, employing some expert dodging as Lana made a grab for them. 'Merry Christmas, Jacob,' she said. 'Thanks again for coming. I really appreciate it.'

Jacob fixed her with a searching gaze. 'We should be together,' he said. 'You know that.'

'Yes.'

He laughed. 'Well, that was easier than I thought.'

'I have a lot to sort out with Ted and Stacey. It's all a terrible mess and I'm feeling very fragile. We should take things very slowly.'

'I'm in no rush.' Tenderly, he moved a strand of hair from her face. 'I've waited a long time.'

'So long that you nearly gave up?'

'Never.' He smiled regretfully. 'I was getting close to Nadia, but we could only ever be friends. You were always there in the background. After Lana, I thought that you and Ted would really make a go of it and, in a weird way, I was happy about that. I wanted your happiness more than my own.'

'Oh, Jacob.'

'It's true. I would have stayed miserably single rather than make someone else unhappy because I couldn't fully commit.'

She put her hand on his chest, felt his strong heartbeat beneath his fingers. 'We have a chance now, we should grasp it.'

'You know that I've always loved you.'

She looked up at him and could see how much he cared for her shining in his face. 'I think I've always loved you, too.'

'That makes this Christmas very special, Chantal. Thank you.'

'Merry Christmas, Jacob.' And when he kissed her, warmly and lingeringly, she felt that she had come home, that this was where she was supposed to be. For her, for Jacob, it seemed that Christmas had worked a little bit of magic.

Chapter Eighty-Six

Nadia was delighted to see the cottage finally come into view. 'I thought we'd never get here,' she said, letting out a relieved breath.

'That's it, guys,' Miles said. 'The end of the road. Thank you for your patience.'

'You've done brilliantly,' Autumn said. 'There'll be a large glass of red wine with your name on it.'

'Amen to that.' He pulled into the sweeping drive. 'But I'm thinking two glasses. At least.'

'You deserve them,' Nadia said. 'That was a hell of a journey.'

The trawl up the motorway had been slow and tedious but otherwise uneventful. Thankfully, Lewis and Florence had dozed on and off in the back seat. When they were awake and restless, she and Autumn had managed to keep them entertained. Miles had made a few stops on the way for them all to stretch their legs. But, if they ever went away for Christmas together again, it would definitely be easier if they went somewhere closer to London.

When they left the M6, they'd taken a wrong turn off the main road and had taken an unexpected detour through the small town of Keswick. It was all pretty stone buildings and had a proper High Street like they used to be. Nadia didn't think she'd seen anywhere quite so lovely. Then they'd climbed, up and up out of the town and into the hills until they'd eventually found Cumbria Cottage.

'Wow,' Autumn said. 'Look at this place. It was certainly worth it.'

'It's stunning,' Nadia agreed, readily. You could always rely on Chantal to pull something spectacular out of the bag. 'There's hardly anything else for miles. This is the epitome of the word remote.' The hill above and the lake below were simply breathtaking. She couldn't wait to get out of the car and have a good look round.

'We won't have too much light left,' Miles said, stretching. 'We should unpack the car as soon as possible.'

Chantal, in boots with a shawl wrapped round her shoulders, rushed out to greet them. 'So glad you made it. Clive and Tristan have just arrived too. They got here a bit earlier than expected and are already on the booze.'

'It won't be long before I'm joining them,' Nadia said. 'A glass of something with bubbles in is calling.'

'Five minutes and it will be all yours. You should see the room you and Lewis have got. It's beautiful. You have a view right over the lake.'

Nadia hugged her. 'Thanks for organising this, Chantal. It was a great idea.'

Her friend held her at arm's length. 'Jacob's here too. I believe I have you to thank for that?'

They hugged each other tightly.

'You should be together,' Nadia said. 'There's no doubt about it. I wanted to see the smile back on your face and no one can do that quite like Jacob.'

'I do love him,' Chantal admitted. 'I think I always have.'

'Ease me in gently, though.' She met Chantal's eyes. 'I had become very fond of him. Please tell me that you're not sharing a room?'

'No,' Chantal assured her. 'Definitely not. I adore Jacob. I always have, but I think I need to get everything sorted with Ted before I even think about pouncing on him.'

'But you do want to pounce?'

Chantal smiled. 'I'm feeling more pouncey than I have in a very long time.'

They both laughed at that.

'Come on in. Don't get cold.'

'I'll help Autumn and Miles to unload first,' Nadia said. 'It won't hurt to let Lewis run off some steam. He's done really well to handle being cooped up in the car for so long, but I don't want him being fractious later.' She glanced over at her son and Florence who were racing round the garden, scooping up snow and throwing it over each other.

Miles and Autumn carried some of the cases into the house and Nadia followed with a box of provisions. 'Stay in the garden, Lewis. I won't be a minute.'

She stood the box on the counter, marvelled at the farmhouse kitchen and then went outside again. As she emerged into the snow there was a man coming up the drive, head down, walking in a determined manner and clutching a bottle. A small black and white sheepdog followed him at his heel. When, eventually, he looked up and saw her, he waved a hand in greeting.

He wore a flat tweed cap that failed to completely cover his dark curls and a green, waxed jacket and green boots. He was also tall, sturdily built and rather handsome. Perhaps he was a little older than her, but not much. His ruddy cheeks showed that he had an outdoor lifestyle. Something inside Nadia did a little somersault.

'Hello, there,' he said as he approached. 'I'm your neighbour, James Barnsworth. Came to see how you're settling in.'

He slipped a hand from his pocket and held it out. Nadia shook it.

'Nadia Stone,' she said. 'We've only just this minute arrived, but some of the others have been here for a little while. It's a beautiful place.'

'My family home,' he said. 'Or it was. I live in the next farmhouse down.' He pointed to somewhere unseen in the distance.

'You still own this?'

He nodded. 'We still farm the land here, but there's just me and my two children now, so this place is far too big for us.'

No Mrs Barnsworth, Nadia noted.

'It looks great but it's a devil to heat in the winter. We have something much more modest.' He glanced over to where Lewis was making aeroplane wings and zooming round the garden like a mad thing. 'Is that your son?'

'Yes.' She risked another appraisal of him while he observed Lewis, a wry smile on his lips. Her first assessment had been right. He really was *quite* handsome. 'The little girl is our friend's daughter, Florence. I don't think either of them has ever seen this amount of snow before. I thought we had it bad in London, but this is something else.'

'It can be harsh up here.' He watched Lewis for another moment and then asked, 'How old is he?'

'He's four. Coming up to five.'

'My son's six and my daughter's eight. I have a houseful today and tomorrow – family – but they'll all be gone by Boxing Day. You should all come over for a drink. Lewis and Florence can meet my two. They'll be unbearably hyperactive by then.'

'That would be great.'

'You might be going stir crazy yourselves by then. We could take a walk beside the lake.'

'I'd like that. It's really very beautiful here. Do you ever get tired of this view?' she asked.

'This?' He gestured at the snow-capped mountains, the lake, and then shook his head. 'Never. I was born and brought up here, yet I still feel my heart beat faster when I look at the mountains.'

'I can't imagine what it must be like to live somewhere like this. My house is a tiny, terraced place in a rather scruffy part of London.'

'Then I'm glad that you've come to see my part of the world.' He held up his bottle. 'Can't stay long, but I thought I'd bring this to wish you all merry Christmas.'

'You must come and say hello to the others. They'd love to meet you.'

'I have things to do,' he said. 'But my mobile number is up on the chalk board next to the big fridge. The signal can be a bit erratic, but text me and we can fix up a time for you all to come over.'

He handed over a bottle of fine port.

'Thank you. That's very kind.'

'No bother.' He turned and started to walk away. 'If there's anything you need, I'm just down the road. I'll speak to you soon. Merry Christmas, Nadia.'

'Merry Christmas, James,' she echoed and was surprised to find herself smiling.

Autumn and Miles came out of the kitchen.

'Wow,' Autumn said. 'Who's the hottie?'

'Our nearest neighbour, apparently. James Barnsworth, gentleman farmer.' She held up the bottle for examination. 'He brought us this to say merry Christmas.'

439

'Hmm. Nice. Him *and* the port,' Autumn concluded. Then she grinned at Nadia. 'He's certainly put a smile on your face.'

Nadia beamed back. 'Yeah,' she said, still aware of the unfamiliar fluttering in her stomach. 'He has.'

Chapter Eighty-Seven

It's Christmas Eve at Chocolate Heaven and I'm rushed off my feet, keeping the café customers happy and serving those simply calling in to collect their Christmas orders or to buy a few last-minute gifts.

After I close up here I have a long drive up to the Lake District tonight. By myself, too. I don't feel like going at all. I was so looking forward to this, being with Crush at Christmas in the company of good friends, surrounded by kids and presents. Now I'll be on my own again and I really hoped that this year things would be different.

It's snowing outside and laughing people laden down with carrier bags filled with presents pass by the window. It's so very Christmassy and I wish with every fibre of my being that I was going home to Crush, that we would make love on the rug in front of the fire with me wearing nothing but a fetching garland of tinsel. But it's not to be. I haven't heard from Crush at all. Not a card with a smiley Santa or a cheeky snowman. Nothing. It's been ages now – I could actually tell you exactly down to the days, hours and minutes, but that would be too, too sad.

The last stragglers are finishing up their coffees now and are heading home for the holidays. As I watch them go out into the snow, my phone pings. For a moment, my aching heart surges with joy. It could be Crush. He could have had a change of heart this Christmastime. He could have heard a sentimental song – 'It'll be Lonely This Christmas', 'All I Want For Christmas is You' or 'Last Christmas' – there are plenty of them to choose from and maybe it made him think of me. Suddenly, he'd be overwhelmed with a sense of loss and realise how very much he missed me and that it wasn't too late to get me back.

That's what it could be.

But, of course it's not Crush. It's Chantal.

Don't you even think about not coming, she texts. *The motorway is clear and the roads up here aren't too bad either. You can still get through OK. Drive safely. We'll see you later. Love you loads. xx*

Sending her two kisses in return, I pocket my phone again. There's no way out. I'm going to the Lake District whether I like it or not.

My mood darkens again. I wanted it to be Crush. I *so* wanted it to be Crush. But if I could will something into being then he'd have phoned me by now.

Instead, before I can think better of it, I pick up my phone and call him. Even though I have vowed not to. It's Christmas and I can't get him out of my mind. I punch in his number. As always, it goes straight to voicemail. I feel he must be screening my number.

Before I speak, I take a deep breath. It was a mistake to attempt this without eating chocolate beforehand – a *bad* mistake – but I launch myself in anyway.

'Hi. It's Lucy,' I say. 'Again. I just wanted to wish you merry Christmas and to let you know that I'm thinking of you. A lot. All the time.' I wait in case he's really listening and may pick up. He doesn't. So I press on. 'I may be ditzy. I may drive you mad. I may do ridiculously stupid things. And I admit that taking my clothes off with a stranger in a hotel is up there among the worst. Letting Marcus trick me into going to Bruges wasn't that bright either, come to think of it. But I still love you with all of my heart and surely that counts for something?' Still nothing. 'Anyway, merry Christmas, Aiden. I hope you have a wonderful time, whatever you do.' He might be making love to someone else draped in nothing but tinsel on someone else's rug in front of someone else's fire. 'And, if you're not busy and you ever feel the need to call me, then I'll be very happy. More than that.'

Then, as I'm in danger of rambling, I hang up. Bugger.

At least I wasn't drunk.

Probably better if I had been.

Then, as if I'm not depressed enough, the now-familiar red Ferrari pulls up outside the door. Marcus. That's all I need.

'Hey.' He comes in as the last of my customers departs, so we're alone in Chocolate Heaven. 'Don't look so miserable, it's Christmas.'

'I had noticed.'

'I've only come to wish you the very best of the season.'

'Merry Christmas, Marcus,' I say. 'Now you can go. I've got to lock up and get on the road.'

'Oh, yeah. You're off to the Lakes.'

'Chantal has rented a cottage for us just outside of Keswick.' Then I realise that I should only tell Marcus things on a Need To Know basis. And he really doesn't need to know where I'm going.

'Is . . . er . . . wotsit . . . not going with you?'

'*Aiden*,' I supply. 'And, no. We're still . . . estranged.' The word cuts me to the very quick.

'Estranged?' Marcus raises an eyebrow. 'That sounds pretty terminal to me.'

'Whether it is or not, it's none of your business.'

'So you're heading up to there alone? It's a hell of a drive. Especially in the snow.'

'That's why I can't stand around chatting, Marcus.' I glance pointedly at my watch. 'I need to get going.'

'I haven't got any plans for Christmas. I'm going to spend it by myself.' Marcus puts on his little-boy-lost face. 'I don't suppose you'd consider squeezing in another small one? I don't take up much room.'

I look at his face and it melts my heart. No one should be alone at Christmas and it's on the tip of my tongue to invite him.

'We could even share a bed, to save space,' he suggests.

Then I remember what Marcus is like and that the girls will kill me if I turn up with him in tow and I step back from the edge.

'I really do have to be going, Marcus,' I say sadly.

'I bought you this.' He hands over a small and beautifully wrapped box. 'Just a little something.'

I stare down at it. I know that from Marcus, it definitely *won't* be a 'little something'. 'I've already got a diamond bracelet from you that I won't wear. You really shouldn't buy me anything.'

'I told you that I'd prove to you how much I love you.'

With a sigh, I go to undo the scarlet red ribbon.

'Don't open it now,' he says. 'Save it until Christmas Day.'

I put the box on the counter.

'Just one Christmas kiss and I'll be gone?'

'A hug,' I say. 'No kissing. No tongues. No nuzzling my neck. Nothing.'

Marcus laughs. 'When did you become such a cruel woman?'

'Shortly after you tricked me into going to Bruges with you.'

Marcus shrugs. 'You can't blame me for trying.'

No, I guess not. Realising that it is pointless resisting, I go round the counter and into Marcus's open arms. He holds me tightly.

'I love you,' he whispers against my neck. Which is very nearly almost nuzzling despite what I said. 'Never forget that.' Then he breaks away from me. 'Merry Christmas, Lucy Lombard.'

'Merry Christmas, Marcus.'

He goes to the door and blows me a kiss and mouths, 'I love you.'

As Marcus leaves, I stand and watch him drive away. He always leaves me in such turmoil – regret, sadness, frustration, exasperation, annoyance, attraction and, maybe deep down in there, still some love.

Heavy of heart, I tidy up inside Chocolate Heaven. It's just me here, alone. I turn off the lights and stand in the café for a moment, thinking about all the fun we've had here, the Chocolate Lovers' Club. It feels as if an era is coming to an end. Things have changed for me, for Nadia, Autumn and Chantal. I suppose that's the fluid nature of friendships. We've been here for each other through thick and thin, but maybe we'll all be moving on now. The ties that have bound us together may be loosening as time passes. Nothing ever stays the same. I'm the best one to tell you about that.

There are other cafés where we could quite happily meet, I know, but there was something very special about this place and, with new owners, that could be lost for ever. I don't even know if they're going to carry on with the business as it stands. As a minion, I'm not even in the loop. For all I know, my dear Chocolate Heaven could be a noodle bar by the end of January. The thought floods me with sadness.

It's Christmas and I should be happy. But I'm not.

I want to stay here, linger as long as I can soaking up the atmosphere, but I can't. I need to be on the road. So I take the goodies that I've packed for the Lake District from behind the counter. We're there for four days and it wouldn't do to run short of chocolate, so I've made sure I've got plenty. No one will go wanting for the lack of a chocolate reindeer. Besides, what am I to do with them in January? Then I realise that it may not even be my problem. I could be out on my ear. I might have been running this place, but I have no contract, no rights, no severance pay. Nothing.

With a weary sigh I head to the door. I have a long drive ahead of me and all I want to do is lie down on the pavement and let the snow fall on top of me.

Possibly for the very last time, I lock the door behind me and then I stand and look up at the sign. Chocolate Heaven. A place of happy times and great memories and exceedingly good chocolate.

'Goodbye Chocolate Heaven,' I say out loud. 'I'm sad to be leaving. You were a lot of fun.'

The tears that roll down my cheeks feel hot against my chilled skin. Well, there's nothing more to be done. Laden with boxes of chocolates and goodies, I go round the corner, find my car which is loaded up to the gills. I'm relieved to see that it doesn't have a parking ticket – perhaps even the vulture-like traffic wardens round here had a bit of Christmas spirit today. I climb into my car and sit and hold the steering wheel, just trying to still my mind. My thoughts are racing, none of them coherent. Some would say no change there. I attempt a bit of deep breathing, but that only steams up my windscreen.

Having failed to reach any sort of inner serenity, I start the engine. I have a long drive ahead of me so I'd better brace myself and get started. It's going to be midnight before I reach the cottage in the Lakes and for one silly, stupid fleeting moment, I wish that Marcus was coming with me.

Chapter Eighty-Eight

It's gone midnight when I finally arrive at the cottage. Despite Chantal's assurances, the motorway wasn't clear and the roads up to the cottage were nearly impassable. More than once I was terrified that I was going to end up in a ditch. At some points on the journey, my poor little car was nearly up to its axle in snow and I was almost driven mad by the constant clacking of my windscreen wipers as they battled to swipe the continually falling flakes away. But I'm here. Somehow, we've made it through.

I nearly weep with relief when I turn into the drive and see the lights of the cottage shining out in the darkness, welcoming me. The moon is high and the snow on the ground glitters like blue diamonds in its light. As soon as I pull up outside, Chantal opens the door and runs out to greet me. She has a shawl held over her head to ward off the snow.

'You made it,' she says.

Now I do cry. Big, fat tears to match the big, fat snowflakes. She lets go of her shawl and holds on tightly to me instead. 'Come on, we've all waited up for you.'

She takes my bag and, huddled together under the shawl,

we slither our way back to the door. The warmth from the massive country kitchen hits me the minute I walk in. I can feel it right down to my bones and it's so soothing, comforting that I can feel all my tension disappear.

'There's some chicken casserole left. Do you want tea or hard stuff?'

'Both.'

'Fab. Start with this.' She sloshes some red wine into a glass and I gulp it gratefully. 'Better?'

'Much.' I take in my surroundings. 'Look at this place. It's fantastic. Did you pick it from the Fantasy Christmas Catalogue?'

'Wait until you see the living room. Go through,' she says. 'We've got a roaring fire going. Move Jacob from in front of it.'

'He's here?'

She looks at me and smiles. 'Nadia asked him.'

'I hate to broach this, but for you or for her?'

'For me.' Unusually, Chantal looks bashful. 'It's early days, but I think we're going to try and make a go of it together, Lucy. Slowly, slowly. I've got a lot to sort out with Ted, but I can see Jacob and I being a couple in the future.'

'That's good to know. You've always had something special.'

'Little steps,' she says. 'But I feel very optimistic.'

I kiss her. 'So you should.'

'Go and get warm. I'll bring your supper through for you.'

So I leave Chantal and head into the living room, opening the latch on the farmhouse-style door.

'I made it,' I announce as I go in. Then I'm stopped in my tracks. The room is so beautiful that it makes me gasp. The huge Christmas tree in the corner sparkles magically, dressed from head to toe in gold and silver baubles, myriad twinkling lights shining out. Beneath it, there's a pile of stylishly wrapped presents. There's a roaring fire at one end, the fireplace dressed with garlands of holly and red poinsettia flowers. On the large coffee table there's a centrepiece of a silver platter with a display of candles and silver stags. All my friends are hunkered down on the cosy sofas: Nadia, Autumn and Miles, Clive, Tristan and Jacob.

'Lucy!'

Nadia and Autumn jump up and come to kiss me.

'We're so glad that you're here safe and sound,' Nadia says. 'Your face is freezing. Come and sit by the fire.'

Clive and Tristan hug me to death, too. Whatever happens with Chocolate Heaven, I know that we'll still be friends.

Sure enough, as Chantal said, Jacob is sprawled out looking very content in one of the armchairs nearest the fire. His cheeks are pink from the heat and, when he sees me, he rouses and comes to kiss me.

'Good to see you.' I wink at him as I hug him and he knows that I'm going to grill him about what's happened the minute I get the chance. 'Did you do all this?'

'Chantal and me. Team Christmas. We only just got it finished in time.'

'Well, it looks perfect. You couldn't have done it any better.'

Chantal follows in with the promised bowl of chicken casserole and a hunk of bread on a tray for me. They're all so kind that it makes me want to cry again. This is where you should be at Christmas, surrounded by family, friends, people who love you.

Then I think of Crush. He should be here with me. He would have loved it. We have all the elements for the most perfect Christmas ever – beautiful setting, fabulous friends, flowing wine, more snow than you can shake a stick at. This is like a dream come true. There is only one thing missing for me. And that's the most important thing. The love of my life isn't here for Christmas and that makes me sadder than you can imagine.

Chapter Eighty-Nine

I wake and, for a moment, I don't know where I am. Then I remember, I'm at a winter wonderland cottage in the Lake District and it's Christmas Day.

There's a hushed silence all around. I kneel up in the bed and look out of the window. The view is incredible. It was dark when I arrived, so I missed all of this splendour. Now it takes my breath away. There's beautiful unspoilt country-side, dusted white, as far as the eye can see. Below us, a broad swathe of shimmering silver water. If I'd looked at Chantal's brochure properly, I could even tell you what lake it was. But I didn't and, therefore, I can't. That doesn't stop it from being hugely impressive, though. On the far side of the lake immense snow-clad mountains rise above a frame-work of bare grey trees. What I've seen of the cottage so far looks amazing and I'm really glad that I did make the effort to get up here.

As I lie back in my bed, luxuriating in my surroundings, I hear movement downstairs and think that I must rouse myself. Chantal, of course, has booked the most splendid accommo-dation which means that I have an en-suite bathroom all to myself. I stand in the shower and let the hot water work its magic.

When I emerge ten minutes later, I feel almost human again. Despite being here alone and despite all the things that you know about, I do feel a surge of excitement. I adore Christmas. Though I'd hoped for a slightly better one this year in the love department, I'm determined to make the best of it. No sulky puss from me! No doubt Chantal will keep me well supplied with champagne, which is sure to help.

Downstairs, I'm the last to arrive in the farmhouse kitchen. Everyone else is assembled round the massive table in the middle and my heart lifts to see them here. It would take very little to make me cry. I'm saved from weeping only by the mouth-watering smell of cooking bacon in the air. Looks like bucks fizz is the order of the day. The table is a clutter of cereal packets.

'Merry Christmas, everyone,' I say.

Then everyone gets up and hugs me and wishes me merry Christmas and I'm nearly in pieces again.

Chantal says as she hands me a glass, 'Did you sleep well?'

'Like a log.' I lift my drink to toast my friends. 'Cheers. Here's to a fabulous Christmas!'

'Cheers!' they echo.

Eventually, after much kissing and hugging, breakfast is resumed. Clive and Tristan budge up and I sit down next to them. Clive puts his arm round me and I lean against him, cosy in his cuddle. I don't really want to talk about Chocolate Heaven now, as reality is a vastly overrated state and I can't face this conversation on an empty stomach, but it must be had.

'Why didn't you sell Chocolate Heaven to Autumn?' I say miserably. 'We'd have made a great job of it. You would have left your business in safe hands.'

'It will still be fine,' Clive assures me. 'I've sold it to a great company. I told them what a fantastic job you're doing as manager. They're still going to run it on the same lines. Things won't change at all.'

'You can't be sure of that.'

'They were so keen to have the business, Lucy – desperate almost – that I can't believe they'll want to change it. When I told them someone else was interested, they just upped the offer. And they're paying cash, which means it could go through quickly.'

'Even so . . .'

'You have absolutely nothing to worry about,' he says. 'Trust me. This is a great solution for all of us.'

'It would have been a good venture for Autumn.'

'It's a massive commitment, Lucy. We're talking a *lot* of money. I'd have worried about Autumn being in too deep.' He hugs me. 'You won't even notice the changeover.'

'I hope you're right.' I'm still not sure if I'm mollified.

'You're our friend. Our *best* friend. We've done this in your interests, too.'

And I should believe in that. The guys wouldn't deliberately let me down. They're great and I should trust Clive's instincts.

In fact, looking round the table, I can't believe how lucky I am to have such good friends and I sit and let the general chatter wash over me, feeling content despite my bruised and battered heart and the inevitability of having a new boss soon. There isn't one of us here who hasn't weathered similar or more difficult storms and I know that with their help I'll survive again.

Nadia looks more relaxed than I've seen her in a long time. She's chatting easily to Jacob and I'm so pleased to see that they're still friends. Lana is on her lap and the baby is dozing happily. Autumn looks quite smitten with Miles and I can see them holding hands beneath the table. Nice. I can also see them down the aisle within a year.

Chantal piles sausages and bacon on a huge platter and puts it in the middle of the table. A few seconds later there's a big dish of scrambled eggs.

'Dive in,' she instructs. Whereupon we all fall on it.

While we eat, Nadia comes and sits next to me and kisses my cheek. Lewis slides onto my lap. 'Hiya, champ. How are you doing?'

'Good,' he says, but he's engrossed with the car he's running along the edge of the kitchen table.

'This is a fantastic place,' Nadia says. 'We drove through the town yesterday. I only got a brief glimpse, but it's so lovely that it makes me wonder why I live where I do.'

'Yeah,' I agree. 'It's a tough choice. Dirty old Camden or rather splendid Keswick?'

'We've had a few holidays up this way,' Chantal throws in. 'The only trouble is that you can buy any product you want in the world – so long as it's made of fleece.'

'And we'd miss you at Chocolate Heaven,' Autumn says.

I don't give further voice to my fears for the future of our favourite chocolate emporium. I'm just going to have to keep my fingers and toes crossed and hope that Clive is right about what will happen there.

'Nadia has already been eyeing up the local talent,' Autumn teases.

'I have not!' Our friend is outraged.

'Tell me more.'

'Gentleman farmer James Barnsworth came calling yesterday,' Chantal fills in.

'He owns this place,' Nadia says. 'But he lives just down the hill. He invited us all there on Boxing Day.'

'All of us?'

'He's just being neighbourly. Nothing more,' she insists. 'And he has children similar ages to Lewis and Florence. I thought it would be nice. He suggested a walk by the lake.'

'You've been quick, Ms Nadia Stone,' I whisper.

'Stop it, Lucy,' she hisses back at me. But her cheeks flame with colour and she looks remarkably coy.

'I have some good news to share with you all,' Autumn adds. 'Nadia and Miles already know, but I had a call yesterday from the Find Families agency. Willow's adoptive mother has been in touch with them. Willow wants to meet me in the new year.'

'That's fantastic.' I give Autumn a hug.

'I hope so. I still can hardly believe it.'

That's the hard thing about Christmas, isn't it? For some it's a time of family, reconciliation, unity and happiness. For others it's a time of loneliness – even in the midst of a crowd of wonderful friends – regret and thinking about what might have been. I have my phone; I could just call Crush and wish him merry Christmas. That would be the thing to do. But I don't know where he is and, what worries me more, he may not be alone.

Chapter Ninety

When our carb levels are topped up with a multiplicity of toast and marmalade to finish off breakfast, we all head through to the living room. The Christmas tree lights are already on and the fire is roaring in the grate. Beneath the tree is a pile of presents, including the mystery one from Marcus, which I put there last night.

There are so many beautifully wrapped boxes that I'm not sure how Autumn and Miles actually managed to fit in the car with them. Supervised by Autumn and Nadia, Florence and Lewis are already over-excited and are ripping open presents at a rate of knots. I think we'd better take them out to play in the snow later to run off a bit of energy. A bracing walk and a snowball fight wouldn't go amiss and, at some point, there's a Christmas dinner to be cooked – my favourite meal of the year.

Before that though, we have important business to attend to. The rest of us sit on the sofas and, while Lana is still contentedly snoozing in her chair, Chantal and Jacob do the honours of handing out the many gifts.

He gives me a present and kisses my cheek. 'Merry Christmas, Lucy.'

I pull him close and, while no one's paying us any attention, whisper, 'It's good to see you here, Jacob. I hope everything turns out well for you and Chantal.'

'I hope so, too.'

'We need a happy ending.'

'It seems to have been a convoluted route getting here,' he says. 'Why do we all make our lives so complicated, Lucy?'

'Sometimes it happens without us really meaning to.' Look at my own scenario. Everything I try to do, however well-intentioned, turns to total disaster. I am the past master of it.'

'Speaking of which, no Crush?' he asks.

'We've split up,' I tell him. 'Sadly.'

'I thought you'd got it right this time, Lucy.'

'Yeah,' I agree. 'Me too.'

'Jacob,' Chantal says. 'Pass this one to Lucy.'

He hands me the box from Marcus. 'This is from you-know-who,' I confide. 'Chantal will kill me if she knows.'

Chantal flops down next to me. 'If I know what?'

Gah. 'This is from Marcus.' I show her the pretty box.

She tuts at me, exasperated. 'It will be something ridiculously expensive and extravagant. More one-upmanship than gift.'

'He's no one to out-do,' I point out. 'Crush isn't here.'

'Sorry, I shouldn't have said that. It's a gift and, even though it's from Marcus, I'm sure it's well-intentioned.'

'You were probably right the first time,' I admit.

'Better get it opened then.'

I do as I'm told, carefully untwining the lavish ribbon. As Chantal has voiced, I bet it's more diamonds or something profligate. That's Marcus's style.

When I lift the lid off the box, I look inside and see a chunky key made out of glossy dark chocolate.

Chantal wrinkles her nose, puzzled. 'Has to be something cryptic.'

'There's a note with it.' Taking out the key, I retrieve the small card from underneath it. A cartoon reindeer grins at me. I open it and read out loud: '*My darling Lucy. This isn't the key to my heart – you already hold that.*'

'I think I might be sick,' Chantal says.

I roll my eyes in agreement and continue, '*I told you that I'd prove to you how much I love you and I only hope this makes you realise that I'm truly sincere. This is the key to Chocolate Heaven. I've bought it for you.*'

I look up at Chantal and Jacob and their mouths have dropped open.

My own mouth has gone as dry as a bone. He said he'd do something to prove that he loved me. I guess this is it. Oh, Marcus. I let out a long and bewildered breath. 'I can't believe this.'

Chantal shakes her head. 'Me neither.'

Now my hands are trembling. Gripping the note, I read on. '*I want you to have it, to run it as your own business. No strings.*'

But there will be strings with Marcus, I'm only too aware of that.

'*Have a merry Christmas, my dearest darling. I love you as I always have. Marcus.*' There are lots of kisses on the bottom.

I hold up the chocolate key, struck dumb. Marcus has bought Chocolate Heaven. I don't know whether to weep with joy or despair.

Chapter Ninety-One

We all sit and stare at the key in my hands, unspeaking.

'Wow,' Chantal manages eventually. 'Is this for real?'

'Of course it is.' I want to bang my head hard on the rather attractive coffee table, but I consider the candles and the stags. 'What shall I do? What *can* I do?'

'It might not be a bad thing,' Jacob says, a hopeful note in his voice. 'You've got to hand it to Marcus. He's big on the grand gesture.'

'There's no way he's going to hand the business over lock, stock and barrel. I know Marcus too well. I'll be his employee, his *serf*.' My heart sinks. 'He'll be my boss. I'll have to see him every day, answer to him. He'll meddle to his heart's content. There *will* be strings.' As many as Marcus thinks he can get away with.

'I could kill Clive,' Chantal says. 'What was he thinking of?'

Clive looks up from his present opening, suddenly aware of our complaining, and grins at us. 'What have I done?'

'You sold Chocolate Heaven to Marcus,' I wail. 'Why would you do that, Clive? Out of all the people in the world you chose Marcus?'

The colour drains from Clive's face. 'Marcus? We didn't. We sold it to an investment company. They assured us they'd still want the business to run as it had been. It's a fantastic deal and I thought that Chocolate Heaven would be in safe hands. I told you this. We recommended you as manager and they sounded thrilled. They seemed really keen for the business to continue seamlessly.'

'Did you ever meet this company?'

'No,' Clive admits. 'We did it all through the agent. They came highly recommended.'

'And what was the company called?'

'Canning Investments,' Clive says.

'*Marcus* Canning,' I tell him. 'Bloody Marcus bloody Canning bloody Investments.'

'Oh.' He and Tristan exchange a worried glance. 'We didn't even consider Marcus might be involved. Why would we?'

'I wish you'd taken Autumn's offer. You know that we would have loved to run it.'

'I'm sorry, Lucy.' He looks distraught at this turn of events. 'We signed on the dotted line before we left yesterday. I think we're fully committed now.'

'I wish you'd talked to us. Given us some time. Autumn could have perhaps got more money and the Chocolate Heaven legacy could have continued unchanged. Who knows what will happen now?'

Clive looks distraught. 'Couldn't you still manage it for Marcus?'

'No.' I shake my head sadly. 'Never.' Knowing Marcus as I do, he'd twist me round his little finger until I didn't know which way was up.

Now Autumn and Nadia come over. 'What's the problem?'

'Marcus has bought Chocolate Heaven,' I tell them, flatly.

461

'He's given me this.' I show them the chocolate key and hand over Marcus's note for them to read.

They scan it, looking increasingly worried.

'We know how much Chocolate Heaven means to you,' Nadia says. 'Think carefully about this, Lucy. Don't be in too much of a rush to say no.'

'You might feel differently in the new year,' Autumn offers.

'I won't,' I vow. 'Marcus has only done this to get me in his grasp again. I'm devastated.'

'There's only one thing for it.' Chantal hands me a chocolate reindeer.

But, do you know, I don't even feel like eating chocolate. My appetite has completely disappeared. That's how bad this is.

Chapter Ninety-Two

When we've unwrapped all of the presents, we manage to drag ourselves away from the heat of the roaring fire and head out into the snow. The day is bright, sharp and there are a few tentative snowflakes falling. It's just how Christmas Day should be.

We bundle ourselves into all the warm clothes we've brought and walk down to the lake in the freezing air. Meandering along the snow-sprinkled shore, Jacob leads the skimming of flat stones into the slate-coloured water. We all try our hand and stand to watch them hop and skip across the surface of the lake. Then we admire the majestic peaks around us beneath a grey-white sky that threatens yet more snow. I show Lewis and Florence, both in colourful wellies, how to stamp on iced-over puddles until they crackle, satisfyingly, under foot.

The beauty of it all makes me forget that I'm unloved and about my dilemma with Marcus and Chocolate Heaven. Almost. Afterwards, we go back to the garden of the cottage and build a snowman, project-managed by Jacob and Miles, who clearly both have degrees in snowman building. He is a fine specimen though, when we've finished. Chantal finds a short, fat carrot from our veg stash for his nose and we use black stones for his eyes. Clive hands over his pink cashmere scarf to bring a touch of Islington to our creation and Miles donates his beanie hat. When we're tired and our gloves are wet through, we head back indoors. The scent of the cooking turkey in the Aga wafts out to greet us and makes us realise that it's been quite a while since breakfast.

We spend ages stripping off our outdoor clothes and hanging them to dry in the utility room where the boiler is kicking out plentiful heat. Everyone's hair is damp or tousled from hats. Our faces are pink-cheeked, raw with cold. Divested, we then pad about the kitchen in our socks, huddling close to the range, while Chantal makes hot chocolate for the children and mulled wine for the adults.

This has been a lovely day and, despite my sadness and the Crush-shaped hole in my heart, I've really enjoyed myself. It would be hard not to fall in love with this place.

Someone puts Michael Bublé on the iPod and he croons out Christmas tunes while we sing along. Once she's had a restorative glass of wine or two, Chantal starts to prepare the Christmas dinner. We all fall into helping her. Clive and Tristan are put in charge of the starters – pea and ham soup or smoked salmon blinis. I peel potatoes and carrots. Jacob is in charge of sprouts. Nadia is slicing parsnips. Miles, with the help of Lewis and Florence, sets the big farmhouse table for us all. It's a lovely time of chatter and laughter.

It's still a hive of activity when there's a knock at the front door and we all jump.

'I didn't hear a car,' Chantal says. 'We're not expecting anyone else, are we?'

'It could be farmer James,' Autumn teases.

'It better not be Marcus.' I wipe my hands on a towel. I remember letting slip that we were heading for Keswick.

Despite my earlier crossness, I had actually managed to push my troubles to the back of my mind – not hindered by three glasses of mulled wine. 'It would be just like him to follow me up here.' He's probably hiding behind a bush waiting for just this moment.

'You stay put,' Chantal says. 'I'll get it.'

'I'll go. If it is Marcus,' and I have a *very* strong suspicion that it is, 'then I'm the one who has to face him.'

So, with a deep breath, I gird my loins – even though I'm not exactly sure what that means – and I march to the door ready for action.

Chapter Ninety-Three

When I wrench open the door, the wind whips up a flurry of snow. It's coming down really heavily now and fat, lacy flakes drift in the air. It feels as if I'm on the inside of a snow globe.

Standing there is a man in a bright red Santa outfit, trimmed with fake fur. His beard curls down to his waist. Despite the disguise, I'd know him anywhere. Also his car is parked on the drive. Which is a bit of a giveaway.

'Hello, little girl,' he says softly through his beard. 'I've come to bring your Christmas present.'

I think about being cool, taking this in my stride. But I can't. That's just not me. Instead, I launch myself into his arms. 'Thank you,' I say. 'Thank you so much.'

'You don't know what it is yet,' Crush says.

'I don't care.' I'm sobbing now. 'You're here and that's all that matters.'

'Don't cry,' he says, wiping away a tear with his black-gloved thumb.

'I can't help it. I'm so happy.'

'You could put me down now, Gorgeous. It's quite cold here and you're letting all the snow into the porch.'

Reluctantly, I unwind my arms from round his neck and he steps inside, shaking the snow from his hat and beard.

'How did you even know where I was?'

Crush sighs. 'I contacted Marcus. I knew that if there was anyone who'd know, then it would be him. Sure enough, he'd somehow managed to find out. I had to threaten him to get the details out of him.'

Oh, Marcus. What are you like? He's probably got contacts in MI5 and, at this very minute, has a drone trained on me monitoring my every move. I daren't even mention the latest revelation about Chocolate Heaven to Crush. That will have to keep for another day.

'I'm sorry that I went off like that,' Crush says. 'I don't know what got into me. I wanted to come back, but my stupid pride wouldn't allow me to. I let you down and I don't blame you for not contacting me again.'

'I did,' I say. 'I rang you all the time.'

Crush looks confused. 'Not me.'

I check my phone. 'Hundreds of calls, none of them answered. The same number of texts, none of them returned.'

Crush takes my phone and looks at the screen. 'That's not my number.'

I grab the phone back. 'Isn't it?' All of the calls have gone to my dad. No wonder Crush didn't answer them. Gah!

I do remember my dad sending me a rather cross text about something now, but in the depths of my misery I didn't actually read it properly. Doh.

'When you called yesterday – that one *was* my number, incidentally – it made me realise that I still had a chance.'

'I came to see you and you were having such a lovely time at the pub with someone else that I thought it was all over.'

'When I saw you, I followed you,' he says. 'I ran up the road after you, but once you'd gone into the Tube, I couldn't find you. Then I thought that you'd think I was just like Marcus and would want nothing to do with me.' Crush manages a smile. 'One Marcus is enough in your life.'

'Oh, God. What fools we've been.'

'But that's behind us now.'

'It was all my fault,' I say. 'All of it. It always is. I know that I'm stupid and irritating, but I love you so much.'

He puts a finger under my chin and kisses me. His fake beard tickles my lips. 'I love you too, Gorgeous. No matter what ditzy things you do, I'm in this for good. If you'll have me back.'

I'm overwhelmed by how much love I feel for this man.

'You never went away,' I tell him. 'Not for me.'

'Oh, Lucy.' He grins at me. 'I have missed you.'

'Come in. Come in.' I pull him towards the kitchen. 'The others will be amazed.'

Almost touching the low beams, Crush edges inside and stands dripping on the stone floor. 'Hi, everyone.' He waves, awkwardly. 'Merry Christmas.'

Instantly, our friends come over and swarm round him, hugging him.

'We're glad you came,' Chantal says when they've finished cuddling him half to death. 'For Lucy's sake. Now take off that rather fetching outfit and let me get you a well-deserved drink.'

He removes his Santa hat and his beard, self-consciously.

'I've just got one little thing to attend to first, if you don't mind,' Crush says. And, with that, he drops to one knee in front of me.

I feel all the breath leave my body.

'Lucy Lombard,' he says solemnly. 'Will you do me the very great honour of becoming my wife?'

'Yes,' I say. 'Yes. Yes. Yes. Yes. Yes. Yes.'

'Lucy, your needle's stuck,' Chantal laughs and then to Crush, 'I think you can safely take that as a yes.'

Crush reaches into the depths of his Santa suit and pulls out a ring box. He flicks open the lid and inside there's a beautiful princess-cut diamond ring.

'It's a new one,' he ventures.

The other one never did see the light of day. It could be lodged in my digestive tract for ever or it could be bobbing its way towards the sea in the sewers of London. I guess we'll never know. But a brand new ring feels like a brand new start.

Crush takes the ring and slips it onto my finger. It fits perfectly, which I think is an omen.

Better still, I don't eat it, drop it, stand on it or break it in any way.

Everyone claps and rushes to give us their congratulations. Crush stands and the men slap him on the back and all the members of the Chocolate Lovers' Club smother me with kisses.

'Let's get married as soon as we can,' he says quietly to me when they've finished fussing over us.

'I'd like that.' I sink into his arms again. This is where I am meant to be. Mr Aiden 'Crush' Holby and me together for ever. This time, you can bet your bottom dollar that I'm going to get him down the aisle as quick as I can before I do anything stupid to mess it up. 'I'd like that very much.'

I look round at my best girls, the Chocolate Lovers' Club, and my eyes fill with tears. I felt as if they were slipping away from me, that everything was changing, but they're not. They're still very much here for me and I know that, whatever happens in our lives, our friendship will always endure. This Christmas has pulled us together again. Chantal, Nadia and Autumn will always be in my life. I don't know what will happen with Chocolate Heaven and right now I'm too happy, too blissed out, to think about what the future might hold, but I do know that our happy little gang of chocoholics will go on. It's not about the place where we meet or what we like to eat, it's about the love that has grown up between us and nothing will change that.

Chantal produces a couple of bottles of champagne and pops the cork. Clive helps her to pour it out. When we're all furnished with a glass, she lifts hers and proposes a toast. 'To Lucy and Aiden!'

'To Lucy and Aiden,' all our friends echo, beaming at us. That makes me cry again and Crush puts his arm round me, protectively.

'To Lucy and Aiden,' I whisper, as I admire my new, sparkling engagement ring. 'I like the sound of that.'

Crush kisses me again.

Outside the snow is still coming down, but we are nestled here in our own cocoon. This is the best Christmas that I've ever had. I'm in love and I'm loved. I'm to become Mrs Aiden Holby. All of my dreams have finally come true.

'Merry Christmas, Gorgeous,' Crush says.

And it is such a very, very merry Christmas that I think I might just burst.

Acknowledgements

To my cherished Team Matthews' Cheerleaders. Thank you so much for being dedicated readers, coming along to events, promoting my books beyond the call of duty, giving me so many laughs, and, most importantly, embracing me as a friend. It's lovely to have you in my life.

Hurrah for you all. Go us!

Acknowledgements

The Chocolate Lovers Rise Again

I came up with the idea for the first book in The Chocolate Lovers' series many moons ago, after a long and slightly boozy lunch with my then agent and editor. We had all ordered very chocolatey desserts and my agent grandly declared that any book with chocolate in the title was bound to fly off the shelves. I found nothing there to argue with.

On the way home on the train to Costa del Keynes, that one sentence had me thinking. I'd been looking for an idea for my next novel that would feature four women and their struggles in life. I've always loved television programmes that dealt with the dynamics between a group of female friends such as *Sex and the City* or *Desperate Housewives* and I really wanted to write something that embraced that vibe. By the time I got off the train, *The Chocolate Lovers' Club* was already half-written in my head.

Thankfully, my editor loved the idea too. Oh, I had such fun with those ladies. Even before I started the book, I'd always been a big chocolate fan, but this took it to a whole new level. I had a great time doing research and fully unleashed the chocoholic within. I also learned a lot about chocolate and how to appreciate the finer chocolatey things in life.

My main character, Lucy Lombard, is, I think, far too much like me and I've always valued my female friends and longed for a group who were as close-knit as The Chocolate Lovers' Club. I like how they are all very different women, only united by their love of chocolate, but sometimes the most diverse people make the best of friends.

Some characters stay with you long after the book is finished and, when I reached the end of *The Chocolate Lovers' Club*, I realised that I hadn't finished with those ladies. Try as I might, they wouldn't leave my head. Their story continued on while I slept at night!

So I went on to write *The Chocolate Lovers' Diet* with more lovely chocolate and mayhem – mainly caused by Lucy. I love how these ladies interact. They have fun and adventures together, they confide in each other and yet are never judgmental. Wouldn't it be nice if we all had a group of friends like that to support us in life?

They proved to be my most popular books worldwide. It seems that women in all countries like their chocolate too – and a good romantic story, of course. As I always had to have a bar of chocolate to hand, I did put on a stone while writing the books, which I never quite managed to lose. Suffering for my art! I still have to write the book about a personal trainer or health spa – or both – to restore my figure to its former glory. Ahem.

A few years went by and I wrote several more books. I got emails nearly every day from readers who were keen to read more about the girls, but I had other tales that I wanted to tell. Then I changed publisher and it seemed as if The Chocolate Lovers' Club would be left behind. But I never quite gave up on them.

Then the joys of social media came along and one day,

quite out of the blue, one of my readers tweeted me, 'Write more about The Chocolate Lovers' Club!' I retweeted it to my editor, Cath, and she sent me one back to say, 'I'm in!' Hurrah!

It seemed as if the time was right. I now write two books a year – a summer book and a very festive Christmas one. It just seemed so obvious to give these ladies a delicious chocolate adventure for Christmas.

So I wrote this book, *The Chocolate Lovers' Christmas*, and it was lovely to take up with them again, just like re-visiting old friends. Plus it meant that I could recommence my chocolate research with renewed enthusiasm. Yay! And what better time than Christmas to have chocolate treats? And I set part of the book in one of my very favourite areas of the country too. My spiritual home is Keswick in Cumbria. I do love it there. There had been a long gap since *The Chocolate Lovers' Diet* but I decided to pick up the story where I left off and delve straight back into their lives. I don't think my readers would have forgiven me if I'd missed a chunk out.

Before the ink from the printer was dry on *The Chocolate Lovers' Christmas*, I knew that these ladies still had more to share and so I went straight on to write *The Chocolate Lovers' Wedding*, which will be out in paperback next spring.

I think the other lovely thing about these ladies is that I, too, have found new friends through our mutual love of all things chocolate. I met Jennifer Earle of Chocolate Ecstasy Tours when she read *The Chocolate Lovers' Club* and invited me on a tour. Now I'm hooked. If you haven't done one yet, definitely put it on your bucket list. I've taken part in several chocolate weekends for the lovely people at the Pudding Club at the Three Ways House Hotel in Mickleton and recently held a Reader Outing there for seventy-five readers and they've become dear friends over the years.

So maybe chocolate – much like love – is a universal language. I think after *The Chocolate Lovers' Wedding* I'm done with the Chocolate Lovers ladies for now. Their story is told. Famous last words. At least, I *think* so. But they're feisty and fun characters and I can never quite be sure . . .

If you enjoyed *The Chocolate Lovers' Christmas*,
you only have to wait until the spring
for Carole's next bestseller,

The Chocolate Lovers' Wedding

Find out what the ladies from
The Chocolate Lovers' Club get up to next in
The Chocolate Lovers' Wedding!

EXCLUSIVE!
Read on to enjoy the first two chapters!

Chapter One

In London you are never knowingly more than ten feet away from a Twix. True fact. There is one, right now, in my desk with my name on it. Third drawer down. Back left hand corner. It's now twelve-thirty and its siren song has been calling me for the last hour.

I'm holding strong. And there's a very good reason for it. I, Lucy Lombard, aficionado of all things chocolate-based, am a recently engaged person and, as such, am of course on a diet. No one wants to sashay down the aisle at their own wedding with the multitude of the congregation sniggering 'lard arse' into their hands, do they?

I sigh with happiness. Not about the diet. I'm not a weirdo. I'm happy because I'm actually to be married to the love of my life, Mr Aiden 'Crush' Holby. After years of unsuitable boyfriends – Marcus Canning in particular springs to mind – and one previous abandonment at the altar – also due to Marcus Canning – I am betrothed to someone who is not only undeniably handsome, but is kind, loving, can cook, likes small animals and, most importantly, is willing to overlook my various foibles and flaws to make me his wife. To the point that he wouldn't *actually* mind if I was packing a little more punch in my wedding frock. Hmm.

Right. That's it. The Twix gets it.

'Lucy.'

Guiltily, my fingers snap back from the drawer. My boss. Wearing his usually expression of harried disdain. How did he know I was about to eat The Forbidden Twix?

'Did you get those figures for me from production?' he growls

Oh, right that. 'Ah, no.'

'I'm sorry to interrupt your daydreaming. Again. But they are quite important.'

In the short time I have worked here at Green Information Technology – or GIT as the employees call it – I have found that Mr Robert Simmonds gives great sarcasm. Sometimes – quite often – he does have a point.

'Sorry. Sorry.' In fairness, he asked me ages ago to get his figures or whatever and I'd completely forgotten. I got a bit side-tracked googling wedding favours and such on the internet. As you do when you are shortly to be a bride. I'm thinking of heart-shaped chocolates or personalised chocolate lollies. It's tough. What would you do?

My boss drums his fingers on the filing cabinet. Mr Simmonds likes to make out that he's a laid-back, hippy person. He brings a quinoa salad in for his lunch, for heaven's sake. But, he's *so* not. He's old, grumpy and is a total stress bunny. He wears a suit and tie when everyone else in this office favours faded jeans and open-necked shirts. My easy-going approach to my job is totally at odds with his uptight, starchy nature. We are terminally unsuited and I should discuss this with my temp agency.

My eyes slide back towards the chocolate bridal favours.

More drumming. 'And you're waiting for?'

'Right. Right.' Must. Stop. Thinking. About. My. Wedding. And. Chocolate. 'I'm on my way.'

With a theatrical tut that's not even necessary, Mr Simmonds – never Rob – slams back into his office. This is a company that is supposed to care about the environment and the planet and all that but, frankly, doesn't give a toss about its employees.

Wearily, I push myself from my desk and head towards the finance department. I could probably just call them, but this will help to fill my endlessly dull day and also burn off some calories to balance out the imminent Twix consumption.

Before I depart, I ease open the desk drawer and take a sneaky peek at it. 'Wait for me, baby,' I coo. 'Mummy won't be long.'

Then I head off to – where was it again? Finance. Finance. That's where I'm going.

I've been working here at Green IT for three months. Three months since Marcus Canning – dastardly ex-fiancé and serial cheat who I may have already mentioned – only went out and bought the best café and chocolate emporium in the whole of London. Chocolate Heaven. This was my sanctuary, my home-from-home, my life, my career. And Marcus has spoiled it all.

I vowed then and there, as long as Marcus was calling the shots, that I'd never darken the door of that blessed place again. True to my word, it's now been three months since I have entered its hallowed halls. Three months. It makes me feel quite dizzy to say it. In all that time, the good ladies of the Chocolate Lovers' Club – Chantal, Nadia, Autumn and my good self – have been wandering the hinterlands of north London like nomads. Having our favourite haunt cruelly snatched from us, we've been meeting at a variety of inferior, less chocolatey cafés across the capital city to indulge our cravings and finding that nothing really floats our boat in quite the same way. No wonder I'm depressed.

During these long three months I have also been back in the dreary, dead-end world of office temping. And, to tell you the truth, I feel as if I'm hanging onto even this poxy job by the skin of my teeth. This could, potentially, be a great company to work for. Saving the planet and everything is very fashionable, right? But the other problem is that, as a temp, I'm given No Responsibility. Therefore, I turn off my brain the minute I arrive at my desk. Then, when I am actually given something to do, I usually make a total cock of it. Vicious circle.

I think I'm skating on thin ice after putting together an important Powerpoint presentation for my boss on the Anthropogenic Effects on the Natural Environment which he was giving to some bigwigs in the industry that, somehow, featured mainly wedding dresses. Gah! I have no idea how that happened. Still, a lot of people found it amusing. Well, some people found it amusing. One in particular didn't though. Ahem. The proper presentation was *really* boring, anyway.

There are some upsides to being at GIT. This is a great building to work in. It's an enormous, contemporary office block right on the river by Blackfriars Bridge – prime location. It's stuffed full of bright artworks and multi-coloured chairs. It has floor to ceiling windows and, because that makes it like an oven, we have the air-conditioning pumping out all day. Which, if you ask me – and no one does – doesn't seem all that green. Clearly, we prefer to tell other people how to cut back on their energy usage rather than have the inconvenience of doing it ourselves. I have, however, connived to surreptitiously manoeuvre my desk further towards one of the said windows so that I can admire the splendid view of the Thames at my convenience.

Before Mr Simmonds can come and chase me again, I scuttle out of the office. Normally, even in the face of adversity, I'm a cheerful soul but I'm out of sorts today, restless and unsettled.

Out in the main corridor, where I'm alone, I hold up my hands and lean against one of the windows, resting my cheek against the cold glass. It's March and it's chilly outside. However, it's one of those days that makes you hopeful that spring is just around the corner. The Thames is a shimmering silver ribbon and trees along the Embankment are shyly coming into bud. The sky is a quite promising shade of blue.

I look down over the river and, on a bench, three floors below me, a figure looks up and waves.

'Marcus?' I jump back from the window and press myself against the wall. I'm sure it was him. Could I be hallucinating due to lack of chocolate? I inch forward and risk a peek.

My phone pings with a text and I glance at it, warily.

Hi, Lucy! Surprise, surprise. M xx

I summon up the courage to look again. Sure enough, it's Marcus who's down there and he's waving at me again.

Go away, I text back.

No, he answers. *Come and talk to me.*

As I watch, he pulls his coat round him and lies down on the bench. He'll freeze out there. When he sets his mind on something, he doesn't falter until he gets the result he wants. He could be out there for days waiting for me to crack. I know Marcus only too well; I will not win this staring contest. I am always the one who blinks first.

With an exasperated sigh, I head downstairs and, after getting my security pass all in a tangle at the gate, flounce outside and into the cold. Marcus sits up, smiling triumphantly, as I approach. His blond hair is tousled by the breeze coming from the river. He's wearing a sharp grey suit and a black cashmere coat. As always, he looks devastatingly suave. This is the man who has broken my heart into a thousand pieces time and time again. I should never forget that.

'I have nothing to say to you,' I tell him firmly.

'Shall we do it over a coffee?' he asks. 'Or I could buy you lunch?'

Lunch. My stomach growls. I check my watch. It is, technically, my lunch time.

'Just hear what I've got to say,' Marcus pleads.

He turns those devastating china blue eyes on me. The ones that I have loved so much. The ones he thinks always reduce me to a quivering wreck of compliance. Ha. Not today, Marcus Canning. Today, I am braced against your wily ways.

'There's nothing that you can say that I want to hear.' I hold up a hand. Talk to that.

'I love you,' Marcus offers.

'Don't be silly. You haven't sat out here in the freezing cold just to tell me that.' I shiver and Marcus, quick as a flash, whips off his coat and wraps it gently round my shoulders.

'I can't manage without you,' he tells me.

I purse my lips. 'Emotionally or physically?'

'Both,' he admits, boyish smile giving it all it's got.

'Stop it, Marcus. I'm immune to your charms these days.' But still my stupid heart remembers how much it once loved him. It's like a chocolate stain on a favourite white blouse that always remains no matter how much Vanish you scrub it with, yet you still can't bear to part with it.

'Half an hour,' he cajoles. 'You owe me that.'

'I don't *owe* you anything.'

Despite my protestations, Marcus takes my hand in his and starts to walk, in a determined manner, towards the bridge. 'This could change your life.'

'It won't.'

'Just hear me out.'

I make some show of resistance, pulling against him. But it's futile. I so desperately want to know how things are going at Chocolate Heaven without me. I want to hear him beg me to go back.

I won't. Obviously.

But I want to hear it all the same.

'Oh, Marcus.' I fall into step beside him.

I'll hate myself for this. I know I will.

Chapter Two

'I thought we'd eat at the OXO Tower,' Marcus says.

'No.' I stop stock still. 'No OXO Tower.'

'It's fabulous there,' he insists.

'And that's exactly why.' Plus it was the scene of my first proper date with Crush, and I don't want to sully that memory. Well, no more than falling down the stairs and breaking my leg afterwards did. 'You think you can ply me with fine food and wine and I'll be putty in your hands. Well, it's not going to happen.'

Marcus's face falls. 'I've already booked us a table.'

I tut. 'Then ring them and cancel.' Does he really think that I'm so malleable?

'OK. Whatever you say, Lucy.'

He looks so miserable that I can't hold my ground. 'We'll grab a sandwich. A quick one, mind you. I have things to do.' Which reminds me that I should be on my way to the finance department right now.

Reluctantly, Marcus calls and cancels the table. He thinks I'm a pushover, I know. Well, I'll show you, Marcus Canning.

We walk further down the Southbank until we come to a

small, chain café. Perfect. Scruffy enough and grubby enough not to impress me. Inside, every table is strewn with the detritus of the previous customers' meals.

'You really want to eat here?'

'Yes.'

Marcus sighs his resignation. 'Grab a table, then. I'll queue up. Coffee?'

I nod. 'Get me something low calorie to eat. I'm on a diet.'

He laughs out loud at that.

'I am!'

I shrug off Marcus's coat so that I can load up a tray swimming in tea with empty sandwich wrappers and crisp packets and move them onto the next table. Then I wait, twiddling my thumbs, until Marcus returns.

He puts a latte and a plate with a giant slice of chocolate cake in front of me.

'I said low calorie.'

'Just inhale it then.'

'I'm *seriously* on a diet.'

'You look sensational exactly as you are. I like a woman with curves.'

'You like a woman who *breathes*,' I counter. As many and as varied as possible all the time we were in a relationship together, if I remember rightly. 'Anything else is a bonus.'

He laughs. 'Oh, Lucy. You can be so very cruel.'

Not cruel enough, I think.

While Marcus faffs with our coffee and sets the cake in front of me, I catch sight of my reflection in the window. I thought I'd melt away to a size eight after leaving the temptations of Chocolate Heaven behind. Truly, I did. But no. I'm curvier than ever. I think I've been comfort eating since I was cast adrift at Christmas. And who wouldn't in my circumstances?

When Marcus bought Chocolate Heaven, I lost the best job in the world and nothing, not even a Wispa and a Bounty bar combo, can make up for that. So I'm not just curvy, I'm heading towards the positively rotund. And no one wants to be a fat bride, right? No one wants to waddle down the aisle next to the man of her dreams. I want to be a sliver of my former self at my wedding and must keep this, at all times, at the forefront of my mind.

'I'm losing weight for my *wedding*,' I remind him.

'Ah.' He stirs his coffee thoughtfully. 'To whatsisname? Still going ahead then?'

'Yes, Marcus. Of course it is.'

'No sudden change of heart?'

'No. I *love* Aiden and he *loves* me. The date is booked. The venue decided. The invitations have gone out.' Not strictly true, I admit.

'I didn't get mine.'

'As if.'

He does his cutest, lost little boy look. 'Not for old times' sake?'

'No. You're the last person I'd want there.'

'You didn't say that last time we were at a wedding together.'

'That's because you were the groom, Marcus. And I was the bride. This is probably a good time to remind you that you didn't actually stay around for the ceremony.'

He frowns. 'You're never going to forget that, are you?'

I laugh, because what else is there to do? 'No. I'm never going to forget that. Or forgive you.' I get an unwanted flashback to the day Marcus jilted me and feel sick to my stomach all over again. It was the worst moment of my life and, frankly, there are a lot of worst moments to choose from. This time it will be different. I know it. Crush is not Marcus. And thank the heavens for that.

Picking up my fork, I toy with the chocolate cake Marcus has bought me. If I eat this and forego the Twix then I'm really no worse off than I would have been. I could just eat half. That's all. I'm thinking that I should order my wedding dress a size too small so that I can slim into it. All brides lose weight, right? I have three months to shed a stone or so. Doable? Tomorrow, I'll really get a grip on it.

Hmm. This chocolate cake is delicious. A moist, light sponge filled with rich ganache – even though we are in a place where I might have expected inferior quality chocolate treats. Marcus grins at me as I eat it. 'What?'

'Come back, Lucy,' he says, earnestly. 'Chocolate Heaven needs you. I need you. It's not the same without you. It's where you're meant to be.'

That, if I'm brutally honest, is music to my ears.

'I bought it for you. So that you could run it. That was the whole point of me owning it.'

'Who's running it now?'

'I've got a manager in.'

'A woman?' As if I need to ask.

'Er... yes.'

'Is she pretty?'

'No, she's French. A double bagger. Awful woman.'

A likely story.

His eyes go all gooey and he reaches out to curl a lock of my blonde hair round his finger. 'Come back,' he pleads. 'Come back to me.'

'Don't do that.' I slap his hand away.

Marcus is unperturbed. 'She doesn't have your way with the customers, Lucy. She doesn't have the vision or the passion for Chocolate Heaven. Without you, it's nothing. You know the business like no one else. You were born for it.'

All of these things are true. There is chocolate flowing in

my veins. I wasn't cut out to be a temporary secretary to a bad-tempered, not very green, IT director. That pulls me up short! Yikes! The finance department! All this banter with Marcus may have slightly side-tracked me.

As the realisation is dawning, my phone rings. It's my Mr Simmonds.

'Hello.' I try to sound as if I am in the quiet of the finance department and not in a noisy café on the Embankment.

'Where exactly are you, Lucy?' my boss asks somewhat tightly. 'I have been down to the finance department to get the figures for myself and they say that they haven't seen hide nor hair of you.'

'I had to pop out. Urgently. I'll be back in five minutes,' I promise. Then I remember that I'm on the wrong side of the river and will have to run. 'Make that ten.'

'Make it that you don't bother to come back at all,' he hisses. 'I'll call the agency and get someone else who's actually interested in doing this job. You're fired.'

He hangs up. Very abruptly. I'm left staring, open-mouthed at the phone. When I look up, I can see that Marcus is grinning.